Choosing You

Books by Stacy Finz

The Nugget Series
GOING HOME
FINDING HOPE
SECOND CHANCES
STARTING OVER
GETTING LUCKY
BORROWING TROUBLE
HEATING UP
RIDING HIGH
FALLING HARD
HOPE FOR CHRISTMAS
TEMPTING FATE
CHOOSING YOU

The Garner Brothers
NEED YOU
WANT YOU
LOVE YOU

Dry Creek Ranch
COWBOY UP
COWBOY TOUGH
COWBOY STRONG

Published by Kensington Publishing Corp.

Choosing You

Stacy Finz

LYRICAL SHINE
Kensington Publishing Corp.
www.kensingtonbooks.com

LYRICAL SHINE BOOKS are published by

Kensington Publishing Corp.
119 West 40th Street
New York, NY 10018

All Kensington titles, imprints, and distributed lines are available at special quantity discounts for bulk purchases for sales promotion, premiums, fund-raising, educational, or institutional use.

Special book excerpts or customized printings can also be created to fit specific needs. For details, write or phone the office of the Kensington Sales Manager: Kensington Publishing Corp., 119 West 40th Street, New York, NY 10018. Attn. Sales Department. Phone: 1-800-221-2647.

Lyrical Shine and Lyrical Shine logo Reg. U.S. Pat. & TM Off.

First Electronic Edition: February 2021
ISBN-13: 978-1-5161-0396-6 (ebook)
ISBN-10: 1-5161-0396-3 (ebook)

First Print Edition: February 2021
ISBN-13: 978-1-5161-0397-3
ISBN-10: 1-5161-0397-1

Printed in the United States of America

Chapter 1

Ethan Daniels reined his gelding to the right, cutting off three stray cows that had broken loose from the herd. "Get!" he shouted, waving his Stetson in the air as he maneuvered them back to the pack.

He wiped his forehead on the shoulder of his ranch jacket and moved to the drag position at the rear of the herd. The ground was still soggy from the last rain but at least he wasn't choking on a cloud of dust.

A few of the neighboring ranchers had come to help move his cattle down from the hills to the lower pasture, where he'd be weaning calves in about a month. The camaraderie of the ranching community was one of the reasons he'd chosen Nugget, California for his new home.

The other reasons had more to do with his six-year-old daughter, Veronica.

Ethan let out a loud whistle to bring up a few stragglers from behind, hanging off the side of his gelding to slap a lollygagging calf on its rump. "Get along now."

Clay McCreedy, owner of a ranch seven miles away as the crow flies, sidled up next to him on his horse. "Watch those million-dollar hands of yours."

Ethan grinned. "I'll do my best." He gazed up at the clear blue sky. "Couldn't have asked for better weather for this."

"Don't jinx it. These mountains are fickle. Ten o'clock sunshine, noon a monsoon."

"Yep." Ethan nodded. It was rainier and colder here than in Reno but according to the locals, they were having a fairly mild February. Still, it had to be forty degrees out.

Greener than the high desert river valley where he'd grown up in Nevada, the landscape here was thick with fir and pine trees and lush with grass nearly year-round. Another reason he was enamored with the place.

The land—two-hundred acres—had been in his family for as long as Ethan could remember. His father used to run his cattle here in summer when the only blades of grass left in Nevada were on city watered lawns.

Last year, he hired a local contractor and carpenter to build a two-story home—rustic farmhouse, Alma called it—and a guest cottage with views of the Feather River and the Sierra Nevada mountain range. The house was finished just in time to enroll Roni in first grade at Nugget Elementary.

Flynn, the point rider, moved the cattle down the gully. It was slow going, as they had to watch their footing on the slippery slope. But Flynn, Ethan's neighbor to the east, knew what he was doing. Like the rest of them, he'd been moving cattle since he was knee high.

They'd been out since sunup; the sky painted a pink and smoky gray. It was Ethan's favorite time of the day, when the land began to wake up from its long night's sleep and the birds stirred, restless.

When they got to the bottom of the ridge, Flynn let out a holler and the herd dispersed, spreading out across the pasture to munch on the tall grass.

Mission accomplished.

Ethan and his neighbors rode back to their trucks and trailers and served themselves coffee from the CaterGator, before loading up the horses.

"I guess we'll be back in a month or two." Clay shielded his eyes and stared out over the fields. Come March, they'd corral the calves away from their mothers for weaning, before trucking them to a feedlot in the Central Valley.

"Yep." Ethan cradled his cup to warm his hands. "Thanks for the help, fellows."

Ethan pushed off the back of the trailer he was leaning against so Clay could pack up his horse.

"Lunch at the Ponderosa?" Lucky Rodriguez hitched his thumbs in his jeans. The former bull-riding champ raised rodeo stock and ran a dude ranch a few miles from Ethan.

"I'm game," Flynn said. "No court today, which leaves me footloose and fancy free."

Ethan laughed. "Nice job if you can get it."

"Yeah, then how come I feel a lawyer joke coming on?" Flynn scraped his boot on a rock and sniffed himself. "I need a shower."

"Why don't we meet in thirty minutes?" Clay led his gelding up the ramp and locked the Dutch doors.

"I'm afraid I have to bow out," Ethan said. "I've got to get to Reno. But lunch is on me. I'll call Sophie and Mariah . . . tell 'em to put it on my tab."

"Nah, not necessary." Clay waved him off. "You helped us; we help you. That's the way it's done around here. But I wouldn't turn down a beer one of these evenings."

Flynn and Lucky nodded in agreement.

"How about the PRCA championship on Saturday?"

"I'm in," Flynn said. "Here or the Ponderosa?"

"Either way." If Ethan asked nice enough Alma might make her legendary *chile con queso.*

"How big's your TV?" Lucky asked.

The corner of Ethan's mouth hitched up. "Big."

"We'll do it here then." Clay opened his door and slid behind the wheel. "See you all Saturday."

After everyone drove off, Ethan mounted up and rode to the stable. Like his house, the gable barn was new construction. Despite housing five horses, it still showed shiny and clean. He'd hired Clay's youngest son to muck stalls a few times a week. Even so, he suspected that by next winter it would feel more lived in.

He unsaddled Reggie, combed the old boy's coat, cleaned his hooves, and turned him out in the paddocks. Leaning against the fence, he watched Reggie nibble on a patch of grass for a while, then turned for the house for a quick shower.

No one was home and he could hear the clicking of his boots on the hardwood floors echo through the hallway. Alma would've had his head for not leaving them in the mudroom.

She'd befriended a group of women who called themselves the Baker's Dozen. They met the first Thursday of the month at the big inn on the square to exchange recipes. Ethan was glad she was making a place here. He didn't know what he would do without his stepmother. Besides helping with Roni, she made the trains run on time and was good company.

At first, he'd worried that Nugget, away from her glittering life in Reno, would be too pedestrian for her. Even when Alma married his dad, she preferred her high-rise condo to his sprawling ranch, sixty miles from the city.

But she seemed to be adapting well to retirement in Nugget, making friends, volunteering at Roni's school. And when she got homesick, it was only a fifty-minute drive to Reno.

He climbed the timber staircase to his bedroom. The smell of fresh paint and floor finish still clung in the air. The master bathroom bordered on the obscene with a walk-in shower three times the size of his old one. It seemed a bit much for a bachelor but the architect had gotten her way, claiming that a stingy master would hurt re-sale value.

He had no intention of selling but secretly enjoyed the decadence of all the water jets and the rain showerhead, not to mention the radiant heated floors. Today, though, he didn't linger. He bathed, dressed and was on the road thirty minutes later.

The freeway was nearly desolate. He watched the view change from forest to prairie to desert and finally to billboards advertising all-you-can-eat buffets and the Gatlin Brothers, who were performing three nights at the Grand Sierra.

Glancing at the time, he was confident he'd make it to his appointment with a few minutes to spare.

His phone rang and the Bluetooth dashboard lit up with caller ID. His ex-wife. For a second, he considered not picking up. But with a sigh he pressed handsfree.

"What's up, Joey?"

"That's a nice way to answer the phone. I was calling about Saturday. I want to take Veronica to The Discovery for the Mindbender Mansion exhibit."

"We talked about this. You're welcome to spend time with her at the ranch as long as Alma or I am there."

"Oh for God's sake, Ethan. She's my daughter. I want to take her to a children's museum, not a brothel."

He tried for patience. "For now, we're sticking with the court order."

There was a long pause and for a second Ethan thought Joey might've hung up on him. It was her MO, after all.

"Come on, Ethan, I've been clean for almost a year. This isn't fair. I could go back to court, you know. Push for fifty-percent custody. My lawyer says I'd get it."

"Your lawyer, huh?" Joey needed to work on her poker game. Her bluff sucked. She was living with her parents and supporting herself with the alimony he paid her, which was a nice chunk of change. But not enough to retain the kind of attorney who could go up against his. "Take me to court, then. In the meantime, we follow the judge's orders. I'll be home on Saturday. Come any time after ten, stay as long as you like."

"Aren't you generous?"

He didn't respond. The whole damn thing exhausted him. "How are your folks?"

"Fine. They miss you . . . they miss Veronica."

"We're fifty miles away. They can visit anytime. How's the job search?"

She huffed out a breath. "Humiliating. Degrading. Yesterday, I interviewed with a toddler for a barista job. Seriously, I don't even think he was old enough to shave."

"You hear from the board about your license yet?"

"Crickets."

He wasn't surprised. "How are you on money?" She had student loans, a new car payment, and had never been much good with a budget.

"Getting by."

He let out a frustrated breath. "My exit's coming up. I'll see you on Saturday . . . and Joey . . . if you need cash I can float you." The minute the words left his mouth, he saw an image of Alma scowling and shaking her head.

He hung up, got off on Mill Street, turned into the parking structure, and slid into his personal space. It was a plum location, just across the breezeway to the lobby.

The double doors swished open when he reached the entrance and he nodded at the senior woman at the volunteer desk before heading for the elevator.

"Afternoon, Dr. Daniels."

"Afternoon." He picked up his pace, hoping he wouldn't get waylaid on his way to the orthopedic unit.

"Dr. Daniels, how are you?!" A nurse stopped him just before he reached the south wing of the hospital.

Ethan flashed a smile and struggled to remember her name. She was one of Joey's friends. Raina? Rosalind? Renee? Yeah, Renee. He was pretty sure that was it. "Hey, Renee."

She beamed back so he must've gotten it right.

"You have surgery today?"

"Just a consult." He tapped his watch. "Gotta go or I'll be late."

"A few of us are meeting for drinks at five if you'd like to join us." Her face flushed red.

"Thanks for the offer. Can I take a rain check?" he asked, walking backwards. He didn't want to seem rude but he needed to get going if he had any hope of reviewing the radiologist's notes before his two o'clock arrived.

"Uh . . . of course. Any time."

He brushed by her and made it to the elevator as the door slid closed. Without thinking twice, he wedged his arm in and forced it open.

"Hope those hands are insured." The chief of staff leaned against the back wall, a stethoscope shoved in the pocket of his white lab coat.

Ethan gave a weak smile. It was the second reference to his hands that day. He hadn't minded when Clay had made the quip. But the joke was getting old.

The door dinged open on the fourth floor. "This is my stop. Catch you later."

Ethan walked to the end of the corridor to the orthopedic surgery center, the crown jewel of Renown Children's Hospital. Its reputation as having one of the finest, most cutting-edge programs in the country—maybe the world—was largely due to his mentor. Five years ago, Dr. Jason Bentley retired, leaving Ethan to carry on his legacy.

He used his keycard on a door off the passageway and bypassed the waiting room. Marjorie, one of the center's receptionists, passed him, carrying a lunch tray from the cafeteria.

"Your appointment is here."

"Already?" He glanced at his watch. "She's ten minutes early."

Marjorie shrugged and went out the same way Ethan had come in with her empty tray. He flicked on the light in his office, took a quick assessment of the mess on his desk, and booted up his computer. The room was smaller than his new walk-in closet but it served him well enough for meeting with patients and referrals. He had a more spacious office at the School of Medicine at UNR, where he was on the faculty.

Ethan quickly called up the radiologist's report and ran through it. He took off his jacket, slung it over his chair, and called the front desk. "Send in Ms. Barnes, please."

A few minutes later, she was led through his doorway. He looked up from the referral notes he'd been reading and suddenly lost his train of thought. Quickly rising, he locked eyes with her, then remembered to shake her hand.

"You look different than your picture," she said. "Younger."

The hospital's profile picture of him had been taken three years ago. He was now forty. In another context her observation would've been a compliment. But age added credibility to his position.

"Have a seat, Ms. Barnes." He motioned to a metal chair and closed the door before taking his own place behind the desk. "How was your flight?"

"Fine. We got in yesterday." Nervous, she fidgeted with the button on her coat and he noted that her hands were delicate and fine boned.

Ethan leaned in. "Ms. Barnes, it'll be okay."

"Will it? I just want my son to be normal again."

He got up, came around the desk, and sat on the chair next to her. He could smell her perfume, something soft and feminine without being cloying. "What is normal, Ms. Barnes?"

"The way Henry was before the accident." She sniffled, drawing her shaking hand across her nose. "Able to walk. Run, jump, ride a bicycle."

"Not being able to do those things does not make your son abnormal. It'll be a challenge for him, sure. But in my experience, children with the proper support and encouragement can rise to meet almost anything."

"I didn't mean normal." She squeezed her eyes shut for a moment, strain tugging at the edges of her mouth. "That was a terrible word to use."

He held her gaze and tried for a consoling smile. "Your son is amazing, no?"

"Beyond amazing." Her voice cracked and her eyes watered but she was holding it together, which impressed him. "He's the love of my life."

He reached across his desk for a box of tissues and rested it in her lap. He felt for all his patients but something about her unguarded vulnerability got to him. "Then no matter what, he'll always be the amazing love of your life."

"He will." She dabbed at her blue eyes with a tissue and turned away to collect herself. Gathering up her courage, she asked, "Are you saying you won't be able to perform the procedure?"

"No, what I'm saying is that even with surgery, Henry might not have full use of his legs. His injuries were extensive and Dr. Brunswick is one of the best pediatric orthopedic surgeons in the country."

"But not better than you." She turned slightly in her chair. "I'm grateful for everything Dr. Brunswick did. Really I am. Because of him and the entire team at Boston Children's, Henry is alive. But . . . Are you a father, Dr. Daniels?" She leaned forward in her chair and he nodded. "Then you understand that I would do anything for my son. Anything."

He not only understood, he felt it in every fiber of his being. The day Veronica was born, holding her tiny body in his arms, he'd felt an overwhelming instinct to protect her. To keep her safe. To love her beyond anything he could've imagined. There wasn't anything he wouldn't do for his daughter.

"I do, Ms. Barnes but there is a lot to consider here. The accident crushed much of Henry's femoral shafts. Dr. Brunswick focused on open reduction and internal fixation, using screws and pins to align his bones together. The problem is the damage was severe and the bones aren't healing."

"Dr. Brunswick explained all this," she said. "He said if anyone can repair the damage it's you. That you have been successful with a new, experimental treatment that could give Henry back full use of his legs."

Successful in the world of science didn't mean a hundred percent. And with a patient as severely injured as Henry the returns were even more diminished.

"Stem cell therapy is not a guarantee and will require hours of post-op physical therapy, not to mention a level of pain that would be difficult for anyone, let alone an eight-year-old. And, at the end of the day, Henry may not have any more mobility in his legs than he has now." He looked at her, assessing whether she truly understood the magnitude of what he was telling her. Every parent of a hurt child wanted a magic bullet and he simply couldn't promise her one.

"What are you telling me, Dr. Daniels? You won't do it? You won't help us?"

"What I'm telling you are the facts. It's my duty as a surgeon to help you make an educated decision about your son's care."

"Tell me this, Dr. Daniels, could the surgery make Henry worse?"

With any surgery there were dangers. Anaphylaxis, infection, heart failure, the list went on and on. But that wasn't what she was asking. "Besides the inherent risks of anesthesia, no. The question is whether the gain will be worth the pain, Ms. Barnes. Your little boy has already been through so much."

Ethan had pored over Henry's case history. An all-terrain vehicle accident eight months ago had left the young boy's father dead and Henry with a severe concussion, broken wrist, and two femoral shaft fractures.

For a long time, she didn't speak and he got the sense she was thinking long and hard about what he'd said. Good. A decision like this should be made with her head, not her heart.

"I need a drink," she said at last.

Ethan laughed. There was no shortage of bars in Reno but he didn't think she'd actually meant liquor. Though he'd known her all of twenty minutes, she didn't strike him as someone who looked for answers at the bottom of a bottle. Considering what she'd been through, she'd sat through their appointment like a steel magnolia. Her clothes—a black pair of trousers, a red silk blouse and a cashmere coat—were impeccable. Her dark hair was neatly tied back from her face and her blue eyes sparked with intelligence.

From the moment she'd walked in the room he'd been rendered speechless by her looks. But now it was her fortitude he admired. As bleak as the picture he'd painted of the bone regeneration treatment Bentley and he had pioneered, he could tell by the set of her jaw that she was still determined to get her son into his clinical trial.

"Let me see if I can scare up a beverage for you. At least a juice box." He grinned and went in search of a bottled water or a can of soda, returning a few minutes later with both.

She chose the water and seemed to get a second wind after a few sips. "If Henry doesn't do it now will he blame me later? Will I blame myself?"

"You'll tell him what was at stake."

She leaned forward in her chair. "But if you do the procedure there's a chance my son could get full mobility?"

"There is a chance." They'd had good results on adolescents and even better results in children five and younger. Bentley, a biomedical engineer and an orthopedic surgeon, started the research specifically to repair severe fractures in toddlers who'd been abused and children with birth defects. "And as I stated before there is a chance that the large gaps in his bone may never be repaired. We just don't know, Ms. Barnes."

"Please call me Brynn. What would you do if you were me, Dr. Daniels?" She looked at him expectantly.

He started to say that he wasn't her but it was a cop out. Ethan knew exactly what he'd do. "Is Henry here?"

"He's in the playroom."

"May I see him?"

"Uh . . . yes . . . of course." She started to get up and he motioned for her to remain seated.

He picked up the phone. "Letty, please bring Henry Barnes to exam room two."

Together, they walked down the corridor, the walls covered in laminated children's artwork. Fish and whales. Somewhere up there was a picture Roni had drawn on a day he'd brought his daughter to work.

Brynn Barnes's high heeled shoes clicked on the linoleum floor beside him. At the exam room, Ethan tapped on the door and went inside. Henry's wheelchair had been pushed to the side and the young boy sat on the exam table, reading a comic book.

"Hey, buddy, I'm Ethan." He bumped fists with Henry, then went to the sink and washed his hands. "Let me take a look at that wrist of yours. That okay?"

Henry glanced at his mother, who smiled and nodded encouragingly. "Uh-huh."

The boy was a good-looking kid, same dark hair and blue eyes as his mother. A little on the slender side. Henry didn't quite make eye contact, leading Ethan to believe he was shy. Or sick of doctors. Lord knew the boy had seen enough of them since the accident.

"This the one?" Ethan lifted Henry's left hand and winked. According to the boy's X-rays the scaphoid had healed nicely. He gently rotated Henry's wrist. "How does this feel?"

"Good." The boy brushed a lock of hair away from his face. Looked like he could use a haircut.

Ethan picked up Henry's comic book. "*Spider-Man Loves Mary Jane*, huh?"

"It was all that was out there." Henry shrugged.

Wheeling a stool over, Ethan sat, facing the exam table so he could be eye level with Henry. "What do you like to read?"

"*The Last Kids on Earth*, *My Big Fat Zombie Goldfish*, books about facts."

Ethan grinned. "What kind of facts?"

Ethan hitched his shoulders again. "Stuff about everything. Sports, whatever."

"You like sports?"

"Yeah. Football and baseball mainly." Henry let his eyes drop to the white paper on the exam table.

"You ever been to a rodeo?"

"No." Henry shook his head. "What's that?"

Ethan rolled around to the foot of the table so he could take a closer look at Henry's legs. The right one was longer than the other. The boy had taken the brunt of the accident on his left side. "Cowboys and cowgirls competing on horses and bucking broncs and bulls. It's something to see."

Henry raised his face to Ethan's, suddenly interested. "Is it on TV?"

"Yep. You've got to look around for it but it's there. Better to watch in person, though." Ethan gently manipulated Henry's left femur. "Can I get you to stand up, son?"

He reached out his hand to help Henry get down from the table but the boy rejected the assistance. Henry scrambled to the edge and used his arms to lower himself down, holding on to the table for stability.

"That hurt?"

Henry nodded and lowered his eyes. Brynn jumped up and started to go to him but Ethan gestured for her to stop.

"Can you get to the door without the wheelchair?" It was roughly eight feet away.

Henry made it a few steps before stumbling and grabbed onto his mother's chair.

"Pretty good there, champ." Ethan helped Henry back to the exam table and resumed his spot on the stool, tilting his head to one side. "Do you know why you're here, Henry?"

Henry played with the pages of the comic book. "So you can fix my legs so I can play Little League when I'm ten."

"Is that the plan?" Ethan mussed the boy's hair.

Henry bobbed his head enthusiastically. "Yep. Shortstop."

"Like Brandon Crawford, huh?"

"Nope, like Derek Jeter."

"The Yankees?" Ethan threw up his arms in feigned outrage. "Then let's see what we can do. In the meantime, do you want to hang out here or in the playroom while I talk to your mom in my office?"

"The playroom, please."

The kid had nice manners. Ethan was working on that with Roni, who couldn't sit still long enough to say please or thank you. His little girl was a bundle of energy.

He got Letty to take Henry back to the playroom, a plexiglass room with colorful carpet tiles and donated books and toys.

"Let's take a walk," Ethan told Brynn. It was too cold for the children's garden. The manicured yard with its flowers, whimsical sculptures and interactive games was often where he took stressed out parents for pre-op discussions. Instead, they strolled in the direction of the cafeteria. "You asked what I would do if I were you."

She unconsciously moved closer. "Yes?"

"I'd do the surgery."

Chapter 2

Brynn rose the next morning in her hotel, wondering if she'd made the right decision. Henry had been to hell and back. But if there was a chance, even a small one, that he'd gain more mobility in his legs wouldn't the surgery and subsequent therapy be worth it? Yeah, easy for her to say. It was Henry's small, battered body taking the hit. Though sometimes she could swear she felt his physical pain right down to her marrow.

Ever since the crash, she'd spent most nights either crying herself to sleep or mentally punching Mason in the face.

She could hear Henry's gentle snores in the bed next to hers. He slept so soundly that she stayed still under the covers just so she wouldn't wake him, when what she wanted to do was lean over and kiss his sweet face. Her beautiful boy.

There were a million things to do today, including arranging shipment of their things. She assumed that after their meeting with Dr. Daniels they'd return to New York until he could fit them in for the procedure. He was a world-renowned surgeon after all. It had taken her two months just to get in to see him, even with a referral from Brunswick. But now everything was moving at warp speed, even arrangements for housing.

Dr. Daniels offered them a cottage. A sort of Ronald McDonald House for the families of the patients in his trial. The cottage was funded by the Bentley Foundation, a charity named after Daniels's mentor to help parents with their out-of-pocket expenses during treatment or just to give them one less thing to worry about. The foundation had housing closer to the hospital but unfortunately it was full. Though she could rent a nearby apartment, it would be difficult on short notice.

When Dr. Daniels said there was a cottage to handle the overflow that was available to trial patients who could provide their own transportation to and from the hospital, she jumped at the chance. The lodging was a good drive from Reno but she could rent a car.

They'd taken a Lyft from the airport to the hospital and Dr. Daniels dropped them off at the hotel after their appointment in his pickup. A beat-up truck with a scraped up back bumper and a crack in its windshield. The distinguished doctor, who'd worn jeans, a Western shirt and cowboy boots to their appointment, was surprisingly down to earth. She liked him more than Brunswick, who had a bit of a God complex and was always rushed and impatient when she asked too many questions.

Daniels, on the other hand, had gone slow with Henry and welcomed her questions. He was certainly easier on the eyes than Brunswick. The fact was Ethan Daniels was easy on the eyes, period. Tall and broad with a thick head of dark hair and hazel eyes that seemed to see inside you.

Not that Dr. Daniels's good looks mattered. Quasimodo would be beautiful in her eyes too if he could help Henry.

She slipped from under the blankets and tiptoed to the bathroom with her phone and laptop, careful not to wake her son. The long plane ride and his hospital visit had knocked him out, even with the three-hour time difference.

She could make her calls while he slept. The bathroom, like the rest of their suite, was awash in marble and mirrors. Her assistant, Zena, booked the casino resort to get them as close as possible to the hospital. Under normal circumstances, she would've preferred something smaller, like a cozy bed and breakfast.

She sat at the vanity and powered up her laptop. While waiting for it to load, she called Zena and gave her a list of the clothes and assorted items to send to the address Dr. Daniels had given her. After Zena, she arranged for a rental to be delivered to the hotel. Then, she made a call to her financial advisor and asked him to arrange for a donation to the Bentley Foundation.

"Mom."

"I'm right here, baby." She rushed out of the bathroom to find Henry trying to walk on his own. "Not without your wheelchair, okay?" She grabbed it from the side of the bed.

"I'm hungry."

The sound of those words made a smile blossom in her chest. In the months following the accident, Henry's appetite had disappeared. He'd lost a considerable amount of weight and his pediatrician wanted him to gain at least ten pounds back.

She grabbed the room service menu off the credenza and leafed through it. "Pancakes, waffles or eggs?"

"Pancakes!" He pumped his fist in the air.

She smooched the top of his head. His hair could use a washing. And a cut. But that would have to wait until later. "Pancakes it is. How about a bath while we wait?"

He pulled a face but didn't argue. She drew the water in the big soaking tub and laid out his clothes for the day. While he washed, she called in their breakfast order.

"Henry, let me know when you're ready to get out." He was beyond the age where he allowed her to remain in the bathroom with him.

"I will."

She stepped out onto the balcony to take in the sights. It was her first time here. She'd been to Vegas with Mason when they first married and Lake Tahoe with her best friend Lexi for a long weekend a few years ago. But never Reno.

The small city stretched out before her. In the distance, the mountains were dusted with snow. She hugged herself from the cold and stared out over the skyline, a cluster of high-rise buildings that stood starkly against the silhouette of the Sierra Nevada mountain range.

A billboard at the edge of the resort's parking lot caught her gaze and she smiled. It was a life-size picture of Megan Rapinoe with the soccer player's foot in the air, shattering the glass ceiling above her. The athletic shoe campaign was one of many that had catapulted the Barnes Group to the top of Madison Avenue.

"Mom, I'm ready."

Brynn went inside and closed the slider behind her. "I'll be right there."

Henry had drained the water from the bath and wrapped himself in one of the hotel's stingy terrycloth towels. She lifted him out of the tub and even as thin as he was, her body strained with exertion. Her little boy was growing up faster than she wanted to admit.

"Can we go to a rodeo?" Her son was a sports nut like his father. "Dr. Daniels said they're cool."

She grabbed another towel and dried his hair. "I suppose that while we're here I could look into it." She assumed they had rodeos in New York, probably Madison Square Garden. But maybe while Henry was rehabilitating from the surgery they could go to one in Reno.

There was a knock at the door. "You need help getting dressed? Breakfast is here."

"I can do it."

She pulled out the vanity bench for him in case he needed to sit and shrugged into one of the hotel robes from the closet, then waited for room service to leave before assisting Henry to the table. He had learned to get around fairly well in his wheelchair but getting into a chair was difficult sometimes.

"This smells good." She took the metal domes off the platters. "You want me to fix your pancakes for you?"

"Mom, I'm not a baby."

She unfolded the napkin and tucked it into his shirt. "You'll always be my baby no matter how old you are."

"Asher Stone's mom lets him stay up until eleven." Henry poured syrup on his stack of pancakes and watched the amber liquid flow down the sides, pooling on his plate in a puddle.

"Does she now?" Asher Stone's mother probably didn't know what time her son went to bed. Between her society events and her globetrotting, Sylvia Stone was rarely home. For the most part, a nanny was raising Asher.

Brynn was probably the only mother among her social set who didn't have a nanny. As soon as she went back to work that would have to change unfortunately. But despite the rigors of running the Barnes Group, she planned to be home in time to have dinner with her son and tuck him into bed every night. When Mason ran the company, he missed most of Henry's bedtimes.

But it was only her now, and no matter how excited she was to go back to work and oversee the firm she and her husband built; her son would always be her first priority.

"Henry, are you okay with all this? Dr. Daniels thinks we'll be able to go home in two months."

Since the accident, he'd clung to their Manhattan apartment as if it were a life raft. Often, she'd find him in Mason's study, curled up in the big leather chair, hugging a picture of his father to his chest. "What if I forget what he looks like?" he'd asked.

"I guess." Henry licked syrup off his fork. Brynn noted that he'd barely touched his food. "Do I have to go to a new school?"

She wasn't sure yet how that would work. Between the surgery, physical therapy and all his medical appointments, it might just be better to hire a tutor. She didn't want him to get behind, but it seemed silly to enroll him in a new school for only two months when he'd have to miss so much of it.

"Let's see how it goes, okay?" She pointed at his plate. "Eat up. We have a big day today."

By the time she showered, dressed and repacked their overnight bags, the concierge called to let her know their rental car had arrived. Brynn made a few more phone calls, including one to her late husband's assistant at the Barnes Group. Monday, when she was a little more settled, she wanted to hold a telephonic meeting with the firm's executives. Rich and Layla would have to run things while she was away. They were used to it. Since the accident, she'd been too preoccupied with Henry's care to pick up where Mason had left off.

The car, a Subaru Outback, was waiting in front of the valet station when they got there. Brynn helped Henry in, folded his wheelchair, and stashed it in the trunk. On the GPS, she punched in the address Dr. Daniels had given her and was surprised when, only a short time later, they'd crossed the state line from Nevada into California.

The truth was everything moved so quickly during their appointment that she hadn't paid much attention to the details of where they'd be staying. She'd just been thankful, and frankly relieved, that it was one less arrangement she'd had to make. But come to think of it, Dr. Daniels mentioned that the cottage was on a ranch, about fifty miles out of town.

The scenery changed from desert scrub to green piney forest as they climbed higher into the mountains. Brynn's ears popped and as they crested the next plateau, she held her breath at the sheer magnificence of her surroundings. There was snow on the tops of the distant mountains and the trees seemed to ascend to the sky. The highway ran next to a rushing river. Occasionally, they passed a home or two but, for the most part, the land looked untouched.

"Look, Henry. Isn't it gorgeous?"

He leaned between the two front seats to see better. "Where are we?"

"I'm not altogether sure." She glanced at the GPS map on her dashboard. "Somewhere in California."

"How come there's no ocean, then?"

"It's a big state. Not all of it is near the ocean. Do you see the river?"

Henry stared out the window. "How soon until we're there?"

"Not long, according to the map." Though it seemed like they were in the middle of nowhere. A beautiful nowhere.

They passed a sign for a small airport and Brynn wondered how it stayed in business. She hadn't seen any towns for miles. Just vast swaths of forest, which would open suddenly to rolling hills and wide-open prairies. Each disparate landscape was more breathtaking than the next.

She'd grown up on Manhattan's Upper East Side with panoramic views of the city, the East River and Central Park. Nothing to sneeze at. But this . . . the only way she could think to describe it was epic.

They crested another hill and in the valley below she spotted a small village. "You think that's it, Henry?"

He sat forward in his seat and peered out the windshield. "It looks small."

"No skyscrapers, that's for sure. Sit back, baby." He had a seatbelt on but she didn't like him perching so close to the front.

The town was Nugget, according to the welcome sign, which proclaimed the place to be "the pride of the West." Before they reached the town center, Brynn's GPS told her to turn off on Banner Road.

"Mom, I have to go to the bathroom."

"Can you hold it just for a few more minutes? According to the map, we're almost there." Besides, she had no idea where to find a bathroom around here.

"Yeah," Henry said. "Or I could get out here and pee behind a tree. Dad taught me how."

Of course he had. The world had been Mason's urinal. She was tempted to pull over but it would be an ordeal for Henry to get out of the car, let alone hike along the rutted shoulder to the nearest copse of pines. And knowing her son the way she did, he wouldn't let her help him.

"Just a few minutes more, buddy."

The thicket of trees opened to pasture. "Look at all the cows, Henry. My goodness, have you ever seen so many?"

The cows seemed to distract him from his pressing need to pee. He stared out the window and appeared to be counting them.

"You have arrived at your destination," came the disembodied voice of the GPS.

The road dead ended at a giant gate. Above the entrance, hung a sign with the letter "D" inside a circle that had been burned into the wood. Dr. Daniels had written a combination to the gate on a scrap of paper with the address. Brynn reached into the back seat for her purse and rooted around until she found the note. Leaning out of her window, she punched in the code.

The gate slowly swung open and she pulled through. A dog jogged up to greet them, barking and yipping at their tires. Brynn let the engine idle, afraid if she drove, she would hit the animal.

She considered opening her door and shooing the dog away but what if it was vicious? What she knew about dogs, she'd learned from watching old re-runs of *Lassie*. Growing up, her family traveled too often to keep a pet and Mason had been allergic.

"Mom, I've really gotta go." Henry squirmed in his chair.

"Okay, baby." She gently accelerated and to her relief the dog moved out of the way.

A woman came down the lane and the pup ran to her, flanking her side and wagging its tail. Brynn rolled down her window.

"Hi, we're the Barneses. My son is Dr. Daniels's patient."

"Welcome to the Circle D. Ethan is at Stanford today but he told me to show you around."

"Oh," Brynn said surprised. "Does Dr. Daniels live here?"

"We live in the house up on the hill." She pointed and Brynn got a glimpse of a roofline through the trees but not much else.

Brynn didn't know how far the cottage was from the house but she could feel Henry getting antsy in the backseat. "I hate to ask, but is there any way my son could use your bathroom?"

"Of course. Go on up. The door's unlocked and I'll meet you there."

"Would you like a ride?"

The woman waved her off. "It's only about two-hundred yards up the hill. I'll be right behind you."

Brynn felt funny about letting herself in but at the same time she didn't want Henry to wet his pants. A few lengths up the road and the house came into sight. It was a two-story timber-frame house with enough decks and windows to take advantage of the glorious view. She could easily see the front facade gracing the pages of *Architectural Digest*. Sophisticated mountain chic.

She also noted that there were stairs up to the front porch, which would be difficult for Henry. There was a Mercedes Benz in the driveway. Brynn pulled up next to the sedan and cut her engine.

"Let's try it without the wheelchair," she said, figuring it would be faster if she carried him up the stairs and helped him to the restroom.

Henry nodded and opened his door.

"Wait for me," she called and went around to his side. "Put your arms around my neck."

Together, they got him out of the car and she helped heft him up the stairs to the front door. The foyer was every bit as impressive as the outside. Beautiful hardwood floors, soaring ceilings with big iron trusses, and incredible woodwork. She wished she had more time to look around but her first priority was finding a bathroom.

"Let's try this way." There was a corridor off the entryway that appeared promising. Her instincts were good because the third doorway down was a powder room. "Want me to come in with you?"

Henry rolled his eyes. "I'm good, Mom."

She waited outside the bathroom door, examining the Navajo rug hanging on the opposite wall. It was evident that the Danielses had exquisite taste. Yet, it wasn't ostentatious. Judging by the earth tones, the rustic touches and the enormous windows, the house was built to pay homage to the outdoors.

Brynn heard the water go on inside the bathroom. "How you doing in there, buddy?"

"I'm done." Henry came out, his shoulder hugging the wall for balance.

They followed the corridor back to the foyer to find the woman they'd met on the road coming in.

"Did you find the bathroom okay?" She took off her wide brimmed felt hat and hung it on the hall tree.

"We did, thank you."

Brynn noted that the woman was older than she originally thought. Maybe mid-fifties and quite beautiful. Jet black hair that fell a little past her chin, big dark eyes, and flawless skin. Though she wore simple khakis and a white blouse, there was a certain elegance about her. She seemed too old to be Dr. Daniels's wife but Brynn could be wrong.

"You have a lovely home."

"Thank you. I'm Alma." She stuck out her hand to shake Brynn's. "And you must be Henry." Alma took Henry's hand in hers and simply held it. "How about a cookie before I show you to the cottage?"

She led them into a grand living room with a big stone fireplace and through the dining room to the kitchen, which was just as impressive. The entire space was open and probably three-thousand square feet. Yet, it felt warm and cozy.

"I just baked them this morning." Alma plated a half dozen cookies from a cooling rack and put them on the table. "Would you like a glass of milk, Henry?"

Henry looked up at Brynn, silently asking for permission and she nodded. "Yes, please."

"What can I get for you, Brynn? Coffee? Tea? Something cold?"

"I'm fine, thank you." She gazed around the kitchen while Alma poured Henry a glass of milk. The cabinets were a dark stained wood and the appliances stainless steel. There was a huge iron pot rack over the center island and a deer antler chandelier that floated over the center of the room.

It was so different than her ultra-modern kitchen back home, which she designed from the ground up. Oddly, she liked this one better.

Alma told them to make themselves at home at the breakfast table and joined them with a mug of coffee. "How was the drive?"

"Gorgeous. How large is the town . . . Nugget?" Later, Brynn needed to buy groceries and a few toiletries to hold them over until their things arrived.

"Tiny." Alma laughed. "A small supermarket, a hamburger drive-through, a sporting goods store, A farm supply shop, a gas station, a barber shop, a Victorian inn and a few other businesses. The hub is the Ponderosa, a sit-down restaurant, saloon and bowling alley."

"A bowling alley, huh?" That sounded fun. "Does Dr. Daniels have an office here?" While the area was spectacular, it was rather remote for a world-renowned surgeon to set up shop.

"His office is at the University of Nevada in Reno." Alma sipped from her cup. "His family . . . my late husband . . . were ranchers. Ethan is carrying on the tradition. The Bentley Foundation has housing in Reno, closer to the hospital. But there is never enough space. The cottage is new and was built as backup housing. And this place"—Alma put her hand to her heart—"is good for the soul. Good for recovery."

Brynn could see that and hoped it would be a morale booster for Henry. Though her boy had grown up in Manhattan, his outdoor getaways with Mason had made an impression on him. Perhaps this place would too. Regardless, it was extremely generous of the doctor to show Henry extra care.

"How was your late husband related to Dr. Daniels?" Brynn asked, curious. A cattle ranching surgeon. It was different, at least in New York.

"He was his father. I'm Ethan's stepmother."

Well, that answered that question. "I'm sorry for your loss."

"Likewise." Alma had clearly been briefed on Mason's death.

"Thank you." She looked away, unable to meet Alma's eyes. The accident had left her conflicted. Sometimes she missed Mason with a bone-deep sadness that made it difficult to get out of bed in the morning. Sometimes she hated him with an intensity that plagued her with guilt.

Henry reached for another cookie and Brynn shook her head. She needed to get some vegetables into her boy.

"We've taken up too much of your time." Brynn rose, not wanting to be an imposition.

"You'll have to meet my granddaughter, Veronica," Alma told Henry. "She'll be home from school around three." She cleared the table and packed up the remaining cookies on the plate in a sandwich bag, which she handed to Brynn. "Let me show you the cottage."

They piled into the Outback and Alma told Brynn to follow the paved road past the big house, down the hill. About a quarter mile away sat a miniature replica of Dr. Daniels's house. This one, though, was built on a slab foundation, so the front door was at ground level. No stairs, thank goodness.

"Oh, it's darling." Brynn couldn't wait to see the inside.

She hurriedly unpacked Henry's wheelchair from the trunk. The pathway to the entrance was paved and he had no trouble making the short distance from the car to the cottage. The entrance was extra wide. Brynn assumed it was to accommodate a wheelchair.

Alma unlocked the door and let them inside. "You're our first guests."

"It's absolutely lovely." Brynn adored the natural light that streamed through the picture windows.

Like the big house, it was an open concept. Though the rooms weren't nearly as large, the cathedral ceiling made the space feel endless and airy. The furnishings, a gray sectional piled with a collection of kilim accent pillows, an overstuffed leather swivel chair and a live-edge wooden dining table and six upholstered chairs, complemented the rustic vibe. Her favorite feature was the wood burning fireplace. The ones she had in New York were gas. Growing up, her parents had had a wood burning stove in their weekend home in the Hamptons. And she missed the comforting smell of wood smoke.

"Did you do all this?" Brynn turned in place, taking in the small but well-appointed kitchen. "The decorating, I mean."

"The Bentley Foundation brought in someone to design the cottage to be ADA compliant. But I did help with the décor. Come look at the bathroom."

It was a large Jack and Jill that adjoined both the master and guest room. The sink, toilet and large walk-in shower were all wheelchair accessible. The bedrooms were bright and cheery. But more importantly, they felt like someone's home, not a hotel.

"You did an amazing job, Alma. It's so warm, so inviting. Are you an interior designer?"

Alma laughed. "Heaven's no. But this . . . both homes . . . have kept me from climbing the walls."

Brynn's expression turned consoling. "After your husband died?"

"No," Alma corrected. "That was three years ago. I'm newly retired. I moved in with Ethan to help with Roni. But when she's in school . . . well, I'm not used to all the free time."

Brynn was curious about what Alma used to do but didn't want to pry.

"I'll leave you two to settle in. On the breakfast counter is a list of phone numbers, including one to the main house, and directions to town. Despite Nugget being mostly a cow town, the food is excellent at the Ponderosa and everyone raves about the burgers at the Bun Boy, though it's take-out only. Please let me know if there is anything you need. I'm sure Ethan will check in as soon as he gets home."

Brynn watched Alma hike up the hill and disappear behind the trees. There wasn't much to unpack but she got their overnight bags from the car while Henry flipped through the channels on the flat screen. Dr. Daniels still had some tests to run but if everything came back normal, Henry's surgery was slated for Wednesday. That gave them a medical-free weekend to explore this wondrous place.

"You thinking about lunch, Henry?"

"I'm not hungry."

"You seemed hungry when there were cookies to be eaten. Don't you want to go looking around, see what Nugget has to offer?"

"I guess," he said, distracted by the TV.

She snatched the remote control away and turned it off. "Come on, let's have an adventure."

Without cartoons, he stared outside the window. In the distance, cows dotted the outlying pastures. A shroud of fog hung over the mountains like smoke. And the river—presumably the same one they'd followed along the highway—narrowed and widened through the property as far as the eye could see.

Somewhere, a train whistle blew.

"Do you think Dad would've liked this place, Mom?"

The question stabbed at her. For an urbanite, Mason loved the outdoors. Skiing, sailing, hiking, mountain climbing, he'd done it all. He once compared the rush of pitching an ad campaign to careening down an ice track on a bobsled.

"Yes, I do." She joined Henry on the couch and snuggled next to him. "He loved you so much, baby."

"He loved you too, Mom."

"I know," she said, wishing with all her heart that it was true.

Chapter 3

It was dark by the time Ethan got home. He parked in the driveway and glanced at his watch. He'd missed supper with Roni and braced himself for a lecture from Alma.

He was halfway inside the door when his daughter flew down the stairs in her PJs and threw herself into his arms.

"Daddy, I've missed you." He lifted her so that they were eye level and she caught his cheeks in her hands and kissed him. "Guess what?"

"What?" He kicked the front door closed.

"Mommy's coming tomorrow and she's taking me to buy a new dress for school."

"Oh yeah." He exchanged a glance with Alma, who also came to the door. She shrugged.

Goddamn you, Joey.

"How's my girl?"

"Good." She squeezed his cheeks together. "Where've you been, Daddy?"

"Work, bonny Roni." He sniffed the air. "Something smells good. Did I miss dinner?"

"We had enchiladas but Grandma saved you some. Did you know there's a little boy living in the cottage? Grandma met him. Can we go over there and see him?"

"Not tonight, Roni. Maybe tomorrow. Are you going to sit with me while I eat?" It wasn't a school night. He told himself that they could let the eight o'clock bedtime deadline slide every once in a while.

"Okay, Daddy. Afterward, will you read me a story?"

"You got it, pardner." He threw her over his shoulder to fits of giggles, then let her down.

Alma made him up a plate while he washed. When he returned to the kitchen, Roni set him a place at the table with the #1 Dad mug she'd given him for Christmas and a drawing she'd made at school.

"This is good, kiddo." He held up the picture, trying to decide whether the crayon sketch was of a horse or a dog. Whichever, one of its legs was missing. "How was school?"

"Mrs. Richards put George Freeman in a time out and we had tater tots for lunch. Cody McCreedy came over to clean the stalls." She stood up on her chair.

"Sit on your butt. All the way down, Roni." He got up to get a beer out of the fridge.

"Use your mug, Daddy." She waved the #1 Dad cup at him.

He screwed off the cap and filled the mug, taking a long slug before shoveling in a forkful of enchilada. "These are great, Alma," he said around a mouthful. The last time he'd eaten was breakfast.

"How was your presentation?" she asked.

"I think it went okay. Just glad it's over. The traffic in the Bay Area sucks. It's a lot worse than when I did my residency. I don't understand why anyone would live there voluntarily."

"Daddy, you said a bad word."

He chuckled. "You're right, I apologize. Did you help Cody with the stalls?"

"He let me ride in the wheelbarrow."

"In her school clothes." Alma grimaced.

His lips twitched. His stepmother had never taken to ranch life. How she and Ethan's father had such a good marriage was a mystery. Ethan supposed it was the whole opposites attract phenomenon. In the beginning, Ethan and his siblings weren't too crazy about Alma Perez. They thought she was a snob and the eighteen-year age difference between her and their father was awkward. Alma wasn't that much older than Ethan's sister, Mary.

But Alma quickly became an integral part of their family. She never tried to replace their mother, who died from breast cancer while Ethan was in college. But she was the only paternal grandmother Veronica and his sister and brother's kids had ever known. And they couldn't get enough of her. Unfortunately, his brother's family lived in Colorado and his sister's in New England, so they didn't get to see a lot of one another.

He finished his enchiladas and though sorely tempted, turned down a second helping.

"You ready for that bedtime story?"

"Uh-huh." Roni wrapped her arms around his neck and he carried her up the stairs, calling down to Alma, "I'll clean up after I get Roni to bed."

But when he came down an hour later, his dishes were cleared away and the kitchen sparkled. He found Alma curled up on the couch with a book. The fireplace crackled. He threw another log on the blaze and planted himself in the recliner.

"So you met the Barneses this afternoon, huh?"

"What a nice little boy. Will you be able to help him?"

"I hope so." Ethically and legally, he couldn't get into the details of Henry's care. But he'd shared enough of the backstory with Alma that she would understand why they were staying on the Circle D Ranch.

The accident was no secret. Some of the media outlets in Maine had publicized the ATV wreck, which had happened in the Jackman-Moose River area. And of course, Mason Barnes' obituary had run in the *New York Times*.

"I didn't realize they were those Barneses." Alma tucked the throw blanket on the back of the couch around her.

"You've been doing your research."

"Old habits die hard. She's quite beautiful . . . much more so than her pictures on the society pages."

"I wouldn't know." Unless his patient's background was relevant to their care, he didn't pay attention to their social standing. He knew that Brynn and her late husband founded the Barnes Group, probably one of the largest advertising agencies in the country. Whether they rubbed elbows with the Rockefellers or the Vanderbilts was of no interest to him.

"You know who her father is, don't you?"

"No idea."

Alma pinned him with a look. "He's Raymond Herman." When Ethan stared at her blankly, she said, "The New York Philharmonic." Another blank stare. "Oh come on, he's only one of the greatest conductors in the world."

Ethan wasn't big on classical music unless you counted Jimmie Rodgers. Now, he was a true classic. "No kidding."

She slapped him with her paperback. "She seems down to earth, not what I would expect from someone with that kind of pedigree."

Ethan liked her right off the bat, which wasn't always the case with his patients' parents. "She's a good advocate for her son . . . wants what's best for him. In my book, that's all that matters."

"And of course you didn't notice how gorgeous she is?"

"I noticed." He grinned. He'd have to be blind not to. "Thanks for taking over my welcome wagon duties today. I appreciate everything you do around here. The truth is I don't know what I'd do without you. But if it ever gets to be too much or if you ever feel like Nugget is too bucolic for you I would totally understand, Alma."

She waved her hand in the air. "And leave my granddaughter? Not on your life. Besides, watching that overly tan, blond Ken doll do the news every night isn't good for my indigestion."

Ethan's mouth quirked and he shook his head. "Get over it, Alma. You're the one who retired from KRNV. No one told you to go. In fact, I bet they'd take you back in a heartbeat." She'd been the most popular news anchor in Reno. Everywhere she went in town, people fell at her feet.

"It was time to go. Besides, I wanted Mariana to inherit my spot. We Latinas have to stick together." She gave him a conspiratorial wink.

"Just as long as you know that Roni and I want you to be happy, even if it means you living in Reno."

She reached over, pulled his head down and kissed him on the forehead. "Your father was so proud of you. And your mother . . . I just know she's smiling down from heaven. I'm not going anywhere, Ethan. I'm very happy here."

She got off the couch and folded the throw into a neat square. "I'm going to start the *chile con queso* for your rodeo gathering tomorrow and turn in for the night."

"Alma," he called as she headed for the kitchen. "What's this bullshit about Joey taking Veronica shopping?"

"She called while you were away and asked to talk to Roni. She must've brought it up on the phone. She's sneaky, that one." There was no love lost between Alma and Joey.

"I talked to her on Thursday, told her under no circumstances were we breaking with the court order." He blew out a breath. "She keeps pushing it."

"What'll you do?"

"What I always do. Be the damn bad guy."

* * * *

Ethan hiked down to the barn the next morning, taking a circuitous route that would have him passing the cottage. He doubted Brynn or Henry would be awake this early. But in case they were, he'd like to check in on the boy.

Much to his surprise, he found Brynn sitting out front on the patio in one of the rocking chairs he'd bought from a local who'd done much of the carpentry in the cottage and big house. She was sipping a cup of coffee and waved to him as he came down the hill.

"Morning. You're up early." He pulled the other rocker over and grabbed a seat.

"It's gorgeous here." She inhaled the air and closed her eyes.

"I like it. The property has been in my family for generations. My father used to run his cattle here in summertime."

"Where did they live in the winter?"

"Nevada. About an hour outside of Reno. That's where I grew up. When my father died, we sold the ranch. It was too isolated. We all wanted something a little closer to civilization, but not too close." He grinned. "This was my compromise."

"Well it's pretty fantastic. We meant to go to town yesterday but never made it. Henry and I plan to go today. Alma said the bowling alley restaurant is good." She held up her mug of coffee. "Thanks for stocking the cottage with the Keurig, by the way. And thanks for letting us stay in such a magnificent place. I slept better here than I have in months."

Brynn smiled, making her entire face light up and her blue eyes sparkle. It hit him in the gut the same way it had in his office that first day.

"Glad to hear it," he said. "How's Henry?"

Her smile slipped away and her expression grew pensive. "He's trying to adapt, he's mourning his father, he's mourning his legs, he's dealing with the pain. It's a lot for an eight-year-old." Her voice quivered and she turned away to stare out over the horizon.

His first instinct was to squeeze her hand, offer comfort, but he stopped himself from anything physical. "Henry's a tough kid. We'll get him through this."

"Thank you. For everything you've done. The cottage . . . well, you've been a lifesaver."

Her eyes swam with tears and again Ethan held himself rigid. Outside the confines of the hospital it was best to refrain from physical contact.

"Let's hope the Circle D has restorative powers." He stood and jammed his hands inside the pockets of his down jacket. "When are you heading to town?"

"Just as soon as Henry wakes up. I thought we'd try the restaurant and buy supplies. Is there anything I can get for you or Alma?"

"Nah, we're good. I appreciate the offer, though. You know how to get there?"

"I think so. If not I've got the GPS."

"You've got our number. If you need anything let us know."

"I will."

As he started to walk away she cleared her throat. "Uh, I think I heard horses this morning."

"Yep." He pointed through the trees at a roofline of a building. "A stable full of them."

"Would it be okay if I took Henry to see them later?"

"Absolutely. Do either of you ride?"

"No, but Henry likes animals. I just thought it would be nice for him to pet them or say hello."

"They're friendly." He walked backwards. "Maybe I'll send my daughter, Veronica, over this afternoon to give you the tour."

"That would be wonderful."

He nudged his head at her cashmere coat. "You might not want to wear that, though. The closest dry cleaner is in Reno."

Ethan tipped his hat and continued to the barn. As he tossed the last flake of hay, he heard a car coming up the driveway. It was a little early for visitors. He started back to the house and saw Joey's Ford Edge parked in front of the driveway.

Lengthening his pace, he braced himself for a confrontation. She was already in the kitchen when he got inside and Roni, still in her pajamas, was all over her.

He had to admit his ex looked good. Healthy. She'd shed the weight she'd gained in rehab and her blond hair was thick and glossy again.

He'd learned to tell whether she was high by looking at her eyes. Today, they were clear.

She looked up from the table where she was studying Roni's drawing. "Hey."

"Hey." He leaned against the counter.

"Daddy, I'm going to give this to Mommy because you already have a bunch. And she needs it for her fidgetrator."

"It's refrigerator." Joey rubbed her nose against Veronica's. They'd been kissing like that since Roni was a baby.

"Okay."

"Can we go shopping now?" Roni asked as she braided Joey's hair.

"I don't think the stores are open yet, sweetie."

"Joe, come talk to me for a minute." He motioned for her to follow him into the living room.

Veronica started to tag along but Ethan sent her upstairs. "How 'bout getting dressed, kiddo? Something warm, it's cold outside."

"Okay, Daddy."

He waited until he heard Roni's bedroom door shut and said, "Why'd you tell Veronica that you'd take her shopping after I explicitly said that the visit was to be here?"

"You said I couldn't take her to Reno . . . to the Mindbender Mansion exhibit. What's wrong with taking her to Nugget?"

He tried very hard not to raise his voice. "Seriously? What part of supervised visitation don't you understand?"

"Fine, come with us, then. For chrissake, Ethan, you can't even trust me to take our daughter on a short shopping excursion, alone?"

"No, I can't. Because when I trusted you to protect our daughter you got her out of bed in the middle of the night, drove her to some fucking hell hole so you could score and you were robbed at gun point. My little girl with a 9 mm in her face."

"I was sick, Ethan. Addiction is an illness." Her bottom lip trembled, making him feel like an asshole.

But this was about Veronica, not them.

He lowered his voice. "I know, Joe. And I'm proud of you. For rehab, for all of it. But it's only been six months since you got out. You've got to give this time, prove yourself. The Circle D is a big ranch. Take Roni riding, go on a hike. She doesn't need more clothes. All she needs is her mother."

Roni came bounding down the steps. She held her hands up high and shouted, "Ready."

"Change of plans," Joey said and wiped her eyes with the back of her hand. "It's too nice a day to waste inside a store. What do you say we saddle up Chuckie Choo Choo and go for a ride?"

"I say, yes!" Roni jumped around in a circle.

"I say we have breakfast first." On his way to the kitchen, he gave Joey's shoulder a squeeze in a silent thank you.

Alma joined them a few minutes later and took over his lame attempt at waffles. She gave Joey a terse "hello" and for the most part ignored her. It didn't help the awkwardness of the situation. They were functioning as a family, even though they weren't one any longer.

But if it was good for Roni he'd go through the motions.

Chapter 4

Brynn found a place to park in front of the Ponderosa. From the outside it looked cute. Kind of rustic saloon with a touch of city tavern.

"What do you think?" she asked Henry.

He craned his neck out the window. "I like it."

On the other side of the square was the inn Alma mentioned. It looked like something out of a storybook with all its gingerbread and its crisp white porch and potted ferns. Maybe after breakfast they'd take a look inside.

Across from the inn was a barber shop and a police station and in the middle of the square, a park. It was too cold to sit outside but Brynn imagined that the grassy plaza was quite the hangout spot in warmer weather.

She opened her car door and went through the routine of unpacking and unfolding Henry's wheelchair from the trunk. Inside, a gust of heat hit them, as did the smell of frying bacon.

"Two?" The woman at the hostess stand gathered up a couple of menus.

"Yes, please. If you've got a table away from the door that would be great." She didn't want Henry catching a chill. All it would take was a cold and his surgery would have to be postponed.

"I've got something in the back," the woman said and led them through a dining room filled with Western-style saloon décor—dark paneled walls, Victorian light sconces, vintage mill work, red velvet curtains, and pleather banquettes.

The restaurant was crowded. There were even people sitting at the bar. She glanced around, looking for the bowling alley, which must've been on the other side of the building.

"You two passing through?"

"We're actually staying at Dr. Daniels's place. My son is his patient."

"The Circle D, huh?" The woman winked at Henry. "His daughter, Veronica, plays with our little girl, Lilly."

"We just got here yesterday afternoon, so we haven't met Veronica yet. But later, we're hoping she'll show us the horses, right Henry?"

He nodded, then turned away to stare at a collection of cowboy hats on the wall. The place certainly made an instant first impression.

"I'm Mariah, by the way. My partner and I own the Ponderosa."

"Pleased to meet you, Mariah. I'm Brynn and my son's Henry. I believe he's already enamored with your restaurant."

"It does have that effect on people. Would you like me to leave the chair or take it away?" Mariah nudged her head at the table.

Brynn turned to her son. "Henry?"

"You can leave it." Using his arms and hands, he lifted himself out of the wheelchair and took a seat at the table.

"Is there a place we can stow the wheelchair, so it won't block anyone's way?" Brynn asked Mariah.

"I'll put it against the back wall."

Brynn started to fold the chair but Mariah stopped her. "It'll be fine like this. I'll send a server over to take your orders. Welcome to Nugget, you two."

"Thank you. We're excited to be here." It was a charming town from what she'd seen so far.

Brynn leaned across the table. "After breakfast let's check out the bowling alley and that big Victorian inn. What do you say?"

"Can I get a cowboy hat, Mom?"

"I think we should both get one. When we leave, I'll ask Mariah where's the best place for cowboy hats."

Henry's face lit up and Brynn could feel the warmth of it in her chest. Maybe this place would be good for him. Their apartment in New York served as a constant reminder of Mason and life before the accident. Her little boy survived that day but he wasn't the same. And she wanted the old happy Henry back.

Despite trying to persuade Henry to try something different for a change, he ordered pancakes. She went with the waiter's recommendation of chicken fried steak. The beef was local. When everything came, Brynn wished she and Henry had shared. The portions were big enough for five breakfasts.

She watched him tuck into the pancakes and turned to her own plate. It was her first chicken fried steak and she wasn't sure whether she'd like it. She didn't know it would be smothered in gravy. But after one bite she was sold.

"Henry, you have to try this." She cut off a piece and tried to coax him into taking a mouthful but he scrunched his nose and shook his head. "You don't know what you're missing."

After a few bites of pancake, he pushed his plate away. "I'm full."

"Just a little bit more, baby." Getting him to eat had become a constant struggle. He always started out gung-ho but lost interest after only a few bites. Part of the reason was he suffered from stomachaches. His pediatrician thought they were associated with post-traumatic stress disorder from the accident.

He played with his food for a few minutes to appease her. But it soon became clear that he wasn't going to eat anymore. She didn't push it. When the server came with their bill, Brynn slipped him her credit card.

A new rush of diners came through the door. Brynn couldn't tell if they were locals or tourists. The previous night, after Henry had gone to bed, she'd done a little research on her laptop about the area. Nugget started as a gold mining town and later, logging. But it wasn't until the Western Pacific Railroad came to California's Sierra Nevada in the early 1900s that the tiny village began to thrive. Now, it was a crew-change site for the Union Pacific and home to cattle ranches. The latest census data had the town's population at around six-thousand people. A far cry from Manhattan, which had more than a million and a half people squeezed into fewer than 23 square miles.

"Shall we poke around?" she asked Henry. When the waiter returned with her Visa card and receipt she asked him where the bowling alley was.

He pointed her to the other side of the dining room where an archway led to a separate space. The two buildings were a study in contrast. While the restaurant looked like something out of the old west, the bowling alley was as modern as any you'd find in a big city, except smaller. Ten lanes, shoe rental booth, video-game arcade, and food concession stand.

About half the lanes were being used. The bowlers wore matching shirts, leading Brynn to believe that Saturday mornings were reserved for leagues.

"Maybe we'll come back one evening and play." She hadn't bowled since she was a child. It might be difficult for Henry from his wheelchair but they could try.

Outside, Brynn zipped Henry's jacket to his throat. And they strolled slowly around the square.

"Mom, you forgot to ask that lady where to buy cowboy hats."

"If we don't find something in one of these downtown shops I'll pop into the restaurant again and ask her. And if she doesn't know I'll ask Dr. Daniels."

He'd been wearing one this morning, looking like a model for a Ram truck commercial, an ad she'd actually created. The thing was the guy in the commercial wasn't nearly as nice looking as Ethan Daniels. "Kay?"

Henry nodded. "Don't forget."

"I won't, I promise."

When they got to the big inn—the Lumber Baron, according to the sign—she was heartened by the ramp that led to a wraparound porch and the entrance to the hotel. The accident had given Brynn an intense course on the kinds of access difficulties a person in a wheelchair faced on a daily basis.

"Isn't this pretty?"

Henry shrugged. He was less impressed with the inn than he had been with the Ponderosa. But the Victorian was right up her alley.

"Let's take a peek inside."

The foyer was gorgeous with nine-foot-high embellished ceilings and corner fans. The parquet floors extended to the front parlor where old photographs of the area lined the walls. Everywhere Brynn looked was the original gumwood millwork. The newel on the staircase was intricately carved and the wooden balustrade had been polished to a high shine. A giant stained-glass window let in a prism of color and light.

"Can I help you?"

Brynn looked up to find an attractive brunette about her age at the reception counter. "We were eating at the Ponderosa and I was dying to know whether the inside of the inn was as beautiful as the outside. Wow, it far exceeded my expectations."

"Thank you." The brunette stepped out from behind the desk. "You should've seen it before my brother and I bought it. It was ready for a wrecking ball."

"You're kidding."

"Nope. The place was a real eyesore. But we brought her back. Well, mostly Colin Burke did. He's a local carpenter and furniture maker." She nudged her head toward the front door. "He made all the rocking chairs on the porch. Also revived the Ponderosa when the new owners bought it."

Brynn gazed up at the stacked crown molding. "He does beautiful work."

"He does." The brunette sighed. "Do you need a room?"

"No, we're staying down the road, over at the Circle D Ranch."

"Ethan Daniels's place."

Brynn noted that the innkeeper had only referenced Ethan and not a Mrs. Daniels. He hadn't worn a ring the two times Brynn had spoken with him but she could think of a million reasons why a surgeon wouldn't wear one.

"That's right. Henry is Dr. Daniels's patient. We're staying in the cottage."

"The cottage is great," Maddy said. "Another one of Colin's masterpieces. The main house isn't too shabby either."

No, it wasn't.

The woman crouched down until she was eye level with Henry. "Are you enjoying your stay, Henry?"

He nodded and let his eyes drop to the floor. Since the accident he'd become shyer, often avoiding eye contact. Brynn was trying to break him of that habit.

"Henry?" She nudged her son.

"Yes, thank you," he said.

The innkeeper smiled. "I'm Maddy Shepard."

Brynn introduced herself and they stood for a while, talking. Brynn told her she and Henry were from New York and Maddy said she was originally from Wisconsin but had moved to Nugget via San Francisco.

"It's such a sweet little town."

"You should come for high tea tomorrow," Maddy said. "In the winter we do one every Sunday at four. A lot of the women in town come and I could introduce you around."

"That's so nice of you. It'll depend on Henry here. But I'll be around for a couple of months while my son recovers from his surgery. So if not tomorrow, I'll come another Sunday."

They were just about to leave when Henry brushed her leg and whispered, "Mom . . . stores."

It took Brynn a second to catch on. The hat. "You wouldn't happen to know where they sell cowboy hats around here would you?"

"Farm Supply. It's just up the road about mile out of town." She went behind the desk, got a map from the brochure rack on the wall and with a pen traced the route. "It's easy to find and Nugget's version of a department store."

Ten minutes later, they were on the road with Brynn glancing at the map every few seconds. A mile in Nugget seemed to go on forever. She guessed that's why they called it a country mile. Either that or it seemed longer because she rarely drove anywhere. In Manhattan, she mostly relied on taxis or a limo service to get around.

"There it is, Mom." Henry pointed, bouncing in his seat.

Sure enough, on the left side of the road was a large Quonset hut, styled to look like a barn, and a good-size parking lot. She pulled into a space close to the building. A set of log rocking chairs, like the ones on the patio of their cottage, sat under the hut's awning. She peeked at the price tag. Not bad as they appeared to be custom made. It was probably the work of that carpenter Maddy had mentioned.

Next to the chairs were a few chicken coops and a rack of cute sweatshirts that were on sale. They came in various colors with the Farm Supply logo. She found a black, extra small for Henry and a pink one in her size. It wouldn't hurt to have something warm to wear until their clothes arrived.

With the sweatshirts draped over her arm, they went inside. Maddy wasn't kidding. The place had a little bit of everything: Pet supplies, horse gear, a whole section of clothing, and even housewares. Henry zoomed in on the rows of cowboy hats and left her at the counter.

"Hi," she said to the cashier, an older woman in a calico smock. "Do you mind if I leave these up here while I look around?"

"Of course. Let me know if you need help with anything."

"My son is desperate for a cowboy hat."

The woman followed Brynn to the hat shelves where Henry had on a black Stetson that fell over his ears and eyes.

"Let's see what size you wear, sweetheart. Then we can get you into something that fits." The lady pulled a tape measure from her apron pocket and wrapped it around the middle of Henry's forehead. "Looks like you're six and three quarters."

"Hey, Grace." A man came from the back, carrying two sacks of grain over each shoulder.

The cashier . . . Grace . . . shook her head. "Why didn't you just pull your truck around back, instead of carrying those heavy bags?"

"I came in for dog wormer. The chicken scratch was an afterthought."

Henry elbowed Brynn and pointed at the man's felt hat, "I want one like that."

"Don't point." She smiled at the man apologetically.

"What do you got on, Clay?" Grace asked him.

"This here is a Resistol." He dropped the sacks of chicken scratch on the floor and began rooting through the children's hats to find a black one that was similar. "Here you go. Is that his size, Grace?"

She checked the inside label. "Sure is. Six and three quarters. Let's have a look." She fitted the hat on Henry's head and pointed him to a full-length mirror next to the dressing rooms.

"It's perfect, Henry," Brynn called to him.

He gazed at his reflection, turning his head from side to side, looking pretty pleased with himself. Then, just as suddenly, he frowned, took off the hat and handed it back to Grace.

"You don't want it, baby?"

He shook his head. "Can we go home now?"

Embarrassed, Brynn took the hat from Grace. "He's just tired. We'll take it."

She paid for everything at the counter and carried their purchases to the car. On the ride home, she slid a glance in her review mirror at Henry, who had turned his face to the side and was pretending to stare out the window.

"What's wrong? The hat looked so handsome on you." She saw his shoulders tremble and knew he was crying. "Henry?"

"Cowboys don't need a stupid wheelchair."

She wanted to say that he wouldn't need one soon but she didn't know that for sure. "Baby, no one cared about your wheelchair. That nice man and lady in the store sure didn't. All they wanted was to help you find the perfect hat." She wanted to tell him that everyone was special, that no one was exactly the same, but she could tell he was in no mood to hear it. "I get this is hard for you. It's a big change, but we'll figure it out together. Promise."

"I want to go home . . . to New York."

She reached back and squeezed his knee. "Just a couple of months, Henry, then we can go home."

They rode the rest of the way to the cottage in silence. When they got there, Henry wouldn't let her help him into his wheelchair. He managed to get inside on his own and went directly to his bedroom. She hoped a nap might change his mood. He'd always been a sweet and happy boy, even-keeled, affectionate, warm and extroverted, never mean or disrespectful. But after the accident and Mason's death he struggled with bouts of depression and had turned introverted.

The doctors, the therapists, all the literature she'd read said it was normal behavior for a child dealing with death and trauma. She tried to be nurturing during these episodes but at the same time, give him his space.

After bringing in their packages, she realized she'd forgotten to shop for groceries. When Henry woke up, they could go back out again. In the meantime, she made herself a cup of tea and drank it on the patio. It was a little cold for outdoor sitting but she adored the smell of the pine trees and gazing out over the river.

She'd always loved Manhattan and the excitement of a bustling city, but a person could get used to this.

A couple of pickups came up the road and disappeared behind the trees. She assumed they were going to Dr. Daniels's house. Perhaps he and Alma were having a gathering.

Not far away, she could hear a cow bellowing. There had been nothing in Ethan Daniels's CV about him being a rancher, she mused. Just a lot of information about his education. He'd gone to Stanford for his undergrad and Harvard for medical school. His residency had been at Lucile Packard Children's Hospital before joining the team at Renown.

He was your basic overachiever, Brynn laughed to herself.

He and his former partner had come up with the experimental treatment of using stem cells from bone tissue to repair severe breaks and deformities. Dr. Brunswick had been convinced that the cutting-edge procedure was a viable option for Henry.

Lost in her own world of hope and what ifs, she didn't hear the woman and little girl walk up until they were standing on the patio.

"Are you the new boy's mother?"

"You mean Henry?" Brynn smiled at the beautiful child, who had Dr. Daniels's hazel eyes, though they were more green than brown, and a dimple in her cheek. "I'm his mother. And you must be Veronica."

Veronica's eyes grew wide. "How did you know?"

"Your dad told me about you." Brynn stood and introduced herself to the child and the woman, who except for the hazel eyes—hers were blue—was the spitting image of Veronica.

"I'm Ethan's wife, Joey." The woman flashed a pleasant smile.

"Oh," Brynn stammered. "It's lovely to meet you. Thank you for your hospitality. We love the cottage."

"How long will you be staying?"

The question threw Brynn. Not because Joey had asked it unkindly but it seemed like a topic her husband would have discussed with her. Brynn and Henry were staying on the woman's property after all.

"Dr. Daniels thinks Henry will be okay to go home in two months."

Joey didn't respond. Brynn got the sense that Joey was sizing her up in the same competitive way that some of the women in her Upper East Side circle did whenever there was a newcomer. It had always bothered Brynn. Women should lift each other up, not view each other as threats.

Perhaps in this case, though, it was only her imagination.

To break the awkward silence, Brynn nudged her head up the hill, "I thought you might be having a party or a gathering."

"The guys are watching the Professional Rodeo Cowboys Association championship. Roni and I went for a ride."

"Where's your son?" Veronica asked.

"He's taking a nap. But he'd like to meet you. Your dad said that maybe later this afternoon you'd show him the horses."

"I could show him now." Veronica jumped up and down as if she was on a pogo stick.

"Roni, honey, Henry's taking a nap." Joey turned to Brynn. "How's he doing?"

"Just tired. We flew in Wednesday night and I don't think he's used to the time change yet. And . . . he's angry with his wheelchair today."

Joey's lips curved up in a commiserating smile, making Brynn reconsider her earlier assessment of Dr. Daniels's wife. "Make sure he gets lots of fluids. That'll help with the jet lag. The wheelchair . . . well, that'll just take time. Make sure he eats plenty of foods with antioxidants. It'll boost his immune system."

"Are you a doctor, too?" Brynn asked.

"An orthopedic nurse practitioner."

"Whoa, you and Dr. Daniels are a power couple."

Joey laughed, then something akin to sadness flickered across her face and the laughter was gone. "We should get going. How 'bout Roni comes back in a couple of hours?"

"That would be great." By then she hoped Henry was in better spirits. If not, the horses might cheer him up.

Joey and Veronica continued up to the big house. And with them went Brynn's theory that Dr. Daniels was single. For some reason the revelation that he was married made her sad. Not because she had designs on her son's doctor. It was something more intrinsic. Loneliness she supposed. Even years before Mason's death, her relationship with her husband had deteriorated. They'd become nothing more than roommates with benefits. And even the benefits had been scarce.

But once the surgery was over and Henry recovered, she'd take over the helm of the Barnes Group and find herself in the work that had once been her obsession.

Her tea was cold, so she went inside for a warmer. The cupboards were well stocked with drinks and a few canned goods and dry provisions. But she really needed to load up on the foods she and Henry liked. They couldn't eat breakfast, lunch and dinner at the Ponderosa, though the prospect of not cooking sounded nice.

In New York, they had a home chef come in four nights a week. The rest of the time, they either ate out or did delivery. Between Henry, her volunteer work and social commitments there wasn't time for her to cook, not that she'd ever been particularly proficient at it.

On Monday, Henry had his pre-op tests. So anything she couldn't find in Nugget, she'd buy in Reno.

Brynn refilled her mug with hot water and while the tea bag steeped, she dashed off a quick email to her mother and then one to Lexi, her best friend since they were freshmen in college. Lexi had offered to come to California with them but Brynn knew she was in the middle of closing a big real estate deal. Lexi's clients owned yoga studios all over Manhattan and were branching out to the Upper East Side. Lexi had found them a former dance studio on Third Avenue. If they negotiated the lease without a hitch the clients would hopefully use her as their agent again.

As far as Brynn's parents, February was a bear for her father, who had a performance nearly every night. So she'd come alone. She'd grown so used to handling everything on her own that it wasn't a hardship, though having company would've been nice.

She quickly perused her inbox and opened an email from Layla.

"Hope everything is going well with Henry. Don't worry about us, the Barnes Group is in good hands. Talk to you on Monday."

Right, the meeting. She'd almost forgotten it and quickly went to add it to her calendar when she saw that Zena already had. What would she do without Zena?

Just as she closed her laptop, Henry came into the kitchen. "I'm hungry."

She went over to him and smoothed his hair. "The bad news is I forgot to buy groceries. The good news is we could try that burger joint and hit the market after we eat. But first, I need you to bundle up." The temperature had dropped since their first trek into town. According to Brynn's cell phone, it was thirty-five degrees out.

Henry put on his shoes and jacket and sat in the car while Brynn loaded his wheelchair into the trunk. They followed the same route they had that morning. This time, the trip seemed shorter.

She found the drive-through, which was at the end of the square. The Bun Boy, she laughed at the burger joint's graphics, a chef with a hamburger bun butt. Ad-wise, there was a lot there to work with.

"We'll have to eat in the car. It's too cold for the picnic tables." She joined a short line of vehicles waiting to pull up to the order window. "Do you know what you want?"

Henry leaned over the driver's seat to read the menu posted on the side of the building. "A cheeseburger, french fries and a vanilla shake."

The line moved at a snail's pace. Brynn unrolled her window and craned her neck outside to see what the holdup was. She saw a middle-aged woman standing next to the pickup that was at the head of the line, gabbing with the driver. If they didn't move it along she was going to toot her horn. A few minutes later, the woman greeted the next motorist in the cue. They too had a lengthy conversation. Brynn noted that the pickup drove around to the front of the drive-through without any food.

"I don't know what's going on here, Henry." They were no longer in Manhattan that's for sure. Apparently in Nugget they took "service with a smile" to a whole new level.

Eventually the woman got around to Brynn, who unrolled her window.

"The speaker is busted. We're taking orders inside. Sorry for the inconvenience."

"Oh . . . okay." Brynn didn't know why they didn't just put up a sign. The poor woman wasn't wearing a jacket and was probably freezing.

The car in front of her pulled around to the front like the pickup, and Brynn followed suit.

"You want to wait in the car while I get our food?" It was only a few steps from Brynn's parking space to the door but why not make it easier on Henry?

"I want to come." He unfastened his seatbelt.

She rushed around back, got his chair and helped him out. By the time they got to the counter, they'd lost their place in line. The lady was back, taking orders while one of the kids in the kitchen went out the door with a piece of construction paper and a roll of duct tape.

The guy from the pickup was wearing a cowboy hat. Brynn poked Henry and whispered, "I like yours better."

"Mom!" He gave her a look. These days anything she did or said embarrassed him, which according to her friends would last for the next twenty years.

"Sorry for the wait," the woman said when she finally got to them and handed Henry and Brynn a cup of hot chocolate. "It's on the house today."

Henry's eyes lit up. "Thank you."

"Would you look at that, a young man with good manners. What's your name, sweetie?"

"Henry," he mumbled.

"And where are you from, Henry?"

"New York City."

"Well we won't hold that against you. What'll you have?"

Brynn rattled off their orders and they huddled in the corner, sipping their hot cocoa while waiting for their food. The woman—everyone called her Donna—seemed to know all the customers at the counter.

An older man came through the door and called to Donna, "What the hell's wrong with that speaker of yours? You got traffic backed up to the other side of the square."

"Oh shut up, Owen."

Brynn and Henry exchanged glances.

"Get the damned thing fixed." And just like that the man sauntered out the door.

Their number was called and Brynn grabbed the white paper bag with their order. They tore into the food as soon as they got in the car. The smell of the grill, a combination of fried onions and sizzling meat, made Brynn ravenous.

"Why was that man so mean to the lady?" Henry asked.

Brynn shrugged. "He certainly seemed grouchy, that's for sure. I suspect there is some kind of rivalry there."

"What's rivalry?"

"Friendly competition. Like when you and Asher play video games."

"Oh." Henry continued to nurse his shake. Under normal circumstances she would've insisted that he finish his meal before ice cream. But at this point she'd take whatever sustenance he got.

"Tomorrow we eat vegetables," she reminded him.

He scrunched up his nose. "Do I still have to go to the doctor tomorrow?"

"Yes, you know that. It won't be so bad, just a few easy tests. And Dr. Daniels will tell us what to expect on Wednesday." Throughout the ordeal, Henry had been so brave that she worried he sometimes held too much in.

Shortly after the crash, she took him to see a child therapist, but Henry was too closed off for it to do any good. When they got back to New York, she planned to set up another appointment. Now that eight months had passed, he might be more willing to open up. For now, though, she didn't want to heap too many doctor visits on him. He'd already gone through more than any eight-year-old should ever have to.

She collected all their wrappers, dumped them in a trash can next to the parking lot and headed to the Nugget Market to pick up enough provisions to hold them for the week. It was a small store but well stocked with everything they'd need, including a decent produce section.

When they got to the Circle D Ranch, Dr. Daniels's old truck was in his driveway but all the other vehicles from earlier were gone. She passed the big house, parked as close to the cottage as she could get without running over the lawn.

Balancing an armful of grocery bags, she raced to the front door to unload before helping Henry in. That's when it dawned on her that she'd never taken the key. She could still picture it on the kitchen counter where she'd left it from this morning.

Hoping that it wasn't a self-locking door, she turned the knob.

Uh-oh.

Chapter 5

Dr. Daniels came down the hill holding a casserole dish in one hand and little Veronica's hand in the other.

"I am so sorry," she said, mortified. "Our door lock in Manhattan is one of those code key deals, so it completely slipped my mind to take the key with me when we left. This time I'll put it on my car key chain."

"No worries." His mouth hitched up in the corners and she immediately thought of one of those silly nicknames from *Grey's Anatomy.* McDreamy. McSteamy. Either applied.

He handed her the covered dish, pulled a spare key from his jacket pocket, and unlocked the door. Scooping up her grocery bags off the patio table, he carried them inside and put them down on the kitchen counter.

"Those are enchiladas." He motioned at the still-warm covered dish in Brynn's hand. "Alma made them and the only thing better in this world is her *sopes.*"

"My goodness, they smell delicious." She sniffed the pan. "That was so kind of her."

"She figured you'd be busy the next few days, too busy to worry about dinner."

Brynn rested the casserole on top of the stove. "Let me just help Henry out of the car." She hadn't wanted him to wait outside in the cold while someone came with the key.

Dr. Daniels followed her down the walkway but Veronica beat them to the punch. She was standing in the doorway, offering a miserable looking Henry her hand while trying to coax him to come out.

"Roni, give Henry some space."

Veronica shrugged and moved away from the car.

"Hey, buddy. How's it going?"

Henry's face flushed and Brynn wanted to go to him and hold him in her arms the way she used to when he was a baby. But she feared that would only compound the situation. Henry had been an independent little boy and having to rely on her . . . and strangers . . . in conjunction with everything else only made matters worse.

She was about to call everyone away when Dr. Daniels discreetly hoisted Henry to his feet in one swift motion. Brynn got the wheelchair out of the trunk and Henry took it from there, Veronica dancing around him.

"You want to see the horses, Henry?"

He wanted to; Brynn could see it in his face. But he held back from saying so. Dr. Daniels also picked up on Henry's ambivalence because he offered to get his truck so they could ride.

"We could go in the Outback," Brynn suggested.

"That works. What do you say, Henry?"

"Okay." He nodded.

"Let me just put the groceries away. Anyone want something to drink?"

"Do you have soda?" Roni hopped up on one of the bar stools.

Her father grabbed her around the waist and swung her down. "What did we say about soda?"

Roni let out an exasperated breath and Brynn smothered a laugh.

"What do we have here?" Dr. Daniels zeroed in on the Resistol hat box that Brynn left on the kitchen table after their first shopping excursion.

Brynn slid the enchiladas into the fridge. "Show him what we got at the farm store."

Henry's cheeks turned red again and he shook his head.

The doctor didn't wait for Henry. He lifted the lid, took out the hat, and eyed it. "This is one good looking Resistol." He popped it on Henry's head and spent a little time adjusting the brim. "Let's get a little steam on it."

Brynn wasn't sure if that was some sort of cowboy euphemism. When she continued to stand there, he pointed to the tea kettle.

"Oh, you want me to boil water?"

"Yes, ma'am."

When the kettle whistled, Dr. Daniels removed Henry's hat from her son's head. Using the steam from the tea pot, he began to shape the rim.

"Come on over here, Henry." He called him closer and fitted the hat on Henry's head. After examining the fit for a few seconds, he took it off again and played with the sides some more, molding the rolls. "No cowboy's head is the same. When I'm done with this, it'll be just for you. Let me see. Put it on."

Henry gingerly fitted the hat on his head, afraid to ruin the new crease in the crown.

"You won't hurt it, just handle it by the front or back brim. And when you take it off don't put it down right side up. It'll ruin the brim. Do it like this." He demonstrated by turning the hat upside down and placing it on the counter on its crown. Then he put it back on Henry's head and eyed it from every angle. "Yep, looking good. Real good. Take a look in the mirror over there."

There was a small mirror on the wall over the coat rack, next to the door. It was probably there for exactly the purpose of adjusting a hat before leaving the house. The best part was it was wheelchair height.

Henry made his way around the counter and stared at his reflection. A grin the size of the Grand Canyon split his face. And in that moment Brynn fell a little in love with Dr. Daniels.

"We better get if we want to beat daylight," he said and turned off the heat under the kettle.

Brynn grabbed her keys, both sets this time, and they were on their way. The horse barn was only five minutes down the driveway in a small valley at the bottom of the hill. It was as pretty as the cottage with a triangular shaped roof, log siding, windows and a lean to under the left eave. Three horses grazed in a corral off the side of the barn, which opened to a larger pasture.

They got out of the car and Dr. Daniels let out a loud whistle. Two more horses trotted out of the stable and came up to the fence, where they hung their heads over the top rail and snorted. Roni climbed up, patted one of the horses on the head, then swung her legs over to perch on the fence. Without saying a word, Dr. Daniels swung Henry up and sat him next to Roni so that his legs dangled onto the horse side of the corral.

It was at least six feet up and Brynn's chest clutched. "Hold on with your hands, Henry."

"He's fine," said the doctor who fixed bones for a living.

She moved closer and even though she knew she was hovering she couldn't stop herself.

The horses crowded around the two kids and pushed their noses into their hands. Henry giggled. Brynn's heart nearly came out of her chest. She hadn't heard that sound in so long that it was like music, like Mozart's "Sonata No. 17" with her father conducting.

Dr. Daniels tugged a baggie full of apple slices from his pocket and gave them to Roni. "Show Henry how to do it."

"You put your hand flat like this." Roni demonstrated with one of the apple pieces, then shared some of the fruit with Henry so they both could feed the horses.

It was about the sweetest thing Brynn had ever seen. She grabbed her phone from her purse in the car and snapped a few pictures.

Roni told Henry the name of each horse and various stories about them. He listened raptly, petting a big brown horse with a white mark on its forehead that had taken a shine to him.

Her son's surgeon leaned against the side of the barn, a whisper of a smile playing on his lips.

"Thank you, Dr. Daniels," she said in low voice, her eyes filling.

"Everyone just calls me Ethan." He held her gaze, then glanced at the brown horse that had become Henry's new best friend. "Maybe after the surgery, when Henry's had a little time to heal, we'll get him up on Choo Choo there. It'll be good therapy."

As much as she wanted to, she couldn't see that far ahead. Today, she was focused on Monday's tests, hoping Henry was healthy enough for the procedure. So she simply nodded and changed gears.

"I met your wife today. She's lovely."

"Joey?" He slanted his head. "She's my ex-wife."

She pursed her lips in confusion. Someone wasn't telling the truth.

"She lives in Reno and visits Roni here." He stared out over the paddock as if he was searching for something. "We divorced a year ago."

"I'm sorry," she said, embarrassed that she'd raised the topic. Clearly, the situation was complicated. "I must've misunder—"

"No worries. What did you think of town?"

"I loved it. Everything about it is so quaint. The square, the Ponderosa, the fact that you can find parking."

He chuckled. "We've got plenty of that. I like the sense of community here. We used to live in Reno, in one of those planned divisions where all the houses look the same because it had lots of kids Roni's age. But it never really felt like home. I wanted my daughter to grow up like I did. Lots of wide-open spaces, neighbors who look out for one another, and a place for the animals." He glanced at the barn. "Good schools without the hour-long bus ride that I had to take on our ranch in Nevada. How about you? You like Manhattan?"

"I do, then again it's all I've ever known. I grew up a few blocks from where I live now. We have a lovely place but it's an apartment." A five-thousand-square-foot apartment but it was an apartment just the same. "No yard other than a rooftop garden and no pets because my husband was allergic. My folks have a weekend home in the Hamptons. That's about as close to the country as we ever got.

"But this place," she twirled in a circle, holding her hands wide, "is wondrous. I love sitting on the patio, watching nature unfold."

His lips tipped up in that signature grin she was coming to recognize. It probably made him the most popular doctor at Renown. "Maybe you should get yourself a cabin in the country."

"Mason used to talk about it. But . . . well, you know how it is."

He nodded politely. "I'm sorry for your loss." He bent his leg at the knee and pressed his boot against the barn siding.

"Thank you." Brynn hadn't fully mourned her husband's death. With Henry's injuries there hadn't been time. So, for the last eight months she'd been stuck in the anger stage of grieving. "Is it unhealthy to be furious at a dead man? For dying. For causing the accident that killed him," she blurted and just as quickly wished she could take back her words. She'd never voiced her rage at Mason for the crash before, not even to Lexi. Maybe it was because Ethan was a doctor, a healer, that she'd been so blunt, so personal. But now she felt awful for having said it.

"Nope, it's pretty natural. I see it frequently." His hazel eyes held hers for the longest time and the knot around her chest began to loosen.

"How do you do that?"

"What?"

"Always make me feel like things are going to be okay . . . That I'm okay."

"You are okay, Brynn. You're brave and Henry is lucky to have a mother like you."

Her eyes watered and she turned to where Henry and Roni were still sitting on the fence. "Look at him. Look how happy he is."

Ethan reached out and took her hand. A shot of heat slid up her spine. As if sensing the weird connection, he quickly took his hand away. "I'll do everything I can for Henry. You have my word."

"I know," she said, letting several seconds of silence pass.

The kids continued to chatter away and though she worried about Henry being out too long in the cold, she hated to interrupt the nice time he was having.

"Shall we go?" she asked, seeing her breath turn white in the air. "It's getting cold."

Ethan gathered the kids and they drove the short distance up the hill.

"Would you like to come in for a cup of coffee or tea?"

"Thank you but Roni and I need to get home." He hooked his arm around Veronica's waist and swung her onto his shoulders.

"Bye, Henry," she called. "See you tomorrow."

Henry waved, his face chapped red from the cold. Brynn bustled him inside and shut the door.

* * * *

Ethan locked himself in his office for a couple of hours while Alma and Veronica made cookies. The smell of sugar and cinnamon wafted under his door.

He shouldn't have said anything to Brynn about his and Joey's divorce. It wasn't wise getting too personal with a patient's mother and one as attractive and single as Brynn Barnes, especially when she was living next door.

Well, he couldn't undo what was already done. Nor could he erase the feel of her soft hand.

But he tried by busying himself returning emails. As usual his inbox was full. He skipped the usual junk mail and opened a message from the executive director of the Bentley Foundation.

"We just received a two-million-dollar donation from a Brynn Barnes. Do you know anything about this?"

He took a deep breath. Two million was a lot of cash and a big surprise. He and Brynn had never spoken about a contribution. The Bentley Foundation was always looking for wealthy benefactors but Ethan had no part in fundraising. He left that to others on the foundation's staff.

Brynn must have done a little background check on her own. The donation was beyond generous.

He sent a brief response to the executive director: "Yes, I know the donor but am not at liberty to discuss details. Don't spend it all in one place."

His phone chimed with a text. He wasn't on call today but when the emergency room was inundated with broken bones it was all hands on deck. The text wasn't from the hospital, though, it was from Joey.

"Thanks for giving me the run of the ranch with Roni. It was a really good day. Our girl is growing so fast. I swear it feels like yesterday that we brought her home for the first time. Our little bundle of joy. I miss those days. Anyway, I wanted you to know how much I appreciate you making things feel normal. You look good, Ethan. Really good. Love, Joey."

He slid the phone across the desk. Joey looked good too, like the nurse he first met eight years ago, doing rounds at the hospital. Even back then she'd been a party girl. Truth be told it was one of the things that had attracted him to her. He'd worked so hard to get through med school, his residency, and then as Bentley's protégé that he'd felt like an old man at thirty-two. But along came Joey to teach him how to be young again.

The sex had been great. And more than that they seemed to have so much in common. Their jobs, their goals, their backgrounds—both grew up in the country outside Reno. Joey loved horses and Ethan's family owned a ranch. It should've been a match made in heaven.

But over time it was hell.

Even before Joey became addicted to painkillers, there were cracks in their marriage. A year after giving birth to Roni, he caught her posting on an online dating site. She swore she'd never be unfaithful that she'd only done it to see if men still found her attractive. He told himself that it was postpartum depression and blamed himself for working too many hours.

But things got worse when Joey slipped on a wet floor in the orthopedic ward and threw out her back. For months she lived with chronic pain and by the time she healed, she was popping opioid analgesics like they were breath mints and injecting herself with the narcotic waste she was supposed to be dumping at the end of her nursing shift.

She stole from him, jeopardizing his career. And she stole from the hospital. When he and hospital staff got wise, she turned to street dealers for her oxycodone. Ethan had begged her to check into a residential facility. He and her friends had even staged an intervention. She promised she'd quit on her own.

Ethan should've known that her words were empty, a junkie's unfulfilled promise. But he wanted so much to believe that she'd get clean for the sake of their daughter. And the idea of deserting her was out of the question. He'd signed on for better or for worse, in sickness and in health, and held those vows sacred.

But when she endangered their daughter while looking for her next fix he couldn't do it anymore. He left her, took Roni with him, and filed for divorce. That was eighteen months ago. It took six more months before she hit rock bottom and entered a six-month program. The last six months she'd been living with her parents and from all outward appearances was clean and sober.

He was beyond proud of her. And as soon she proved herself to the judge and Roni's legal advocate, his ex would get joint custody. Ethan knew that. All Joey had to do was stay clean. In the long run it would be best for Roni. She'd missed her mother desperately and Ethan had suffered terrible guilt for separating them and breaking up their family.

But joint custody would be a logistical nightmare. And the damned truth of the matter was losing Roni, even for only half the week, was going to kill him. His daughter was his life and the idea of them missing holidays together and only seeing each other every other weekend made him sick to his stomach.

Still, it was inevitable. He'd have to suck it up but it didn't mean he'd have to like it.

"Ethan." Alma tapped on the door and let herself into his office. "How were the horses?" She sat in the big chair by the fireplace. Simba, their Australian shepherd, moved out from under his desk and laid at Alma's feet. Who said dog was man's best friend?

"The horses were good." Alma's interest wasn't in the horses but Ethan planned to make her work for it.

"And Henry? How is he?"

"As well as can be expected. Brynn thanked you for the enchiladas, by the way."

"And how is she?" Alma's mouth curved up in a teasing smile.

"Fine. Of course, you could always walk down there and ask her yourself. What did you think of Joey today?"

Alma let out a huff. "What can I say, Ethan? She seems sober. She seems like a doting mother. She seems like a woman who isn't done with you yet."

"What's that supposed to mean?"

"It means that she wants you back. She wants this big house and everything that goes along with it."

"Nah, it's not like that, Alma. We weren't good even before the pills."

She arched a brow. "*La cabra siempre tira al monte.* A leopard does not change its spots. She wants what she wants and she will pull out all the stops until she gets it."

"I don't understand why you never liked her. Before the pills she was a great nurse, a wonderful mother, and a good human being."

"But a terrible wife. *No hay peor sordo que el que no quiere oír.* You made yourself blind to it. But it was there. I saw it, your father saw it, your sister saw it."

There was truth in what she said. But he shouldered much of the blame. "How do you say in Spanish that a husband's no good if he's never around?"

"Bah, you were around plenty. And when you weren't you were doing important work."

"Spoken with the bias of a mother." He loved her for that but a man faced his foibles. And Ethan had plenty.

"Don't believe me." She shrugged. "You'll see. She's starting her campaign." Alma got to her feet and headed for the door. "We're having milk and cookies in twenty minutes. Then it's Roni's bath and bedtime. She wants you to read to her."

"What's your plans tomorrow?" If she didn't have any Ethan wanted to take her and Roni on a drive to Glory Junction to have lunch at their favorite Indian restaurant. The ski town was only thirty minutes away and Alma enjoyed the shops.

"I'm going to Reno to lunch with my old colleagues and gossip about the Ken doll, then catch a show at the Events Center with an old friend. You and Veronica are on your own. Don't burn the house down."

"I'll try not to." He wondered if that old friend was male. It had been three years since his father died. It was time for Alma to start dating. She was only fifty-nine and still caught plenty of men's attention. He would hate to think she wasn't moving on because of him and Roni.

Alma left, shutting the door behind her. Simba let out a whine.

"Traitor," he told the dog and opened the French door to give her a bathroom break. "Go on out, girl."

Simba got up on shaky legs, stretched and took her sweet-ass time going outside, letting the cold in. Ethan followed her, walked to the end of the yard, and gazed down the hill. There was smoke coming from the cottage's chimney.

He lingered there for a few minutes, then went back inside.

Chapter 6

Monday came fast. Brynn spent much of Sunday putting out fires at the Barnes Group. At the last minute, a client wanted to change his ad strategy. The creators of the campaign had to come in over the weekend, tear up their entire pitch and start from scratch. But nothing was working.

Desperate, they called Brynn. She spent much of the day video conferencing with the team and reworking the message and graphics. In the end, she thought the campaign turned out better than the original. Henry kept busy with Veronica, who showed up at the door at eleven, asking if he could play with her.

At five this morning, Brynn was up to do it all over again. It was difficult running the agency from the opposite coast but what choice did she have?

Mason was the agency's rainmaker, splitting his time between schmoozing new clients and working on the biggest campaigns, including Super Bowl and Black Friday ad strategies. Until she left to be a full-time mom, they shared those duties.

Now, it was Rich and Layla, who needed her help. The four of them had started the Barnes Group after leaving the Omnicom Group. She'd met Mason her first year working at the mega global marketing firm. Fresh out of school, they were ready to take the advertising world by storm. And they had.

Between Mason's brilliance tracking trends and her creativity, they quickly moved up the ranks, working on some of the agency's largest accounts. And somewhere along the way, they fell in love. But when the thrill of building their own agency and competing against their former employer for the biggest jobs in the business was gone, so was their desire for each other.

"You almost ready, baby?" she called to Henry in the other room.

They were stuck wearing the same clothes they'd worn to their first appointment until their things came. But Brynn took special care with her hair and makeup, telling herself that it was for Henry. She was putting on her best face for what would probably be a trying day.

He came into her bedroom in the new sweatshirt she bought him, wearing the cowboy hat.

"Looking good, buddy. Oatmeal or eggs?" She wanted him to have a good breakfast before they left. There was no telling whether there would be time at the hospital to have lunch.

He scowled. "Can't I just have cereal?"

"Yes, if you promise to eat it all."

They went to the kitchen where she pulled out the box of Cheerios she'd gotten at the Nugget Market and fixed him a bowl. While he ate, she made herself a cup of coffee. They had ninety minutes to get to the hospital and Brynn was a little nervous about finding her way. That was what the GPS was for, she reminded herself.

She checked twice to make sure she had the house key before they were on their way. The drive didn't seem as complicated—or as long—as it had the first time. She found the highway with ease and from there it was a straight shot to the Nevada state line.

"Mom, will it hurt?"

"Today? Or the stem cell procedure?"

"Today."

"I don't think so. It's just tests to make sure you're healthy enough to be treated. But we'll ask Dr. Daniels just to be sure."

She found parking easily enough in the hospital structure. And even though they'd been there last week, she needed directions to the orthopedic surgery center again. Though modern and quite nice, the hospital reminded her of an antiseptic maze.

They sat in the waiting room as they had the first time. The sound of trickling water from a table fountain on the reception counter was supposed to be soothing, she presumed. Instead, it increased her need to use the restroom. Too much coffee.

She leafed through a parenting magazine and tried to focus on the eighteen fast and fun breakfasts that children were guaranteed to love. But her gaze kept skipping to the window behind the reception desk, hoping to catch a glimpse of Ethan.

He called Sunday but only to ask her to send Roni home. Otherwise, she hadn't seen him. She knew she was being silly. He was a busy man, after all. And Henry's doctor, not a friend. But Saturday at the horse barn he'd been such a comfort.

For the first time, she hadn't felt like the responsibility of Henry's care was hers and hers alone. Her parents and Lexi had been enormously supportive during the ordeal. But she hadn't been able to confide in them what she had in Ethan. Maybe it was easier because Ethan was a stranger and hadn't known and loved Mason. He wasn't judging.

In fact, he even validated—or at least normalized—her resentment toward Mason for the accident. So many nights Brynn went to bed chastising herself for being a terrible person. Her husband paid the ultimate price for his irresponsibility. Yet Brynn still couldn't help blaming him—who careens down a mountainside on a three-wheeler with a child? Because of Mason's recklessness, Henry might never have full use of his legs again.

"Ms. Barnes, Dr. Daniels will see you and Henry now."

Brynn and Henry followed the nurse through the doorway to the exam rooms. They wound up in the same room they'd been in the first time they came.

"Dr. Daniels will be right with you." The nurse left and shut the door behind her.

Brynn helped Henry up onto the table and tucked his wheelchair out of the way. "You want to take off your hat. I can hold it for you."

"Uh-uh." Henry shook his head. "I want Dr. Daniels to see it."

The door swung open and Ethan came in. He smiled and she felt her pulse quicken. Suddenly everything seemed okay, like he had this and she could breathe again.

"Ms. Barnes." He nodded.

It did not escape Brynn that he'd reverted to using her surname, a signal that he wanted to keep things formal at the hospital. "Dr. Daniels."

He turned his attention to Henry. "The hat looks good, partner. How we doing today?"

"Good. Is it going to hurt?"

Ethan winked. "Just a little pinch when we take blood. You've had that done before, right? The rest of it is easy peasy. Did the nurse take a urine sample?" He addressed the question to Brynn.

"No. Would you like for us to do that?"

"Yep. You want Mom to help you, Henry, or you think you can do it by yourself?"

"Myself." Henry started to get down from the table and Ethan lent him a hand.

Brynn got up to go to him but Ethan gestured for her to remain in her chair.

"Let me show you where the bathroom is." Ethan got Henry his wheelchair and pointed him in the direction of the men's room.

"He might have trouble standing by himself." She worried about him holding himself up while trying to collect a sample at the same time.

"Then he'll sit. It's good to let him do things for himself."

He hadn't said it to chide her, but Brynn still felt as if her mothering was being called into question. Her first inclination was to let him know that how she chose to handle her son's needs was her business. What did he know about having a disabled child anyway?

He gently touched her elbow as if he could feel her hostility emanating across the room and just as gently said, "It's important for Henry to be and feel self-sufficient."

There was something about his touch and the empathetic way he spoke that made her anger melt away.

"I just . . . if I could replace his legs with mine I would."

"I know. Let's see if this works instead, okay?"

She nodded, trying to appear stronger than she felt.

Henry returned and Ethan helped him onto the table. A nurse came in to take his blood and for the next hour Ethan conducted a series of tests, explaining each procedure as he went along.

"In most cases, after a fracture is treated the bone grows new tissue, which for all intents and purposes glues the broken pieces together," he explained to Henry. "But in about ten percent of the fractures we see there's delayed healing or nonunion, which is a fancy way of saying your bones aren't getting better. More than likely the impact from the crash impaired blood flow to your femoral shafts." He laid his hand on Henry's thigh to show him where the femur was. "Blood supply is vital to repair breaks. So, we're going to use something called stem cells to regenerate that tissue.

"What we do, Henry, is we take the cells from your bone marrow, isolate them, then inject them into the missing section of your bones, where they become healing blood vessels and begin filling the gaps."

"How long does that take?" Brynn asked.

"On Wednesday we'll do the harvesting, then give Henry a week to recover while we isolate the cells. During a second surgery, we'll reinject the stem cells directly into the site of Henry's injuries. Recovery time is about eight weeks."

"Will it hurt?" Henry scooted to the edge of the table.

"I'm not going to lie to you, buddy. It's painful. But we'll put you to sleep with a general anesthesia during the surgery, so you won't feel anything until you wake up."

"Henry," Brynn got to her feet, "we talked about this, baby."

"I know." He wiped his eyes with the back of his hand and her heart folded in half.

"You know what?" Ethan said. "We're done for the day. Why don't you two get lunch and head home. This evening, I think we should visit the horses again, maybe get a picture of Henry on top of Choo Choo. How's that sound, Henry?"

Henry rubbed his nose on the sleeve of his sweatshirt. "Okay, I guess."

Ethan motioned for Brynn to stay behind after he sent Henry to the front desk for a treat. "You okay?"

"Nervous. Questioning whether I'm doing the right thing."

"You're doing the right thing. Henry's a brave kid, he'll do better than you think."

Though his words were meant to comfort, the idea of putting Henry through yet another medical procedure was overwhelming.

"There's a good Italian place a block from the hospital." He pulled his cell phone from the pocket of his lab coat and showed her how to get there on a Google map.

"Sounds good," she said.

But at the last minute she couldn't bring herself to eat in a strange restaurant in a strange town. Instead, she found herself in Nugget, parked in front of the Ponderosa.

It was less crowded than it had been on Saturday. Given the time, Brynn assumed the lunch crowd had come and gone. Mariah greeted them like they were old friends. The warm welcome made Brynn's throat constrict.

Mariah took them to a table not far from the man who had helped Henry with his hat at the feed store. He winked at them as they walked by. There were two other men sitting with him.

"Henry, you should take off your hat when you're inside."

He lifted it off his head by the brim, like Ethan had showed him and put it down on the chair next to him on its crown. She reached over and stroked his hair.

"Can I have ice cream?"

"Sure, but not until after you have real food. What about soup and a sandwich? That sounds good, doesn't it?"

He pulled a face and glanced at the table where the three men sat. "I want what they're having."

Brynn discretely turned to look. "I think it's chili." As far as she knew her son had never eaten it before. Beans had never been a staple in their home. "Did you order it with Dad?"

"No."

She wondered if the only reason why he wanted it was because they were men. Symbols of the father he'd lost. And that too made her throat tighten.

After the server came to take their order she went to the restroom, locked herself in one of the stalls, and cried.

* * * *

"Hang on to the horn." Ethan swung Henry onto Choo Choo's back, careful of his legs. "Can you get your feet in the stirrups?"

"I'll help." Roni climbed through the fence and held one of the stirrups while Henry searched for it with his foot.

"There you go. How does it feel? Good?"

There was no hiding Henry's smile. All that angst from earlier was gone, which Ethan tried to tell himself was the sole objective of this outing.

Ethan was getting too involved with the Barneses but couldn't seem to stop himself. Their vulnerability in the hospital today had been palpable. But it was more than that. The fact was he was drawn to Brynn Barnes. He admired her strength, her compassion, and her grace under fire. Her beauty.

The attraction was dangerous. As a doctor who'd already been called before the medical board, he should know better. But here he was, spending the evening with Brynn and her son.

"Let me get a picture for Grandma and Grandpa and Aunt Lexi. They'll love this." Brynn bent down and squeezed between two of the fence railings to get inside the corral.

Ethan reached down with one hand to help her through. "Watch behind the horse, Brynn. Tap him on the rump and let him know you're there."

She searched for the best light before the sun made its final descent and pointed her phone in the air. "Look over here, Henry." She got a couple of shots and said, "Now you get in the picture, Roni."

Veronica scrambled up the fence and leaned against Choo Choo with a toothy grin.

"Nice one," Brynn called.

"Ethan, you too."

He posed next to Veronica until she got her shot and said, "Your turn." He took the phone from her, waited until she got in spot and took a few frames.

The sun had turned into a flaming red ball and the sky was streaked in purples and blues. Another one of the things he loved about Nugget. The sunsets.

"Shall we head up? It'll be dark soon."

"But I want to ride," Henry protested.

"How about a turn around the ring and then we call it a night? Next time, we'll do this earlier."

"I'll lead him," Veronica shouted.

"You can help me." At seventeen hands, Choo Choo was too big for Roni all by herself. Ethan slid the reins over the gelding's head and led him in a circle. "Henry don't press against the saddle horn, scoot back just a little. There you go. Looking good."

Brynn took a few more pictures. Without the proper light, he doubted they'd come out. But there would be other opportunities. Even though he shouldn't encourage them spending time like this, he knew he would.

After the ride, he removed Choo Choo's saddle and let the kids brush him out with the curry comb.

"I can't tell you how much this meant to Henry." Brynn moved next to him as he supervised Choo Choo's grooming.

She'd changed from this morning into jeans, knee-high boots and a puffy jacket. Alma said a delivery for them had come. Ethan assumed it was their clothes. He liked her like this. Casual but sexy. He wondered if this is how she dressed in New York.

"When we do it again, I'll let him take the reins."

She hugged herself.

"You cold?"

"A little."

"All right, guys. It's time to head up." He took Choo Choo's lead and led him to a stall.

They drove to the cottage in his truck.

"Mom?" Henry leaned over his mother's seat. "Can Roni and Dr. Daniels have hot cocoa with us?"

"Of course they can." She turned to Ethan. "Is that okay? If you need to get back I don't want to keep you."

Against his better judgment he said, "Sure, we have time for a cup."

They went inside the cottage where Ethan made a fire while Brynn made the chocolate. The house smelled like her perfume, something floral that reminded him of springtime.

"It won't be as good as the cocoa at the Bun Boy but it's the best I can do on short notice."

"You've been to the Bun Boy, huh?" He came up behind her. "Did you meet Donna Thurston? She owns the joint and is a real character."

"I think so. Blond, middle aged, yelled at some guy named Owen."

"That's the one. So you met Owen, too?"

"Not really. He came in, they had a spat, and he left."

Ethan chuckled. "He's an institution in Nugget, owns the barbershop, though he's constantly threatening to retire. His daughter does hair too. I guess it's a family tradition. He and Donna are like dog and cat. But don't let them fool you. They'd go to the mat for each other.

"Owen hangs out with a bunch of the other old guys in town, playing cards at either the barbershop or the Gas and Go. Folks around here call them the Nugget Mafia."

"Seriously?" She laughed. "Do they shake people down? What an amusing little town."

He supposed he'd thought the same thing when he'd first moved here. Now, Donna, Owen and Nugget's other resident characters were just part of the fabric of the town. And a large part of the reason he liked it here so much.

"Nah. But they like to think of themselves as big honchos."

She grabbed a bag of marshmallows from the cupboard, popped one in her mouth, and dropped a small handful in each cup. "Come and get it," she called to the kids but brought Henry his cup to the living room where he and Roni were playing a board game.

"Brynn, don't wait on Henry. He has to learn to do things himself."

"I can't help it," she said tersely.

He put his hand on hers. "As his doctor, I'm asking you to try."

Besides touching her, they'd slipped back to using first names. This morning he'd tried to set some boundaries—for him, not her. It was a ridiculous tactic, though, as he'd been on a first-name basis with many of his patients' parents. Then again, they hadn't looked like Brynn Barnes or lived less than a quarter of a mile away.

He took his hand away, searching for a neutral topic that would still tell him more about her. "So you're an advertising executive, huh?"

She sat on one of the stools at the bar. "I guess I am again. For the last eight years I've been on the mommy track, working a little here and there from home."

"Alma says you're the woman behind the Nike and Capital One ads." He'd actually been the one to look her up. It was because he was curious about the Barnes Group, he told himself. He didn't know much about the faces behind the catchy taglines of the products he bought. But as it turned out she was responsible for a good many of them. Her late husband too.

"Ram, Ford, McDonalds, Apple, you name it."

"Wow, impressive."

She shrugged. "I don't save children's lives."

"Neither do I," he said. "I just fix their bones. I'm basically a mechanic." She arched a brow. "You're the most modest doctor I've ever met." A smile played on his lips. "That's not saying a whole lot. We're an arrogant bunch."

"Not you." She took a sip of her cocoa and eyed him over the rim of her cup.

"I can be. It's hard to help when you're the best." He winked.

"Yes, you are. That's why I picked you."

Their eyes locked and for a few seconds he let himself enjoy the moment—because they were definitely having a moment. He couldn't remember the last time a woman had captivated him this way.

His conscience told him to collect Roni and go. But he didn't want to. The fact was he could stay up all night, talking to Brynn, having a few more moments.

Chapter 7

Joey leaned against her steering wheel to peer out her windshield. It was a madhouse in the Nugget Elementary School parking lot. More cars than she'd ever seen on a Tuesday afternoon. And not the usual moms and dads in their cars and trucks, picking up their kids after school. She knew their faces by heart because for the last month she'd been secretly loitering in the lot just to catch a glimpse of Veronica.

If Ethan ever found out there would be hell to pay. And Alma would take great delight in ratting Joey out. But the risk was worth it to see Roni running across the grass with her blond hair flying and her backpack bouncing in the air. Even if it was only for a few minutes.

Sometimes, if Joey was lucky, Alma would stand at the curb, gabbing with a couple of moms. That would give Joey just a little extra time to watch her daughter.

So what if she felt like a stalker?

She'd missed Roni's entire year of kindergarten. That first day, when all the parents went to see their children's classrooms, Joey had been in a rehab facility in the middle of the desert.

"What the hell is going on?" she muttered to herself as motorists cruised through the lot, looking for parking only to wind up on the street.

Adjusting a pair of oversized sunglasses on her face, she unrolled her window and craned her neck outside. She spotted Ethan's Ford crawling behind a line of cars. "Shit." She pulled her head in and ducked low enough to be concealed by the dashboard.

Maybe it was parent-teacher night or some kind of an assembly or talent show. What she wouldn't do to sneak inside. But she was already pressing her luck by being here in the first place. It wasn't as if there was a restraining order against her. But responsible adults didn't lurk in school parking lots, shadowing their little girls.

Weekends. Those were the conditions of the supervised visitation schedule the court had set forth for her. You'd think she was a serial killer. But if she didn't abide by the rules, she'd never get joint custody.

She'd been working so hard to prove herself. And though she still hadn't found a job, she'd been hyper vigilant about keeping a routine. It was one of the keys to success for a recovering addict.

So every morning she went to the gym at nine and was at her computer by ten-thirty to further her search for employment, which included compulsively checking her inbox for any word from the California Board of Registered Nursing about her license. By two, she was on the road to Nugget, a fifty-minute drive from Reno just to spend a few precious seconds watching Roni get into Alma's car.

Well, today it didn't look as if it was going to happen. And sitting in the lot, amongst the empty vehicles, didn't seem prudent. Perhaps she could grab a bite to eat and come back in an hour. By then, whatever the event was might be over. If she timed it right, she could still catch sight of her daughter.

She turned on her ignition and headed for town. Though the hamburger joint would be faster, she was trying to eat healthy. Another one of her post-rehab obsessions. At this time of the day the Western place, the one with the bowling alley, would probably be empty.

Joey parked on the square and went inside. A Willie Nelson song played on the jukebox and the smell of fried food floated through the air. There were two men at opposite sides of the bar, one wearing a gun and police badge and the other a cowboy. Rugged face, square jaw, and broad through the shoulders. They held eye contact, then she looked away.

Other than a few couples at tables, the place was empty, as per her prediction.

The bartender told her to sit anywhere she wanted, so she grabbed a table not far from the restrooms, away from the bar. She ordered a Caesar salad with grilled chicken and carbonated water.

The cop took a brown bag to go. The other guy, the cowboy, asked for the remote and changed the channel on the TV over the bar to ESPN, which was airing a Professional Bull Riding event. She watched out of boredom, keeping one eye on the cowboy.

He seemed to know the riders and cheered a few of them on. "How 'bout that? That brings Cody Teel's world ranking up to number six."

The bartender joined him and Joey could hear them discussing PBR scores. Those bull riders were a bunch of idiots if you asked her. She'd seen enough broken bones to know what kind of damage a fifteen-hundred-pound bull could do. These riders spent half their time with concussions or in traction.

Her food came and the salad was better than she expected. Not too heavy on dressing, which in her experience was the problem with most Caesars. That and soggy croutons. But these were crisp with a hint of herb and garlic.

The cowboy got up and passed her on the way to the bathroom. When he came back out, he lingered at the jukebox.

"Any requests?" he asked her. "You look like you could use a song."

As far as lines went it was pretty lame. But she told him to play something by George Jones.

"Old school, huh?"

"Not really, just in the mood." She knew she was opening the door by interacting with him, handing him an invitation to make conversation.

He put a dollar in the machine, a restored Wurlitzer that played CDs instead of 45s, and "She Thinks I Still Care" came on. Then he surprised her by returning to the bar and the PBR without so much as a smile.

She finished her salad, glanced at the time, and motioned to the bartender for her check. On her way out, she caught the cowboy's gaze and he nodded. Outside, she took in the semi livestock trailer taking up most of the street adjacent to the one she'd parked on and wondered if it was his.

Fifteen minutes later, she sat in front of the school again. The parking lot, still jammed with cars, was as quiet as the Reno Public Library. Whatever was going on inside was important enough for Ethan to break away from work. Between his patients, consults, students and speaking engagements, he kept a full schedule. Most of the time, at least when they were married, he didn't get home until well after dark. Then there'd been the weeks he went out of town.

She rooted through her purse for her phone, opened up her picture gallery, and brought up a photo of Ethan, Roni and her on vacation in Hawaii. Roni had been barely four years old. Her little belly round as Buddha's in her pink polka-dot bikini. Looking at her made Joey's heart swell. She missed being a family and the life she'd taken for granted before the pills. Before everything fell apart.

More time passed and she started feeling silly for waiting. For what, a fleeting glance of her daughter tucked between Ethan and Alma before they were gone? She nosed out of the illegal space where she'd parked her car and started for home.

Maybe if she asked real nice Ethan would let her have dinner on a weeknight with Roni at the Circle D. Maybe he would even be there too.

* * * *

That night Brynn put Henry to bed, praying that he would actually sleep. They were both so nervous about tomorrow that it had been difficult getting through the day without having an anxiety attack. Twice, she'd almost picked up the phone to call Ethan for reassurance.

The last thing a busy surgeon needed was a pain-in-the-ass mother who needed hand holding. She'd gone over the instructions, which were basic. Henry couldn't eat after midnight. Ethan explained the procedure step by step, so she didn't know what she was getting herself all worked up about.

She fixed herself a cup of tea and tried to read a romance novel she picked up in the airport but had never opened. The phone rang and she jumped, then looked at caller ID. Lexi. Thank God.

"Hey, Lex, what're you doing up so late?" It was midnight in New York and Lexi was an early riser.

"As if I'd go to bed without talking to you first. I just got home. How's Henry?"

"All things considered, good. You were out?" Lexi was a workaholic but she was also a homebody. Brynn had to beg and plead to get her to meet her for a drink after eight o'clock.

"You don't want to know."

"A date with someone from that matchmaker site?" Brynn took her tea to the sofa. This was just the distraction she needed. "Well, how was it?"

"Let's put it this way: I'd trade places with Henry tomorrow over another date with this guy."

Brynn curled up with one of the throw pillows under her head. "That bad, huh?"

"So bad that I excused myself in the restaurant to use the bathroom and never went back."

"Seriously? Do you think he's still sitting there? Come on, what was so horrible about him?"

"He talked about himself incessantly. It would've been one thing if he was interesting . . . He gave me the entire synopsis of a book he someday plans to write. It's a really bad book, Brynn. Enough about my excruciating date, tell me everything."

"There's nothing more that you don't already know. Except my parents want to come now."

"Oh shit."

Brynn sighed. "I don't have the heart to tell them that they're too high maintenance."

"I do. Want me to call 'em?"

"Yeah, sort of . . . no. I'll come up with an excuse. It's a difficult time for my father anyway. And Henry doesn't need my mother hovering. He's got me."

"Want me to come, Brynn? Fuck this deal. It's taking too long anyway. I could be there by tomorrow night and Uber to that little town where you're staying in time to tuck Henry in."

"Uber?" Brynn laughed. "You'd die here, Lex. There's no takeout and the nearest Blue Bottle is more than two-hundred miles away. Seriously, you'd go into cardiac arrest."

"You said there are cowboys. Are they single?"

"I don't know. But you should see Henry's doctor."

"The surgeon? The one with the ranch and the cottage?"

"Uh-huh," she said and immediately wished she hadn't mentioned Ethan. Brynn told Lexi almost everything but she felt weird discussing Henry's doctor like a high school girl with a crush. "Wait to come, Lex. Henry and I may need you more after the second surgery."

Ethan had made it clear that the stem cell procedure was by no means a guarantee. They were taking a leap of medical faith and if it didn't work out as well as Brynn prayed it would, she'd need moral support. Perhaps even her parents.

"Whatever you need you know I'm here for you."

"That's why I love you."

They talked more about Lexi's real estate deal and by the time Brynn hung up, her anxiety level had faded to a dull niggle. She slept through the night without having a panic attack and woke the next morning ready to put Henry in Ethan's capable hands.

Henry came into the kitchen, reached into the cupboard for the box of Cheerios.

"Baby, remember what Dr. Daniels said? You can't eat until after your surgery. I'm sorry. But later, we'll go anywhere you want for dinner." She smoothed his hair away from his forehead. He really did need a trim. "In the meantime, let's get you into something warmer." He'd emerged from his bedroom in a thin T-shirt and jeans.

She found a sweater from the carton of clothes Zena sent, tugged it over his head, and grabbed a pair of socks from the dresser drawer. "Put these on and your tennis shoes. We've got to get going if we want to make it on time."

To Henry's credit, he didn't complain and followed Brynn out to the car. They made it to the hospital in less than an hour. She tried to block out the institutional smells and sounds as they navigated the maze to the OR. Henry was taken immediately into an exam room where Brynn helped him undress and put on a hospital gown.

She was sitting next to Henry's gurney, trying to distract him with a childhood story about her appendectomy when Ethan came in. He had on green surgical scrubs and seeing him instantly bolstered her confidence. It was a lot to put on one person. He was a doctor after all, not a superhero. And yet, the anxiety that had been eating away at her subsided the second he walked in the door.

"How is everyone this morning?" Ethan winked at Henry but Brynn got the distinct impression that the question was for her.

"Good," Henry said. "But I'm hungry."

"Sorry, buddy. When this is over we'll order you up a pizza. How does that sound?"

"With pepperoni?"

"You bet." Ethan turned, taking Brynn in for the first time since he walked into the room. "How's Mom holding up?"

Better now that you're here.

"I'm fine. How long will the surgery take?" He'd told her earlier but now she couldn't remember.

"About an hour." He squeezed her shoulder reassuringly.

In theory, an hour wasn't that long. But as Brynn sat in the waiting room, watching the clock, each second seemed to take an eternity to tick by. She tried to remind herself that this wasn't a life-saving measure, and attempted to pass the time by reading a long memo from Layla on her phone about the Barnes Group's newest client. But she had trouble retaining any of the information. Instead, she returned a text to her mother with an update.

"Still waiting."

Finally, at a little after one, Ethan emerged in the waiting room with a face mask hanging around his neck, a scrub cap on his head and surgical booties. He gave Brynn a double thumbs up. She rose so fast that she nearly dumped the contents of her open purse on the floor.

"He's still out and is on his way to the recovery room. A nurse will take you back there in a little bit. Everything went well and we got what we needed. We'll see how he responds in the next two hours. If he's feeling okay, we'll clear him for takeoff and let him get that pizza."

"Okay. Thank you."

"Brynn"—he was back to using her first name—"for the next five days or so don't be surprised if Henry has trouble sitting and sleeping on his side. His hip will hurt. We'll stick with Tylenol for now . . . see how he does. Maybe sponge baths for the first few days, so he doesn't get the bandage wet. Other than that, he can go back to his regular routine. Next Wednesday, we'll transplant the stem cells into both breaks and wait."

Wait.

She had never been good at waiting.

"Brynn?" He cocked his head to one side. "Breathe. We're halfway there."

"I'm trying." She forced a smile but her eyes filled with tears. A man sitting across from them eavesdropped while pretending to be reading a book.

"Let's step in here for a second." Ethan ushered her into a small conference space off the waiting room and shut the door.

"I'm sorry." She searched her purse for the small packet of tissues she always carried. "I was fine and then . . . Please don't think I'm a drama queen." She thought of Marlo Thomas and the St. Jude commercials, the kids dying of cancer, and wanted to smack herself.

"I don't think you're a drama queen, Brynn. If I was in your position I'd be reacting the same way." He took her hand and held it in his much larger one. It was warm and strong and even a little calloused and she wanted to hold on for as long as he would let her. "Henry's a great kid. He's going to come through this just fine."

"I'm the one who's going to have a heart attack." She laughed, trying to make a joke of it.

"You've got a lot on your plate. How about talking with one of the hospital social workers?"

"Oh no. I'm okay, really I am. I think mostly this is relief you're seeing." She took another swipe at her eyes with the tissue. "It's been a lot. These past eight months . . . I'm still adjusting." For some reason she didn't want to say grieving. "Henry is such a little trooper and I'm . . . babbling."

"Nah, you're stressed is all. When was the last time you ate?"

Now that she thought about it, she'd skipped breakfast along with Henry. "Dinner. I'll grab something as soon as I see Henry."

Ethan let go of her hand to glance at his watch. She wanted to grab it back. "I'll take you to recovery myself."

She followed him through a long, narrow hallway, behind a room walled off by a curtain. There lay Henry under a heap of blankets, looking so small it put a lump in Brynn's throat.

"Hi, baby."

He lifted his eyelids for a second, then they fluttered closed. She moved closer and tucked the blankets around him tighter.

"He'll be in and out of it for a little while." Ethan pulled up a chair for her. "A nurse will be in to check on him. And I'll be back before he's discharged."

Brynn wished he would stay but wasn't foolish enough to think Henry was his only patient. Her fixation on Dr. Daniels was getting absurd. She'd only met him less than a week ago and he was Henry's doctor for God's sake. A kind, compassionate surgeon. And here she was, mistaking her gratitude for something else. Wasn't that a cliché? The patient falling for the doctor?

"We'll be here," she said.

He returned thirty minutes later, said something to Henry's nurse, and handed Brynn a protein bar. "Eat."

She unwrapped the bar and obeyed. The truth was she was starved. "Thank you. Do you have more surgeries scheduled for today?"

"Nope, just Henry's. I promised Roni I'd be home early enough to take her to dinner. Tuesdays are our going out night. But yesterday she was in a play at her school and there was a party afterward. So I promised we'd make up for dinner today."

"Did she have a big part?" Brynn glanced at Henry to see if he was still sleeping.

"Nah. Pretty much the whole elementary school was in it. The first graders were all flowers. She was a damned good petunia, though." Ethan reached over her and gave Henry a gentle nudge. "You up yet, buddy?"

Henry murmured something and his eyes fluttered. Brynn could tell it was taking effort for him to keep them open.

"You did great, Henry."

"Hi, Mom. Is it over?"

"It sure is. How are you feeling?"

Henry tried to sit up but could only manage coming partly up on his elbows. "Good I guess," he said in a sleepy voice. "I'm thirsty."

Brynn looked to Ethan and he nodded. There was a plastic pitcher of water on the bed table. She poured a half cup and gave Henry a sip from a straw.

"Not too fast, baby."

When he finished drinking his head fell back on the pillow. "Can we go home now?"

Brynn wasn't sure if Henry meant the cottage or New York. "Soon," was all she said.

"As soon as the anesthesia wears off and we're sure there are no side effects, I'll release you, buddy. Then you can get that pizza."

"Will you come with us, Dr. Daniels?"

"Oh, Henry, Dr. Daniels has his own plans."

Henry looked up at Ethan. "Can't you come? Please."

"Sweetheart, Dr. Daniels has his family . . . Veronica. Maybe another time. Besides, let's see how you feel before committing to a pizza." Brynn had stocked up on soup, worried that Henry's stomach would be a little off from the anesthesia.

Ethan leaned against the wall. Even in his scrubs, his loose-limbed stance reminded her of a cowboy. "I could pick up a pizza on my way home and the four of us can eat at the cottage."

"We don't want to impose," Brynn protested. Henry had put Ethan on the spot and he was too nice of a man to say no.

"No imposition," he said in a low voice that made Brynn wonder if he didn't want any of the nurses roaming the floor to hear. "We've got to eat and Roni loves pizza. How about seven? I don't have any more surgeries but I still have a few patients. It'll allow me time to get home and clean up. That work?"

"Yes, of course. But are you sure? We really don't want to impose." She held his gaze, trying to silently convey that while thankful for the offer there was no obligation for him to have dinner with them. He'd already gone above and beyond, including the horse and barn outing and the small fact that he was her and Henry's salvation.

"I'll see you at seven." He walked out, leaving no doubt that their dinner plans were final. Not that she'd put up that big of a fight.

Chapter 8

Ethan stood at the door, juggling two large pizza boxes and a container of salad. "Knock, Roni."

His daughter, who couldn't do anything halfway, pounded on the door. Brynn answered in a pair of exercise pants and a blue sweater that matched her eyes. He continued standing there, maybe gawking, until it got awkward and finally went in.

"I don't think they're hot anymore." He put the pizzas down on the counter. It had been more than an hour since he'd picked them up at Giovanni's in Reno, drove home, showered and changed.

"No worries. I'll just reheat them." She set the temperature and popped both boxes in the oven.

"How's Henry?" He looked around the room and found that Roni had joined Henry on the couch to watch a Nickelodeon show.

"Good, I think. The pain meds probably haven't worn off yet, though."

When they did, Henry would feel pain from the area where Ethan had gone in with the needle. But he already warned them of that. No need making Brynn any more anxious than she was already.

He walked to the back of the sofa and put his hands on Henry's shoulders. "Looking good, partner." He dropped a kiss on Roni's head and went back to the kitchen where Brynn was setting the small table.

"My guess is they'll probably want to eat in there." He pointedly gazed at the living room where the two kids were so absorbed in their television program that they didn't know anyone else existed.

"You're probably right. I don't usually let Henry eat in front of the TV but I suppose today would be a good day to make an allowance."

Brynn glanced at the sofa where Roni had crawled under Henry's throw blanket. "She is so adorable and so sweet to Henry. I just want to squeeze her up."

Ethan flashed a smile. "Not to brag but she's a great kid."

"You can brag all you want about your child. Lord knows I do. Alma didn't want to come?"

"Alma left for Reno the minute I got home. I'm not sure but I think she may have a gentleman friend she's seeing there."

Brynn got down four glasses. "Is that weird for you, uh, because of your dad?"

"It's been three years since my old man passed." He shook his head. "Anything that makes her happy makes me happy. How about you? Are you working through your husband's death?" The question was wholly inappropriate. He was her son's doctor, not hers. He could pretend that he was merely checking into the wellbeing of Henry's family for the sake of the boy. But his question had nothing to do with Henry.

She sighed. "It's complicated. We weren't on the best of terms when he died."

Despite himself, he asked anyway. "How's that?"

"We'd grown apart and were mostly together for Henry . . . and the business. We built it together and we had a strong sense of stewardship."

"What'll you do now? Run it on your own?"

She shook her head. "We started the agency with two others. They came over with us from the Omnicom Group. Although Rich and Layla were never principals in the Barnes Group, they served as senior executives. They've approached me about buying in as equal partners. Although Mason had rejected that proposal in the past—he enjoyed his autonomy too much—I think they'll leave and start their own agency if I say no. And while I'd like to protect Mason's legacy for Henry, I don't want to lose them."

"You can't just hire senior executives, lure them away from another ad agency?" Ethan had no idea how it worked. He was only going on what he knew of other large businesses.

"I could. But they've been with us from the beginning. They know how we do things and they're an integral part of the Barnes Group. Besides, they make up for my weaknesses."

"And what are those?" He was interested because from where he was sitting, she was strong in all things that were important. Strong mother, strong advocate for her son, strong enough to weather a devastating crisis.

She checked on the pizzas, then took the barstool next to him. "I've always been the creative force behind the Barnes Group and not particularly good on the business end. That was Mason, Rich and Layla's strength. Mason was our rainmaker; he brought in the clients and sold them on what we had to offer. I would sooner lock myself in a studio to work on campaigns than have to schmooze prospective accounts. Rich and Layla have picked up where Mason left off. They already succeeded in bringing in a couple of Silicon Valley Fortune 500 companies, which was no easy feat with Mason gone. He was the draw."

"Why's that if you were the creative force? Aren't companies attracted to ad agencies with a track record, agencies known for creativity?"

Her lips curved up in what Ethan could only describe as a wry smile. "The general consensus was that Mason was the creative force, the one with the track record." She said it as if it wasn't exactly true.

"But he wasn't?"

"He was brilliant. Some of our best campaigns were his and the ones that weren't . . . " She didn't finish and instead got up and pulled the pizzas from the oven.

He planned to circle back around to the conversation, even though her issues with her late husband were none of his business. Any further inquiry would cross the line from professional to personal. But it intrigued him. Everything about Brynn Barnes did. And that wasn't good.

As predicted, Henry and Roni opted to eat in front of the television. Like Brynn, he didn't usually allow Roni that preference. In fact, he curbed her TV time to two hours a day. He moved to the country so she'd have plenty of land to roam on foot or horseback and to fish and swim in the Feather River. It's the way he'd grown up and he wanted to pass that down to his daughter.

"What about you?" she asked as they ate their pizza at the bar. "What made you want to become a doctor?"

A soft chuckle escaped his lips because for all intents and purposes his future should've been ranching. His older brother carried on the family profession in Colorado and his sister and her husband owned a dairy farm in Vermont.

"Yeah, unfortunately I don't have a great story. It's as simple as I spent my youth around livestock and slowly took on the role of tending to the sick animals on our ranch. We had a vet on speed dial but he was a busy man, making house calls to ranches all over northwestern Nevada. So when he couldn't get to us, the chore fell to me, whether it was dealing with a colicky horse or delivering a breech calf.

"Once, one of the calvings was so difficult that the calf fractured his femur on the way out. I went online, searched a couple of cattle websites, figured out how to set the calf's leg with little hope that I would do it right or that the calf would even survive. But damn if that femur didn't heal just the way it was supposed to. I guess from that day on I knew what I wanted to do. I probably should've become a veterinarian but somewhere along the way little humans interested me more."

"What are you talking about? That's a great story," she said.

He loved the way a smile spread across her face and made her blue eyes twinkle. The fact was he liked her face—with or without a smile.

"And how did you meet Joey?"

Ah, she was working herself up to the big stuff far more adroitly than he had. "The hospital. Pediatric orthopedic surgeon." He pointed to himself. "And pediatric orthopedic nurse." It was your run of the mill office romance. But he really didn't want to talk about Joey.

"And?" She wasn't going to let him off the hook. It was only fair after he'd pried first.

"We were once very much in love. But it sounds like you know how that goes."

She nodded. "I was curious about Roni. She seems to be with you fulltime." Her cheeks pinkened and her gaze fell to her untouched salad. "I'm crossing a line, aren't I?"

"I started it," he said. "Joey got sick last year and needed time to recover. I suspect that our custody situation will change in the near future."

"I'm glad she's okay." She dropped the topic, probably sensing that Ethan was uncomfortable with it.

He in turn reverted to medical mode, talking about what Brynn should expect next Wednesday and explained how Henry's therapy would work. A physical therapist would come to the ranch and work with Henry under Ethan's supervision while he documented the progress as part of his research.

"Hey, Roni," he called to his daughter, noting the kitchen clock. "Time to go."

They both had an early morning. Roni for school and him for a lecture to a group of pediatric orthopedists in San Francisco about his stem cell research.

"Five more minutes, Daddy." She held up her hand and through her missing front tooth said, "The thow is almost over."

He nearly gave in because it was five more minutes with Brynn. But his parenting skills—and a nagging conscience that he was crossing the line into unethical territory—had him scooping up his daughter like a sack of grain and tossing her over his shoulder. "Nope, it's bedtime for you, bonny Roni."

He squeezed Henry's shoulder. "Take care of your mom."

On his way out the door, Brynn thanked him for the pizza. "And the conversation."

"*De nada.*" And because he was a masochist said, "Let's do it again Friday."

* * * *

The next morning, before he even had time to go downstairs for a cup of coffee, his phone dinged with a text. A part of him hoped it was someone canceling his talk, which would save him a four-and-a half-hour drive to the city and an overnight stay in a hotel.

But the text was from Joey.

"*Any chance I could come Friday afternoon to visit Roni? Maybe I could make everyone dinner?*"

He jogged down the stairs, texting her back at the same time. "*You can't come Saturday?*"

Alma was standing by the three-thousand-dollar coffee maker—another thing his architect insisted he had to have—when he got to the kitchen. She automatically grabbed his insulated to-go cup and filled it from the machine.

Over the whirring of grinding beans, his phone dinged with a reply from Joey.

"*Yes, but I was hoping for Friday, too. I miss her, Ethan.*"

"Everything okay?" Alma asked.

"Yep, it's Joey." He gave Alma a quick once over. "What time did you get in last night?"

"None of your business." She pinched his cheek and pulled him in for a peck on the forehead. "Roni's getting dressed. Do you want me to take her to school?"

He usually did it on his way to work. "If you wouldn't mind. I've got to hit the road." He wanted to avoid rush hour near Sacramento.

"Do you have time for breakfast?"

"Just something I can take with me." He stuck his head in the pantry and filched a cereal bar and a banana.

"Clay's youngest is coming over tomorrow to ride the fence in the back forty." It was something he liked to do but was always short on time. "I should be home tomorrow evening in time for dinner. This isn't going to get in the way of whatever you've got going in Reno?" He waggled his brows, letting her know that he was onto her.

"Of course not. Veronica and I will hold down the fort while you're gone, like we always do. Right, sweetie?" Veronica came in, wearing an ill-fitting dress that she'd gotten two Christmases ago.

"Roni, that dress is too small. How about something else?" He'd been having this fight with her a lot lately. Ethan believed a kid should have some independence, including picking out her own clothes. But he drew the line at shorts in the dead of winter, shoes she'd outgrown a season ago, and clothes in the wrong size.

"Mommy got me this dress." She pouted.

"It doesn't fit you anymore, Veronica. Please go upstairs and change."

"You get going. I'll take care of it." Alma clasped both of Veronica's small shoulders and walked her up to her bedroom.

His phone dinged again.

"Well, would it be okay?" Joey was getting impatient.

She'd just have to wait.

He climbed the stairs, checked on how Alma was doing with the dress situation, and kissed Roni goodbye. On his way out, he swiped the overnight duffle he'd left by the door and stashed it on the front seat of his pickup. He'd been eyeing a new Ford F-150 Raptor but didn't have the heart to put his old truck down. Despite its wear and tear, it still got him where he wanted to go.

He got to the highway and called Joey. "Does it have to be Friday?"

"I can't do it tonight. I have a meeting." Meeting he knew was AA, which was good. She was working to maintain her hard-won sobriety and Ethan was proud of her for that.

"I can't do it tonight either. I'm lecturing in San Francisco and won't be back until tomorrow."

"Then what's the problem? I'll make dinner on Friday, one less thing you have to worry about when you get home."

"I have plans Friday night."

The words dropped like a thud and a long stretch of silence ensued. Then finally, "Can't Alma chaperone?" Joey asked, her tone dripping with sarcasm.

"I'm doing something with Roni."

"Oh." Her voice brightened. "Maybe I could tag along."

Ethan blew out an audible breath.

"Come on, Ethan. I miss her so much that it hurts. I literally walk around with an ache in my chest all day. Sometimes I call your house, hoping she'll answer just so I can hear her voice. Sometimes . . ."

"Sometimes what?"

"Nothing. I just don't want to miss out on any more of Roni's life. The whole time I was in rehab, Veronica was my north star. Ethan . . . please."

"I guess we can cancel our plans." He didn't want to. From the moment he'd mentioned Friday night to Brynn, he'd been looking forward to it. Ah hell, who was he kidding? He'd been counting the minutes like a kid waiting for Christmas morning.

But Joey. How long was he going to make her pay penance? Even after everything she'd done, he'd never doubted her love for Roni. But more importantly, Roni loved Joey.

When he'd separated with Joey and had gotten a court order barring her from seeing their daughter until she got herself into rehab, Roni constantly asked about her mother. One day Joey was there, the next she was gone. Confusing didn't begin to cover it. Especially for a four-year-old.

Roni became withdrawn. It took all he had, along with Alma's help, to coax her back to her precocious self. The thing about kids was they usually bounced back. He always told his patients' parents that and it was the truth.

But, now, he owed his daughter a relationship with her mother. Something more than insubstantial weekend visits.

"Why don't you come over around four," he said, telling himself that it was probably better that he put some distance between him and Brynn Barnes anyway.

"Great. I'll bring stuff to make that pasta dish you like."

She used to make it when they first got married. It was the only dish in her cooking repertoire and they'd sometimes have it three nights a week.

He hung up and realized something that had been hovering in his subconscious ever since Joey's last visit to the ranch. Then, it hadn't been anything he could clearly identify, just a lightness of being. But now he knew what it was.

He wasn't angry with her anymore.

Chapter 9

On Thursday Henry felt well enough to get a haircut. Brynn considered driving to Reno but remembered the barbershop in Nugget on the square. She'd seen it when they'd walked to the Lumber Baron. A small, western-style storefront with an old-time red, white and blue barber pole and a wooden bench outside. Ethan had said the owner's name was Owen.

Henry protested but with a little coaxing Brynn got him to sign on. If he got tired or the pain got too overwhelming they could come right home, she promised.

It was thirty degrees, according to her phone, the coldest day since they'd gotten here. Brynn pulled out their warmest coats and made Henry wear a hat and gloves.

She got the car as close to the barbershop as she could—not difficult in the land of abundant parking. A blast of heat greeted them in the cozy shop and to Brynn's surprise there were three customers ahead of them. She'd assumed that the shop would be empty in the middle of a workday.

Owen, the man they'd seen in the Bun Boy, gave them a cursory glance, landing for a beat on Henry's wheelchair. Then he waved them toward a cluster of plastic chairs while he finished with the police officer, whose hair he was cutting. Henry caught Brynn's eye and she gave him a reassuring nod.

In Manhattan, Henry went to Mason's stylist for haircuts, where you were as likely to run into one of the Yankees as you were Bill de Blasio.

The men here were more of the rugged variety as evidenced by their wardrobes. Lots of flannel, denim and work boots. Owen and the police officer were deep in conversation with a man sitting a few feet away from Henry.

"What you ought to do is raffle off one them houses and drum up a little publicity," Owen told him. "That's what they do on that home network Darla watches all day."

"I don't think giving away a house is going to help Griffin kick up his sales." The police officer swiveled around in his chair, using a hand mirror to check the back of his head. "Owen, take a little more off the bottom, right here around my neck."

Owen spun the chair so it was facing front and clipped away at the man's gray hair.

"I've got to do something," the man named Griffin said. "When I bought Sierra Heights I thought it was a good investment. Now I'm stuck with two dozen vacant homes. Yo, Jake, I thought your daughter and her boyfriend were interested in one of the Pine Cones."

"My daughter has big eyes and a small bank account," the police officer said. "What about Dana? She's your real estate agent. What does she think?"

"She thinks the market's tough right now, especially for homes in the middle of a forest." He glanced out the picture window at the towering pines in the distance. "No one can get fire insurance, not since half the state burned to the ground. Another reason I've got to unload these places. I'm paying through the nose to insure them."

"What about those BYOBs?" Owen asked and the two men . . . Griffin and Jake, who exchanged glances.

"Do you mean VRBOs?"

Brynn noted that Griffin was trying not to laugh.

"How the hell should I know what they're called? The places you rent out to vacationers. What about that?"

"I've thought about it. But Lina thinks it'll piss off the actual homeowners."

"I can see that." Jake, the police officer nodded. "Who wants to pay close to a mil for a house on a golf course and live next door to a constant barrage of frat boy shindigs, family reunions, and bachelor parties?"

"Not me." This from another one of the waiting room men, who until now had been reading a magazine and ignoring the conversation. "Griff, bro, love you like a brother. But if you go the VRBO, Airbnb route you can forget me ever cooking for you again."

"Don't worry, Brady. Not happening. I don't want to be a property manager. I just want to run my gas station, build custom bikes, and live large."

"Come live large in my chair." Owen waved Griffin over and went to the cash register to take Jake's credit card.

During the transaction Jake looked over at Brynn, bobbed his head, and winked at Henry. "Got to go protect and serve. See y'all later."

There was a chorus of "Bye, Jake" and Brynn watched through the picture window as he got into a Nugget Police SUV and drove away. Henry was watching too.

"I've got to go back to work." An older man about the same age as Owen got up, crunched a Styrofoam cup in his hand, and tossed it in the trash can.

"Bye, Dink," everyone said in unison.

Brynn was starting to think that she'd landed in another dimension. It was like a re-run of *Petticoat Junction* on Hulu.

"I still think you should raffle one of them off." Owen snapped a cape around Griffin's neck. "Make a big to-do about it, get yourself on TV."

"It sends the wrong message," Brynn blurted as three pairs of eyes locked on her.

Griffin swiveled around to face her. "It looks desperate, right?"

She shrugged not wanting to offend Owen. "From the discussion I assume this is a luxury community, yes?"

"As luxury as it gets around here."

Owen slapped Griffin. "Learn to talk without moving your head."

"Golf course, swimming pool, tennis courts, riding stable," Griffin continued, ignoring Owen.

"It sounds lovely. And it's near here?" Griff nodded, provoking yet another slap from Owen. "What kind of people has it attracted so far?"

The man . . . Brady . . . lifted his head from the magazine again. "Me."

"What do you do for a living?" Judging by the tattoos up and down his arms he could be anything from a bouncer to a rock star. "And what are your hobbies?"

"I'm an executive chef for a hotel group and I like to run, hike, ski, fish. Not necessarily in that order."

"And would you say that most of the other homeowners have the same interests?"

"Yeah, most of us like the outdoors or else we wouldn't be here."

"Are there ski resorts close by?"

"About a half hour away in Glory Junction," Griffin said.

Okay, too far to really promote the area as a ski destination. "How's the real estate market in Glory Junction?"

Everyone laughed.

"Those crazy Trekkies from the city will pay seven figures for a shack." Owen rolled his eyes.

"Trekkies?"

"He means Techies." Brady shook his head. "But, yeah, the market is red hot there. Same outdoorsy feel as Nugget. We've both got a river and a lake. The only thing lacking in Nugget is the ski-in ski-out resorts, the fancy shops and the froufrou."

"Is it mostly second homes? People who come up from the Bay Area for the weekend to play?" She figured it was a lot like the Hamptons where her parents had a second place.

"Exactly," Griffin said. "Not enough jobs to live in Glory Junction or here full time unless you can telecommute."

"Is it correct to assume that the homes you're selling here are less expensive than the ones in Glory Junction?"

"Yep." Griffin gave her a thumbs up. "But still too expensive to appeal to railroad workers and ranchers."

"Then you need to make your community an alternative to Glory Junction. Sell it as a less expensive option that still offers an outdoorsy lifestyle. I don't know, call it something like a spa experience for the nature lover. Buy up ads in travel and luxury magazines. Tap the weekend get-away market."

"Whoa, I like it."

She'd just been riffing off the top of her head. Without having seen the place, she was at a disadvantage. But if Griffin's planned community was anything like the Circle D Ranch it had to be breathtaking. All this countryside was.

"That's just an example. The point is not to rely on traditional real estate listings but to target people who don't even realize they want a second home. You have to make them want one and persuade them that not only can they afford it but it's a good investment."

Brady gave her a once over. "Are you in marketing or something?"

"Advertising."

"You up on vacation?" Brady smiled at Henry who had been staring at his tattoos. "I didn't notice you staying at the Lumber Baron. I work for Breyer Hotels. They own the Lumber Baron."

"Henry's Dr. Daniels's patient." By now she'd learned that everyone seemed to know one another in this small mountain town. "We're staying in his cottage."

"Can I hire you?" Griffin asked as Owen brushed hair off his neck.

"Uh . . . I'm pretty tied up with my son." Telling him that the Barnes Group's clients were typically major corporations would've sounded snobby. "But a local agency should be able to handle your job just fine."

Owen finished with Griffin and all but pushed him out of the chair, signaling for Brady to climb up. Griffin joined them in the waiting room, pulled up one of the plastic chairs, turned it backwards, and straddled it.

He was a nice-looking man, younger than Brynn, and kind of a Charlie Hunnam look alike.

"Hey, Henry." He shook Henry's hand and from Henry's reaction Brynn could tell that the attention made her son feel important. "Griffin Parks. Nice to meet you both. How you liking Nugget?"

"I like it," Henry said. "Dr. Daniels has horses. I got to ride one the other day."

"Ethan's got some nice horses all right. We've got some too over at Sierra Heights and a lady who gives lessons. How long you staying in town?"

Henry looked to Brynn. "About two months while my son recuperates from his surgery."

"Come on over and see us." He tugged his wallet out of his pocket and scrounged through it until he found a business card and slipped it to Brynn.

He paid up at the cash register and waved his hand in the air as he went out the door.

Brynn turned the card over. Apparently, Griffin was Nugget's resident businessman. According to his card, he owned the local gas station, a convenience store, a custom motorcycle shop and Sierra Heights. From an advertising standpoint, she didn't know if she would've put all that on one business card. But it was economical, she would at least give it that.

She turned her attention to the assortment of reading material while Brady and Owen discussed the weather. There were a few *People* and *Cosmopolitan* magazines that were months old. But the bulk of the selection were about hunting and fishing.

Henry was occupying himself with a year-old *Highlights*. So far, his hip—the spot where Ethan had harvested his bone marrow—didn't seem to be bothering him. But she'd given him Tylenol before they'd left the Circle D.

An attractive woman pushed a stroller through the door. "Hey, Owen. Hey, Brady. Darla wouldn't happen to be here would she?" She craned her neck, searching the back of the barbershop.

"Day off." Owen stopped cutting Brady's hair and crouched down in front of the stroller. "You're getting big there, Paige."

The woman glanced curiously over at Brynn and let her gaze fall on Henry.

"What do you need from Darla?" Owen asked.

"Shampoo. I forgot which one I get and she keeps a list on the computer."

"Can't help you there. Don't know how to use the thing." He eyed the iPad next to the old timey cash register with distaste. "Don't know why she needs a computer to keep track of these things. Shampoo is shampoo."

"This one is specially for color treated hair and has some kind of UV protection." She slipped past Owen and perused a shelf of shampoos, conditioners, hair gel and mousses.

Brynn recognized some of the brands from the salon she went to in the city and was surprised to find luxury hair products in a country barbershop. It was good to know she could get them here, though Zena had sent Brynn's from home.

"It's either this one or this one." The woman held up two bottles. Both had similar packaging. "I'll wait until she's in. Otherwise, I'm liable to get the wrong one."

"Suit yourself, missy."

The cowboy . . . Clay . . . who'd helped Henry with his hat came in. "You get what you need?" he asked the woman.

"Nope. I have to wait for Darla. You ready to go?"

"Yep." Clay tipped his hat at Owen and Brady, then at Brynn and Henry, who instantly recognized the man. "We've got to stop meeting like this. How's the hat working out?"

Henry once again looked to Brynn, who silently told him to answer for himself. "Good. I didn't wear it today because I'm getting a haircut but Dr. Daniels made the sides better."

"Yeah? He use a little steam?"

Henry nodded. "It's like his now and kind of like yours."

"Ethan knows what he's doing. You all staying up at his place?"

"Yes," Brynn said and introduced herself and Henry.

"Clay McCreedy." He gestured toward the woman, who'd been observing their conversation with interest. "This is my wife, Emily, and that right there is Paige, our little girl."

"Hello." Brynn smiled at Emily. "Your husband helped Henry pick out his first cowboy hat at the store up the road."

"Oh yeah? Clay's had a lot of practice picking out cowboy hats." She put an arm around her husband and inexplicably Brynn felt a tinge of melancholy. "How are you liking the Circle D? Are you staying in the cottage?"

Clearly, she and her husband had figured out the situation. If nothing else the wheelchair was a dead giveaway.

"It's lovely. We're from Manhattan so this is quite a treat."

"Ethan's got a great spread," Clay said, slinging his arm over his wife's shoulder. Both smiled in that pure way that told Brynn that they were very much a unit.

"I don't know how long you're here for but we have a great high tea at the Lumber Baron every Sunday." Emily looked at Brynn expectedly.

"Yes, the innkeeper . . . Maddy, right? . . . told me about it. I'd love to go but it'll all depend on this guy here and how he's feeling." She mussed Henry's hair.

"If you like sweets, Henry, you'll want to come," Emily said. "Or we can send Alma home with treats."

People were unbelievably nice here. Brynn attributed it to the slow pace of living in the country. Home in Manhattan, everyone rushed around so much no one had time to reach out to a neighbor or a stranger.

"We will do our best to make it, won't we Henry?"

Henry gave a small nod. He was holding up so well that Brynn wondered whether Ethan exaggerated the aftereffects of the surgery. Either that or Henry had been through so much these past eight months he'd become immune to pain.

But an hour later both theories proved wrong. As they returned to the cottage Henry sat in the backseat, rocking back and forth, silently crying.

"We'll be home soon. I'll get you some Tylenol and you can lie down." She slid a look in the rearview. "Your hair looks great."

He wasn't listening, lost in a world of hurt. She kicked herself for taking him to town, seeing now that the trip and the haircut had been overly ambitious just a day after surgery. But he'd seemed fine this morning.

As she ushered Henry inside, she thought about calling Ethan. Maybe he could prescribe something stronger. Honestly, she just wanted to hear his reassuring voice. But she didn't want to take advantage of the fact that they were living on his ranch and had struck up a friendship. At least she thought it was a friendship. Perhaps he had dinner with the families of all his patients.

She doubted it, though. The pizza was one thing. But the flash of guilt that flitted across his features when he'd invited them to do it again on Friday was a pretty good indication that he didn't typically fraternize with the mothers of his patients. She may have been married to Mason for ten years but that didn't mean she was clueless.

She was attracted to Ethan Daniels and she was pretty sure he was attracted to her. She also knew it wasn't anything either of them could act on. Perhaps her little crush felt safer for that very reason.

Henry curled up on the sofa while she went to get the Tylenol. If it didn't help with the pain, she'd go to plan "B."

A short time later, he was out, his arms clutched around one of the throw pillows like he used to hug his stuffed bear when he was a tiny boy. She stood there, watching him sleep, her heart moving in her chest. Her sweet little boy. Unable to resist, she dropped a small kiss on the top of his head. "Sleep tight," she whispered.

She made herself a sandwich in the kitchen and ate it in front of her laptop. On a lark she Googled Sierra Heights, finding only a story about the gated community in an old *Nugget Tribune* article and an even older real estate ad in the classifieds.

Why wasn't there a website, a Facebook page, or an Instagram account? No wonder the man wasn't selling houses. If she ran into Griffin Parks again she planned to tell him to take advantage of social media—it was free!—and investing in building a good website.

She checked in with Layla and Rich, made some minor tweaks to a new campaign for Apple, and left a message for Lexi. She read the *Time's* review of Berlioz's "Symphonie Fantastique," which waxed poetic about her father. Not surprising.

Funny, for all her father's musical talent, Brynn couldn't so much as hum in tune. Mason used to joke that to save them all, Brynn should refrain from singing in the shower. Unfortunately, Henry had taken after her. His rendition of "Für Elise" bordered on painful.

So, her son would never be a pianist. Henry had other talents. He drew beautifully for one and he was such a compassionate little boy, never mean to anyone. His teacher called him the classroom peacemaker. Perhaps he'd be a diplomat one day.

There was a soft rap on the door and Brynn's pulse quickened. It was still relatively early, only four. But she hoped it was Ethan. She fluffed her hair, trying to remember if she'd even put on makeup before they'd gone to town, and answered to find Veronica standing there.

"Can Henry come out to play?"

"Oh, honey, Henry's sound asleep." Brynn went outside and quietly shut the door. "He's not feeling so well after his appointment yesterday. Are you out of school for the day?"

"Uh-huh. My grandma said I could come over but only if it was okay with you."

"Henry will be disappointed that he missed you. But we're having dinner tomorrow." It was ridiculous but she'd already planned her outfit. A simple pantsuit that according to Lexi, showed off Brynn's curves.

"My mommy's coming tomorrow. She's making patha for me and my daddy. My grandma can't come."

Ethan hadn't said anything about canceling. The possibility filled her with disappointment, a disappointment too deep for a woman supposedly mourning her dead husband.

Roni jumped up with excitement. "Henry can come."

"That is very nice of you to invite him, Veronica." Brynn wiped a smudge of dirt off Roni's nose. The girl was too adorable for words. "Let's see how Henry feels, okay?"

"Okay. When he wakes up can he play?"

"If he's feeling up to it, absolutely. We'll call up to the house."

Brynn watched Veronica skip up the hill and tried to imagine living in a place where children had backyards the size of Central Park and could safely run free.

She went inside and debated whether she should send Ethan a text about Friday. It wasn't as if the need to know was pressing. She and Henry would simply have dinner together, alone. But she secretly hoped Roni had gotten the date wrong.

It turned out texting him wasn't necessary. Ethan had sent his own message.

"Sorry, but I have to cancel Friday. Something's come up. Ethan."

It wasn't a something, Brynn told herself. It was Ethan's ex-wife.

Chapter 10

Joey was running late. She'd spent too much time getting ready, changing at least four times before settling on what to wear. Even now, forty miles from Reno, she second guessed her selection. The red sweater dress said first date, not casual dinner at home with her daughter and ex-husband. She should've stuck with jeans and a fitted tunic—her first choice.

And she'd gone too heavy on the makeup. She grabbed a tissue from her visor dispenser and began blotting red from her lips. In the review mirror she caught her reflection and cringed. The 90s called and wanted its eyeliner back. Seriously, she looked like she was on her way to a dance club.

She thought about stopping in town, finding a bathroom, and washing her face clean. But Ethan hated unpunctuality more than he did overly made up women. Though the two were nearly neck and neck for his least favorite things.

She'd just have to suck it up, maybe say she was coming straight from a job interview. Yeah, for a part in a drag show. She glanced at the clock on her dashboard, took a deep breath, and tried to stop being so hard on herself.

The groceries for a delicious dinner sat in her trunk, including Ethan's favorite dessert. Coconut cream pie from the best bakery in Reno. She'd even gotten Roni a cupcake decorated in butterflies, her daughter's latest obsession.

For once in her life she was organized and there was nothing Ethan loved more than organization. Despite her poor wardrobe decision, she could pull this off and prove to Ethan that she truly had her act together.

But as she drove through the Circle D's gate, she could feel a trickle of perspiration collect in the bridge of her bra. Simba—another thing Ethan had gotten in the divorce—greeted her in the driveway.

She was halfway out of the car when Roni flew down the porch steps and into her arms. And suddenly Joey's clothes and her makeup didn't matter anymore. Instead, she filled herself with Roni. The smell of her sweet baby shampoo hair, the feel of her small body vibrating with excitement and the way in that mini voice of hers she said, "Mommy, Mommy, you're here."

"I'm here. And I'm so, so happy to see my best girl."

"I'm you're only girl, Mommy."

"Yes, you are. But you're also my best girl. My best everything." Joey wrapped Roni in a hug and held her tight.

When she looked up, she found Ethan standing on the front porch, watching them. His expression, a combination of something Joey couldn't quite identify—sadness maybe—made her suddenly feel self-conscious.

"Want to help Mommy carry up the groceries?" She popped the trunk and handed Roni the pie box. "Careful with that. It's Daddy's surprise."

"Did you get me a surprise?"

"Of course I did."

"What is it?" Roni tried to wedge herself between Joey and the trunk to peek.

"If I told you it wouldn't be a surprise, now would it? Take that to the kitchen, Roni."

When Joey turned around Ethan was there. He took two grocery bags out of her hands. She picked up the bakery box with Roni's cupcake and followed Ethan into the kitchen.

"Where's Alma?" she asked, silently hoping that Ethan's stepmother wasn't joining them.

"She had plans."

"Too bad, I brought enough food for all four of us and then some."

He raised his brows to let her know he knew she was lying. She and Alma had never made a secret of their dislike of each other. Alma had never thought Joey was good enough for Ethan and Joey didn't appreciate Alma's meddling.

She started to unpack the bags, making neat little piles on the counter, all the while trying to gauge Ethan's mood. Unlike her, he'd dressed casually. Faded jeans, a Stanford sweatshirt, and his ranch boots.

"Where are your pots?"

He nudged his head at the enormous pot rack over the center island. *You're an idiot, Joey.* No, she was just incredibly nervous.

It never used to be that way between them. In fact, during their marriage, Joey had always suspected that Ethan had loved her just a little more than she had loved him. Though it was a sad statement on their relationship, it had always given her a slight upper hand.

"You look nice," he said as she took off her coat and draped it over one of the breakfast table chairs.

"I kind of over did it." Why not just put it out there? "I was nervous about making a good impression." The last months of their marriage, she'd rarely washed her hair. Most days she was lucky to summon enough energy to put on an old set of scrubs.

"You could come in a gunny sack. It wouldn't make a difference to Roni." She wasn't trying to impress Roni.

"It is what it is." She Vanna Whited her hands over the red dress. "Next time I'll wear jeans."

"Wear whatever makes you comfortable, Joey."

She wanted to tell him to stop being so agreeable. She wasn't going to break, or worse, sneak through his drawers, searching for pills, if he looked at her sideways. Yes, she had bad days. All addicts did. But she was committed to her recovery.

"Let's get this party started," she said, wanting to change the topic.

He reached up and unhooked a pasta pot from the rack. The kitchen was twice as large as the one they'd had in Reno. Joey suspected Alma had had a say in the design. For all her faults, Ethan's stepmother was an amazing cook. Joey was more of the make-it-from-a-box or stick-it-in-the-slow-cooker kind.

The whole house was gorgeous. Much posher than what Joey would've expected from Ethan, who was a no-frills guy. Even though he made crap loads of money, he'd always liked to live light on the land. He wasn't stingy or cheap, mind you. Just not showy.

After they'd had Roni, she'd bought herself a seventy-five-thousand-dollar Mercedes GLS 450. Her push present to herself. He hadn't complained about the price. But he'd asked her to keep it in the garage. Not for security reasons but because he was embarrassed of the SUV. He thought it was loud.

They'd both been raised land rich, cash poor, though Ethan's family had made a killing in the beef cattle industry. Her reaction to their newfound prosperity had been to spend with wild abandon. His was to live exactly the way he had growing up.

The Circle D Ranch was a departure from that. It was exactly what you would expect from a world-renowned surgeon.

She used the fancy pot filler and put the water up to boil. Roni raced up to her room to get her own surprise for Joey. Ethan sat at the counter on his phone, texting as nimbly as a teen. It reminded her of what his fingers—and hands—were capable of in and out of the operating room.

"What's going on?" She gestured at his phone.

"Nothing." He quickly put it away as if he'd been caught doing something he shouldn't. "Just a patient."

"The little boy at the cottage?" It was just a weird gut feeling.

"Uh, no. Someone else."

She was pretty sure he was lying. It was the little stutter in his voice. Ethan had never been duplicitous, never one of those husbands who played around on the side. But occasionally he'd circumvent the truth to avoid an argument when it came to him choosing work over her.

"How is he?"

"Who?"

She pierced him with a look.

"Good but hurting from a bone marrow harvest on Wednesday. But you know I really shouldn't talk about it."

She nodded. Even when she'd been a practicing nurse, he'd been tightlipped about his patients, a stickler for HIPPA compliance.

"You hear anything about your license yet?" he asked.

"Nope. I'm starting to think I should give up, find a new vocation."

"Would you go back to the hospital if the board reinstates you?"

"I don't think so." She'd actually been giving it considerable thought. First, there was the mortification of facing her former colleagues. Then, there was the stress of those long, demanding shifts. But mostly it was for the sake of Ethan. After what she'd done to him, working at Renown again would surely make him uncomfortable. "I've been looking into home nursing care. There's a big need, it pays well, and I might have better control over my schedule." To be with Roni. She didn't say it but she knew she'd gotten her point across.

"Sounds like a decent plan. And what are you considering if the board rejects your appeal?"

She blew out a breath. "Don't know. Pharmacist?" It was joke of course. But Ethan didn't laugh.

Roni bustled in, carrying a booklet out of folded construction paper. "I made you this, Mommy." She hopped up next to Ethan and began turning the pages. "Thee, it's our family." She'd drawn a series of stick-figure pictures of her, Ethan and Joey. One with them under a big yellow sun, another with them standing next to a brown house with a dog. Presumably Simba.

"These are beautiful, Roni. And this is for me?"

"You can thare it with Daddy." She swiveled her stool to face Ethan. "Daddy, can Henry come over for dinner?"

"Nah, honey. Henry's with his mom and needs to rest."

"I'm going to make him a card." She jumped down from the stool and ran off, looking for Crayons.

Joey flipped through Roni's booklet. This is what she'd missed. Whole chunks of her daughter's life. "I'm keeping it."

Ethan laughed and bobbed his head at the refrigerator door covered in Roni's artwork.

The water boiled and Joey poured the penne in and got to work on the salad. "You want to eat in here or the dining room?"

"It's up to you."

She chose the dining room. It was more formal and she wanted her dinner to make an impact. Not the meal so much as the statement it made. She was back in her daughter's life for good. And if Ethan let her, she could be back in his, too.

She hunted through the cupboards to set the table.

"What are you looking for?" Ethan got up to help.

"Our wedding china."

After a long silence, Ethan said, "I boxed them up and put them in storage. If you want them, they're yours. If not, I'll save the dishes for Roni."

She didn't say anything at first. It shouldn't have surprised her. What single man had use of fine china? Especially Ethan, who had scoffed at the idea of registering for them in the first place—"What do we need china for?" But the fact that he'd packed them away was more of a metaphor of his feelings toward her. She'd been relegated to the dusty attic like an old toy.

"That's fine. I guess I don't have any use for them either. I'll just use these." She stacked four white plates from the cupboard that could've come from anywhere. They seemed well made and practical, exactly the kind of thing Ethan went for.

She made the table look as nice as she could with the plain Jane ironstone, kicking herself for not picking up flowers. Dinner was served and she noticed that Ethan paid more attention to his phone than he did to her meal or contributing to the conversation. She and Veronica kept up a steady stream of chatter, though.

Her daughter spoke in stream of consciousness, veering from the topic of school to getting a pony without taking a breath. Joey loved every minute of it.

"Did you like the pasta?" she asked Ethan as she cleared the table.

"It was great. Thanks for making it."

She hadn't expected him to go into raptures over her dinner. But there were a lot of memories wrapped up in that pasta dish. They'd practically lived on it in their first few years together. It became an inside joke whenever one of them asked what they were having for dinner. Even still, Ethan swore that he would never tire of it.

She had hoped that by making the dish tonight, it would evoke those memories and remind him of the good times. The fun they'd had before everything went to shit. But no. He frankly seemed distracted, like his mind was somewhere else altogether.

"Is everything okay?"

"Of course. Why wouldn't it be?" He loaded the plates into the dishwasher while she rinsed.

"I don't know. You just seem absorbed by something."

"Just work stuff." He didn't elaborate. There was a time when he used to confide in her, even if it was only in vague terms to protect a patient's privacy.

She surprised him with the coconut cream pie and Roni with the butterfly cupcake. After dessert, she played a game of Candy Land with Veronica. Ethan disappeared into his office and shut the door.

The night wasn't going as she'd planned and she tried not to let disappointment ruin her time with Roni. She'd won a major victory, getting an extra day of visitation with her daughter. Stay focused on that, she told herself.

Yet, when the hour grew late she pressed her luck and tapped on Ethan's door. "Hey, I was wondering if instead of me driving all the way to Reno, only to come back first thing tomorrow to spend the day with Roni, if you wouldn't mind if I stayed the night?"

He looked taken aback by the request and didn't answer right away. Then came around. "Yeah, okay. You want to bunk with Roni or take the guest room?"

"Um . . . I'll stay in Roni's room on the trundle." It wasn't the bed she'd been hoping for but she still added it to her victory list.

* * * *

On Saturday, Henry spent most of the day on the couch either watching TV or reading books. Brynn's assistant had the forethought to send them with Henry's clothes. Another reason she loved Zena.

By Sunday, she was climbing the walls. She went outside for a short walk, afraid to leave Henry alone in the cottage too long and noticed the red Ford Edge that had been parked in Ethan's driveway since Friday evening hadn't moved. And there'd been no sign of Ethan.

She reprimanded herself for being ridiculous. It wasn't Henry's surgeon's job to keep them entertained.

There was smoke coming from the big house's chimney. It was definitely a day for curling up by a fire. Cold and gray. Still, the ranch was beautiful. Green and lush. She walked along the river's edge. There was an old frayed rope tied from a heavy branch of a huge tree where the river had formed a natural pool.

"My dad put it up thirty years ago."

Brynn jumped, caught off guard by Ethan's voice behind her. "How'd you sneak up on me like that?"

"Sorry. I should've made my presence known. You were off in your own little world." He sat down on a big flat rock near the tree and skipped a stone across the water. "I saw you from my office, walking, and came down to ask about Henry."

She tucked a strand of hair that had come loose from her ponytail behind her ear. "It's what you predicted. He's sore and sleepy."

"Sleep's good. By tomorrow he should be feeling a little better and likely get some of his energy back. How 'bout you? How are you holding up?"

"Fine." She found a spot near him on another smooth boulder and sat. "This place has healing powers. All morning I watched three deer outside the window. And the squirrels are twice as fat as the ones in New York."

"Yep. Unlike everyone else in California, they don't eat kale and own a Peloton."

She laughed, then turned her attention to the big tree. "Why'd your dad hang the rope?"

"We used to move the cattle here in the summer. He put the rope up so my sister, brother and I could swing into the river . . . cool off after riding fences. Looking back, it was probably a bribe to get us to help out." He grinned at the memory, accentuating the cleft in his chin. "Maybe this summer I'll replace it with a new one for Roni."

"It must be a wonderful way to grow up, having all this space."

"I liked it." He glanced over at her, holding her gaze. "I wanted to apologize about Friday. My ex-wife offered to make dinner and . . . it made my daughter happy."

"What about you? Did it make you happy?" The question was too personal, Brynn knew it the moment she asked. But it was too late to take it back now.

"That's a tough one. I'm thankful Joey's better and I'm thankful Roni has her mother back. So the abridged answer to that question is yeah, it made me happy to have her here."

It seemed like a convoluted answer to Brynn, peppered with ambiguity. But it wasn't her place to press. "I'm glad she's better, too. Your ex seems like a lovely woman," she said and he gave an imperceptible nod.

"You cold?" He must've seen her shiver.

There was a thin layer of frost on the rock and it had bled through her jeans. But she shook her head no, afraid that saying yes would result in him suggesting that they both return to their respective homes.

He moved over to her rock, stripped off his field coat, and draped it around her shoulders. It was still warm from his body heat and large enough to wrap around her twice.

She tried to hand it back. "You'll freeze."

"Nah, I've got thermals on and thick skin."

She motioned for him to lift up, took off her woolen shawl and used it as a cushion for the both of them. He found that amusing, she could tell.

"I should've brought folding chairs."

"I don't know, this is pretty comfortable." She wiggled into the soft, warm cashmere of her scarf.

They were so close now that their arms touched. And for a long time they didn't say anything, just stared out over the river, listening to the sounds of nature.

She sensed that he wanted to tell her something but was holding back. Intuitively, she knew not to broach whatever it was. That if she did, it would put an end to this thing they were feeling toward each other and weren't supposed to.

"I should get back," he finally said.

"Me too." But neither of them attempted to get up.

She inhaled his smell, a combination of soap and leather from the cowboy boots he had on. Their hands inched closer. And she wondered if he realized what effect he was having on her.

The sound of a vehicle coming up the driveway broke the spell and Ethan quickly got to his feet. "I better see who that is." He held his hand out for Brynn and swiped her scarf off the rock.

"Let me give this back to you." She started to shrug out of his jacket but he stopped her.

Fastening the top three buttons, he said, "I'll get it from you later."

Although she had her shawl, she didn't argue with him, hoping it was an excuse for him to come to the cottage soon.

He walked her home, stopped at the door, and waited for her go inside. She stood at the window, watched him crest the hill, and tried to keep her heart from racing.

Chapter 11

The Ford Edge was gone. It was the first thing Brynn noticed Monday when she and Henry passed Ethan's house on their way out to get breakfast.

"Mom, can I get a new book?"

Dismissing her absurd obsession with Joey's car, she turned her attention to Henry. "Of course you can. I didn't see a bookstore in town, though. Did you?"

Henry shook his head. Ethan had been right about Henry. He was feeling much better today. In fact, it was Henry's idea to go to the Ponderosa.

"Maybe there's a library nearby." If not they could always go in search of a mall. There had to be something local.

The Ponderosa had a good crowd. For fun, Brynn counted the number of cowboy hats hanging from the hooks on the wall. It appeared that they'd walked into some kind of meeting.

"Plumas County Cattlemen's breakfast," Mariah said as she followed Brynn's gaze to the wall. "Third Monday of every month. Good to see you again."

She settled them at a quiet booth in the corner. Without having to be reminded, Henry took off his hat and carefully hung it on a lower rack already littered with Stetsons. His mouth tipped up in a small confident smile.

Clay waved to them from across the dining room and Brynn waved back. It was as if she and Henry were part of this little town.

A waitress came and took their orders and returned a few minutes later with coffee for Brynn and juice for Henry. As soon as Mariah sat the party behind Brynn and Henry, she dropped by their table to chat.

"Is there a bookstore around here?" Brynn asked.

"No, but we've got a small library next to the Western Pacific Railroad Museum." Mariah gave her directions and ran off to seat the next wave of diners.

Their food came and Brynn was heartened to see Henry demolish his pancakes. He'd barely eaten over the weekend. They idled over coffee and hot cocoa, watching the people who came into the restaurant. Her son couldn't take his eyes off the group of men. She supposed all little boys loved cowboys.

After paying their bill, they went in search of the library. It wasn't far from the grocery store. She parked as close as she could and she and Henry went inside. It was a newer building that didn't match the Western flavor of the town. Just a non-descript two-story wooden structure filled with books.

The librarian pointed them to the children's section, a ten-by-ten area with a small table, a few chairs and a couple of large stuffed animals that toddlers could sit on. It was cheery enough but Henry groused at the lack of selection.

They went to the front desk where Henry applied for a California library card. And in the end, he left with two books and a promise to return soon.

On the way back to the cottage, she took a detour.

"Where are we going, Mom?"

"I want to take a look at those houses the man at the barbershop told us about. Just a quick drive by."

She'd managed to get an address off the real estate classified ad she'd found online and plugged it into her GPS. A short time later, she came to an empty guard kiosk and an open security gate with a "no trespassing" sign next to the one that read "Sierra Heights."

"Should we go through?"

Henry shrugged. "Will we go to jail if we get caught?" Her son was the ultimate rule follower.

"No." She chuckled. "I'll just say we know the owner."

Brynn took the tree-lined road and threaded her way through the development. It was gorgeous. Big log houses on equally big lots clustered around a woodsy golf course.

"What do you think, Henry?"

He pressed his face against the window. "It reminds me of Aunt Virgie's house."

Mason's sister and husband lived in a golf course community in Massachusetts. But it wasn't nearly as rugged or as beautiful as this.

"A little bit."

"How come we're looking at this?"

"The owner is having trouble selling some of the houses. I thought if I saw them, I might be able to suggest some good advertising ideas."

He slumped back in his seat and returned to his book. She continued along the main road, which wound around the golf course. On a lark she flipped a turn up one the side streets, which took them away from the links, into the forest. She marveled at the large, wood-frame houses with their enormous picture windows, wide decks and porches. Whoever designed the houses did a wonderful job of taking advantage of the breathtaking views. The homes were like elaborate treehouses.

No manicured lawns or flower beds in the front yards. Just natural landscaping that took advantage of the pine trees and native plants. She liked the way the garages were angled to the side of the homes, instead of being the first thing you saw.

She wended her way back to the development's main road, taking a series of side streets, passing more homes on her way. Most of the driveways were empty but it was approaching noon on a Monday. So it was difficult to tell whether the places were vacant or the homeowners were at work.

Once back on the major thoroughfare, she followed the signs to the lodge and pulled into the generous parking lot.

"How do you feel about waiting in the car while I take a quick look around?"

Henry barely glanced up from his book. "I'm good."

As long as Brynn had a visual of the car, she wasn't worried about leaving Henry alone for a few minutes. The place appeared deserted anyway.

She took the path to a big timber and stone building and peeked inside the windows. It was a clubhouse with chunky wooden and upholstered furniture and a mammoth double-sided fireplace on the interior and exterior of the building. She assumed the entire setup was used for parties and outdoor events.

At the back of the building was a fully equipped gym with glass doors that opened out onto a deck with an Olympic-sized swimming pool, outdoor kitchen and cabanas. Several yards away sat a series of lighted tennis courts.

The entire complex, which was situated on a plateau, overlooked the golf course and the surrounding snow-capped mountains.

Brynn had been to some of the most exquisite resorts in the world but Sierra Heights was awe inspiring. With the right advertising campaign there was no reason the gated community shouldn't have a waiting list for homes.

Back at the car she did a quick Google search on her phone for the nearest airport. There was a small one—the landing strip they had passed when they'd first come to Nugget—only a few miles away. It was unclear whether it was private or public but it didn't really matter. The convenience would appeal to wealthy buyers, looking for vacation homes. To everyone else it gave the area a degree of gravitas.

On the drive out, she stopped at the stables. The barn was similar to Ethan's but the corral was made of metal pipes instead of wood. No one appeared to be around. She and Henry got out of the car to pet the horses.

"They're pretty, aren't they?"

A dark horse with white on his legs that looked like socks pushed his nose between the bars into Henry's hand, making him giggle.

"He likes you." Or maybe it was a she. Brynn didn't have a lot of expertise in determining horse gender. But he looked like a he to her.

"Can I have a horse, Mom?"

"Sure. Should we keep him in your bedroom at home?"

He giggled again, a sound that never failed to make her happy. "We could keep him at Dr. Daniels's and I could come visit him on school vacations."

"And who would take care of him in the meanwhile?"

They went back and forth for a while. Henry had many ideas of how he could keep a horse for a pet in Manhattan. And while Brynn should've found the discussion delightful it made her return to the dark hole of fear that she'd been living in ever since she'd gotten that first call from the Somerset County Sheriff's Department.

"Mrs. Barnes, your son and husband have been in an accident."

Would her son ever be able to actually ride a horse? Sitting on one's back and being led around a ring for ten minutes was one thing. But would his legs ever be capable of accomplishing the kinds of things he'd imagined for himself? The kinds of things she'd imagined for him?

"There is a chance that the large gaps in his bone may never be repaired. We just don't know." Ethan had been straight with her. And on Wednesday they would once again put Henry's fate in Ethan's hands.

"We should get home," Brynn said, afraid that if they stayed out any longer it would push Henry's limits.

But he proved her wrong, spending the rest of the afternoon playing with Veronica, who came over after school with another casserole dish from Alma.

It had been a good day, Brynn told herself. First, Henry ate all his pancakes at breakfast. Then, for the first time since the bone marrow procedure, he made it through a full day without napping.

They were small wins in the scheme of things. But Brynn took solace in them just the same.

* * * *

Ethan managed to sidestep another happy hour invitation Monday evening. This time, from an ER doctor he went out with once after his divorce from Joey was final. He didn't remember much about the date, only that he hadn't had a desire to ask her out again.

Since then, he could count on one hand the number of dates he'd had in the last year. He told himself between work and Roni he didn't have time. But he knew if he'd met Brynn Barnes under different circumstances, he would've made the time.

He also knew he was playing a dangerous game where she was concerned. Sunday, he'd nearly kissed her. But as he left work, he vowed to keep things more professional in the future. If he dropped in at the cottage when he got home it was simply because he wanted to look in on Henry and make sure the boy was ready for Wednesday.

That was if he ever got home. Traffic was bad, at least by Reno standards, and it took him twice as long to get to the interstate as it usually did at this hour.

He'd been cooped up at the hospital all day and was surprised to see that the weather had gone from semi-cloudy to stormy. It wouldn't surprise him if they got snow. They'd been lucky to have gone most of February without it.

His phone rang and his caller ID lit up with Joey's number.

He answered on handsfree. "What's up?" He'd left the house before she had this morning.

"I just wanted to thank you for the weekend. I can't begin to tell you how much it meant to me to have three consecutive days and nights with Roni."

"You get off okay this morning?"

"Uh-huh. I tagged along with Alma to drop Roni off at school and met a few of her friends."

Alma must've loved that. "I'm sure that made Roni happy."

"First grade, Ethan. She's growing up so fast."

"I know it. Half her clothes don't fit, yet she insists on wearing them anyway."

"I'll get her some things in Reno. But Ethan, it would be easier if she could try them on. Let me take her shopping this weekend."

He wasn't ready for that, not unless he was there to supervise. He wanted to believe Joey had her issues under control. He really did. But he wasn't willing to gamble with his daughter's safety.

There'd been so many lies, so many false attempts at getting clean, so many times that Joey had let him down that who could blame him for being cynical where she was concerned?

"Let's take it one step at a time," he told her, trying to keep the irritation out of his voice. He'd given her complete run of his home and not even a full day later she was angling for more.

There was a long pause, then, "Ethan, she's my daughter and you're treating me like a criminal. Can't you see that I want to make up for lost time with her?"

"And you will. But you can't rush this, Joe. It's not good for Roni and it's not good for you. It's too much pressure."

"First of all, I'm not some fragile flower who will go back to popping pills at the first sign of stress. It's not like that and it never was."

"Then how was it? Because from where I'm sitting you went from a responsible, loving mother to someone who would do anything, including throwing me under a fucking freight train, to get a fix. You yourself said it was pressure—the pressure of being married to me. Is that no longer your story?"

He didn't know why he was dredging all this old shit up. It was over now. She'd beaten the odds and gotten herself clean. And he wanted to celebrate that with her. For Roni.

"I said a lot of shitty things back then that I'm now ashamed of. And I blamed a lot of people for a situation I brought on myself. I'll forever be sorry for that. You were never the reason I became a drug addict. You were the best thing that ever happened to me and I was too stupid and too self-centered to appreciate it at the time." She stopped, letting a long silence stretch between them, then said, "I wish we weren't doing this over the phone. My therapist thinks you should come to one of my sessions. I have amends to make, things I need to tell you."

She'd already done that as far as he was concerned. But if it would help her with her recovery he'd go, even though he was tired of talking about their past. All he wanted was a fresh start.

"If you think it will help, I'll come to a session," he said. "And, Joey, we'll work things out with Veronica too . . . more time for the two of you to spend together . . . but this is all new territory. Let's do it right and not rush it."

"Thank you for agreeing to sit down with my therapist. I'll talk to her, check with Rita about your schedule, and set up an appointment. But Ethan, let me take Roni shopping. It's only fair that I get a few hours alone with my daughter. It's a mall for God's sake, a mother-daughter rite of passage. And I promise to have her back whenever you say. Please, Ethan."

His hands gripped the steering wheel tighter. Even though she was only asking for a small concession, he wanted to continue the way they were going. Supervised visits. Nevertheless, he felt himself caving. Joey made a good case and despite his ambivalence, he knew it was better to pick his battles.

"Just a few hours, Joey. You can take her on Saturday. But I want her home before dark. This is a big step for me . . . Please, don't push for more."

"Thank you, Ethan. It means a lot to me."

By the time he arrived home and pulled into the driveway, a flurry of snowflakes clung to his windshield. A sheer layer of silvery white covered the eaves of the house. He sat in his truck in the driveway for a few minutes, watching the way the snow trimmed the trees, making their branches glisten in the dark.

It was a garage night, he decided and pressed the clicker on his visor, slipping in next to Alma's Mercedes Benz. The house was quiet when he went inside and for a few seconds he thought he was alone. Then Alma drifted down the stairs.

"Hello." She greeted him like she did most evenings with a kiss on the cheek. "How was your day?"

"Fine and yours?"

"Quiet. Roni is having dinner with the Barneses. I figured one of us could walk down and get her in a little while."

"I'll do it. It's snowing."

"I noticed." Alma started for the kitchen. "I made lasagna."

"Sounds good. Just let me change and wash up."

He went upstairs and returned a short time later. The kitchen smelled of garlic and warm bread. Alma had put down two settings at the center island and placed the lasagna dish on a trivet.

"Dig in," she said.

"It looks delicious." He served them both.

"I made one for Brynn and Henry too."

"That was nice of you."

She shrugged as if it was no big deal. "The poor woman has enough to think about. I heard from Owen that he cut Henry's hair the other day. Griffin Parks was there and she gave him some advertising tips on moving some of those homes he's sitting on."

"Oh yeah? Seems like small potatoes for her. Sierra Heights sure isn't Coca-Cola."

"I think it was just off the cuff, nothing formal. He wanted to hire her, though."

Ethan laughed. "Does he even know who she is?"

"I have no idea, though I doubt it. I only knew who she was because I read her husband's obit in the *Times*. It's not like advertising people, even the big ones, are household names. I couldn't tell you who came up with 'Got Milk?' Could you?"

He thought about it for a moment. "Nope. But I can't look at a carton of milk without seeing that slogan in my head."

"That's why it's good." She got a French bread out of the oven, put it on a cutting board, and sliced it. "Compliments of Emily McCreedy."

He got the butter out of the refrigerator, unable to resist Emily's homemade bread. Clay's wife was a well-known cookbook author. She used to ghostwrite recipes for some of the biggest celebrity chefs in the business but had begun penning her own books.

"So, did Griff hire her?"

"According to Owen, she said she was here to focus on her son. She suggested that Griffin hire someone locally."

"Tactful."

"Why do you say that?" Alma blew on a forkful of lasagna.

"She could've always referred Griff to her own agency but I suspect the Barnes Group might be overkill for Sierra Heights, not to mention a fortune." Though according to rumor, Griffin was loaded.

"I don't know. Right now, her focus is on her son. Anyone can see that she's feeling the weight of the world on her shoulders."

He most of all.

After dinner he helped Alma with the dishes, grabbed his jacket, and hiked down to the cottage. Both kids were outside on the patio, twirling in circles—Henry in his wheelchair—with their arms held wide, trying to catch snow. He stood hidden behind a tree, listening to them laugh as pure joy streaked across their small faces.

Brynn called to them and he waited for them to go inside before making his presence known.

"We're having hot cocoa," Brynn said. "Join us."

He peeled off his jacket, stood by the fire to warm up, and watched her prepare drinks. Roni was telling Brynn how she liked her chocolate—"lots of marshmallows but no whipped cream."

Henry chimed in. "I like both."

Brynn listened carefully and fixed each cup accordingly. "How about you, Ethan?"

"I'm with Henry. Marshmallows and whip."

"Both it is." She floated around the kitchen in a pair of houndstooth leggings and a black sweater.

Though casual by any standard, Ethan thought she was elegant. Elegant and approachable at the same time. Every time he saw her, he became a little more infatuated. The smart thing would be to stop seeing her but Ethan had never been accused of being smart. At least not where women were concerned. Look at his track record with Joey.

The kids took their drinks to the living room where a deck of Go Fish cards were spread across the coffee table. He joined Brynn at the breakfast counter, noticing that she hadn't fixed a cup for herself.

"You don't like chocolate?"

"I do and tonight's perfect for it." She gazed out the window as the snow continued to fall.

"But?"

"My stomach's upset."

"Something you ate? Or nerves about Wednesday? Because, Brynn the procedure is fairly straightforward and not as painful as the bone marrow harvest. Using image guidance, I'll inject the stem cells into the precise area of Henry's breaks. We're talking a thin needle and eighty minutes max. The next day, we'll draw blood from Henry's vein and in the orthobiologics lab a technician will process it into platelet rich plasma, which will work with the stem cells to hopefully expedite Henry's healing. We'll inject Henry with the concentrated blood platelet on Friday. And that's it. We wait and see."

He'd explained this to her already but knew it was a lot to take in. Most parents needed him to repeat the steps over and over again.

She nodded but Ethan could tell she'd gotten lost in the details.

He reached across the counter and took her hand. "I've got this, Brynn. It may be new science, but I've done it hundreds of times. That's why you came to me, remember?"

She flashed a small and slightly sad smile and continued to hold his hand. She didn't ask, even though he knew she wanted to.

What if it doesn't work?

"One step at a time," he said softly and then waded into a less serious topic. "I heard you met Griffin Parks at the barbershop and gave him a marketing plan for Sierra Heights."

"Just a few tips. Hardly a plan. For the hell of it I drove over there today. It's fantastic. I can't believe buyers aren't snapping up homes there. Is it haunted or something else terrible that Griffin isn't divulging?"

"Nah, it's just isolated. And we don't have the perks or cachet of Glory Junction or wine country."

"That's the thing about cachet, you can create it with the right imagery and the right words. I'm tempted to take it on just for fun."

Ethan quirked a brow. He loved being a surgeon. The high he got from healing a child was unrivaled. He could safely say he found great reward in his work.

But fun?

She laughed at his quizzical expression. "If my work involved as much pressure as yours I wouldn't think of it as fun either."

"I suspect there is plenty of pressure in advertising." But yeah, fun to him was teaching Roni to ice skate. It was riding Reggie across a field at breakneck speed. It was watching the National Finals Rodeo from a lower level seat in front of the bucking chutes. It was sex in the bed of his old F-150 under a full moon.

"There is. Lots. But it's a different kind of pressure. It doesn't involve life or death situations."

Once again, she'd exaggerated. Like any surgery there were risks of fatality. But for the most part, he fused bones back together. His pressure came from the devastating disappointment his patients had when he had to tell them they'd never walk or throw a ball again.

"What's the strategy then . . . for Griff's houses?"

"First thing is identifying a target audience. I don't know that he's done that yet. From what I can tell Sierra Heights has been marketed the way you traditionally sell real estate. Classified ads in the local newspapers, open houses, all the typical stuff. Unfortunately, that only works to attract buyers in the general vicinity. But if it turns out that his target audience is an avid outdoors person who has a home on the beach in Florida but likes to spend his or her summers in the forest on a river then Griffin has to figure out how to let those folks know Sierra Heights is here and what it has to uniquely offer."

"Ah, and that's where you come in."

"Sort of. Most of my clients have that end already covered. My job is to come up with catchy jingles and taglines that hold the brand together, basically give consumers a reason to choose my client over the competition. But in a case like this I can do the marketing and advertising."

He added ardent to his list of the many things he found attractive about her. She'd said she had been working behind the scenes while raising Henry. Yet, she still seemed to have her finger on the pulse.

"Is this to get your feet wet before diving back in?" he asked.

"No, I wouldn't say that. Before Mason . . . before the accident I worked on a number of campaigns from the sidelines. Even here . . . well, I never completely left it."

"That's good because it sounds like you enjoy it."

"I do." She beamed.

He'd been so engaged in their conversation that his hot chocolate had gotten cold. Ethan drank it anyway, raising the mug to his lips one handed. His other hand was still wrapped around Brynn's.

Chapter 12

It snowed all day Tuesday, covering the fields like a white goose-down blanket. Brynn and Henry stayed in, cuddling up in front of the fire, reading books and watching TV. Soon, Brynn would have to brave the weather to get more logs from the wood pile.

She wanted to clear the walkway but didn't know where to find a shovel. And no one was home at Ethan's.

It was pretty as a post card, she thought as she stared out the window, looking at the white capped mountains. They looked as if they'd been dipped in whipped cream. And the trees flocked in pearly white powder.

It was her idea of a perfect day if not for the fact that first thing in the morning they'd have to drive nearly an hour in this weather. She didn't need the stress on top of everything else. But what could she do?

Maybe by tomorrow the temperature would rise and the sun would come out and melt the snow. The forecast on her phone promised clear weather after midnight.

But it only seemed to get worse as the hours passed. The wind blew so hard she could hear it whistling through the trees. And the sky was so dark it felt like night at three in the afternoon. When Brynn finally reached Alma she was reassured that it was just a passing storm.

"I'll send over Cody to shovel the walkway. He's the teenager Ethan hired to muck out the barn."

At this point it seemed like a waste of time. The snow was coming down so fast and hard that by the time he cleared the path it would only get covered again. But she thanked Alma anyway, hoping that it would let up soon.

She switched the television to the local news and waited for the weather report. The forecast echoed what everyone else said. The weather would be clear by morning.

By the time the eleven o'clock news rolled around, though, the forecaster had changed her tune, predicting another snowstorm was moving in and the state put out a high-winds alert and might even close Donner Pass. She had no idea where Donner Pass was and pulled up a map on her laptop. From what she could tell Nugget was past the pass but she'd never been great at geography.

She deliberated on whether to call Ethan but decided it was too late. Besides, if there were any changes in the plan the hospital would've notified her.

She checked in on Henry, who was sound asleep. After an hour of obsessing, she turned in for bed. But sleep evaded her. She got up regularly to peer outside the window where all that stared back at her was a blur of white. And judging by the whooshing—it sounded like a freeway outside her window—the wind had picked up.

Her heart sank. What if they canceled the procedure? Was that even possible? She had no idea if there was an expiration date on Henry's stem cells. The idea of him having to go through another bone marrow harvest made her chest ache. She wasn't even sure it was possible. How many stem cells did an eight-year-old have?

She had just drifted off to a fitful sleep when she was awakened by a banging on the door. At first she thought she'd dreamed it but someone was calling her name. She bolted upright and glanced at the time. Four o'clock.

She got up and padded to the door in her bare feet. Ethan was there, bundled up in a down jacket and a plastic cover over his cowboy hat.

"Come in, come in." She moved out of the doorway while he knocked the snow off his boots. "Have you come to cancel?"

"I don't want to but I'm not sure the roads will be passable."

"Do we take Donner Pass? I heard on the news that they're closing it."

"No, Donner Pass is about ten miles west of Truckee. But we've got our own challenges."

He unzipped his jacket and hung his hat on the hook by the door. She had the heat cranked up for the sake of Henry and it was hot.

"What if we can't make it to the hospital?"

Ethan let out a breath. "Then we'll have to postpone."

"Will the stem cells keep or will you have to do the process all over again?"

He motioned for them to sit in the family room, his eyes drifting over her, making her suddenly aware that she was in her nightgown. She excused herself, threw on a robe, and returned.

"I can bank Henry's stem cells," he said. "Frankly, I don't think it'll make a difference in his recovery. But if we postpone I'll have to exclude Henry from the trial. All our subjects were injected exactly seven days after harvest. We can't deviate from that. It will skew the data."

Brynn was fully aware that the cottage, and more importantly Ethan, were the fringe benefits of participating in the study.

"And what would that mean for Henry?" They both understood what she was asking. If Henry could no longer be part of the trial would Ethan still be his doctor?

He shrugged out of his jacket and hung it over the back of the sofa, then glanced at the time. "I could use a cup of coffee."

Apparently, Ethan wasn't planning to go back to bed. She went in the kitchen and put a pod in the Keurig.

"Cream? Sugar?"

"Just black, please."

She brought him the mug and remained standing until he answered.

"I'd finish the procedure and refer you to a new orthopedic surgeon in New York."

She hung onto the words "finish the procedure." At least he wouldn't abandon the treatment altogether. From what she could tell the experimental surgery was Henry's only chance for a full recovery. But Brynn didn't want a new surgeon. She wanted Ethan.

"I understand that we would have to leave the cottage. But we could get a place in Reno, even here if it's more convenient for you. But why couldn't you remain Henry's doctor?"

"Sit." He took both of her hands in his. "I'll complete everything we talked about. It will be the same as if he was still in the trial."

"But afterward you won't monitor his progress to make sure it's working?"

There was enough pain in his expression that Brynn knew the answer before he spoke. "There's still a chance we'll make it in time, Brynn. We'll keep watching the weather."

"Ethan?"

He squeezed the bridge of his nose. "The heavy lifting will have already been done, Brynn. The rest is recovery. I'll find you someone with excellent credentials to monitor that. Someone even better than Brunswick. And make no mistake about it, Brunswick is one of the best. I will be there for consultation every step of the way."

"Consultation," she scoffed. "But you will no longer be Henry's doctor?"
"We're jumping way ahead of ourselves here. But no, I can't be Henry's doctor if he's not part of the trial."
"So you won't even be part of his physical therapy?"
"Brynn, I was only going to be part of Henry's therapy in a tangential way. Only to document his progress."
If she wasn't Henry's mother she might've understood. The study was integral to Ethan's life's work. But all she felt was discarded. It was as if Henry's well-being didn't count unless he could be a statistic for Ethan's study.

She began to cry, despite her best effort not to break down in front of him. "Brynn . . . ah, Brynn." He pulled her into an embrace. "It'll be okay. This won't affect Henry. He'll have all the treatments that he's supposed to. Very little will change. You have to trust me on this."

"I did trust you and now you're deserting us." She was angry with him and should've pulled away, yet she remained nestled against his chest.

"Shh." He rocked her. "Please don't cry. All I care about is making Henry well. That's why I do this, that's why I became a surgeon. But the rules are the rules."

She didn't care about the goddamn rules. She only cared about her son. "If I have to crawl to that hospital tomorrow with Henry on my back, I will. Just tell me you'll do the same."

"I will do whatever is humanly possible to get there. I have a friend with a plane who used to be a fighter pilot . . . was awarded a damned Silver Star for his bravery. Even he won't fly in this."

He absently ran his fingers through her hair. It felt so good that she burrowed in deeper, resting her cheek against his flannel shirt. Her body shuddered with new tears. She knew it was a combination of exhaustion, fear and disappointment. Of shouldering all of this—the accident, Mason's death, and Henry's injury—on her own. Her parents, Mason's sister and Lexi had all done what they could but in the end only she could fight for Henry.

Ethan pulled her closer. "I'm so sorry, Brynn. No one could've predicted this, not even the weather guys. According to the chief of staff, they've gone to their back-up generator at the hospital. Still, they're encouraging anyone who can, to reschedule."

Weather conditions and other unforeseeable situations happened all the time, but she couldn't help but feel like the world was conspiring against her. The last eight months had felt hopeless until two weeks ago when Ethan had agreed to accept Henry into the Osteoform trial. Getting a surgeon of Ethan's caliber and renown and being part of an experimental treatment with an almost miracle track record had given her something to cling to. And living here in this sweet little cottage in this welcoming town had been idyllic. Healing for a child who not only lost full use of his legs but had lost his father.

And now, because of one stinking storm, this second chance for Henry stood to be ripped away.

"I'm so angry," she said and whimpered as her body spasmed with a new set of sobs.

"Me too." He lifted her face away from his chest and brushed away her tears with his thumb. "If I could change it, I would. I swear to you."

They locked eyes and then his lips were against hers, soft and pure and perfect. She closed her eyes and let his kiss take her away to a place where there were no worries and no hurt little boys.

She heard her own hums of pleasure as his lips moved over her, as his tongue explored.

Reveling in the strength of his arms, acting on two weeks of pent up attraction, she wanted the kiss to go on forever. For the hot pull of his mouth to take until she had nothing left to give.

But just like that he stopped and jerked away from her so fast she didn't have time to catch her breath.

"Ethan." She reached for him. "Please. I—"

He shook his head. "This is wrong . . . unethical. I'm Henry's doctor. You're upset and I took advantage."

"We're friends," she protested lamely.

"Friends?" He shoved his hand through his hair and quickly pushed to his feet. "Jesus Christ, Brynn, we both know what's going on here. We've been dancing around it for days. And here we are at your most vulnerable and I—"

"Nothing. You didn't do anything. You were comforting me, that's all."

"There are rules, Brynn. Rules designed to protect the patient. I broke them." He hurriedly put on his jacket and collected his hat off the hook. "Try to get a couple of hours sleep and I'll monitor the roads and the weather."

He walked out, leaving her alone to repeat her earlier sentiment. She didn't care about the goddamn rules.

* * * *

At dawn the weather hadn't improved. If anything it was worse. Brynn switched between the morning news and her phone for updates. None of them good.

The entrance to US Route 395 from Highway 70 had been closed. It was the road Brynn needed to take to get to Reno.

Ethan had called three times to keep her informed that there hadn't been any changes. But he hadn't come in person. It didn't matter, she told herself. The bottom line was that they were stuck here.

Henry, oblivious to how this would complicate things, celebrated the postponement of what he called "his shot" by eating packaged coffeecake from the Nugget Market for breakfast. Brynn was too glued to the weather report to insist on something nutritious.

The wind blew so hard that it was a wonder that one of the enormous pine trees didn't crack in half. The sky had turned pink from the reflection of light from the falling snow. Any other time it would've been beautiful. Now, it only served as a reminder of how much Brynn's life sucked.

At ten, she changed out of her wool slacks and cashmere sweater into jeans and a fleece hoodie. The chance of them making it to the hospital looked bleaker every second. Even Nugget schools had closed, which according to the local news site was a rarity. Challenging weather was nothing new here. But from what Brynn had ascertained the roads were typically cleared in a matter of hours as many people in the region commuted to Reno for their jobs.

In this case, though, the problem wasn't so much the snow. It was the visibility factor.

Unable to look at her laptop anymore, she broke away from the latest update on road conditions and made herself another cup of coffee. She deliberated on whether to scramble a couple of eggs and make toast but settled on the same packaged coffeecake Henry had eaten for breakfast. It tasted like bitter disappointment.

By noon she lost all hope and curled up with Henry on the couch. They would get through this, she told herself. Even without Ethan they would get through this. Yet, the voice in her head told her she had failed her son.

She considered calling Ethan and begging him to break the rules just this once. He would argue that it was twice. But she refused to think of their kiss as breaking the rules. Despite all the reasons why kissing her son's doctor was a bad idea, Ethan had not taken advantage. In fact, the kiss was the best thing that had happened to her in a long time. And, yes, he'd been right. They'd been dancing around it for days.

Forget about the kiss, she told herself. She needed to channel all her energy into Henry. Now more than ever.

His head was in her lap while he played Froggipedia on the iPhone 11 Pro Mason had gotten him for his seventh birthday. She and her late husband had fought over the iPhone. It was too extravagant for a child, she'd argued, worried they weren't teaching Henry the value of a buck and that they were turning into the same materialistic parents she abhorred. Mason hadn't been moved.

"He's a kid, Brynn, and all his friends have the same phone. He has plenty of time to learn the value of a buck. Why do we have to start that lesson on his birthday?"

Ironically, that phone had become her salvation in the months following the accident. Ever since the crash, she had a desperate need to know where he was. At school, she'd called him at least five times a day.

She played with his hair, letting his baby fine strands sift through her fingers like silk. She used to do this when he was a toddler, sitting in her lap while they glided back and forth on his rocking chair, singing "Baa Baa Black Sheep."

The memory warmed her as she started to nod off, exhausted from her restless night. She was somewhere between that gauzy floating feeling and actual sleep when Henry shoved her awake.

"Mom, there's a police car outside."

She jerked up, cleared her eyes, and went to the window, her chest tightening with dread. The last time a police officer had called her it had been the worst day of her life. Her mind immediately went to her parents, then Lexi.

The lights flickered on and off as they had been doing for most of the morning. And for a second, she convinced herself that the police were here to warn her of a pending power outage. But of course that didn't make sense. Law enforcement did not run the local utilities.

Ethan's old truck gingerly made its way down the road and parked next to the Nugget Police SUV. Ethan and the officer exchanged words through their open windows.

Brynn slid into her boots and hurriedly shrugged into her coat but Ethan and a plain-clothes officer met her at the door.

"Let's go inside." Ethan brushed the snow off his jacket.

The two men made the cottage feel small.

"What's going on?" Her voice trembled with concern. "Is everything all right?"

"This is Rhys Shepard, Nugget's police chief. He's going to try to get you and Henry through the closure."

She blinked in confusion. "I thought they weren't letting anyone through."

"They might with a police escort for a medical emergency," Ethan said, then drew his mouth into a straight line and looked away. They both knew this wasn't a medical emergency.

"What about you? Are you coming with us?"

"I'll follow in my truck . . . show the CHP my hospital credentials. There's no guarantee they'll let either of us pass and if it's too unsafe to drive we turn around. You understand?" This time he looked her straight in the eye.

"Oh my God." She flung herself at him. "Thank you, Ethan. Thank you."

Chapter 13

Brynn had held her breath as the police chief explained the situation in somewhat exaggerated terms to a California Highway Patrolman whose job it was to turn back motorists where Highway 70 met US Route 365. The twenty-three-mile stretch of road emptied into Reno.

She held her breath a second time when Ethan was stopped behind them.

"What if they don't let him pass?" The police chief had had no qualms making it sound like Henry's injections were a matter of life or death. He gave a complicated dissertation on Henry's stem cells and how they were being kept at Renown on ice until he got there. By the time he'd finished, the CHP officer had probably thought Henry's procedure was akin to a heart transplant. Brynn didn't think Ethan would go that far.

The rules. He was a stickler for them. Then again, he'd probably broken them today. For Henry. And for her.

"He'll get through," said the police chief, who'd insisted she call him Rhys. "And if for some reason he doesn't make it, he said there's another surgeon who can do the injections."

But Brynn wanted Ethan. Only Ethan.

The air was thick, a shroud of white fog, and she could no longer tell whether Ethan was still behind them. The road was deserted of course. Brynn wasn't sure whether that was a blessing or a burden. At least if there was someone in front of them Rhys could follow the red glow of their taillights.

"Thank you for taking us. I feel terrible that you're out in this." The air was so soupy it made her claustrophobic.

"No worries. It really isn't that bad. And I have a kid." He looked back at Henry.

They crawled along with only hazy visibility. Even Henry, who was usually too absorbed in a book or a game app on their drives to pay attention, sat forward in the back seat, staring out the window. He didn't look scared, just interested.

The snow had begun to taper off and Brynn wondered if at some point, before the fog had rolled in, a plow had come through to clear the road. Rhys's studded tires appeared to be providing plenty of traction.

They'd gone only a few miles when the veil lifted enough that Brynn could see headlights in the rearview mirror.

"Do you think that's him?" she asked, breathless.

Rhys squinted into his rearview and his lips tipped up. "Looks like a Ford to me." He patted her leg. "We're practically home free."

She hoped so but didn't want to celebrate yet. They still had a way to go, according to Rhys's odometer, which she'd been watching like a hawk.

To distract her, the chief made light conversation. She was a little in awe of how he could drive in this and talk at the same time. But he navigated the icy, whiteout conditions like a pro.

"How old is your daughter?"

"Emma's five, going on twenty. My wife Maddy and I are also raising my little brother. Long story."

"Maddy who owns the Lumber Baron?"

"Yep." He beamed. "You met her?"

"Just briefly. Henry and I wanted to see the inside of the inn. It's gorgeous and she's lovely."

"No argument from me on that score," he said and grinned. "And the inn is her pride and joy. Tell your friends. Business is good but they could always use more, especially in the off season."

"I will make a point of it," she said, turning around to see if Ethan was still following. If she looked hard she could still make out the faint glow of his lights. "I'll have my parents stay there when they come to visit. My mother is an avid antique collector and my father loves history."

Lexi was more of an Intercontinental girl but as far as Brynn could tell, the Lumber Baron was the only game in town.

"He's back there," Rhys said as he peered in his mirror.

"Do you know Ethan well?" Brynn assumed they had at least a passing relationship for the chief to have come to the rescue like this. It was above and beyond duty to taxi people to Reno in a storm.

"Everyone in Nugget knows everyone. There are fewer than six thousand of us, so we stick together. Ethan, Alma and Veronica are recent transplants. But I knew him when we were kids. His father used to run cattle up here and would hire a couple of us in summer to do small jobs around the property. I always liked Ethan. Even back then, you could tell he was destined for big things."

"Really? Why?"

"There was a kind of intensity about him and a loyalty you didn't see too often in kids that age. My old man was for lack of a better description the town outcast. I got a lot of crap about it from the other kids. Ethan stood up to them . . . had my back. I was sorry when he stopped coming around."

"Why did he stop coming around?"

Rhys laughed. "High school, rodeo, girls. The usual suspects. And not long after, I left and Ethan went off to college, then med school. I'm glad we're both back. He and his family are great additions to our town."

It answered the question of why Rhys was helping them. Though it sounded like this is the way things were done in Nugget. One for all and all for one.

She turned around and Ethan was still there. Her chest hitched at the sight of him following slowly behind them. Yes, Rhys was right. Ethan Daniels was loyal and he'd had her back. A surgeon superhero if there ever was one.

* * * *

The sound of Brynn's boots echoed through the hospital hallway. It was quieter than their previous visits, which she attributed to the storm. The lights were on, though, and she took it as a good sign.

Rhys had dropped her and Henry at the hospital entrance and said he had errands to run in Reno before heading home. By then, he hoped the road was open.

She hadn't seen Ethan's truck come through the portico and assumed he'd headed directly to the parking structure and into the building.

The way to the orthopedic clinic was now engrained in her head. "How you doing, Henry?" Even without a major medical procedure staring him in the face, today had been taxing enough for both of them.

"Dr. Daniels said it won't hurt."

"Nope, they're going to numb your legs with a local anesthesia, like what the dentist does when you get a filling." Perhaps she shouldn't have used that analogy. Henry hated the dentist.

A nurse was standing in the waiting room the minute they got there to take Henry back to an exam room.

"Should I go back with him?" Brynn wanted to be there in case Henry needed help with undressing and putting on a hospital gown.

"We've got it covered, Ms. Barnes. Dr. Daniels is scrubbing in and will come out when he's finished with the injections to talk to you. It should only take about an hour. Afterward, we'll need Henry to stay in recovery for another hour. I heard you had a harrowing drive in. Why don't you go down to the cafeteria and get something to eat? If Dr. Daniels needs you for any reason we'll call down to the cafeteria on the intercom."

Brynn kissed Henry and forced herself to go. She hadn't eaten much for dinner and her breakfast had consisted of a few bites of coffeecake. There was a sandwich shop next to the cafeteria. She ordered at the counter and found a quiet table in the corner to dash off a group text to her mother and Lexi.

We made it! Henry's getting his injections now. Will update you later.

She sent a second text to Zena, asking her to book them a suite at a nearby hotel for the next few days. Brynn wasn't taking any more chances with the weather. Henry still had two more days of treatments to go.

Ethan came through. He pretty much made the impossible happen. For the second time that day, she flashed to their kiss. No one would accuse her of kissing Ethan because she'd confused gratefulness with attraction. At the time, she'd been anything but grateful.

But now she could see it from Ethan's side. His attraction to her had made him break the rules not once but twice. She had no illusions. The only reason they were here was because Ethan had pulled strings and been less than truthful about the seriousness of their situation with the authorities.

It was heady, knowing he'd done that for her and her son. At the same time, she had come to understand Ethan well enough to know that he would beat himself up over exaggerating the facts and bending the rules while making Rhys an accessory. He'd barely been able to look her in the eye when he showed up at the cottage that morning.

She ate half her sandwich and wrapped the rest for later. Maybe Henry would eat it when he came out of recovery.

On her way back, her purse began to vibrate. She rummaged through her bag and sighed with relief when she saw the caller ID.

"Hey, Lex."

"I can't believe you made it." Lexi sounded out of breath. "Did the weather let up?"

"Not exactly but Ethan got us a police escort."

"Ethan, huh? You're now calling your son's doctor by his first name?"

If Lexi only knew. "Where are you? It sounds like you're hiking. Or at the gym."

"I'm showing office space and the elevator is out of order. I just climbed twelve flights of stairs. Hopefully, unlike me, my client's in good shape. Hang on a sec." Lexi switched to the other line and came back a few seconds later. "That was him. He's in the lobby and on his way up. I just wanted to say yay! I'm so glad you made it to the hospital. I'll get all the details from you tonight. Give Henry a kiss for me."

"Bye, Lex. Good luck with your client."

The waiting room was empty. She took a chair in front of the TV and switched on the weather. The power was still out to more than a thousand homes on both sides of the Nevada-California line but the winds had died down and the fog had lifted. Ethan would be able to get home.

She scrolled through her emails and messages. Nothing from Layla or Rich. Thank goodness. Brynn didn't know if she could multitask today. Her nerves were already on overload. She swiped a magazine off one of the side tables and thumbed through the pictures. That's all she could manage.

For the next thirty minutes, she watched the clock. She was just about to visit the restroom when Ethan came in. He'd changed from his jeans and cowboy boots into a pair of scrubs and tennis shoes, like he'd worn the first time. Until now, she'd never found scrubs particularly sexy.

"All done." He smiled. "Come on back. You can hang out with Henry."

"How did it go?"

"It went great. I'm real happy with how clear everything was on the ultrasound and how precisely we were able to inject the stem cells in relation to the fractures."

Brynn was aware of how Ethan always said "we." With him it was a team effort. With Mason everything had always been "I."

"Tomorrow, we'll draw Henry's blood, send it to the lab, and mix up a nice concentrated blood-platelet cocktail. Friday, we'll inject him with it. The whole thing shouldn't take more than thirty minutes."

"What about pain?" she asked as Ethan took her back to the exam rooms.

"His joints at the site of the injection will be sore for a few days. Tylenol should be fine but avoid NSAIDs. One of the nurses will give you a list but stuff like aspirin and Ibuprofen. No baths for three days. Henry can take short showers, starting tomorrow afternoon. And I want him to limit activity on both legs for twenty-four hours. Ideally, I'd like to see him go home and stay in bed until our appointment tomorrow."

"We're staying in a hotel tonight, close to the hospital."

Ethan nodded. "That's wise. At least until this weather clears up."

Brynn noted that he didn't mention what he was doing as far as sleeping arrangements. She supposed he wasn't needed to draw blood. A phlebotomist would likely see to that task. More than likely he wouldn't administer the blood-platelet injection on Friday either.

"How long until we know whether it's working?"

"Times vary. But in a few weeks we will hopefully see signs of improvement."

"When does Henry start physical therapy?" She was sure they'd discussed all of this and that she'd even been given written materials that laid out her son's post-procedure schedule. But with everything going on, those details were as hazy as the fog they'd driven through to get here.

"Soon. For now, though, I want him to take it easy." If Ethan was tired of repeating himself Brynn would never know it. His patience was one of the many things she admired about him.

They found Henry propped up on both elbows, drinking water from a straw.

"Hey, baby." She kissed his forehead. "How do you feel?"

"It hurts." His bottom lip trembled.

Ethan asked the nurse to get Henry Tylenol, then came around to the other side of his bed. "Charlotte's going to hook you up, buddy. You hungry? I can have something brought up from the cafeteria."

Brynn held up her leftover half sandwich. "I saved this for you."

Henry got one whiff of the tuna and turned up his nose. "Can I have pizza?"

Her son was clearly milking this for everything he could.

"I'll trade you." Ethan unwrapped the sandwich and took a bite, then asked the nurse's station to have a hospital service worker bring up a slice of pizza. "We're like the Four Seasons here." He winked at Henry and polished off the rest of the tuna melt.

"Let me get you something," Brynn offered. There were a couple of restaurants across the street from the hospital. Her lousy half sandwich would only tide him over for so long.

"Nah, I'm good. I'll grab something on my way out." He didn't mention when that would be.

Brynn was tempted to ask, even invite him to have dinner with them in their hotel suite. But he had his own family to get home to. Besides, he'd been all business today and she got the strong impression he wanted to keep it that way.

* * * *

At the end of the day, Ethan debated whether to drive back to Nugget. The weather had improved and for now it had stopped snowing.

In the end, he drove to Alma's townhouse in northwest Reno and collapsed on the sofa. Though Alma offered him unfettered use of the swanky apartment, he only stayed when he had a late surgery. Now that he'd seen how bad the drive from Nugget could be in a snowstorm, he'd probably make more use of the townhouse in winter.

He hated missing dinner with Roni and tucking her in for the night. But it was convenient having the option to crash here when he needed to. And the place sure didn't lack amenities. Giant flat screen, wet bar, food delivery and only a ten-minute drive to the hospital.

It was a little feminine and fussy—lots of white carpeting and floral upholstered furniture—for Ethan's taste. The townhouse had been Alma's before she'd married Ethan's dad and it reflected her glamorous anchorwoman lifestyle. There was one wall dedicated to her Emmys and other journalism awards as well as photos of Alma with celebrities, governors, and even two presidents.

In summer, Roni liked to visit and use the complex's swimming pool. Joey's parents had one too, but Veronica was partial to Alma's. It might've been the over-the-top waterfall or the fact that Alma's neighbors had a daughter Veronica's age.

He grabbed a beer from the fridge, flipped on the TV with the sound muted, and called home.

"Hi, Daddy. Grandma said I could talk to you first. I have another looth tooth."

"You do? Which one?"

"The front one. Grandma told me not to wiggle it. When are you coming home, Daddy?"

"Not until tomorrow. Is it still snowing there?"

"I can't tell because it's dark outside. I've got to go and have ice cream now. Love you, Daddy."

"Love you too. Sleep tight, bonny Roni."

Alma got on the phone. "How did it go with Henry?"

"Piece of cake." The drive in not so much. But it was done now. He'd ignored his conscience so he could continue being Henry's doctor. The reason for that was even less forgivable than the lies he'd told today. "I've got a few patients tomorrow but I'll be home for dinner. Thanks for holding down the fort."

"Of course. Get some rest."

"Kiss Roni for me."

He turned up the sound on the TV, channel surfed, and landed on a cop show, which he halfheartedly watched. Midway through, he rummaged through Alma's freezer. There wasn't much there.

He considered ordering in but found a can of chicken noodle soup in the pantry. According to the expiration date, it was still good. While he heated the soup on the stove top, he called Brynn, telling himself it was only to check up on Henry.

His lies today were legion.

She answered on the second ring with a bright hello.

"I wanted to see how Henry's doing?"

"The day knocked him out. We'd barely finished dinner and he fell asleep."

"That's good . . . sleep I mean. Where you guys staying?"

"The Sierra Grand again. How was the drive home?"

"I stayed at Alma's place here in town. Didn't want to risk the drive again tomorrow."

"Oh." She sounded surprised. Maybe even a little disappointed. "Had I known I would've treated you to dinner."

"Probably a good thing you didn't know then. Because I would've taken you up on dinner and that's a bad idea, Brynn." Everything involving her was a bad idea, including the phone call. Because now he wanted to find an excuse to meet her at the hotel.

"It's just dinner."

"You and I both know it isn't."

There was a long pause on her end, then, "Thank you for everything you did today. I know . . . it made you uncomfortable. I hope I didn't guilt you into doing something that went against your honor."

"It had nothing to do with guilt" and everything to do with her. Which they also both knew.

He stirred his soup as it began to bubble. In the top cupboard he found a bowl, also floral, and ladled himself a serving.

"Will you be there tomorrow when Henry gets his blood drawn?"

There was zero reason for him to be present. It was a simple routine lab procedure. "Yes. I'd like to see Henry beforehand."

He took his bowl to the table and waited for the soup to cool. If he had half a brain he'd hang up now. But he wasn't ready to let Brynn go. If nothing else, he liked hearing the sound of her voice.

A text chimed on his phone. While Brynn launched into a story about her ride with Rhys, he put her on speaker and checked to make sure the message wasn't from home. Not home. Joey.

"Heard about your dreadful drive from Alma. She actually said more than three words to me today. Shocking. I guess that's Progress. In any event, I wanted to make sure you made it okay. If you need a place to stay there is always room at my folks' house."

The text reminded him of all the reasons getting too involved with Brynn was wrong. After the debacle with Joey he was lucky to still have a job. At the time, he'd been in the dark about the ways Joey had jeopardized his career. It was only later that he'd found out. But with Brynn he'd have no one to blame but himself.

So, was he going to put the skids on whatever this was with Brynn? His head said "yes." But the rest of him screamed a resounding "No."

Chapter 14

The sun peeked out of the sky Saturday for the first time that week. Joey hoped it was a sign, a good omen that today marked a new beginning with Roni.

She'd planned the entire day up to the last detail. And if everything went well, she hoped to close out the evening with some alone time with Ethan.

But Roni was her priority. This would be their first unsupervised outing together and she planned to make it the ultimate bonding experience.

Joey could never make up for the eighteen months she'd lost from Roni's life. But moving forward, she vowed to be the mother her daughter deserved.

She glanced at the clock on her car's control panel and grimaced. In her exuberance to see Roni, she'd left Reno at the crack of dawn and now realized it was too early to show up at Ethan's. He'd specifically asked her to give him the morning with Veronica because he'd been gone most of the week.

Granted, it was Joey's weekend. But as long as Ethan was willing to loosen up on the court order, she didn't want to piss him off.

She bypassed his road and continued to downtown Nugget, hoping the Ponderosa was open for breakfast. Joey could while away the time drinking coffee.

Judging by all the parked cars in the square, one of the shops was doing a brisk business. The big semi livestock trailer she'd seen last time was hogging a good chunk of the street in front of the restaurant. She wondered if it permanently lived here.

A rush of warm air greeted her as she went inside. The place was packed. Folks up from the city to play in the snow, she presumed. Though with the sun out, it would soon be a slushy mess.

"It's a twenty-minute wait," the hostess informed her. "Or you can sit at the bar. It's first come, first served."

Yeah, why not? Though her sponsor would probably have something to say about it.

She grabbed a menu from the hostess stand and hopped up on a stool. The good-looking cowboy who'd played her a song on the juke box sat in the corner, four seats away. They made eye contact and he tipped his hat. Then, as if he'd remembered his manners, took off the Stetson and hung it on a hook on the wall.

He scrubbed his hand through a full head of dirty blond hair. He needed a haircut. And a shave. But he reminded her of Matthew McConaughey before the creepy Lincoln commercials.

The bartender came over to take her order. She decided to go whole hog with the egg, bacon and pancake special. In her rush to get out the door, she'd skipped breakfast and her morning fix of caffeine.

Smart man that he was, the bartender quickly returned to fill her cup. She fluffed her hair in the backbar mirror and caught the cowboy watching her. Absently, she rubbed her empty ring finger.

The bar was beautiful. Hand carved mahogany that looked leftover from the Gold Rush days. She didn't know why she hadn't noticed it before. There was an overloaded coatrack near the front of the restaurant. She got down from her stool and found room to hang her jacket and scarf.

Without having to look, Joey knew the cowboy's eyes were on her. Call it a woman's intuition or just years of attracting male attention. It wasn't because she stood above the rest. No, she wasn't beautiful by any stretch. But she had a nice figure, golden blond hair with the help of a really good colorist, and a manner that invited interest.

She'd spent a lot of time in rehab and counseling exploring these facts about herself and why Ethan had ever loved her in the first place. A truth not lost on her was that he could have had any woman he wanted. A doctor with a resume equally as good as his. A supermodel. A movie star.

Yet, he chose her, loved her like crazy, and even stuck by her when she railroaded his career. If only she could get him back and the three of them could be a family again.

Her food came and she ate while watching a team roping competition on the flat screen suspended from the ceiling. The bartender refilled her coffee and moved on to the other side of the bar where a couple asked for directions to Glory Junction.

The cowboy paid his bill, got his hat and jacket off the hook, and strolled out the door. Joey couldn't help noticing that his backside was as nice as the rest of him.

She, too, squared up and headed for her car. It was past nine. She still needed to kill another hour or so and decided to tool around town. Other than the square, she hadn't done much exploring.

The truck with the semi-trailer started up, spitting out diesel fumes. Joey glanced over and saw the cowboy in the cab, then watched him deftly pull away from the curb and hang a U-turn. Apparently, Matthew McConaughey hauled livestock for a living.

She started her own vehicle and went exploring. The area was beautiful. Tall pines and regal mountains. It was so different from the desert bedroom community where she'd grown up. She found a large feed store. There were a few sale racks outside with sweatshirts and jackets. She started to park to go inside, then thought better of it. Shopping was her weakness and she wanted to conserve her money to buy Roni new clothes.

She managed to burn an hour and decided it was safe to show her face at Ethan's, even if she was still a little early. When she got to the house, Simba raced down the porch stairs, and jumped on her, licking her face.

"Where's your manners, girl?" She gave the dog a hug.

The front door opened and Queen Alma swept onto the porch. Joey waved, trying to be friendly. She craned her neck past Alma, looking for Roni.

"They're down at the barn." Alma buttoned up her wool coat, put on a pair of designer sunglasses and headed to her car, which was parked on the other side of the driveway.

Neither one of them said anything as Alma pressed her clicker and got inside the driver's seat. Joey wrapped her scarf tighter and made the trek to the barn on foot. Despite the cold, it was a gorgeous day. Crisp and clear, scented with pine.

She definitely could get used to living here.

As she got closer, she heard Roni's high-pitched laughter and her heart swelled. Through the trees she saw Ethan standing at the corral next to a woman. Though they had their backs to her, the woman had the same dark hair as Brynn Barnes, the mother of the boy with the leg injuries.

She and Ethan were so close that their arms touched. It was innocent, Joey told herself. Or a trick of the light from this distance. Ethan would never so much as flirt with a patient's mother. Never.

But as Joey got nearer her stomach sank. There was no question that Ethan and the woman, who Joey could now plainly see was Brynn, were in each other's personal space. He reached up to brush a lock of hair out of Brynn's face and Joey froze. That emptiness in the pit of her belly turned sour.

No, it wasn't what she thought. It couldn't be. Ethan was just offering support to an overcome mother, that's all.

She continued down the hill, reassuring herself that it was nothing. That she'd misconstrued a simple gesture of comfort.

But as soon as Ethan and Brynn realized Joey's presence they abruptly pulled apart. And that's when panic rose in Joey's throat. She knew.

* * * *

At seven o'clock Ethan was ready to murder his ex-wife. For the nineteenth time that evening he tried to call her again and like all the other calls it went straight to Joey's voicemail.

He hung up, having already left a series of messages. Each one more heavily worded than the last. He called Joey's mother, Lou Ellen. Again.

"Did you hear from her? Please, God, tell me you heard from her."

"Nope." He moderated his voice to keep the anger out. This wasn't Lou Ellen's fault. "I'd hoped maybe you'd heard something."

"Nothing. But Ethan, I know my daughter. She wouldn't take Veronica. She's worked so hard . . . with the meetings . . . with the therapy. This . . . . well, it's crazy. She's a good mother, Ethan."

Good mothers didn't take their daughters in the middle of the night to score oxycodone in a part of town even he wouldn't venture to alone. But that was the problem with Lou Ellen and Ace. They were blinded to Joey's faults.

First, they'd denied she had an addiction and backed her initial refusal to go to rehab. "She'll kick this on her own," Ace had sworn. Thank God, she'd finally realized she needed help and enrolled herself in a program.

After she got out, he had allowed Roni to stay at her grandparents', trusting that Lou Ellen and Ace would abide by the court order to supervise their daughter when she was with Roni. What was the first thing they did? They left Joey alone with their grandkid.

They were good people but classic enablers. They spoiled and indulged Joey so much that she never needed to take responsibility for her actions.

You fuck up, you own it. That had always been the Daniels family moto.

"Lou Ellen, call me if you hear from her, okay?"

"Of course I will. I'm worried sick that something happened to them."

Ethan didn't need to hear that now. He was banking on the stronger possibility that Joey was just being her irresponsible self.

His phone beeped. "Lou, I'm getting another call. If it's her, I'll call you." He switched to the other line. "Hello."

"Anything yet?" It was Alma.

"Nothing." He could hear his own disappointment. "I thought you might be her."

"I think it's time to call the police, Ethan."

"You think she would actually take off with Veronica? Steal her?" Ethan didn't believe it. Under the influence, she was capable of doing all kinds of irresponsible shit. But clean, no way.

Then he remembered the hurt he'd seen in her eyes when she'd found him and Brynn together. Could this possibly be some kind of warped payback? No, Joey was a lot of things but vindictive wasn't one of them. The more likely scenario was she lost track of time. Or . . . she'd fallen off the wagon.

"I don't know what she would do," Alma said. "Maybe there was an accident . . . call the police, Ethan."

Ethan went out on the front porch. It was dark and there were still berms of snow on the edges of the driveway where he'd plowed. He could smell the wood smoke from the cottage's chimney. Brynn had made a fire.

"Ethan? Are you still there?"

"Yes. I'll call the police."

"I'm on my way."

"No, stay at the townhouse. If they're in Reno it'll be better if you're there."

"Call me the second you hear something."

"I've got you on speed dial," he said, trying to sound less panicked than he felt.

The second he got off the phone with Alma he rang Rhys's cell and explained the situation.

"I'll make some calls," Rhys said above a lot of loud voices. A party maybe.

Ah, shit, Ethan was pulling Rhys away from a celebration for what would probably turn out to be nothing. But it didn't feel like nothing. Ethan's premonition told him it was something. Something bad.

"Hang tight," Rhys said and signed off.

Ethan paced until he thought he'd worn out the floorboards on the porch. Inside, he paced some more. For a fleeting second, he considered calling

Brynn. Why? She wasn't part of this. But he knew she would empathize. And right now, he needed someone to talk him off a ledge.

At the last minute, he reconsidered and put down his phone. Brynn had enough to deal with. The sound of a car came up the driveway and Ethan felt a rush of relief so strong it nearly knocked him over.

But the relief was short lived when Ethan went out onto the porch again. It was Griffin Parks's pickup. What was he doing here? Ethan liked Griff but they were merely acquaintances. Occasionally they shot the breeze while Ethan filled up at the Gas and Go. As far as he could remember Griffin had only been to the Circle D Ranch one time. He'd come for a housewarming party a few of the ladies in town had hosted for him.

Griff got out of his truck. "Evening. Hope I'm not bothering you but I was looking for Brynn." He shoved his hands in his pockets and rocked on his feet.

It seemed late for a house call to Ethan.

"Donna stopped by at the Gas and Go a little bit ago and happened to mention who Brynn was." Griffin let out a whistle. "I had no idea she was like the real-life version of Don Draper when I met her at the barbershop the other day." He rubbed his hand over his face. "I want to hire her agency but never got her number."

Ethan guessed that Alma had mentioned who Brynn was to Donna and it was off-to-the-races. He'd learned early that folks around here loved their gossip.

But he didn't have time for this now. And it wouldn't be right to send Griffin down to the cottage without first getting Brynn's permission.

Griffin must've seen something in Ethan's expression because he said, "Too presumptuous to just drop in?"

"She's dealing with her kid and it is kind of late. Why don't I ask her tomorrow if I can pass you her number?"

"Sure, that sounds good. I guess I got a little overanxious when Donna gave me the news. I was on my way home and thought what the hell?" Griffin looked up at Ethan, who hadn't even bothered to come down from the porch. "Hey, is everything okay?"

Jeez, Ethan was a surgeon. He was supposed be cool under pressure. He let out a breath. "My daughter and ex-wife were supposed to be here two hours ago and I can't reach them."

"Ah, man." Griffin didn't wait to be invited and climbed the stairs. "You call Nugget PD?"

"Yeah, Rhys."

Next thing Ethan knew, they were in the kitchen and Griffin was making coffee.

"Where were they supposed to be?"

"Reno. They spent the day there, shopping." Ethan wished he'd never given in to Joey's plea to take Veronica for the day. If he had only adhered to the court order, they'd both be safe.

"They could've broken down, got caught up in traffic, went to see a movie. There are a million innocent explanations why they're not here. It's too soon to panic."

Ethan had considered all those possibilities. But why wasn't Joey answering her phone? He once again checked his cell for a missed call or text. Still nothing.

Griffin poured them both a cup of coffee, found a bottle of brandy in the cupboard, and splashed a generous portion into Ethan's mug.

He took a visual spin around the room. "Colin Burke do your cabinetry?"

Ethan knew Griff was just trying to distract him with small talk. But he wasn't in the mood. "Yeah."

"The guy is good." Griffin opened one of the cupboards and admired the wood. "He and Harlee went to Mexico for a week. Puerto Vallarta. They wanted to get away from the cold. Can't say I blame them."

"Nope." Ethan peered out the window into blackness. He went into the mudroom and turned on the house's side lights. The floodlights weren't going to help Joey and Roni get home but at least it was something to do.

"I can't sit here any longer. I think I'll search the roads in my truck." Ethan swiped his keys off a hook.

"Let me drive," Griffin said. "That way you can focus on looking."

They were both out the door when Ethan's phone rang. Rhys.

"You find them?"

"Just heard back from the CHP. They got a flat just outside of Vinton. Your ex's cell phone died and they had to wait for help. That stretch of road can get pretty lonely on a Saturday evening. They're on their way to you now."

Ethan let himself breathe again. "Thanks, Rhys. This is two times in a row. I owe you big."

"Just doing my job. Have a good evening."

"Rhys found them?" Griffin asked as soon as Ethan got off the phone.

"Joey got a flat and her cell phone died."

"Does she have a spare? I can go back and get one." Griff ran a tow service and repair shop out of the Gas and Go.

"I don't know but they're on their way here." Just as he said it, Joey's Ford Edge crested the hill.

A rush of emotions hit Ethan like a monsoon. Mostly relief but there was a good dose of anger mixed in there, too. How the hell had Joey let her phone die? She couldn't have plugged into her brand-new car's USB port?

They're home safe. That's all that matters.

Ethan met them in the driveway, flung open the passenger seat door, and scooped up a sleeping Roni.

One look at Joey and he knew that she knew she'd blown it.

"I'm sorry," she mouthed.

Griffin, sensing the tension in the air, said goodbye and made a quick getaway.

"Ethan, I obviously didn't mean for this happen. Will you just look at me?"

He put his finger to his lips. He didn't want her to wake Roni and frankly he needed a little time to cool off.

He took Veronica upstairs, laid her on her bed, and covered her with a blanket. Later, he'd come up and change her into her PJs. Joey was in the kitchen, pouring herself the coffee Griffin had just brewed.

"I am so, so sorry. I know you must've been freaking out."

"Freaking out doesn't even begin to describe it."

She turned to face him, leaning her back against the counter. "Did you actually think I would steal our daughter?"

He backed up, trying to tamp down his fury. "No, Joey, I didn't." Though admittedly he had gone there for an instant. "I spent most of the evening visualizing the two of you, lying dead in a ditch. Do you know what that fucking looks like?"

"Oh God, Ethan. I screwed up. I forgot my phone charger. I tried to change the tire myself, but I couldn't make the jack work. And the truth is I don't know how to change a tire—because I used to have you." She broke down in tears.

"Don't." Out of instinct he went to her and wound up pulling her into a reassuring embrace. "Shh, I overreacted."

"No, you didn't," she said into his chest. "I'm a colossal screw up. Everything was going so well. Roni loved all the new clothes I bought her. We had a really nice lunch on the Riverwalk. Afterward, I took her to that museum exhibit I told you about. It was perfect. Then it all went to crap on the way home."

"Look, these things happen." He started to rub her back the way he used to when they were married and she'd come home from a long day at the hospital upset over some asshole doctor who'd yelled at her or a patient that wasn't getting better. But he couldn't bring himself to be that intimate with her again. He just couldn't. "I'm sorry I went off on you. And I'm glad you and Roni had a good time. But most of all, I'm so freaking relieved that you're both all right."

"Thank you for being understanding." She fisted her hands in his shirt and sniffled. "You're such a good man, Ethan Daniels. You're such a good father. And I'm . . . inadequate."

He lifted her chin with his finger. "Don't do that. You've never been inadequate. Never. You were sick and you got yourself help. Not a lot of people are strong enough to do that. But you were. Look at all you've overcome."

"I did it for you and Roni."

"I'm glad you did it for Roni but you should do it for yourself, Joey. You should do it because you're a special person and the world would be worse off without a sober you in it. You should do it because people love you."

She rested her cheek against his chest. "I want you to love me again."

"I do love you. I never stopped loving you as a friend . . . as the mother of my child."

"But you don't love me the way a husband loves a wife." She choked on a sob.

"Ah, Joey, you left our marriage long before the pills. We both know that. The divorce . . . well, that was just a formality."

"I was terrible to you. But I want to be better. Let me be better."

He didn't know what to say to that. At one time she'd been his everything. But now . . . "Hey, you need to call your mother and I need to call Alma." He pushed away and went for his phone.

She tore a piece of paper towel off the holder, wiped her eyes and disappeared into the other room. He phoned Alma, explained what had happened, and wished her a good night.

Joey returned to the kitchen. She'd washed away her smeared makeup and had combed her hair, looking much younger than her thirty-seven years. For a fleeting few seconds he got lost in her face, transported back to a time when she'd been his world. He dug into himself, curious if those feelings were still there, lying dormant beneath the surface. But he couldn't find them.

It would've been so much easier if he could.

"You talk to Lou Ellen?" he asked, putting a few steps of distance between them.

"Yeah." She took a sip of her coffee, which by now had probably gone cold. "I have a problem. My spare is one of those donut tires. I probably shouldn't drive all the way back to Reno on it. Do you know where I can get my tire fixed or get another one?"

Griffin had offered but by now he was likely home, drinking a beer around a fire or on a date with his girlfriend, Lina. It was Saturday night after all. Ethan wasn't even sure if the repair shop was open on Sunday, though Griff would probably help them out if Ethan asked. That's how things were done in Nugget.

"Not tonight," he said, bracing himself for what was coming next.

"Would it be a horrible imposition if I slept over?"

"Stay," he said, resigned. "I'll take care of your tire in the morning."

The rest of the evening passed awkwardly. Joey settled next to him on the couch, nestling against his side, like she'd done a million times during their marriage. She was working him, not even being particularly cunning about it. That had always been one of the things he'd admired most about her. When she wanted something, she went for it. Hard.

He knew he could never love her the way he used to. The damage had already been done. But was companionship enough to make them a family again? For Roni. To assuage his guilt over all the things he could've done to be a better husband.

He went to the kitchen to get himself a beer and her a glass of water and used the opportunity to relocate to the chair by the fire. The blaze had dwindled to a mere flicker. Instead of stoking it with another log, he let what was left go to embers.

When it came time to turn in for the night, she asked, "Where do you want me to sleep?"

The tenor of the question was not lost on him. It would've been so easy to take her to his bed, try to revel in the familiarity of her body and wake up as a couple again. But he couldn't pretend. There was no desire for her left in him.

"Roni's room," he said.

Chapter 15

The next morning, Ethan rose before the sun came up and headed to the barn to saddle up Reggie. Most of the snow had melted, leaving puddles of brown slush along the sides of the driveway. It was still chilly enough to warrant a jacket, though.

In the east, the sun began to rise, turning the sky a fiery red. Ethan loved this time of day, when the ranch hadn't fully awakened, and he could be alone with his thoughts. Before his father died, they used to ride fences in the predawn hours, checking for chinks in the barbed wire. They'd rarely talked on those rides, yet they were the times he'd felt closest to his dad.

When he got to the barn, he let out a low whistle and good old reliable Reggie came trotting up to the fence.

"Ready to ride, boy?"

The horse nickered and obligingly trotted into the barn. It didn't take long to tack up. Ethan had been doing it since he was old enough to walk. He climbed into the stirrup and mounted up, leading Reggie to a narrow trail.

They walked for a while, taking their time, following the river as it snaked through his land. Joey would've enjoyed the ride. She wasn't much of a morning person but the chance to ride could usually get her out of bed.

But he hadn't wanted her company. The truth was another woman was occupying his mind. Lately, all he could think about was Brynn Barnes. He'd become a little obsessed with her. And trying to fight his fascination wasn't working out too well. It was like taking on a six-hundred-pound grizzly, bare handed.

When they got out on the range, Ethan gave Reggie his head and they loped until the gelding was good and lathered. Ethan didn't know who'd needed the run more. Him or Reg.

He reined the horse around, backtracking to the trail. Judging by the position of the sun, Roni would be up and wanting breakfast. Then he'd get Joey's tire taken care of.

The house smelled like frying bacon when he got home. He found Joey at the stove, making breakfast. And Roni up on the counter, telling her mom a story about a playmate at school. His daughter was lit up like a Christmas tree.

He lifted her off the granite island and sat her down on a stool.

"You smell like horse, Daddy."

Joey glanced over at him. "You went riding without me?"

"You were asleep." He aimed his chin at the mixing bowl beside her. "What do you have going there?"

"Waffles. Buttermilk, your favorite."

She was pulling out all the stops and at some point, when Roni wasn't around, he'd have to talk to her about it. He didn't want to confuse their daughter.

"Do I have time to shower first?" He poured himself a mug of piping hot coffee.

"Yep. But don't take too long. The bacon is almost done."

He jogged up the stairs with his cup of coffee. One hot shower later, he returned to the kitchen and got himself a refill.

"Wow, that was fast." Joey turned off the skillet and plated the bacon. "You must be hungry."

Not as much hungry as he wanted to get the morning over with. But the way his daughter clung to Joey made him feel like a weasel for wanting to rush his ex off. "Starved. You want me to set the table?"

"Nope. You relax. Roni and I are going to do it, right baby girl?"

Roni held her arms open for Joey to stack the plates. He watched as she carefully put each one around the table, then placed the napkins Joey had folded just so. Roni wasn't that conscientious when she helped Alma or him set the table.

Throughout the meal, Roni monopolized the conversation, switching back and forth from a story about a boy who made her cry on the playground to what she wanted for her birthday, which wasn't until June. Joey, to her credit, managed to follow the random bursts of non sequiturs, chiming in every once in a while with a reply. Ethan ate, grateful to Roni for filling the room with conversation.

"You're awfully quiet," Joey said when Roni stopped talking long enough to take a bite of her food.

"Just enjoying my breakfast." He held up a forkful of waffle smothered in syrup as proof. "As soon as we're done, I'll call the local repair shop, see if I can get your tire fixed."

"Great. I appreciate it," she said tightly, like she knew he was in a rush for her to leave.

He gave a short nod and went back to silently eating his meal.

Afterward, Joey insisted on her and Roni doing the dishes. When they'd been married, they'd equally shared in the household chores. Though there were times when Joey had had to pinch-hit while he got called away on an emergency.

"I'll try the Gas and Go to see about that tire," he said and escaped inside his office. The domesticity of the morning was getting to him. It was forced and uncomfortable.

He was more than aware of what Joey was doing and instead of feeling manipulated, he felt a deep abiding shame. Shame for having left Joey when she needed him the most. Shame for having deprived Roni of her mother. Shame that his decision had shattered their nuclear family

Yet, he resented Joey's attempts to win him over. And for that, he felt shame too.

He found the number for the Gas and Go in the Nugget directory, an old-fashioned booklet collated and stapled together by the chamber of commerce and available in all the town's businesses. Nugget was still light years behind the digital age, though the local newspaper was online.

"Hi, this is Ethan Daniels over at the Circle D Ranch," he told the person who answered the phone. "Any chance Griffin Parks is around?"

"No, but Skeeter is. You want to talk to him?"

Ethan had no idea who Skeeter was but perhaps he could fix a tire. "Sure."

In the background he heard someone call for Skeeter and a few seconds later, a man greeted him with "Yo."

He launched into the reason for the call, hoping he didn't have to go to Reno on his day off.

"What kind of car is it?"

"A Ford Edge, this year's model."

"Yeah, I can hook you up. If I can't fix it, we've got Bridgestone and Goodyear touring tires that'll work just fine. Can you drive it to the shop?"

"Yeah. I'll be over within the hour." It was only a few miles and a good excuse to get out of the house for a while.

Ethan got Joey's keys and told her he'd be back soon.

Skeeter was something else. He looked like a hoodlum. Baggy pants cinched across his ass, badly done tattoos, and a few piercings. But he knew his cars. In less than a half hour, he'd fixed Joey's tire and threw in a free rotation.

Before Ethan left, the kid showed him his refurbished Camaro and a before picture when the vehicle was a junked-up primer gray. Ethan wasn't much into muscle cars but the now banana yellow Camaro was impressive, especially given what it had looked like originally.

Ethan considered going over to the Ponderosa for a beer to give Joey more alone time with Roni. Technically, she got Sunday visitations, too. But he knew the Ponderosa was just a convenient excuse to hide instead of having an unpleasant conversation with Joey to set some new guidelines. He wasn't sure he was ready to go with completely unsupervised visits. But how did he get the horse back after it had left the barn? And this staying the weekend bit . . . well, they had to talk about that too.

He forced himself to go home and take the bull by the horns. Roni was giving Joey a fashion show with all the new clothes her mother had bought her. Joey had probably spent a month's worth of alimony.

"Daddy, watch this." Roni strutted across the floor, climbed up on the coffee table, and did a twirl. She reminded him of a miniature version of a drunken super model.

"Nice. Hey, bonny Roni, you think you could give Mommy and me a little alone time?"

"Why? Are you going to kiss?" She hopped down from the table and threw herself in Ethan's lap. "Give Mommy a kiss, Daddy."

A part of him wondered if Joey had put her up to this. But one look at his ex and he dismissed the idea out of hand. Her face was the color of a pomegranate. The color of mortification.

"Hey, Roni, skedaddle." He put her down on the floor and patted her behind. "Take all this stuff up to your room."

Ethan motioned for Joey to follow him into his office and shut the door. "Your tire is fixed. The kid at the repair shop says the other three are fine."

"Thanks for taking it in. What did you want to talk about that you didn't want Roni to hear?"

He sat behind his desk, once again putting distance between them. She took one of the leather chairs, sitting stiffly across from him in a borrowed flannel shirt from his closet.

"How are we going to do this, Joey? How do we move forward from here? I don't think these weekend overnights are a good idea."

"Why not?"

"You saw why. It gives Roni the wrong idea."

"Why is it wrong? Is it so terrible, Ethan, for her to see us as a family?" She tilted her head to one side in challenge.

He glanced at the ceiling and then back at her. "Don't do that, Joey. Don't make me the bad guy. It's wrong if it's not true."

"You're the father of my child, therefore I consider you my family."

"You think a six-year-old gets those nuances? Because I sure the hell don't. We're confusing her."

"We owe it to her . . . to us . . . to see if we can be a family again. I want us to try, Ethan. I know it's a lot to ask after . . . everything. But we were happy once. And look how happy it makes Roni when we're together."

"That's the thing, Joe, we weren't happy. Maybe in the beginning. Maybe in that first year. But then things started to change. Subtly at first. But little by little I could see you growing bored. With me, with marriage, with our life. I tried to tell myself that it was because I worked too much. That I wasn't home enough. Then you got pregnant with Veronica and I thought . . . we both thought . . . a baby would fix things, would fix us. Perhaps it was postpartum depression but the old Joey seemed to disappear. You started going out at night, spending more time with your nurse friends than with us. There was the stuff on the internet that I pretended was innocent. But was it? Was it innocent, Joey?" He held up his hand when she started to talk. "Don't answer to me. Take a hard, honest look inside yourself."

He scrubbed his hand down his face. The divorce had destroyed him. But in many ways, he was just as much to blame as she was. He didn't hold up his end of the bargain. He'd walked away when he should've stood by her.

"It wasn't just you, Joey. I'm responsible too. I was unhappy and instead of trying to fix us, I turned my back, told myself that it was normal, that marriage was hard. And it is hard. But in the end, I don't think either of us felt a strong enough bond to make it worth fighting for."

"We're different people now, Ethan. I like to think we've learned from our mistakes. And it's not just us anymore. We have a daughter. I don't want her to grow up in two single-parent homes. I don't want to celebrate her birthdays separately or sit on opposite sides of the aisle when she gets married."

He didn't want that division either. The idea that all of his daughter's milestones would be tainted by divorce left a gaping hole in his heart. But did he want to live a lie? Did he want his daughter to grow up in that lie?

Her eye caught the clock on the wall. "Shit, I have to be at a meeting at four." She hurriedly got to her feet. "Ethan, think about what I said. We could love each other again. I know we can."

He looked away, wondering whether it was crueler to respond that no he couldn't, not in the way a married couple should love each other. Or just leave it alone and let the silence speak for itself.

She didn't wait for his reply. Upstairs in Roni's room, he heard her tell their daughter goodbye.

"Don't go, Mommy. Stay the night."

"I have something I have to do in Reno, baby. But I will see you on Saturday. We'll make cookies together."

He couldn't make out the rest of their conversation. But judging how long it took Joey to come down the stairs, Roni must've pitched a fit. The gap in his heart deepened.

"I'll walk you out." Ethan shrugged into his jacket.

Joey slid into her driver's seat and before shutting the door said, "Since when do you get involved with your patient's mothers?" There was no animosity in her voice, just that same wounded look he'd seen in her eyes the day she'd found Brynn and him standing together at the horse corral.

He didn't answer because he didn't want to lie. While he wouldn't call what he and Brynn were having a relationship, it was something. Something that he couldn't seem to let go of.

"Are you willing to risk your career for something that in the long run won't mean anything?"

"A little rich coming from you, don't you think?" She flinched and he felt like a mean bastard. "Go to your meeting, Joey."

* * * *

By eight, Roni crashed and Ethan was restless. He sat with Alma in the family room and absently listened to how her weekend went. Apparently, it had been better than his.

He toyed with his beer, which had gone warm. "I think I'll catch up on paperwork."

As he made a beeline for his office, he heard Alma flick on the TV. The house still smelled of onions and peppers from the frozen bag of fajitas he'd made for dinner.

He started to boot up his computer but picked up his phone instead and tapped out a text.

Can we meet? I need to get your permission for something.

Griffin was a handy excuse. And a ridiculously thin guise. But Ethan clung to it like religion. All day he'd wanted to see Brynn. Joey's words had met their mark as she surely intended for them to do. But they hadn't stopped him from thinking about Brynn. From obsessing over her. It had only been one day since he'd seen her last but it felt like an eternity.

Not five minutes after he hit the send button, she texted him back.

"Henry's out like a light. How about the horse barn so we don't wake him up?"

"There in five," he wrote as he took the stairs two at a time and grabbed a penlight on his way out.

Brynn was waiting at the wooden corral in her red woolen coat. Seeing her with her dark hair loose and her cheeks rising with color from the cold took his breath away. For a moment he stood back so he could drink her in. Then she caught sight of him, a smile lighting her face, and she waved.

Something in his chest clenched and he hurried toward her. Without a thought, he swept her up into his arms and covered her mouth with his. It was as if he needed to inhale her.

She twined her arms around his neck and his hands moved over her coat, searching for the buttons. He wanted to touch her skin, feel her breasts, taste them, and bury himself in her warmth.

Suddenly, he was carrying her inside the barn, his lips still pressed against her, tasting. Devouring. His tongue slid inside her mouth and tangled with hers. She was kissing him back with a desperate fervor.

He laid her on a mound of straw and came down beside her. Undoing her buttons, he pushed open her coat and slid his hands inside her sweater, letting them rest on her ribcage. Her skin was soft and warm to his touch. He could smell a hint of her perfume, the same floral scent that filled the cottage.

Her blue eyes held his, pleading. She unzipped his jacket. And in one fluid motion he yanked it off, then pulled his shirt over his head. Her hands glided over his chest and he sucked in a breath.

He rolled her under him, pressing his arousal into her groin. She whimpered and he kissed her again. This time, deeper, until they were fused together as one. He wrestled her sweater off, leaving her in a gauzy black bra. With his finger he edged the lace, loving the sounds she made every time he touched her.

He moved to her neck, kissing that tender spot behind her ear. She reached for his belt and fumbled with the buckle. Pushing her hands away, he unzipped her jeans and pulled them down her legs where they bunched up around her boots. She kicked them off and wiggled out of her pants.

He wanted to lift up on his elbows and gaze down on her, take in her beauty. But his need for her overrode his desire to look. He pushed one leg of her underwear aside and felt her with his fingers.

She was wet and ready. The knowledge that he could arouse her that way, that quickly, made his chest swell with pride.

He reached up with one hand to fondle her breasts and she moaned, continuing to ride his finger. She shoved down her panties, giving him better access. But he wasn't finished with her breasts yet.

He unclasped her bra so he could give them his full attention, taking each perfect globe in his mouth. Her body arched up, letting him have his fill as she rubbed against him, silently begging for him to fill her.

He hurriedly unfastened his belt and opened his fly just enough to free himself. And in one powerful thrust he entered her. She clung to his shoulders as her legs came around his hips, allowing him to go deeper.

Enveloped in her tight warmth, he plunged into her faster and harder. She matched each one of his strokes, running her hands over his bunched muscles. Both were so consumed in their primal dance that nothing outside of it, or them, existed.

He caged her face in both his hands and kissed her until they were both breathless. Then he
spread kisses down her neck, her clavicle, her chest, and her breasts. He combed his hand through her silken hair as her breath quickened and she started to clench. He reached down and worked her with his finger as he continued to thrust inside of her. Then her body began to quake as he felt her let go.

He followed her a short time later with a climax so intense that for a few seconds he saw stars.

They laid there, trying to catch their breath, their limbs tangled together. Despite how wrong it was, he'd lost himself in her and thrown all ethics to the wind. He'd never done anything like that before. Ever. It showed how caught up he was in Brynn Barnes.

An unwelcome picture of Joey drifted into his head and made him question whether he could give up the kind of passion he'd just had with Brynn for mere companionship to hold his family together?

Brynn wiped a piece of straw from his hair.

He buttoned his fly and cinched his belt. "Brynn, we need to talk about this."

She rolled onto her side and touched her finger to his lips. "No we don't. Let's just enjoy it."

"First off, we didn't use any protection." A hell of a doctor he turned out to be.

"I'm on the pill and I don't have any diseases. How 'bout you?"

"Not on the pill but healthy." He sighed. "But there's the small matter that I'm your son's surgeon."

She leaned over and kissed him. "I'm okay with that. So we're all good."

"That's the thing, Brynn, we're not all good. This shouldn't have happened. You trust me to care for your son and I took advantage. I could lose my license for what we just did . . . You're a vulnerable mother of a patient. While it is true that Henry's procedure is completed, I'm still technically supervising his recovery. He's still part of the clinical trial."

"We've been over this before. You didn't take advantage of me. I slept with you because I wanted to. And I won't tell, if you don't." She found her sweater and dragged it over her head, then wriggled into her jeans. "Are you saying you're sorry that you slept with me?"

"Come here." He crooked his finger at her and pulled her into his arms. "I love what we just did. The fact is I'd do it again in a heartbeat. But it's wrong. It's wrong for a very good reason. I want you to know that it's never happened before. That I don't do things like this." He scrubbed his hand down his face because now he just sounded like an asshole. *I don't do things like this.* Well, he just had. And he was already thinking about when they could do it again. This time on a bed.

"You don't do things like what?" She was laughing at him. "Can you grab my boots for me? I should get back home in case Henry wakes up."

He handed her her shoes. "These aren't boots. They're some kind of fashion weirdness masquerading as boots."

"First you're sorry that you slept with me and now you're criticizing my footwear." She imitated his finger crook and kissed him again.

"Listen," he said. "There's something else I need to tell you. About a year ago my license was nearly suspended." He paused, then waved his hand between them. "Not for this. For opioid analgesic prescribing offenses."

She froze, her boot midway on her foot. "What does that mean? Like Oxy? To children?"

"Yes, like oxy. Not to children, to my wife. Now my ex-wife."

He waited for her to process the information, then continued, "I don't want to get into details because it's a privacy issue but I didn't do it. I eventually cleared everything up with the Medical Board. I just wanted you to know."

She handed him his shirt and jacket. He could see the wheels spinning in her head.

"Your ex-wife did it, didn't she? She wrote scripts under your name for herself. That's what you meant when you said she was sick. She was hooked on opioids."

He didn't answer. He didn't need to; she'd figured it out.

"Oh, Ethan. That's just awful."

He got dressed, rose to his feet, and gave her a hand up. "Let's go check on Henry."

They walked to the cottage together. Neither spoke but both were cognizant of all the things that were going unsaid. Henry was still asleep, so they sat out on the patio, even though it was too cold.

"Is she still addicted?"

"No, she's clean. She's a good person, a good mother."

"She seemed lovely to me. But writing those prescriptions . . . Oh, Ethan. You're a little bit of a saint, aren't you?"

He laughed. "You're kidding, right? I'm your son's surgeon and I just seduced you in a barn. I'm a regular Mother Teresa."

She blushed, clearly remembering every detail of what they'd done on that bail of straw. He took her hand. And for a while they just sat there, staring into each other's eyes.

Then in a low voice, not quite a whisper, she asked, "Is that why you left her? Because of the prescriptions?"

He shook his head. He'd stood by her for that. It had been the carjacking with Roni that had broken him. "No, it was later. There was an incident . . . it scared the shit out of me. I had to think about Roni. And the truth was even before the pills, we'd grown apart. After Roni was born we were barely hanging on."

"I'm sorry. I know how hard that is." Her eyes darted to the cottage's window, checking to see if Henry had stirred. "Before the accident, Mason and I had grown so far apart that we hardly talked to each other. We were basically roommates who weren't even friends. Except when he needed my help with an account. Then he happily . . . confiscated my ideas and pitches."

"He stole your work?"

"I wouldn't say stole. We owned the company together. His success was my success and vice versa. And that success supported us. Lavishly."

Ethan remembered the two-million-dollar donation to his foundation.

"But he allowed people to believe that he'd come up with taglines or jingles that were in fact my creations," she continued. "While it's not anything close to what happened to you with your ex-wife, I can relate to some extent. Part of it was my fault. I should've spoken up. I should've played a larger role in the business. But I'd committed to being a full-time mother and I tried to convince myself that it didn't matter who got the credit. There is no 'I' in team, right?" She rolled her eyes. "And later, I despised myself for becoming"—she made quote marks in the air—"the woman behind the man."

"Why didn't you leave him?"

She shrugged. "For Henry. For all the reasons people don't split up even though they should."

He drew in a breath, knowing first-hand what that wrenching dilemma was like.

"Taking credit . . . it happens all the time in academia," he said. "Unfortunately, more to women than men. I'm sorry, Brynn. A husband should prop his wife up. Always. But it's your time now. My hunch is that the world will soon know that Brynn Barnes is the real king of advertising."

"Thank you for saying that. I don't ever really talk about it . . . about Mason I mean. I only told you about us because you confided in me about Joey. For the most part, he was a good man. A good father when he wasn't racing down mountainsides with his son in tow. He did love Henry with all his heart and would be devastated to know that he'd hurt him. And I don't think he meant to overshadow me. He was just caught up in his own myth." She smiled sadly. "But I'm back to steer the ship now. So, hey, Madison Avenue, watch out."

Madison Avenue.

The words were a wake-up call, almost identical to what Joey had said.

"Are you willing to risk your career for something that in the long run won't mean anything?"

This thing between him and Brynn was transitory. They were here now, living in the moment. Even though, for all the obvious reasons, they shouldn't be. But it had happened and he knew it would continue to happen. And in April, she and Henry would leave.

He was a realist. Her life was in New York and his life was here. Hell, they hardly knew each other. And they both had a lot to unpack. He was still trying to sort out his divorce and she was grieving the loss of a husband.

Yet, the reminder had inexplicably been like an ice bath.

"I better get back to the house before Alma calls out a search party," he said.

"What was it you wanted to ask me permission for?"

He shook his head, confused. Then it came back to him. Griffin. He'd almost forgotten.

"Griffin Parks stopped by last night, looking for you. Sounds like word got out about you and the Barnes Group and now he wants to hire your ad agency. I told him I'd run it by you and get your permission to give him your contact info. Or if you'd prefer, someone at your firm."

"I have his business card. I'll call him tomorrow."

"Okay." He leaned over and kissed her, wishing he could stay. But if he wasn't careful, he could fall even deeper. As it stood, he was already in over his head.

Chapter 16

Brynn wandered around the aisles of the Gas and Go convenience store while Henry perused the candy shelves. Today was the first time he'd been out since his stem cell injection.

The headmaster from his school had emailed Brynn homework assignments so Henry wouldn't fall too far behind. She'd granted him one more day of freedom and then they were hitting the books. To celebrate, she told him he could have a chocolate bar and he was taking his time choosing from the wide variety on display.

The store was about half the size of a 7-Eleven. A counter in the center of the store held a self-serve hot dog machine, a nacho cheese dispenser, coffee maker and soda fountain. Next to it, sat the chip and candy aisle. A refrigerator section filled with bottled waters, soda and beer covered the back wall. Near the cash register was a few racks of magazines, maps, and sundry items. And there was an ice cream freezer by the door.

A sign on the wall advertised bait and tackle but Brynn didn't see any.

Griffin came through the garage. He was wearing blue coveralls stained with grease. It was hard to reconcile him with the owner of a luxury planned community like Sierra Heights.

"Hey, Barnes family. Sorry to keep you waiting. I thought my morning was clear then things sort of blew up. But Skeeter's here now. He'll hold down the garage while we talk." He eyed Henry's wheelchair and scratched his chin. "It's a flight of stairs up to my office."

"That's all right, we can talk in here."

There was a nice gust of heat blowing through the vents and no one had come in the store since Brynn had gotten there. Henry could keep himself occupied with one of the magazines.

Griffin grabbed a chair from behind the cash register. "You take this one. I'll be right back with another."

A short time later, he returned with a desk chair he must've gotten from his office.

Henry brought her the Snickers bar he'd spent so much time picking out and Brynn went searching through her purse for her wallet.

"Don't even think about it." Griffin took the candy bar from her and handed it back to Henry. "It's on the house." He strolled over to the fountain drinks. "You want a soda with that, Henry?"

Henry gave her a pleading look and she acquiesced, even though she didn't like him drinking sugary drinks. The candy bar alone would have him bouncing off the walls and he was supposed to be resting, according to Ethan's instructions.

Ethan. She wondered what he was doing today. Was he seeing patients or working on his research?

After yesterday, she'd hoped he would call or text. *Stop being needy.*

Griffin got Henry a soda and straddled his office chair. "Thanks for meeting with me. The other day at Owen's I could tell you knew your stuff. But"—he let out a whistle—"I had no idea you were the one who put Verizon on the map or did all those Nike ads. Jeez, you're a freaking legend."

She laughed. People rarely knew the names behind the jingles. Everyone knew Rice-A-Roni was the "San Francisco treat." But few knew that Charles Foll, vice president of the McCann-Erickson ad agency, had made it so. Or that Forest Mars, of the candy dynasty, came up with M&Ms "melts in your mouth, not in your hand" all on his own.

"I don't know about a legend," she said.

"No need for modesty. I looked you up. Oh man, that beer Super Bowl ad with the lost dog. I freaking cried my eyes out."

"That was a good one." She'd loved that ad.

He hopped up. "You want a cup of coffee or something? Jeez, I didn't even ask."

"I'm fine, Griffin."

He grabbed the chair again. "I want to hire the Barnes Group to work up a marketing plan for Sierra Heights. I just can't let any more houses sit another year."

"Henry and I took a drive through it. I hope that's okay. The gate was open and no one was in the guard kiosk, so I assumed—"

"Of course." He waved her off. "Whaddya think?"

"I thought it was gorgeous. I'm far from an expert on California real estate . . . any real estate for that matter . . . but I can't believe they're not selling."

"It's the location. We're too far from the city, too far from the slopes, too far from the ocean. We're not known for our wine or our five-star accommodations, though the Lumber Baron is a gem. The best we have to offer is that a few miles away from here, in 1847, the Donner Party came through, got stranded in the snow and had to eat each other to stay alive. Unless you're a Stephen King fan, probably not a huge draw."

"I see the dilemma. But Griffin, the Barnes Group is an advertising agency and what you want is a marketing firm. A good one will cost a fortune. I'm not sure it's cost effective. You can do this yourself and I can give you guidance. The trick here is not to just sell homes but to sell a lifestyle. First, you have to figure out what that lifestyle is. Is it luxury living? Is it getting in touch with the great outdoors? Is it retiring in the country?"

"Yeah, it's all of those."

"I think you're right but you have to condense it down into one message that will resonate with buyers. Something simple, like "Life on a Vineyard" or "Life at the Lake" or the "Nature of Happiness," or "Wild at Heart." See how those taglines evoke a vision? Basically, you're branding Sierra Heights, creating a story that calls to buyers and differentiates your planned community from the rest."

"Okay, how 'bout we use one of those last ones? I like 'Wild at Heart.'"

She laughed. "I think those have all been taken. We can come up with something unique to Sierra Heights. Something that tells the story of the Sierra Nevada and compels people to want to live here. Let me kick some ideas around. Once we know the story, you have to build a website that conjures the brand. Lots of pictures and a narrative that sets expectations for what it would be like to live in Sierra Heights. Then, you decide on a budget and advertising strategy of where to place ads. I'd start with luxury magazines that cater to the Bay Area and Los Angeles. Maybe some high-end nature magazines. But first we have a lot of work to do."

"Does that mean you're on board?"

She hadn't meant to be. Her focus was on getting Henry well. But the challenge spoke to her. Besides, she needed something to occupy her time while she was here.

"As much as I can be. My first priority, though, is Henry."

"Got it. We need to work out a payment arrangement."

She waved her hand in the air. "Let's see how much time I can dedicate to it, first." This was for fun, not money.

Henry started giving her that look. The one that told her he was bored senseless and they needed to go.

"I'll call you later this week with some ideas. How's that?"

He made a heart with his fingers and pumped it next to his chest. She found him utterly charming.

"You ready to go, Henry?" As if she had to ask.

She checked her phone on the way out. Still nothing from Ethan. Maybe he had such deep remorse over what they'd done that he was distancing himself from her. The possibility of that filled her with regret, which was ridiculous. She hardly knew him. Yet, from the moment they'd met she'd been attracted. Once again, she questioned whether she was experiencing some sort of savior complex but knew she wasn't. Since the accident there'd been lots of doctors traipsing through their lives. ER, neurologists, specialists of every stripe and color, including a psychologist.

She hadn't slept with one of them. Only Ethan.

"Mom, I'm hungry."

"Okay, we've got three choices: The Ponderosa, the Bun Boy, or I could heat up soup at home."

"The Bun Boy."

"We'll have to eat in the car."

He thought it over. "Let's eat at the Ponderosa, then."

Good choice. She wasn't in the mood for munching on hamburgers and greasy fries in a cold car. They drove the few blocks to the square and Brynn did the wheelchair shuffle. She was going to look great in a sleeveless dress this summer.

Alma was in the restaurant at a table of women. Three of them Brynn had met, including Maddy from the Lumber Baron. They waved her over to join them. Even though she and Henry had only been in Nugget a few weeks, she already felt like she belonged.

"Is there room for Henry's chair?" She didn't want to crowd them.

Donna, the woman from the Bun Boy, dragged another table over and everyone rotated chairs to redistribute the seating.

"This okay?" she whispered in Henry's ear.

He shrugged, realizing his fate had already been sealed and that perhaps he could work the situation to his advantage by pressing for apple pie for dessert. She remembered the candy bar and soda at the Gas and Go.

"Let's see how you do with real food, first." She wasn't above bribing him. His appetite had continued to wax and wane. Mostly wane. Unless of course sweets were on the menu.

Maddy introduced Brynn to everyone. Brynn, who was usually good with names, got lost at about the third new face. Her mind was elsewhere today. She'd been sneaking furtive glances at her phone since they got to the table.

The women were talking about someone named Raylene, which reminded Brynn of the Dolly Parton song, "Jolene." Raylene was expecting and they were planning a baby shower.

"We could do it at the Lumber Baron or at the rec room at Sierra Heights," said a red-haired woman who looked vaguely familiar. Maybe Brynn had seen her around town before.

"I guess under the circumstances, Lucky's barn is out of the question," Donna said and threw her head back and laughed.

"She, Lucky and Tawny are fine now," said Clay's wife, Emily. "But I like the idea of the inn, especially if we do just women?"

The red head nodded. "For sure. But before we make a definitive decision we should talk to Annie. She might want to have it at The Farm."

A server came to take their orders and the discussion moved from shower planning to Brynn. Everyone was curious about her life in New York and what it was like to be an advertising executive.

"Who came up with the Bun Boy logo design?" Brynn asked Donna.

"Me, myself and I. I consider myself a connoisseur of buns."

Everyone at the table laughed.

"It's fabulous." Brynn got a kick out of it every time she drove by the hamburger stand. That little bun butt was quite clever.

"My husband, Nate, and I should talk to you," The red head . . . Sam . . . said. "Nate's the founder and CEO of Breyer Hotels. We have eleven properties, including the Lumber Baron, the Gold Mountain resort in Glory Junction and the Theodore, our flagship hotel in San Francisco. We could use a branding facelift."

"The Theodore?" It couldn't be. The Theodore she knew was one of the most storied hotels in San Francisco. It had played host to some of the most famous people in the world, including presidents, royalty and Hollywood starlets. It had to be owned by Wyndham or Hilton or one of those other giant hotel conglomerates.

Sam broke into a big smile. "Yep, that Theodore. We're so proud of it."

"Wow. It may just be my favorite hotel in the world." A few years ago, she'd stayed there with her parents while her father was guest conducting at the San Francisco Symphony. A dozen taglines came to mind. *A place for kings. A mark above the rest. Luxury unrivaled.* "Anytime. I'll be here awhile." She slipped Sam her business card.

"Don't forget the Lumber Baron," Maddy said. "The Theodore gets plenty of love. My sweet little B&B could use some, too."

"You don't need me for the Lumber Baron. You've got that lovely husband of yours. When he drove Henry and me to Reno he couldn't stop talking about the inn. You should put him on your marketing payroll."

Maddy grinned. "He is pretty great, isn't he?"

Now there was a couple still in love, Brynn thought with a pang of envy. "He told me about your scary ride. I'm so glad he could get you there."

"Me too," Brynn said. "Thank you for having such an amazing husband."

The conversation and wine flowed. These women could drink. Brynn had to drive so she didn't even try to keep up. But the afternoon had been lovely. She'd learned that Alma was an Emmy Award winning journalist, Emily a popular cookbook author and Samantha Breyer was the chief event planner for Breyer Hotels. There was nothing like the camaraderie of women. Smart, accomplished women.

Most of all, though, the afternoon had taken her mind off all the possible reasons Ethan hadn't contacted her.

She gave Henry a sideways glance. "That was fun, wasn't it?"

"It was kind of boring. And that one lady, the one from the Bun Boy, she talks a lot."

Donna Thurston was a kick, that's for sure. She reminded Brynn a little of Lexi. Both ballsy women, who suffered from the lack of a filter. It's what Brynn loved most about Lexi.

She still hadn't decided whether to tell her best friend that she'd slept with Ethan. It wasn't that Lexi would have a problem with the ethics of it. It was more that Lexi had always adored Mason. Even though Lexi had been aware that Brynn's marriage was on shaky ground, she'd dismissed their problems as a rough patch. Despite the situation, Lexi had still held Brynn and Mason up as her model of what a perfect couple should look like. Sleeping with Ethan so soon after the accident would probably weird Lexi out.

But it had been eight months.

Mason's dead. Am I supposed to stay celibate forever?

And it wasn't as if she was certain of Mason's fidelity in those last years of marriage. Though her gut told her she'd probably been wrong, there was a time or two that she suspected Mason of having affairs. There'd been no tell-tale signs—no lipstick on his collar, phone calls in the middle of the night, or discrepancies in their checking account—but his emotional absence from their relationship had been suspicious.

It was as if he'd turned into a ghost, occupying their Manhattan penthouse, a translucent fixture that rarely spoke and only stayed because he didn't know how to leave.

Oddly, despite the tension—or maybe because of it—they'd still slept together. But the sex had been perfunctory, like two strangers looking for physical contact without an actual connection.

Although he'd vehemently denied it, Brynn thought he might suffer from depression. The only time he seemed happy or present was when he bagged a big account or had gone on one of his adventure trips. It was as if he needed that adrenaline rush to make him feel alive.

There was one constant in their marriage, though. And it was Mason's love for Henry. He doted on their son. And Henry loved his father so much that it had been the hardest part of losing Mason.

On their drive home, she made a decision not to tell Lexi. Her one time with Ethan—and it appeared that there would only be a once, judging by his radio silence—would be Brynn's secret.

"How you feeling, baby?" She subconsciously smoothed Henry's hair as they pulled through the Circle D gate. "You tired?"

"No. When we get home can we go see the horses?"

"Sure. I bet they'd like a treat." She'd bought a bag of baby carrots that Henry hadn't touched. At least they wouldn't go to waste.

She noted Ethan's old truck was parked in his driveway. There went her rationalization that he'd been too busy to call. She felt her heart shrink.

When they got to the cottage, she unloaded Henry's chair, thinking again about the boon to her biceps. In Manhattan, there was always a driver or doorman to do the heavy lifting.

She got as far as the front patio when she saw it. A bundle of flowers. She called it a bundle because it wasn't your garden-variety FTD bouquet. Wrapped in a handtied burlap bag was every kind of bloom imaginable. It looked like it weighed more than a small child and had that farmhouse country style—the pretense of being rustic and haphazard when it was anything but—that was all the rage in New York.

It was either from her parents or Lexi. Though Layla and Rich were also a possibility.

Henry was as intrigued as she was. "Read the card, Mom."

Instead of the obligatory white envelope, it was a simple cardboard tag that had been stamped with black typeface that read, "Made with love by The Farm." At the bottom of the tag, someone had scrawled a signature. She read it a few times before she made out the name. Ethan.

That was all. Just Ethan. And her shrinking heart began to soar.

Chapter 17

Henry didn't seem to find it strange that his doctor sent his mother flowers (Brynn assumed they were for her and not Henry). With the mystery of who'd signed the cardboard tag solved, he wheeled his chair into the living room, flopped onto the couch and flipped on the TV.

"Take off your jacket," she told him and quickly switched on the heat. In one of the cabinets she found a vase she hoped was large enough. On second thought, she went outside and fetched a galvanized metal watering can from the patio. She fussed with the arrangement for a little while and stood back to admire how pretty it was.

Then she took her phone to her bedroom and called Ethan.

"I got your flowers. They're beautiful."

"I'm glad you like them." She could hear a smile in his voice. "I wanted to call but had back-to-back surgeries starting early this morning. I just got home about thirty minutes ago. Stopped at The Farm on my way."

"What exactly is The Farm?" Its delightful packaging had her intrigued.

"It's Annie and Logan Jenkins's place. She grows everything from produce to flowers and sells them, along with other local delicacies, at a farm stand at the road's end of her property. I'll take you there sometime. You'd like it. What are you doing for dinner?"

"We don't have plans. We had lunch at the Ponderosa. We saw Alma there and a few of her friends and wound up joining them. Why? You have something in mind?" She hoped so. It had barely been twenty-four hours since she'd seen him last and was jonesing to see him again.

"There's a Mexican place a few towns down. Just a *taqueria* but it's good. Even Alma likes it and she's pretty particular about her Mexican food. I thought the two of us could take a ride later. Alma volunteered to babysit the kids. She's making her famous mac and cheese."

The only time she'd left Henry since the accident was while he was at school. The idea of leaving him now terrified her.

Ethan must've sensed her discomfort with leaving Henry because he said, "Brynn, he'll be fine. Alma will take good care of him, just like she does Roni." It was a reminder that he trusted his stepmother with the day-to-day care of his daughter.

But it wasn't Alma she didn't trust. It was the never-ending loop that ran through her head of Henry flying off an ATV at eighty mph—the speed authorities said Mason was going—and her not being there to save him.

"Brynn, if you're not comfortable with it the four of us can go together."

"Um, if we're not out too long it might be okay."

"Whatever you want to do. It's your decision."

"I promised I'd take him to see the horses. Can we do that first?"

"Roni and I will be right over."

A short time later, he and Veronica came down the hill and something in her tummy did a back flip. Brynn wasn't sure whether it was his rugged good looks—that square jaw got her every time—or the way he carried himself with all the confidence of a man whose life work was saving children.

He looked at her like he wanted to take her in his arms and kiss her but for the children's sake settled for a big, sloppy grin. That smile did funny things to Brynn's insides.

"Let's giddy up," he said and with one arm, swung Henry into his chair, making him giggle.

"Can I ride Reggie?"

"Nope, not for a few more days. Then, we'll get you up on a horse. But not Reggie." Ethan ruffled Henry's hair.

"What about me? Can I ride Reggie?" Roni bounced up and down on her toes.

Ethan hefted her onto his shoulders and pushed Henry's wheelchair out the door. "No one rides Reggie but me."

"What about Mommy? Can she ride Reggie?"

Suddenly, Brynn felt her happy balloon deflate. It was absurd. Veronica was a little girl. She hadn't mentioned Joey to be malicious. She'd mentioned her because she was Veronica's mother. And children loved their mothers.

Brynn noticed that Ethan avoided the question, which for some odd reason bothered her more. What did she want him to say? No, your mother can't ride my horse? She forced herself to brush any thought of Joey away.

When they got to the corral, Reggie and Choo Choo trotted up to the fence and blew through their noses, looking for snacks.

"Shoot, I forgot the carrots."

Ethan put his hand at the small of her back and walked her to the barn. The strong smell of straw brought her back to the previous night and she could feel her face flush. She chanced a glance at Ethan and he winked. He was remembering too.

Roni followed them in, interrupting their walk down memory lane. "What are you doing in here?"

"Hold out your hand," Ethan told her and filled it with a fistful of oats. "Share with Henry." Roni raced out of the stable.

Ethan moved closer to Brynn, leaned in, his lips touching the whorl of her ear, and whispered, "Later."

Brynn wasn't sure if it was a promise or a warning but it sent a delicious shiver down her spine.

They went outside to find Henry feeding Choo Choo, who had lowered his head over the fence to reach his wheelchair. Roni had climbed up and was braiding Reggie's mane. The scene was so adorable that Brynn snapped a few pictures with her phone and hastily texted them to her parents and Lexi.

Lexi immediately replied. "Too cute. Now, tagline that."

"What's so interesting?" Ethan looked over her shoulder at her phone.

"I sent my best friend pictures of the kids."

"Dr. Daniels, can I sit up on the fence with Roni?" Veronica had climbed all the way up, like she had the last time.

He swung Henry up onto the top railing next to Roni. "Next week, you start work with the physical therapist."

Brynn could feel her son's resistance from only a few feet away. In New York, he had weekly sessions with an occupational therapist and hated them. Roni must've sensed his hesitation too because she put her hand on his leg and patted it, which didn't improve Henry's mood.

"I don't want to," he whined.

Before she could explain to him why it was important, Ethan hopped up on the fence.

"You trust me?" Henry nodded yes. "Good. After all that hard work you and I did last week we need to get you moving. Otherwise how are we going to get you onto the back of a horse, huh?" Ethan playfully messed up Henry's hair. "Where's your hat?"

"I forgot it." Henry touched the top of his head just to make sure it wasn't there.

Ethan's lips curved up and for a second she was blinded by his wide smile. It was an irresistible combination of boyish and manly and it made her heart hammer in her chest.

"Who wants mac and cheese?" he asked and jumped down from the fence.

Both kids shouted, "I do. I do."

They walked to the big house, Ethan pushing Henry's wheelchair up the long driveway.

"I want to ride, too." Roni tried to jump up on the footplate but Ethan wouldn't let her.

Instead, he swung her up on his shoulders again and in a tenor, sang a bluegrass version of "Baby Shark." Brynn liked it a heck of lot better than the original, which wasn't saying a whole lot.

The kids joined in. Roni had clearly grown up with country music because she was laying on the twang. And Brynn had never seen Henry laugh so hard.

As soon as they got in the house the aroma of good cheddar cheese hit her so hard that for a second she considered suggesting that they stay in and eat at home. But the prospect of being alone with Ethan was too good to pass up, even for really killer mac and cheese.

Alma came out of the kitchen to greet them and Brynn wondered what Ethan had told her about them. He'd made it clear that their relationship, or whatever they were calling this, was an ethical breach. Were they supposed to be secretive about it? Or had he confided in Alma? She had to suspect something because how normal was it for a doctor to take his patient's mother out for Mexican food?

Brynn realized the dynamic was a little different because she and Henry lived next door and that for all intents and purposes they were neighbors in a small town. Didn't that allow them to be friends?

She also wondered what kind of relationship Alma had with Joey. It was silly, Brynn knew. But she couldn't help wondering if the two women were close.

Later, in the cab of Ethan's truck, as they drove along a windy two-lane highway in a part of the area Brynn had never been before she asked him, "What did you tell Alma about us?"

He was quiet for a few minutes, then said, "That I thought you needed to get out . . . have some time to yourself."

But she wasn't by herself, she was with him. "And she bought that?"

He chuckled. "Probably not. But for both our sakes she's pretending to."

"Because of your job?"

He gave a small shrug. "That and because my love life is my own."

Love life. It was just an expression for any kind of romantic entanglement, even a one-night stand. Still, Brynn was surprised that he would use those words. It gave her a secret pleasure that he had.

"Was she close with your ex?"

Ethan stole a sideways glance at her and answered succinctly, "No."

She wanted to ask more about that, but his body language told her in no uncertain terms that the conversation was off the table. He was protective of his ex, a trait Brynn found laudable. But also gave her pause.

It wouldn't do to fall for a guy who belonged to someone else already. And from their first and only meeting Joey made it clear that she still considered herself Mrs. Daniels, despite what she had done.

Brynn turned so she could look out the window at the scenery. Except for the slim light of the moon it was tough to make out much. From what she could tell, the land was similar to Nugget. Lots of tall trees and white-dusted mountains. She touched the window with her hand, trying to assess the temperature. It was just as cold as well.

"Where are we?" she asked.

"A few miles from Clio. That's where the Mexican joint is." His hand moved to her lap. "You hungry?"

"I could eat." But mostly she wanted to spend time with him. "How were your surgeries?"

"Okay. A little girl whose mother's boyfriend beat her so badly that both her femoral shafts were shattered."

"Oh my God. That's horrifying."

"Ah, Jesus." Ethan rubbed his hand down his face. "I shouldn't have told you that."

"No, it's okay. That must be awful for you." What kind of person did something like that? Not that Brynn was shocked altogether. Even at Henry's hoity toity private school there was an incident a year ago where the staff had to notify social services about a student's suspicious bruising. It showed it could happen anywhere. Abusers came in all shapes and colors and all socio-economic groups.

"Unfortunately, it's a lot of my practice. That and bone deformities. It's why this stem cell research is so important."

"Thank goodness all these poor children have such a great doctor."

"Yep, there's that." She saw him wink at her in the pale light of the truck cab.

He pulled off the highway into a dirt parking lot right off the side of the road. Next to the lot was a low-slung wooden building with a blinking neon sign. Roberto's.

It wasn't much. In fact, it was more like a taco stand with a drive-through than a restaurant. Inside, there was a walk-up counter, concrete floors, and a few tables covered in oilcloths. Bright Mexican tiles and Day of the Dead skulls adorned the walls, and a big sombrero hung over the door. In the corner was a drink station with *aguas frescas* and *horchata* in big jars.

"You'll like it, I promise." He squeezed her neck, letting his hands linger on her skin, giving her goosebumps.

The man behind the counter flashed Ethan a big smile, making it evident that Ethan was a regular. "*Hola. Donde esta la señora?*"

Despite her limited Spanish, she knew what the man was asking. The question was whether la señora referred to Joey or Alma.

"Home with her granddaughter," Ethan said and introduced Brynn to Roberto himself.

They ordered their food and took a seat at one of the empty tables, waiting for their name to be called.

"I think old Roberto has a crush on my stepmother."

"Well of course he does. She's beautiful. And I had no idea she was famous."

A look of pride flooded his face. "Famous in Reno, anyway."

Their food came—Roberto brought it to their table. Ethan hadn't been exaggerating, the *chile relleno* was the best she'd ever had. There was a place she and Mason used to go on 13th Street that wasn't bad. But nothing compared to this.

They ate until Ethan broke the silence. "You talk to Griffin?"

"Uh-huh. Met him at the Gas and Go. I'll try to help him out while I'm here."

"That's nice of you. Be sure to charge him handsomely. From what I hear he's rich as the Sultan of Brunei."

"Griffin?" An image of him in his greasy coveralls flitted through her head. "I mean, I figured he had some money to own a place like Sierra Heights or at least inherited well. But like really, really rich?"

"Yup. Word on the street, which isn't always the most reliable, is that he's descended from the Ramsey band of the Wigluk Nation. They own one of the largest casino resorts in California and Griffin gets dividends."

"Wow. Do you believe it?"

"Yeah." He said around a mouthful. "I sort of do, though he's always struck me as salt of the earth. A really good guy. Besides the Gas and Go, he owns the only tow truck company in town. Drives the trucks himself. But I didn't take you on a date to talk about Griffin Parks."

"Is this a date?" Though the question came out slightly flirtatious, she hadn't been exactly sure what this was. Maybe, like he'd told Alma, he was simply trying to give her a short respite from motherhood. A doctor taking a holistic approach. Keep the family happy and healthy, cure the child.

He looked at her with amusement, clearly finding her question funny. Or absurd. "Hell yeah it's a date." He swept his arms across the restaurant and his mouth quirked. "Only the best."

She leaned across the table, admiring his handsomely chiseled face, the lips that had kissed her so thoroughly the night before, and the hazel eyes that seemed to see everything. "It might not be the Ritz Carleton but you were definitely right about the food."

"I like it." He gave her a slow perusal. "I like the company even better."

Their eyes locked and she suddenly wanted to eat as fast as possible so they could leave and she could tear his clothes off inside his truck. She couldn't remember ever being this attracted to a man. Not even Mason, who had been the love of her life once.

But he seemed to want to linger, unwrapping his burrito a few inches at a time. She liked staring at his hands. Strong, steady, healing hands. The hands of a surgeon.

"What?" He looked down at his burrito to see what was so interesting. "You want a bite?"

"I like your hands, that's all."

"Yeah?" He hitched his brows, checked out his hands, and returned a cocky grin. "Brynn?"

"Hmm?"

"You want to get out of here?"

"I thought you'd never ask."

He devoured the last bite of his burrito and drained his Dos Equis. Nudging his head at her *chile relleno*, he asked, "Do you want to take it for later?"

He didn't wait for her to answer, just walked to the counter and asked for a to-go box. She wrapped up the rest of her dinner, waved goodbye to Roberto, before climbing into Ethan's truck.

"Where now?" she asked. Going back to the cottage would be awkward with Alma just up the hill.

"We could go somewhere and park." He laughed. "Or we could go to the Lumber Baron."

Normally, she wasn't the type to rent a room by the hour but the idea tempted her. She chewed on her bottom lip, debating with herself.

"I was kidding, Brynn."

"You were?" she asked, disappointed. She wanted him to be as desperate for her as she was for him.

"We'll go back to the cottage."

Her eyes grew wide but she didn't question it. Perhaps he didn't have the same thing in mind as she did. But when they got to Nugget, he turned off on a road she didn't recognize. A shortcut, maybe. Not a very good one. The road was rocky and rutted, bouncing them like a basketball. Without four-wheel drive, she was certain they would've gotten stuck.

"Where are we going?"

"You'll see."

They came to a fence. Ethan put on the brake, hopped out of the truck, and opened a big metal gate under the glare of his headlights. As soon as he drove through, he locked it closed.

They continued on what appeared to be a riding or foot trail, lurching back and forth every time Ethan hit a pothole or bump. She could see the Feather River on her left and figured they were somewhere on the ranch. Probably a back entrance.

"Is this your land?"

"Yup. The gate is so a livestock trailer can get into the pasture to load the calves for market."

"How far are we from the cottage?"

"Not far. Two or three miles." He slanted her a sideways glance and took her hand.

She felt like a teenager, skulking around in the backyard of her parents' Hamptons house, making sure the coast was clear before slipping off to a party she'd been forbidden from going to. It was a little silly. They were both single, consenting adults. Still, the sneaking around sort of added to the excitement. The anticipation.

The truck went over something hard, possibly a mound of dirt, and Brynn was momentarily vaulted out of her seat, which sent her into a fit of giggles.

Ethan caught her with his arm and started laughing too. "I guess this whole covert thing is a little overkill, you think?"

She held her fist to her mouth to try to stifle the laughter. That's when he stopped the truck, reached over, and kissed her.

It was slow at first, just a mere touch of his lips to hers. Almost tentative. But then he caged her face in his hands and the kiss became urgent. Deeper and needy. He pulled her over the console on top of him while one of his hands searched the floor. And just like that the back of his seat reclined.

Then their hands were everywhere. Hers under his jacket and shirt, touching his taut, muscular abdomen. His, first in her hair, then on her breasts. She tried to remember whether she'd ever done anything like this in a car but had no recollection of it. The truth was her sex life had never been particularly adventurous.

But now she wanted to do everything. With Ethan.

Soon, their clothes were strewn across the cab as they reached for each other, desperate and needy. He was touching her again, kissing her breasts as his hands stroked her bare back. She rocked against him, feeling denim scrape against her legs.

"Ethan." She wrestled with his jeans.

"I've got 'em." He lifted up, taking her with him, and deftly pulled his Levi's down with one hand. The boots were the problem. He couldn't get his pant legs over his heels, not in the confining quarters of his truck.

While he struggled to untangle them, she got the giggles again.

"Shush," he hushed her with his lips while managing to knock one boot off on the dashboard, then tossed it into the back seat. "Dammit." The second boot wouldn't budge.

Finally, he opened the door and by some miracle kept them from both tumbling out. "Hang on." He slid her over to the other seat, turned sideways with his legs dangling out of the truck and pried off the other boot.

The pants came next, leaving him in a pair of black jockey shorts that barely contained his erection. He slammed the door shut. But the whoosh of cold air had turned her flesh to goosebumps.

He pulled her over him again, rubbing her arms and back until she was warm. Then he slid her panties down her legs and tossed them so that they landed next to her bra, which was hanging off the rearview mirror.

He spread her legs until she was straddling him and thrust up, letting her feel the length of him pressing against her groin. She moaned, frantic for more. He tested her with his fingers and she nearly climaxed right then and there.

"Please," she whispered.

He freed himself from his shorts and impaled her. Neither of them moved at first. He just stayed inside of her, breathing hard. Then, slowly, she began to rock back and forth. He held her hips, guiding her so he could go deeper.

She whimpered with pleasure. Her head fell back as he began to thrust up, bouncing her on his lap. His hands moved up her rib cage and fondled her breasts as she cried out.

"Good?"

"So good," she whispered and grasped his broad shoulders. "Don't stop."

"You don't have to worry about that." He kissed her, his tongue delving inside her mouth while she rode him.

She could see him watching her in the moonlight, his eyes pools of desire. Having him look at her with such heat and arousal, took her higher. She arched her back and he took one breast and then the other in his mouth, sucking and laving them with attention.

His hands had moved to her backside and he began easing her up and down. Faster, then harder. Building until heat coalesced in the pit of her stomach and her body began to seize with release.

"Ethan, oh Ethan."

"I've got you, baby. Let it go. Let it go."

She felt herself clench and spasm as a torrent rolled through her.

His strokes quickened, hard and strong. She held on with each powerful thrust. He grunted, threw his head back, and called out her name. Then they collapsed against each other, her head nestled against his chest.

He wrapped his arms around her back and held her close. The windows were fogged from the inside but Brynn could tell that a thin layer of frost had begun to cover the glass on the outside. Ethan grabbed his jacket from the backseat and covered her with it. For a long time, they just snuggled together, oblivious to the cramped quarters.

"You okay?"

"Never better." She burrowed deeper into his chest and could hear the beat of his heart.

Ethan tried to stretch his legs but hit the dashboard with his knee. "Shit. I'm too old for truck sex."

She laughed. "I don't know, you're pretty good at it if you ask me. But we should get home. I don't want to leave Henry too long." Though it had been well worth it, she'd already been gone more time than she'd planned.

Ethan righted his seat and she crawled out of his lap into the passenger seat, immediately missing the heat of his body and the safety of his arms. With the cold came the sharp slap of reality. She had not come here to fall hopelessly infatuated with a man. She'd come for the sake of her son and the possibility that he would one day walk again.

And as soon as Henry was better she would be leaving to take the helm of her company, her legacy to her son.

Chapter 18

The days got longer, the grass grew taller, and the cacophony of cattle crying for their babies filled the air on the Circle D. According to Ethan, April was weaning season, when mamas were separated from their calves.

Watching the babies and their dams stand on opposite sides of a fence broke Brynn's heart.

"It's life on a working cattle ranch," Ethan had told her. "A month from now we'll send them to market."

The weeks had passed quickly in Nugget. Between working on Griffin's campaign, spending time with the women in town and stealing away with Ethan in the evenings whenever they could, Brynn's life was full to bursting.

But she'd begun to worry that Henry's legs weren't healing the way they were supposed to. A physical therapist came twice a week but Henry still hadn't graduated from the wheelchair to a walker. Every time she broached the subject with Ethan, he told her to be patient.

Today, though, the X-rays would give them a clearer picture of his progress. The films would show whether new bone tissue had begun to form.

And after their appointment, she and Henry were picking up Lexi at Reno-Tahoe International Airport.

"Mom, do X-rays hurt?"

She parked the car in the giant structure at Renown Children's and turned to him. "No, baby. They're just going to take a picture of your bones. Do you remember when Dr. Brunswick did it? It didn't hurt then, now did it?"

"I don't remember."

She leaned over, took off his cowboy hat, and kissed the top of his sweaty head. "You want to leave this in the car or wear it in?"

"Wear it." He'd asked for boots too. Brynn suspected that he was trying to emulate Ethan, who he'd begun to idolize. He followed him everywhere. The cottage, the driveway, anywhere Henry's wheelchair could go.

Ethan had taken him and Roni fishing last Friday. Though Brynn wasn't ready to let Henry go on outings—especially of the adventurous kind— without her, she'd relented. Only because it was Ethan. Henry caught two rainbow trout, which she suspected had been reeled in by Ethan. But the look on Henry's face when they brought the fish home was priceless.

Sometimes, at the height of her guilt, she wondered if it was a mistake letting her son get attached to a man they would leave ultimately. Henry had lost enough already. But if she banished Ethan from Henry's private life, she would have to remove him from her own. And she couldn't. This thing between them had become more than an obsession. Ethan Daniels had become her lifeline.

She was assailed by the antiseptic smell of the hospital as soon as they passed through the double doors. The volunteer at the desk smiled at them. Brynn wasn't sure if the elderly woman recognized her and Henry from past visits or if that's how she greeted everyone.

In the radiology waiting room, they fell into their usual pattern. Henry chose a comic book while Brynn scrolled through her phone, pretending not to be anxious. Twenty minutes later, they were led to a room and asked to remove Henry's pants.

It was cold from the air conditioner and she worried about Henry and his bare legs.

The technician, who said Brynn could stay in the room with Henry while the X-rays were taken, fitted them both with lead aprons. The whole thing took less than fifteen minutes.

The technician asked them to wait while the images were processed. "Just want to make sure we got what we need."

"We're all good," he said a few minutes later.

"How soon until Dr. Daniels gets the results?" They could grab a bite to eat in the cafeteria while they waited.

"One to two days."

Brynn jerked back, surprised. She'd just assumed they would get the results today. "Why so long?"

The technician shrugged. "It's how long it usually takes."

She helped Henry put his pants back on, disappointed. Today, she'd hoped to be reassured, told everything was healing just as it should.

She didn't like to take advantage of her relationship with Ethan but instead of going back to the car, she wheeled Henry to the Orthopedic Surgery Center.

"Is Dr. Daniels in?"

A receptionist who had seen them several times before typed something into her computer. "I don't see you on the schedule, Mrs. Barnes. Did we make a mistake?"

What she meant was did Brynn show up on the wrong day.

"Henry had a radiology appointment today and I just wanted to ask Dr. Daniels a quick question about it."

"Let me check if he's available."

Brynn waited, feeling foolish. For all she knew Ethan was with a patient and she was interrupting him.

"Mom, can we go now?"

"Soon, sweetheart. I just want to ask Eth . . . Dr. Daniels a question."

Ethan opened the door to the waiting room. Unlike at home, he was in full doctor attire. White lab coat, stethoscope stuck in his pocket, and a pair of dark colored slacks. At least he wasn't in scrubs and she hadn't pulled him out of a surgery. Not that he would leave in the middle of a surgery but . . . she felt pushy. And presumptuous.

"Hey," he said, smiling. "Come back to my office."

He ushered them through the door. Brynn noticed he was careful to keep his distance as they walked down the hall together, passing exam rooms on their way. He shut the door behind them and motioned for Brynn to have a seat.

"I'm sorry to bug you like this."

"You're not bugging me." But he sounded harried as if she'd caught him in the midst of something. Or maybe it was just her imagination. But he was acting so stiff and professional. "Did everything go okay with the X-rays?"

"Yes, but the technician said it'll take one to two days to find out anything. I thought we'd know something today."

He nodded patiently. "It's not my call, Brynn. It's up to the radiologist. Two days is pretty standard unless it's an emergency."

"This is an emergency." Her son wasn't getting better.

He just gazed at her with the same patient expression he'd used before. "I'll see what I can do, but it won't be today." He reached over and adjusted Henry's hat. "Nothing's going to change between now and then, anyway."

She wanted to scream at his blasé attitude but held herself in check. It wouldn't do to make a scene.

"Brynn," Ethan's eyes darted to the closed door and then to Henry, "It'll be okay."

Then why wasn't there any improvement?

"I'm sorry to have bothered you." She got to her feet and grabbed the handles on Henry's chair.

"You didn't bother me," he said but didn't reach out to console or stop her from leaving.

She made it all the way to the airport before calming down. It was early. Lexi's flight didn't get in until one. They probably should've grabbed a bite but she'd been too upset to think straight.

"Are you mad at Dr. Ethan?"

"No, of course not. I was just frustrated is all." And on edge. And probably overbearing. She didn't know what she'd expected of Ethan. Was he supposed to drop everything and demand that the radiologist read Henry's X-rays?

"Mom . . . was the accident Dad's fault?"

"What?" Although she prepared for this question—a cadre of medical experts said it would come—she hadn't expected Henry to raise it while sitting in a cell phone lot at the airport.

Momentarily thrown, she caught herself and recited the answer she had rehearsed for months. "Of course not. It was an accident, baby." Yet, resentment for Mason festered in her like a disease.

Be careful, she told herself. Children had an uncanny way of sensing a parent's anger.

"Was it my fault?" he asked, his blue eyes, so much like hers, watched for her reaction. It was as if he was waiting for her to lie.

"Absolutely not. What would even make you think that?" She turned in her seat and brushed his cheek with her thumb.

He hitched his slender shoulders. "I don't know. But why did I have to be in an accident, Mom? Why did Dad have to die?"

"Oh, Henry, I wish I had an answer for you. Sometimes, bad things just happen, even when it's no one's fault. Daddy loved you so much. You were his pride and joy. You know that, right?"

He nodded and sniffled, wiping his nose with the back of his hand. She searched her purse for tissues and wiped his eyes.

"Do you know how we keep Daddy alive in our hearts?" She touched her chest with the flat of her hand.

"How?" His bottom lip trembled.

"We live a happy life for him. Can you remember that?"

"Yes," he said, trying to hide his tears.

"Come here." She pulled him into her arms. "I love you, Henry. You're everything to me."

* * * *

"How many more miles?"

"What are you, twelve?" Brynn poked her best friend in the arm.

"I have to pee. I drank four cups of coffee and a can of ginger ale on the plane. You didn't tell me there was nothing between Reno and Nugget but desert."

"And forest. Oh, Lexi, wait until you see the trees. Pines as tall as a high rise."

"And the horses, Aunt Lexi. You'll love the horses."

Lexi turned to the backseat. "What about cowboys? Are there any of those?"

Brynn elbowed her in the arm and rolled her eyes.

"Dr. Ethan is a cowboy. There are lots of 'em in Nugget."

"Oh yeah?" She raised her brows. "Well get me to Nugget. Stat!"

"You're a nut." Brynn shook her head. "Have I told you how happy I am that you're here?"

"About a hundred times. And I've got presents," Lexi said in her best Oprah singsongy voice.

Henry leaned into the front passenger seat. "What did you bring me, Aunt Lexi?"

"It's a surprise."

The landscape turned from scrub to dense thickets of trees as they climbed into the mountains.

"See that?" Brynn pointed. "It's the Feather River. It flows right by the cottage."

Lexi gazed out the window. "Good job. Now I'm going to pee my pants."

"We're almost there, you can hold it. Later, we'll go to town and eat dinner at the Ponderosa. It's Henry's and my new home away from home. Isn't it, Henry?" Brynn looked at Henry in her rearview mirror.

"And the Bun Boy," Henry said.

"Afterward we can check you in at the Lumber Baron."

Lexi was only staying three days but Brynn planned to make the most of every second. She needed her best friend now more than ever.

"How did the X-rays go?" Lexi slid Brynn a glance. Brynn confided that Henry was taking longer than anticipated to heal, which was a bad sign.

"We didn't get the results yet. It'll take another day or two." She tried to sound optimistic for Henry's sake. But Brynn heard the despair in her own voice.

Lexi reached over and squeezed her hand.

When they got to the cottage Lexi declared it adorable. "It's like a storybook house in the woods."

"I want to show Aunt Lexi the barn," Henry said.

"In a little while, baby. Let's let Lexi settle in first. She's been traveling since early this morning." Brynn pulled a cheese platter she'd prepared earlier from the fridge and opened a bottle of wine to let it breathe while Lexi used the restroom.

Lexi joined them in the kitchen and rooted through her purse. *"Voila,* a gift for *Monsieur* Henry."

Henry tore through the wrapping. It was the most enthusiastic Brynn had seen him in days. The truth was, her worries about his legs had begun to rub off on him. She'd seen it in subtle ways, including making excuses not to play with Roni on the afternoons she came knocking on their door.

She needed to stop wearing her every emotion on her sleeve. It wasn't good for her son. It wasn't good for anyone.

Going off on Ethan earlier had not only been petulant, but it had put him in an awkward position. She'd acted entitled, an attitude she abhorred in the Upper East Side set with whom she socialized.

"Lexi!" Brynn shot her friend a look as Henry exclaimed over his new smart watch. "A little extravagant, don't you think?"

"That's what aunties are for." She helped Henry put it on and kissed him on the cheek. "Go set it up and give your mom and me some alone time."

When Henry dutifully left for his bedroom, Lexi flashed a smug smile as if to say, *See, I'm keeping him busy so we can talk.*

No, it wasn't easy gaining privacy in the small cottage. In the last weeks, Brynn and Ethan had been extremely inventive to meet the challenge.

"You look miserable." Lexi got two wine goblets down from the cupboard and brought the bottle to the coffee table, where she poured them each a healthy glass. "What's going on?"

I had my first fight with the man I'm crazy about. She could still see his face as she'd walked out of his office. His expression was a mixture of anger and pity.

"I'm disappointed that I couldn't get Henry's X-ray results today. If it's not working . . ." Brynn's eyes welled. "I just had so much faith in this, Lex."

"It may simply be that Henry is a slow healer. Did you ever think about that? What does the doctor say?"

"That Henry may be a slow healer." Brynn tried to laugh but it came out more as a sob.

"Ah, Brynn." Lexi wrapped her in a hug. "I can't believe you're doing this all on your own."

Not alone, she had Ethan. But after today who knew. Perhaps he'd want no part of her after she'd thrown her little spoiled stunt in his office.

Brynn got up and went to the bathroom to blow her nose. On her way back, she grabbed the cheese platter. She thought about making a fire to give Lexi the full Nugget winter wonderland experience. But it was in the high sixties, hardly fireplace weather.

Her phone rang and she jumped up, hoping it was Ethan. But it was her mother, who plied her with questions about Henry's X-rays, Lexi's flight and whether she and Brynn's father should book a flight in the next week or so.

"Why don't you wait, Mom? I don't know what our schedule is yet."

For the next ten minutes, her mother talked about everyone and everything in New York, including news about Brynn's father's latest performance. Brynn mouthed "help" to Lexi, who mouthed back, "You're on your own."

There was a knock on the door. "Mom, someone's here. I have to go."

Lexi followed her as if she was Brynn's second line of defense in case they had to take down an intruder. She wanted to tell her that they were no longer in Manhattan.

It was Roni. School had gotten out about an hour ago.

"Henry," Brynn called. "Veronica is here. Why don't you guys play outside for a little while?" She wanted Henry to get fresh air.

To her surprise, Henry acquiesced. She was sure it was the new smart watch that did it. He wanted to show it off.

"She's darling," Lexi said when Henry and Roni were out of hearing distance. "She's younger than Henry, isn't she?"

"She's six. But the nearest kid for miles. Henry's very sweet with her and she's very patient with him. I think it's because both her parents are in the medical profession."

"Her mom's a doctor, too?"

"No, an orthopedic nurse. But they're divorced. She sees her daughter on weekends."

"The doc got custody. That's unusual, isn't it?"

"She had an addiction problem. Opioids." Brynn felt like she was betraying a confidence. But this was Lexi, her best friend. Besides, by Thursday, Lexi would be on the other side of the country and Ethan and Joey would remain mere strangers. No one for Lexi to gossip about with their New York friends.

"Wow, how'd you find all that out?"

She nonchalantly hitched her shoulders. "Dr. Daniels and I have become friends." It wasn't a lie, just a slight obfuscation. "He's my only neighbor for miles."

"Is the ex still a pill popper?"

"I don't think so." Brynn didn't tell Lexi the rest of the story about how Joey had forged Ethan's name on prescriptions. That would've been a true violation of her and Ethan's friendship.

"Well, their daughter is cute as a button."

She was the apple of her daddy's eye, there was no question about that. Watching him with his daughter was one of the things she found most appealing about Ethan. And Lord knew there were plenty of things to find appealing about the man.

"You should see her with the horses. She's fearless."

Lexi pushed the cheese platter at her. "Eat. You could stand to put on a few pounds."

Henry wasn't the only one who had lost his appetite. In the last two weeks, Brynn had shed five pounds.

"Is that your tactful way of saying I look like shit?"

"Have you ever known me to be tactful?" Lexi had a point. "But while we're on the topic you could use a touch up." She openly stared at Brynn's roots, the curse of being a brunette. "Some highlights and a trim."

"Yeah, I'll get right on that with all my extra time." Frankly, Brynn had never had so much time in her life. Even after she left the Barnes Group to be a full-time mom, she rushed from Henry's activities to her various volunteer meetings. There had never been enough time in the day.

Other than taking Henry to his appointments and helping Griffin with his ad campaign for Sierra Heights, she didn't have a whole lot left to do, except obsess over whether her son was improving. Even infinitesimally.

And when she wasn't doing that, she was watching the clock for Ethan.

"There's got to be a place around here or Reno. I'll tell you what. We'll leave early for the airport Thursday and I'll take you to a salon. My treat. Come on, Brynn. It's at least something. Something to make you feel a little bit better."

She agreed, mostly because Lexi wasn't the type to take no for an answer. "There's actually a place here. It's a barbershop but the barber has a daughter who's a stylist."

Lexi laughed. "I think we'll hold out for Reno."

"All the women around here rave about her, including Dr. Daniels's stepmother who is a former TV anchorwoman. Her hair looks great."

"All right, I'll check this place out when we go to town. See if it gets my stamp of approval."

Lexi got her hair done at one of the best salons in Manhattan. It was the same stylist who did Jerry Seinfeld's wife. He charged an obscene amount of money, which in Lexi's case was a complete waste. Lexi had the kind of looks—tall, curvy, big boobs, big green eyes, naturally curly red hair—that made men stop in the street. And yet she was still single. Sometimes Brynn thought Lexi intentionally sabotaged any chance at a real relationship to protect herself from getting hurt.

In Brynn's darkest, loneliest days living with Mason, she'd actually envied that fact about her best friend.

From outside she could hear the kids calling to someone and peered out the window. Ethan was walking down the driveway. It was early for him to be home and Brynn wondered if he'd come to retrieve Roni for a special school function.

But he waved to the kids, stopped for a beat so Henry could show him his new watch, then continued to the cottage.

"What's so interesting out there? Are the kids okay?" Lexi came over to the window to see what had caught Brynn's attention. "Oh my. Is that Dr. Daniels?"

"Uh-huh."

"Holy crap, you weren't kidding. Why don't I have a doctor who looks like that?"

Before he could knock, Brynn opened the door. "Hi."

For a few moments they just stood there, eyes locked.

Then he looked over Brynn's shoulder. "You must be Lexi." Ethan stuck his hand out to shake Lexi's. "Brynn talks about you all the time. Welcome to Nugget."

"Thank you." Lexi shot Brynn a quick, quizzical look.

"Come in," Brynn said.

"Actually, I was hoping we could talk." He smiled at Lexi. "It won't take long."

The context was clear. He wanted to speak to her alone and it was going to be a short conversation. Afraid that he'd come to break it off with her, she nearly told him now wasn't a good time.

Brynn stepped outside. "I'll be right back, Lex."

"Take your time."

Brynn told the kids to keep Lexi company, and she and Ethan walked to the barn. He didn't try to eat up the distance between them, letting her hug one side of the trail while he kept to the other side. Neither said a word until they reached the corral. The horses grazed in the pasture and started to slowly make their way to the fence.

Ethan hung his arms over the top rail. He was still in his dress pants from work. "I got the radiologist to prioritize Henry's images."

Caught off guard, she sucked in a breath. "Oh, Ethan, I should have . . . I was awful . . . I'm so sorry."

"Yeah, you can't do that again, Brynn."

It was the second time she'd thrown what amounted to a tantrum to get her way. The first, he'd called out the cavalry to drive them through a snowstorm.

"I don't let my staff play favorites. Yet here I am doing it."

"You're right," she said, ashamed. "But please believe me that it's about Henry. I push for his sake and would do the same with any of his doctors. What I'm attempting to say is that I'm not trying to take advantage of the fact that we're . . . you know."

He held her gaze. "But the problem is I'm giving in because we're involved. And it's not right. You should feel completely justified pushing the limits and I should be able to put my foot down. I should be able to say that you have to wait in line like everyone else. But I can't where you're concerned." He sighed. "And it's wrong."

"What are you saying?" Her chest squeezed even tighter. "You want us to stop being involved." *Involved.* It was his word, not hers. She'd crossed over to head over heels the first time he'd kissed her.

He didn't say anything and with each second of his silence, she felt her insides collapse.

He blew out a breath. "I think it's too late for that. But I didn't come to talk about us. I came to share the results of Henry's X-rays."

Her mouth fell open. When Ethan had said prioritize, she'd gotten the impression that the radiologist would get to it first thing in the morning. Not today. "You got them already? What did they say?" There was an empty feeling in the pit of her stomach.

"The results aren't as good as I had hoped."

"But they're not bad?" She asked even though deep down inside she suspected that it was her worst fears.

"I would've preferred to do this in my office where I could show you the images." He gave her a pointed look. "It appears that new bone tissue has begun to form but it's microscopic. I had hoped that by now we would've seen some significant changes."

A wave of nausea overtook her. Was it hopeless? Or was Henry a slow healer, like everyone had implied. "Does this mean the stem cells aren't working?"

"No." He shook his head. "I'm somewhat optimistic given that there has been some change. We have to be patient. That's all we can do."

She nodded, holding onto the word "optimistic" like a rope. "Have you had other patients who started out slow like this and made a full recovery?"

He deliberated. Brynn wasn't sure if he was trying to remember or was quickly trying to fabricate something uplifting to protect her from the truth.

"Every patient is different, Brynn." He moved closer and took her hand. "You have to stay positive. In a week, two weeks, we could see real improvement."

She nodded again, though she was sure her disappointment was as transparent as film. "I wasn't expecting much," she said tearfully. Though she'd prayed that the X-rays would show she was wrong.

"Brynn?" Ethan took her in his arms. "A little faith, okay?"

She laid her head on his shoulder. "I know."

Chapter 19

The whole way home Ethan worried that he was giving Brynn false hope. Henry's fractures were severe. In both femoral shafts the distal, middle and proximal sections of the bone had been shattered like a plate glass window that a truck had driven through. Only jagged pieces of the bone were left.

The last time he'd seen breaks that serious was in a five-year-old who'd been in a head-on collision and hadn't been wearing a seat belt.

He questioned whether he would've been more direct with Brynn if she and Henry hadn't come to mean so much to him. Because there was a significant chance that this was as good as it got for Henry.

But watching her fall apart . . . He couldn't do it. Every day they'd been together, he'd become more enamored with the woman Brynn Barnes was. Funny, bright, clever, beautiful, kind. But it was her strength that he most admired. With all that had happened to her in the last year she'd carried on like a fighter in the face of adversity. Not once had she given up or backed down. Her determination to protect her son was fierce and unrelenting.

It made him want to fix everything for her. Not like a doctor with a patient. But like a man. It was visceral. He wanted to be her hero. Her protector.

Joey's Ford was parked in the driveway when he got to the house. He'd forgotten that he granted her a dinner visit with Roni. They'd come to a tacit agreement that Joey could spend unsupervised time with Roni on weekdays as long as she gave him a day's notice. She'd been coming and going as if the Circle D was her second home.

"Hey." He found her in the kitchen, sipping a cup of tea at the breakfast table while Alma snapped peas into a big pot. "Roni's down at the neighbor's. I'll text Brynn to send her up."

"Before you do, I wanted to talk."

"Okay." He exchanged a glance with Alma, who shrugged, then slipped out to give them privacy.

"What's up?" He grabbed a beer from the fridge, took one of the stools at the center island, and swiveled around to face her.

"I'd like to discuss our custody agreement."

"It's not an agreement, it's a court order."

"My lawyer says we can renegotiate the terms on our own and bring it to a judge to vacate the original order. It'll save money and it'll be better for Roni than a family court battle."

"Your lawyer." He cocked his brows. "I wasn't aware you had one."

"I do. She's a volunteer for Legal Aid. Her day job is working for one of the best family law firms in Reno." She jutted her chin at him in challenge. "I want to do this amicably, Ethan. Please."

"I hope she has a bar card in California." He was acting like a douchebag but he didn't like being sandbagged.

"The custody ruling was made in Nevada."

Technically. But Washoe County District Court had been apprised of his move to California after he was awarded full custody. Chances were, he'd be granted a request to move the case to his new jurisdiction. "I guess we'll see."

"Ethan, don't do this."

He rubbed a hand down his face. "It's too soon. Come on, Joey. I've been fair. You're here now, aren't you? I've even backed off the supervision. It's working. Why rush into anything?"

"It's working for you. And rushing? You try going without your daughter for more than a year."

He wanted to say, whose fault was it that she'd lost her daughter? Who was the one who was so stoned she couldn't function as a mother anymore? Who was the one forging bogus scripts, putting their livelihood at risk? Who was the one who nearly got their daughter killed in the middle of the night?

But he didn't say any of those things. They were past blaming each other, past fighting.

"Just until the new year. Then we'll sit down and work out a new schedule."

She shook her head. "That's eight months away, Ethan. You know what got me through rehab? Roni did. Knowing that getting well would mean I could wake up every morning and once again see our daughter's beautiful face. I'm not going another eight months."

He didn't want a second court fight—the first one had been worse than hell—but he wasn't ready to divvy up his time with Roni. And he didn't believe it was unreasonable for his ex to give her recovery another eight months. In the meantime, she could visit with Roni as much as she liked.

"I guess we're going to court, then," he said.

Joey took her cup to the sink. "There's another solution you know."

"What's that?" He knew, of course. He'd toiled over the idea and rejected it a million times.

"We could try to start over. For the sake of Roni. It would be different this time. We would be different."

She wasn't trying to extort him. Ethan knew that as well as he knew his own heart. She truly believed they could make it work. But a working marriage wasn't enough for him. And it shouldn't be for her either.

He followed her to the sink and clasped both her shoulders in his hands. "You deserve more, Joe."

She blinked up at him, her eyes welling with tears. "I know you think you're in love with her, Ethan. I haven't missed the way you look at her when I see the two of you together. The way you care for her son. But it'll never work. She won't leave her big Madison Avenue company for you and you'll never abandon your research for her. And when she leaves, I'll be here. And there will just be us and the family we made together."

"And you'd settle, knowing that I loved someone else?"

"You wouldn't." Her voice was hoarse. "With time you would love me again. I know it."

She was fooling herself. About him loving her again. About her loving him. Because that ship had sailed a long time ago. For both of them.

Veronica rushed into the kitchen, her face red, breathing hard. "I ran the whole way to see you, Mommy." She threw her arms around Joey.

He watched them hug, his heart cracking a little at a time.

* * * *

Joey left after dinner. She'd been invited for dessert but she couldn't bear to sit across from Ethan while he pined for someone else. At least four times during the meal he'd checked his phone. The rest of the night he spent staring vacantly out the window.

If Joey was a vindictive person, she'd turn him into the ethics committee at the hospital. But she'd already gotten him into enough trouble. Besides, what difference would it make? Brynn Barnes had bewitched him. Knowing what the woman had been through, Joey couldn't even hate her. That didn't mean she didn't want Brynn to pack up and leave. And she would. As soon as her son had finished his course of treatment, Brynn would go back to her glamorous life in New York City.

In the past couple of weeks, Joey had been preoccupied with reading up on the Barneses and their ad agency. How Brynn's father was a famous conductor. How her late husband was one of the top advertising executives in the nation. And how Brynn rubbed elbows with the rich and famous. No way would she give that up to live in a small town in the middle of nowhere.

It was still light out and Joey didn't feel like going home. By now her parents were sacked out in their recliners with a cable news show blaring. As soon as she got her nursing license reinstated or a decent job she would start looking for a place of her own. A two bedroom for her and Roni.

She found herself parked in front of the Ponderosa. One cup of coffee, she told herself. At least she could lose herself in the din of the restaurant. She flipped down her visor, reapplied her mascara and lipstick, and finger combed her hair.

The place was busy for a Tuesday evening. Families, truckers, even a few backpackers. She didn't bother waiting for a table and grabbed a stool at the bar. A Giants game played on a flat screen in the corner while pro rodeo aired on another set.

"What can I get ya?" the bartender, a woman in her early forties, asked.

"A cup of coffee, please." And because Joey felt funny about taking up valuable real estate during the dinner hour for a paltry two-dollar beverage she ordered a slice of rhubarb pie.

"Never met a woman who wasn't watching her weight. Good for you."

Ah, jeez, how had she missed Matthew McConaughey?

She turned to her left and stared into the oddest shade of blue eyes she'd ever seen. They were pale, the same color as that slice of sky underneath the horizon. "You must live here."

His mouth tipped up and he gave her a once over before responding, "You too."

"I live in the neighborhood," she lied. "With my husband and daughter."

"Oh yeah?" He made a show of scanning her naked ring finger. "Where's the hubby?"

"He's a surgeon. He works a lot." The minute she said it she wished she hadn't. It was a small town with probably only one surgeon as its resident. The likelihood that Cowboy McConaughey knew Ethan was strong.

Her coffee came and she busied herself doctoring up the cup with cream and sugar. He went back to watching the rodeo.

When the bartender delivered her pie, he glanced over and said, "Looks good."

She dipped her fork in and took a bite. It was good. "A word of advice?"

"Yeah?"

"Don't patronize women for eating pie. It makes you sound like a caveman." And an asshole.

"Noted." He grinned again. His teeth were blindingly white, like a toothpaste commercial. He looked up at the TV and let out a sigh. "That's the second time he broke the barrier."

She glanced up at the roping event and went back to eating her dessert, trying to ignore the scent of her cowboy neighbor's aftershave. Everything about him put her on edge.

The bartender returned to their end of the bar. "Anyone need anything?"

"Yeah, I'll take a piece of that pie." He gestured at Joey's plate.

When the bartender left to put in his order, he asked, "You like pro rodeo?"

"I'm an orthopedic nurse, so no."

He laughed. "Seen a lot of injuries, huh?"

"My fair share." Though she'd never treated a rodeo cowboy in the PRCA.

"You work in the emergency room?"

"I did early on in my career. More recently in pediatrics."

"Ah, kids. That's gotta suck." His pie came and he tucked in. "How long have you been nursing?"

She wasn't sure if he was really interested or fishing for her age. "A lot of years."

He glanced at her. "A lot of years, huh?"

More than ten. But not anymore. She still hadn't heard from the board and suspected that meant she wasn't getting recertified. At least in the meantime, she'd gotten some temp work answering phones and taking orders for a catalog company. The pay was shit but it got her out of the house during the week.

"How old's your kid?" He began eating the pie the bartender had set in front of him.

"Six." She didn't know why she was sharing personal stuff about herself. She chalked it up to boredom. "How 'bout you? You have any kids? A wife?"

"Nope." He didn't offer up any more information than that.

"You live around here?" Joey asked, trying to sound as if she was merely making idle conversation.

"No. I'm a long-haul trucker. Nugget's on my way through."

"What do you truck?" She already knew it was livestock but didn't want him to think she'd paid that much attention.

"Cattle mostly. Sometimes I stay at that inn across the square." He locked eyes with her, letting the words hang in the air.

Joey hadn't missed the inference. The invitation. "Oh yeah. Nice place?"

"Very. You'd like it." Those pale blues eyes of his twinkled and she knew he was testing her.

A woman still in love with her ex-husband should've walked away. Later, she would examine that a little closer. But right now, she was enjoying the game too much.

"Maybe I'll book a room for me and my husband on our wedding anniversary."

He raised his brows, clearly dubious about her marital status. Of course, a caveman cowboy would find it odd that a married mother of a six-year-old would repeatedly eat in a bar, alone. He clearly had never been married to an orthopedic surgeon.

"I'd say that was an excellent plan." He waved to the other end of bar. "Hey, Sophie, can I get my bill?" The bartender brought over the check and he slid her his credit card.

When the paperwork was done, he turned to Joey. "It's been a pleasure." He grabbed his hat off the rack, put it on, and tipped the brim, then walked out the door.

She fought off a wave of disappointment, telling herself the man was trouble. And disreputable.

"Could I get my check, too?" she called to the bartender . . . Sophie, the cowboy had called her.

"Your friend took care of it."

Friend? He definitely wasn't a friend.

She hopped off the stool and stepped outside into the cool air. The sun had gone down and only the street and shop lights illuminated the square. Matthew McConaughey's rig was parked a few spots down from her Ford. The semitrailer was missing, probably the reason she hadn't noticed it when she'd first gone into the restaurant.

He was still here.

She stared across the greenbelt at the hulking Victorian that took up the entire street and for a minute considered his proposition. Then she got in her car and headed back to Reno.

* * * *

"This place is amazing," Lexi said, gazing up at the stained-glass window. "Who would think a little town like this would have such sophisticated accommodations?"

"I wasn't sure if you'd like it." Brynn whispered because Maddy, the innkeeper, was only a room away.

One look at Henry and Maddy had ushered him to the den to meet her daughter, Emma. It was like that around here. Parents brought their kids to work and welcomed other parents' kids as if they were family.

"Are you sure you're not hungry? We can still go to the Ponderosa for dinner. I feel like a terrible host."

"First of all, I didn't come here to be entertained. And second of all, did you expect me to eat after all that cheese and wine?" Lexi put her hand to her stomach. "I'm stuffed."

"I would've had you stay with us but I thought you'd be more comfortable sleeping here, instead of on a sofa bed."

"Brynn, stop apologizing. I love the inn and I'm here for you. Not the other way around. Come up to my room. Henry will be fine."

"Okay." It had been a difficult day and Lexi had been Brynn's rock. "Let me tell Henry where I am."

She had just started for the den when a man came through the entrance into the foyer and Lexi's mouth dropped. Brynn shoved a fist in her mouth to keep from giggling out loud.

"Holy shit," Lexi whispered. "Did he just come from central casting? You weren't kidding about the hot cowboy thing going on here."

Brynn didn't remember describing the men of Nugget as hot cowboys. But this one certainly was.

He tipped his hat at Brynn and Lexi and continued up the long flight of stairs with his duffle slung over his shoulder. Lexi followed him with hungry eyes.

Brynn elbowed her. "Someone might get lucky tonight."

She left Lexi at the foot of the staircase to ogle the man's backside and found Henry in the den with Maddy's little girl, playing a board game. Brady, the chef she'd met at the barbershop, brought them out a plate of homemade chocolate chip cookies.

"This okay?" he asked her.

She nodded and mouthed, "Thank you" and turned away so Brady wouldn't see the tears in her eyes. Something about this town . . . the people . . . made her feel optimistic even after getting today's depressing news.

"Maddy's in the kitchen. I was just on my way out."

"Nice seeing you again."

He grabbed a windbreaker from the closet. "Griff's pretty revved up about the work you're doing for him. Thinks he's going to sell the rest of those houses."

"I don't know about all of them but I think we'll sell a few."

He gave her a thumbs up and made for the door. She told Henry she was going upstairs for a few minutes to help Lexi get settled. "Don't eat too many cookies."

Lexi was unpacking enough clothes for Paris Fashion Week when Brynn got to her room, which was as gorgeous as the public spaces. Furnished impeccably with a Queen Anne bed and highboy chest, it reminded Brynn of a London hotel she'd once stayed in.

"He's two doors down," Lexi said.

Brynn rolled her eyes. "You're bad."

"But he is oh sooooo good. Come here." Brynn walked into her best friend's arms.

"Everything will be okay. I know today was rough but Dr. Hottie's right. You have to be patient."

"I know. Thank you for flying six hours across the country to be here with me."

"Always." Lexi sat on the edge of the bed and patted the spot next to her for Brynn. "So without Henry's big ears around, what's going on with you and the doc?"

"What do you mean?" Brynn feigned ignorance.

Lexi pinned her with a look. "Seriously? You're planning to keep this from me?"

"You're imagining things."

"I'm not imagining the way he looked at you. Or you at him. If you haven't already gotten jiggy yet, you're about to. So why don't you just come clean and tell me about it?"

Brynn laid back on the bed and stared up at the ceiling medallion. It was quite intricate. Flowers and leaves and swirls. "It's just something that happened, something to complicate everything else I'm going through."

"What do you mean? Oh God, you said he was divorced. Please tell me he is."

"Lex, I wouldn't lie about something like that. But the ex would very much like not to be his ex. And I have a son who is completely reliant on him to get well. And then there's the fact that I'm newly widowed."

"Mason's gone, Brynn. You're a beautiful, talented woman. No one expects you not to move on. Does this man make you happy?"

"Yes. But it's hard to be happy when my son may never walk again. And he . . . Ethan . . . could lose his license if anyone ever found out." She covered her face with her hands. "It's a complicated mess. And to add to it, today we got in a fight and I thought he was going to end it with me. And I kind of lost my mind over it, Lexi?"

"What was the fight about?"

"I was one of those mothers we hate. I pushed my way into his clinic and threw a hissy fit because the radiologist was going to take two days to read Henry's X-rays."

"What did he do?"

Brynn laughed, hearing the rusty hollow sound of it in her throat. "He called in a favor and got the results today. Such as they were."

"He sounds like he really cares about you."

"I really care about him." She let out a breath. "What am I going to do, Lexi? I've fallen for an impossible situation. He's got a daughter who adores her mother, who isn't completely out of the picture. And I've got a son who is still grieving the loss of his father. And to complicate things further we live on opposite coasts."

"Can I ask you a question?" Lexi gave Brynn that pensive look she always did when she was about to say something unpopular. "Is there a chance that your feelings for this man are wrapped up in him helping Henry? Don't get me wrong, when Dr. Hottie came walking down your driveway it was love at first sight for me. But, Brynn, you've got a lot going on right now. And here's this famous surgeon who's come into your life to fix the things you can't."

Brynn sat up and rested her elbows on her knees. "Believe me, I've given that a lot of thought."

"And?"

"It's real. As much as I wish it wasn't, it is."

Lexi seemed to take that at face value and didn't try to argue or analyze Brynn's feelings further. She simply knew her too well. Even in college, while Lexi and Brynn's other dorm mates had fallen in love with the same ease as changing a lightbulb, she'd been cautious to the point of staying a virgin until she was twenty-one. Mason had been the second man she'd slept with.

"What are you going to do?"

"Nothing." Brynn stared at the pattern in the needlepoint rug. "What can I do?"

"Enjoy it. Think of it as the ice breaker to your new start in life. Your rebound man so to speak. And keep the lovely memory of him with you when you leave."

Lexi made it sound so simple. You just walk away. No regrets. No heartbreak.

Unfortunately, Brynn wasn't made that way.

Chapter 20

Lexi went home on Thursday. After their trip to the airport, Brynn sat in the car long after Henry had gone into the cottage and cried. Her parents would come without hesitation if she asked them. But she was saving their visit in case Henry's situation hit rock bottom.

Other than a brief text asking how she and Henry were doing, she hadn't heard from Ethan in two days. She had, however, noticed Joey's red SUV in the driveway every evening this week. The possibility that he was going back to his ex was too painful to bear.

She told herself that she had no right coming between a family. That if Ethan and Joey could make things work it would be best for Veronica.

Absurdly, she wondered what she would do if Mason came back from the dead. Could she go on living in her empty marriage for the sake of Henry after experiencing a real emotional connection again? No, she didn't think so.

She spent the rest of the afternoon catching up on Barnes Group work. Rich had signed two new clients: a startup air-fry chip company that was about to go public and Ohm, who in the eleventh hour had decided to do a Super Bowl ad for its latest electric car. Though the biggest single day in advertising was nearly a year away, it took months, even years, to hammer out the right campaign. Especially with a social media component.

Fatigued from working on food and car messaging by the late afternoon, she turned to Griffin's campaign. It had become a project of her heart. She pushed herself hard, hoping she'd chosen the right target audience.

At five she checked her phone one last time before giving up on Ethan and deciding on dinner.

"Should we stay in tonight, Henry? Or eat at the Ponderosa?"

"Pizza," he shouted from the couch while playing a video game on his smart watch.

"The closest pizza place is Reno. I don't want to drive all the way to Reno. How about we go to the market and buy a frozen one?" She should've gotten one when she'd gone shopping for snacks for Lexi's visit.

"Can I stay home?"

As safe as it was here, she wasn't about to leave an eight-year-old home alone. "No. Come on, it won't take long."

"I'm tired," he whined, throwing his head against the back of the couch.

"Now how can you possibly be tired? You've been sitting on the couch all day." As soon as she said it, she wanted to kick herself.

In the last months, she'd been careful about her word choices. She never wanted Henry to feel less because he couldn't walk. And she had just made him sound lazy and listless. But to suddenly correct herself would come off patronizing. Her son might only be eight but he was pretty damned intuitive.

"Come on, Henry, I could use the company."

"Why? Are you sad that Lexi's gone?"

"I am. I miss her already. But I have you." She leaned over the back of the couch and kissed him on the forehead.

"What about Dr. Ethan. How come he doesn't come over anymore?" It had only been two days, yet Henry had noticed.

"Dr. Ethan is a very busy man. He has patients all over the country and other doctors rely on him to help them with their patients." If only she could convince herself that that was the reason he'd been missing in action.

"What about us? We're his patients, too."

She gave him a watery smile. "Yep, and we get to live here, right next door to Dr. Ethan. Not all his other patients are that lucky."

"Can we go see him?"

"Ah, honey, Dr. Ethan needs to spend time with his own family."

Henry seemed to accept that. Still, Brynn wondered whether she'd done her son a disservice by letting Ethan get so close.

"You ready to go?"

She helped Henry into his wheelchair when her phone dinged with a text. Her heart raced as she reached for the phone. It was him. Ethan.

Did Lexi get off okay? What are you and Henry doing for dinner? I'm about an hour out but if you can wait that long I'd love to see you.

Two hours later, they sat outside the Bun Boy at a picnic table, eating burgers and fries. Though it was a little chilly, the fresh air was lovely. And Henry latched on to a dog named Max. The dog's owners sat at a table next to them and according to Ethan, the man was the local carpenter who made the rocking chairs. His wife owned the *Nugget Tribune*, the online news site Brynn read every morning with her coffee. They didn't seem to mind that Henry and Roni had made themselves at home at their table.

"I guess you must've been overwhelmed with work these past few days." She tried to sound conversational and not like a bottomless pit of need. Though it hadn't escaped her that he'd come calling on an evening when Joey's Ford was missing from the driveway.

"It hasn't been too bad."

She hoped his idea of "bad" was a commentary on the criticalness of his patients and that the dark stubble that covered his chin proved he'd been too swamped to call. *Just ask him.* "I was surprised I didn't hear from you" was the best she could muster, afraid a direct question would force his hand. *Brynn, I didn't call because we need to shut this down.*

"I didn't want to get in the way of your time with Lexi."

She studied his face, trying to determine whether it was a handy excuse. Or just a flat out lie. But she saw no deception there.

"Brynn?" He tilted is head. "Are you pissed off that I didn't call?"

"Not pissed off. Just worried I guess."

"Worried about what?" He straddled the bench and pulled her into the V of his legs. "Brynn?"

"I thought you might be exploring getting back with your ex-wife." She'd gone straight to the heart of the matter. But she wasn't altogether convinced that her tantrum over Henry's X-rays hadn't triggered a come-to-Jesus moment in him about all the reasons they were a bad idea.

He didn't respond, which in her mind spoke volumes. She'd nailed it. Her heart hammered in her chest.

"Just say it." His silence was killing her.

"There's nothing to say, Brynn. Joey has raised the possibility but I'm with you."

A rush of relief flowed through her and for a few fleeting seconds she rejoiced. But just as quickly a sad sense of remorse filled her, even shame. How selfish was it to keep Ethan from his family? How foolish was it to pretend their feelings for each other could go anywhere?

She forced herself to ask the question. "What about when I leave?"

He ran his hand down his face, looking as pained as she'd ever seen him. "I don't know. Why do we have to think about that now?"

Apparently, he subscribed to the Lexi school of thought. Live in the moment.

That night, while Henry was fast asleep, they made love. It was urgent and emotional, as if it could be their last time. Ethan moved over her, his back muscles bunched with every stroke. His hands cradled her face as they kissed. Slow, passionate kisses that went on forever and ever. She whimpered his name, running her hands up and down his back. Arching against him, she took him deeper inside of her. She felt every intake of his breath and every beat of his heart.

His hands moved over her, touching reverently. Desperately. Taking and giving pleasure as if it were his last breath.

She tipped her head back on the pillow and closed her eyes while he left a string of kisses across her neck. Her feet curled around his calves and his course hairs tickled her skin.

His lips crawled down her chest to her breasts. "You're beautiful," he said, his mouth pressed against her skin, making her body flush with heat.

She rocked into him, clinging to his shoulders as his thrusts grew more powerful. More frenzied.

He murmured his need for her against her ear. Praised her body, her eyes, her hair. "Oh, baby, this is good. You're so good, Brynn."

Soon his words became nonsensical and then lapsed into a series of grunts and moans. His feverish arousal fed hers, taking her higher and higher.

His body, slick with perspiration, strained to give her as much pleasure as she could take before he took his own. But she didn't want it to end. She didn't want to go back to real life, to injuries and death and broken families and decisions that would only end in heartache. So she held on for as long as she could, drawing out each kiss, each touch, each stroke.

She guided her hands over his impossibly perfect backside, reveling in his fierce thrusts. His hands moved back to cradle her face and for one heart-stopping moment he stared into her eyes. The tenderness of it, the sheer emotion etched across his expression broke her.

Her eyes pooled as she peaked, her body shuddering its release. She turned her face and pressed her lips against his neck, uttering the words "I love you."

* * * *

The next morning, Brynn reached across the bed to find Ethan gone. He must've snuck away some time during the night. She leaned over to sniff his pillow, getting a hit of manly shampoo and aftershave. It's a smell she had come to associate with him and just the mere scent of it made her pulse quicken.

A glimmer of sunshine seeped through the blinds, the first hint that it was later than her usual wake up time. She listened for any sounds of life in the kitchen or living room and didn't hear any. Henry was probably still asleep.

She stretched, touching her toes to the edge of the mattress, then rolled out of bed. Shrugging into her robe, she cinched the belt around her waist. Despite it being the middle of nowhere, she didn't want to get caught in her nightgown. Once, in her Manhattan penthouse, eighty-five floors above the ground, she'd been making toast in her underwear and a window cleaner, harnessed to a scaffold, appeared out of nowhere. Boy, had she given him a show. It was the last time she ever went into her kitchen without being fully dressed.

She padded into Henry's room and as she thought, he was sound asleep. Standing next to his bed, she watched him breathe and listened to his little boy snores, her heart bursting. She brushed a strand of dark hair off his forehead and quietly closed the door on her way out.

In the kitchen, she waited for the Keurig machine to fire up and popped in a pod. Soon, the sweet smell of coffee filled the air.

It was nine o'clock. By now Ethan was either at work or on his way in. She peered out the window to the cottage's driveway where his truck had been parked next to her Outback the evening before. Gone.

Her mind shot to their night together. The way he made her feel. She tried to remember if it had been that way with Mason in the beginning. No. Their love had been built around a mutual interest. Advertising. All their excitement had been directed at jingles, taglines, mottos and messaging. At the end of the day, there wasn't much left for each other.

But there was no question that she'd loved Mason. His drive, his creativity, his excitement, and his entrepreneurial spirit. For the first few years, as they built their agency, they'd been happy. Even blissful. Then Henry came along and life changed and so did her and Mason's relationship.

A part of her wondered if that's how it always was. That with time, love waned. But her parents were proof to the contrary. Forty-five years and still going strong.

Her phone rang. It was a Reno area code, which she now knew by heart. "Hello."

"Mrs. Barnes?"

"Yes?"

"Hi, this is Dr. Daniels's office. He wanted me to set up an appointment with Henry for a few tests."

This was the first Brynn was hearing of this. "What kind of tests?"

"Nothing invasive. Just a DXA to test his bone density for osteoporosis and a vitamin D blood test."

Osteoporosis? She thought that was something middle aged women got, not eight-year-old boys. "I don't understand."

"Dr. Daniels will explain it to you when you come in. He has you down for Monday at ten a.m. Will that work?"

"Yes. Yes of course."

The second she hung up she started to text Ethan and stopped herself. She was doing it again. When she saw him tonight, she would ask him, not interrupt his busy day.

In the meantime, she booted up her laptop and jumped on Google, a thing she'd repeatedly been warned not to do. Last year, Lexi discovered a raised, dark colored growth on her hip. After trolling the internet, she began making funeral arrangements, convinced that she was dying of melanoma. It was a benign mole.

Henry came in. He was still in his pajamas and she would bet her checking account that he hadn't yet brushed his teeth. She closed her laptop, kneeled, and laid a sloppy kiss on his cheek.

"You need help with the shower?"

"No, but can I have breakfast first?"

"Absolutely." She opened the pantry door. "What would you like? How about oatmeal?"

He scrunched up his nose. "Cap'n Crunch."

She didn't like him eating sugary cereals, yet she'd given into him on their last visit to the Nugget Market.

"Okay but enjoy it while you can because we're not making a habit of junk food for breakfast. Got it?"

He nodded and pulled his wheelchair up to the table. "Mom, can we go fishing today?"

"Fishing?" Other than the seafood counter at Whole Foods, she knew absolutely nothing about their fine finned friends. "We don't have any poles, baby."

"Dr. Ethan does. Can we ask him if we can borrow them?"

"He's at work today. Maybe Saturday . . . with Dr. Ethan. How's that?" She liked the idea of Henry being outside and getting exercise. So, if it meant her learning how to fish and putting a slimy worm on a hook, she'd suck it up for her son.

"Dr. Ethan won't be home Saturday."

"How do you know that?" She brought Henry's breakfast to the table and got out the container of milk.

"Roni told me. He's taking her to her grandparents' anniversary party. It's at a restaurant in Reno."

Grandparents.

Brynn assumed the plural there meant Joey's parents. She wondered why Roni's mother couldn't take her daughter to the party. Why did Ethan have to go? Her resentment surprised her. It was uncharitable and out of character for her. These people used to be Ethan's in-laws and were still Veronica's grandparents. Of course he would attend.

She suspected she'd be attached to Mason's sister forever, even though she'd never really cared for Virginia. But her sister-in-law was Henry's aunt and the only remaining member of Mason's family. So, if Virgie and her husband were having a big anniversary party, she and Henry would be duty bound to go.

"Well, then maybe Sunday," she said.

"We could go buy fishing poles at that sports store in Nugget. They have 'em. I saw 'em when we went with Aunt Lexi to her hotel. Then we wouldn't have to wait until Sunday."

He had her there. She propped her elbows on the table and rested her chin in her hands. "I suppose we could check it out. But not until after you do your schoolwork. And your exercises. Your physical therapist said you're supposed to do them every day." She wasn't above a bribe. "But first, breakfast, then brushing your teeth, and a shower."

She'd never seen Henry more enthusiastic about filling in his worksheets and doing his stretches. He finished in record time and practically pushed her out the door.

On their way to town, she came clean. "This is the thing, Henry, I don't know anything about fishing. I've never even been before." Unlike Mason with Henry, Brynn's father had not been what you would call an outdoorsman. She'd been raised in symphony halls, opera houses, theaters and museums. The closest she'd ever come to anything remotely considered a water sport was summers in the Hamptons.

"That's okay. I know everything about it. Dr. Ethan taught me. I can show you."

His confidence warmed her. In some ways he seemed like his old self again. The happy, outgoing boy he'd been before the accident. She had Ethan to thank for that. He showered Henry with attention and had become the surrogate man in her son's life. Henry imitated everything Ethan did right down to the tilt of his cowboy hat.

The sporting goods store was surprisingly well stocked for such a small town. Brynn supposed there was a large market for kayaks, mountain bikes, bear spray and fishing gear in a town surrounded by lakes, rivers and forest trails.

They wandered aimlessly around the shop, clueless about which of the dozens of fishing poles to choose. She waited for the lone salesman to finish helping a customer. He was leafing through a catalog of what looked to her like tricked-out golf carts. From the two men's conversation, Brynn determined that the little buggies were designed to carry around hunters and deer carcasses. She shuddered at the thought.

The police chief came into the store and bobbed his head in greeting when he saw Brynn and Henry. "How are you two doing?"

"We're shopping for fishing gear," Henry volunteered.

"Yeah?" Rhys winked at Brynn. "What are you looking to catch?"

"Fish," Henry said as if the chief was daft.

Rhys chuckled. "Salmon or steelhead?"

"I don't know."

He looked at Brynn and she shrugged.

Rhys eavesdropped on the salesman and his customer for a beat. "Looks like Carl's going to be a while. Let's see what he's got." He examined the array of rods on a rack against the wall and pulled one out. "This'll work. Not too heavy for Henry with enough fighting power for salmon and steelhead." He flipped the rod over and checked out the tag. "And it's a nice price."

Rhys put the pole down on the counter by the cash register. "Let's find you a couple of lures and some good line."

"You don't have to. Really, I'm sure you have better things to do with your time." He was the chief of police for goodness sake.

"I have to wait for Carl anyway and I'm always happy to help another fisherman." He squeezed Henry's shoulder.

An hour later, they left the store weighed down with everything a beginner angler needed to catch his first fish. She loaded the car and stopped at the grocery store for a few assorted things. By the time she was ready to leave, Henry was hungry for lunch. They went back to the square for burgers and fries at the Bun Boy.

"Two days in a row." She rolled her eyes at Henry. "Tonight, it's something healthy."

Donna Thurston dropped by their picnic table—the same one they'd eaten at with Ethan and Roni. "Nice day." She shielded her eyes from the sun.

"We're going fishing," Henry said.

"You are? Well, stay away from that bunch." She bobbed her head across the square at the barbershop, where Owen and his Nugget Mafia crew were sitting outside, playing cards on a folding table. "They'll scare the fish away with their big mouths."

The barbershop reminded Brynn she still needed a cut and color. She'd been so busy showing Lexi around that they hadn't had time for a salon visit. Maybe one day next week.

"Are you coming to high tea this Sunday? It's the last one until next fall."

"You're kidding?" It seemed like just yesterday that Maddy had invited Brynn. "Well then I'll be there." She'd have to drag Henry along. But it would be a shame to miss it.

"Donna, any chance Owen's daughter does hair on Sundays?"

"I'm sure she would if you asked her. Everything is pretty informal around here."

Brynn strolled over to the barbershop after lunch and left Henry outside with Owen and the boys to talk fishing while she went inside to check with Darla.

Brynn got a two o'clock Sunday appointment and left with a new skin-care product Darla swore by. She found Henry playing a rousing game of War with some of the members of the mafia, including Dink the mayor.

"We've got to go, buddy. I've got perishables in the car."

"Now don't go telling anyone you're fishing without a license," Owen warned as Henry pulled away from the table.

Brynn hadn't even considered a license. "We need one even if it's on private property?" Rhys hadn't said anything about it and he was the law.

"Yep. But your secret's safe with us, missy."

Driving home, she thought about this funny little town and its characters. The way they'd accepted her and Henry as if they were one of them. It was different than the mores of the Upper East Side, where it took money and status to belong. She saw why Ethan was so enamored with the place.

And for a wild second she tried to imagine what life would be like here, away from the city she loved and the company she and her late husband had built from the ground up. And just like the idyllic storybook nature of Nugget's town square the prospect was a fairytale.

Chapter 21

Ethan found them by the river, a fishing rod in Henry's hand.

Brynn sat on a rock, staring out over the water, her dark hair windblown, her eyes the shade of zircon in sunlight. She was such a vision that it made his chest hurt. He hung back, taking the opportunity to drink her in.

She must've sensed him because she lifted her head and startled at his shadow. He stepped out from the thickets and grinned.

"You're home early." She rose to her feet.

"I had surgery at eight this morning."

Guilt streaked across her face and then red flushed her cheeks. She was remembering how they'd spent the night. Neither got a wink of sleep until he stole away at three in the morning.

"Dr. Ethan come look at my new fishing pole."

He exchanged a glance with Brynn, who gave a little shrug, and hiked over to the flat bank where Henry had parked his wheelchair. "When did you get this, buddy?"

"Today at the sports store. The police chief said it was good for . . ." He looked at Brynn. "Steelhead and salmon," she finished.

Henry handed him the pole and he weighed it in his hand. "Nice. But I would've lent you one of mine."

"I needed my own." Henry puffed out his chest.

"Fair enough. What are you using for bait there?" Ethan eyed Henry's hook, which was bobbing on the surface of the water.

"Grapes. We couldn't figure out how to put the lure on."

"Grapes, huh?"

"Yeah, it was my mom's idea."

Ethan caught Brynn's eye and grinned. "Clever."

She hitched her shoulders. "We tried cheese but nothing happened."

Ethan went over to the big rock to sit next to Brynn while Henry attempted to cast his line. Later, he'd show Henry how to tie a lure and teach him a couple of knots.

"Where's Roni?"

"She went into town with Alma to do some grocery shopping. Did my office call you?"

She nodded and simultaneously pulled a face. "Osteoporosis?"

"It's fairly rare but not unheard of. It starts about Henry's age, though I have no reason to suspect he has it. I'm just checking off a box, Brynn."

"If he did have it, though, it would explain why his bones aren't healing, right?"

"It could be a factor, yes."

"And the vitamin D test. Rickets?"

"I'm looking at everything, Brynn. Let's not get ahead of ourselves. These are routine tests so we can eliminate even the slightest possibility and move on."

She scrutinized him, waiting for a tell. But the man had a poker face. "You're not keeping anything from me, are you?"

"Nope." He cupped her chin in his hand and leaned in until their lips were almost touching. Then he quickly remembered Henry and pulled away. "I promise. Besides buying a fishing pole, what did you two do today?"

"You're looking at it." She leaned back on her forearms and turned her face up to the sun.

With her lips half parted and her blue eyes filled with contentment she took his breath away. "I missed you this morning," he whispered.

"Me too. What time did you leave?"

"Around three. Felt like a high school kid, sneaking in the house before dawn."

She laughed, then turned circumspect. "I heard you're going to your former in-laws' anniversary party tomorrow."

Word spread fast. He figured it was most likely Roni, who couldn't stop talking about the party. "Yeah, it's their fiftieth. Joey and her brother, Jay, decided last minute to do something and rented out the party room at a steakhouse."

"Sounds nice." She was trying to sound gracious but Ethan heard an undercurrent of . . . something. Not resentment or even jealousy. It was more like sadness. But given the circumstances it wasn't as if he could invite her to be his date.

"Look, I divorced Joey, not her parents. And they are Veronica's grandparents."

She touched his arm. "It's lovely that you're going. Truly." She turned away and searched the horizon. "Mason's mother died when he was in college and his father a year before we married. It's just his sister now. That's the only part of Henry's paternal family he'll ever know. It's wonderful that Veronica still has three grandparents."

"I don't think Lou Ellen and Ace have fully forgiven me for moving away." Or divorcing their daughter. Ace in particular had made his feelings known on that count. "And there's an unspoken rivalry between Lou Ellen and Alma. Though it's mostly on Lou Ellen's end. So, I try to keep the peace."

"Of course. And they're your family . . . Roni's family."

One of the things he'd never gotten used to after the divorce was the division of family and friends as if they were assets. *You get the house, the time share in Hawaii, and Vicki and Bob.* At least Lou Ellen tried to remain neutral. But in cases involving Veronica, they almost always sided with Joey, even when it wasn't in their granddaughter's best interest.

Jay, less subtle than even Ace, made no bones about calling Ethan a prick. He thought Ethan should've stood by his sister even while she self-destructed, taking everyone down with her.

Ethan held on to a lot of guilt over that decision. But not because of anything Jay had to say. Ethan knew for a fact that his ex-brother-in-law had been at his car dealership, fucking his secretary—probably still was—while his wife was at the hospital, giving birth to their first child. So it wasn't as if he relied on Jay to be his moral compass.

His family, who'd never cared much for Joey in the first place, cut bait with her before the ink even dried on their divorce papers. Especially his sister. It bothered him—still did—because Joey could've used their support, not their derision.

"What are you doing tomorrow?" he asked, wanting to change the subject.

"No plans. Sunday I'm going to that high tea they serve at the Lumber Baron. According to Donna, it's the last one until fall."

Alma went sometimes and she had taken Roni once or twice. Other than the sweets, Veronica had loudly deemed it boring. "Why don't Henry and I find some guy things to do while you're at the tea?"

"Really?" Her face brightened with interest. "Like what?"

"I don't know. Wrestle steers, ride a few bulls, throw back a couple of beers, hit the blackjack tables in Reno." His mouth curved up in a teasing smile. He watched Henry absorbed in dragging his line across the water.

The grapes weren't getting so much as a nibble. "Or maybe I'll show him how to tie a jig and perfect a San Diego Jam knot."

"Excuse me, were you just speaking in Greek?"

"Nah, fishing talk." He quickly flicked another glance at Henry, pulled Brynn towards him, and kissed her softly on the mouth. "If you don't know what this means, allow me to interpret," he said against her mouth. "You're beautiful Brynn Barnes and later, I plan to take you to bed."

* * * *

"Roni, we're going to be late. Five more minutes, then I'm coming up there and carrying you down." When had his daughter become obsessed with clothes and dressing up?

Wasn't it only yesterday that she'd worn denim Oshkosh overalls everywhere she went? Today, she'd spent more than an hour in her bedroom, in front of a mirror, consumed with which outfit to wear to her grandparents' party.

"I'm ready." She came down the stairs in a frilly black and white polka dot dress with a satin bow he'd never seen before.

"Look at my bonny Roni. Where'd you get that?" He waved his hand over the ensemble, which included a pair of white sandals that seemed too summery for April.

"Mommy. She got me three new dresses and these." She stuck her foot in the air. "She said I could wear whichever one I wanted."

"Yeah? What happened to overalls?" He hoisted her up on his hip. Pretty soon she'd be too big for him to do that anymore.

"Daddy, those are for little kids."

"Who says?"

"Everyone." She rolled her eyes. "Danica gets to wear high heels."

"Oh yeah. Is she coming tonight?" Danica was eight, going on sixteen. Jay and Moira spoiled her rotten and the kid had an attitude. Ethan didn't want it rubbing off on Roni.

Roni nodded. "Teddy too. Mommy says we're all getting our picture taken with Geema and Geepa. It's going to be this big." She spread her hands wide. "That way they can hang it on the wall and always remember us."

"I bet they'll love that. You ready to giddy up?" He grabbed her denim jacket from the hall closet.

"Daddy that doesn't go." She squirmed out of his arms and shot upstairs.

"Since when?" he called to her back, once again wondering where the new obsession with matching clothes had come from.

She came down with a black fuzzy cardigan.

"Let me guess. Mommy got that for you, too." Joey had always been a clothes horse. It appeared she was passing on her love affair to their daughter. "Let's get, kiddo, before we miss dinner."

An hour later, he took his place next to Joey at a forty-foot-long dinner table.

Jay was at the far end, holding court, letting everyone know he was paying for the party. "Jim, what are you doing with beer? Get a mixed drink. You want a Jack and Coke?" He turned to the waitress whose ass he'd been ogling the entire time she'd been taking orders. "Honey, get my friend here a Jack and Coke."

"You look nice," Joey whispered in his ear.

"You too," he said, though to be truthful he'd been too busy trying to avoid Jay to notice. "Is this going to be okay for you?" The booze was flowing like the Feather River.

"Is what going to be okay?" Someone passed her a bottle of red wine. "Oh, this. Drinking was never my problem." She handed him the bottle and in deference to her, he sent it down the table.

Alcohol may not have been what ultimately brought her down but Joey had always been a drinker. He suspected that if it hadn't been the pills, liquor would've been her drug of choice. It ran in the Nix family. Ethan had never seen Ace without a bourbon in his hand and Jay when he wasn't sloppy. Lou Ellen could drain two bottles of wine by herself in one sitting.

Ace, who was making the rounds, came over and slapped Ethan on the back. "Glad you could make it, son. We miss not seeing you."

"Happy anniversary, Ace. Great party."

"We must've done something right." He swept his hands in the air at the forty or so guests who'd come to celebrate. "And Joey . . . a father couldn't ask for a better daughter."

She stood up and kissed him on the cheek. "Love you, Pop."

"And Jay. Stand up, Jay." Jay rose and because no one knew what to do next, everyone applauded.

Except Ethan. If he was being a dick, so be it.

Joey elbowed him and shook her head, laughing. He covered his mouth, laughing too. Despite the love she had for her brother, she knew he was a pompous ass. Jay had always been their inside joke.

Both turned to the section of the table where Veronica sat with her cousins. Like her Uncle Jay, she was telling a loud story while Teddy blew bubbles in his Sprite with a straw.

"That dress kills me. She picked it out that time I took her shopping. All she wants to wear are dresses now. Remember when she used to be a little tomboy?"

"Yeah, I miss it. How long until I have to lock her inside the house?"

"I know, right?" Joey sighed. "She sure is growing up." Joey looked at him and he knew instantly what she was suggesting.

He knew her mind set. That was the thing about being married to someone for eight years. You knew what they were thinking even before they did. *Not tonight, Joey.*

He didn't want to talk about custody arrangements at Lou Ellen and Ace's anniversary celebration. Frankly, he didn't want to talk about it at all. But especially not here.

A few chairs down, one of Lou Ellen's friends struck up a conversation and Joey moved to the empty seat next to her in order to hear the woman over the noise of the party. It was a good time for Ethan to hit the head, maybe send a text to Brynn, who he hadn't stopped thinking about.

On his way, he bumped into Jay near the bar. He tipped his head in greeting and tried to keep going but Jay wanted to talk.

"How's business?" he asked, sloshing whiskey on Ethan's boots. *Business.* As if more kids with broken bones equated to a better bottom line.

"How's yours?" Ethan returned without answering. Jay only wanted to talk about himself anyway.

"Never better. You ought to come in, take a look at some of the new Fords. I got Joey a great deal."

"Maybe I will." Ethan started to step away.

"Hey" —Jay stuck his arm out to stop Ethan, sloshing more of the whiskey—"what are your intentions with Roni? Are you going to jack my sister up as far as custody?"

Ethan tried to keep his cool. As much as he wanted to knock the son-of-a-bitch on his ass, this was not the time nor the place. He eyed the two drinks Jay fisted in both hands and with all the calm he could muster said, "Not here, Jay."

"Here seems as good a place as any, you sanctimonious piece of crap."

"You're shitfaced, as usual. You really want to ruin your parents' party . . . do this in front of the kids?"

"What are you afraid of Daniels? You afraid I'll mangle those hands of yours?"

Jesus, what was it with Ethan's hands that everyone was so obsessed with?

"You fight Joey on this, and I'll hire her the best lawyer money can buy."

"You do that." Ethan started to walk away but couldn't help himself. He grabbed Jay by the collar. "Next time you want to make a scene in the middle of a gathering, I won't be this restrained."

He bypassed the bathroom and went back to the party. As much as he hated to admit it, Jay was looking out for his baby sister's best interests. Even if Jay was a world-class douchebag, it was hard to fault a guy for that.

"What's wrong?" Joey asked as he took his seat next to her.

"Nothing."

She tilted her head to the side and locked eyes with him. "Come on, I know you. The minute you walked in the room I could tell something was up. Is it a patient?"

"No, I had words with your brother," he said in a soft voice as not to be overheard.

"Oh, Jesus. What did he say and why were you even engaging with him? You know how he gets."

"Yeah, I shouldn't have. It's fine." He brushed her arm. "What did I miss while I was gone?"

"The kids and my folks posed for a picture. Mac Murphy spilled red wine on his wife's new outfit and my Aunt Dorothy made a toast that was pretty much incoherent. Other than that, nothing." She motioned to the head of the table. "Looks like our salads have arrived."

Good, he was anxious to get home. If he timed it right, he could get to Brynn's before she turned in for the night.

He rushed through dinner, wished Lou Ellen and Ace a happy anniversary again, collected Roni, and said goodbye.

"I'll walk you to the car." Joey followed them out to the parking lot.

He belted Veronica into her booster seat and came around to the driver side, where Joey was waiting. Clearly, she had something she wanted to talk about out of earshot of Roni because she moved away from his truck.

"It was a nice thing you and Jay did for your parents. I could tell it meant a lot to them."

"Have you thought more about our discussion?"

So much for small talk. "About Roni and custody?" He huffed out a breath. "Joe, let's end the night on a high note." Though that ship had sailed with Jay. But it wasn't Joey's fault.

She shook her head. "About us . . . trying again."

"We talked about this and all the reasons it was a bad idea."

Her bottom lip began to quiver and his night went from bad to worse.

"How can putting our family back together be a bad idea?"

Because he wanted more than to merely exist in a marriage. But maybe he was being selfish. Who the hell knew? What he did know was he didn't want to do this now in a Reno parking lot. He wanted to go home.

He wanted Brynn.

As if reading his mind, which Joey had always had a knack for doing, she said, "It's because of her, isn't it?"

He was afraid to answer the question. The last thing he wanted to do was hurt Joey. He'd loved her once and still cared about her deeply. "It's not about Brynn. She's leaving, Joe. You know that."

"But you're in love with her, aren't you?" Her eyes filled with tears. "Just say it. You're choosing her over me, the mother of your child, the wife who used to be the love of your life. You're choosing a woman you barely know, a woman who more than likely has distorted feelings for you because of her son."

He'd spent a lot of time thinking about that, wondering whether Brynn's feelings for him were tied up in the complexities of savior syndrome. It wasn't unusual in his field. It was one of the many good reasons doctors weren't supposed get involved with their patients or their patients' parents.

"Let's not do this," he said, drying one of her tears with his hand. "Please, Joey."

"Go, just go." She turned from him and crossed the parking lot.

He watched her disappear inside the restaurant and got inside his truck.

Roni was asleep in the backseat, her head crooked against her shoulder in her pretty polka dot dress. Her face rosy, covered in a sheen of little girl sweat. Ethan sat there for a while, watching her breathe, his heart coming out of his chest.

Chapter 22

Brynn waited until she could no longer keep her eyes open for Ethan. But he never came. It wasn't until the next morning that she saw his text—*"Roni and I are turning in for the night. I'll be over to get Henry in time for you to make your hair appointment."*—and spent most of breakfast analyzing it.

It was nothing, she told herself. They had been exhausted from the party, though the text came in only a little after ten. Maybe Alma went to Reno for the weekend, leaving Ethan without a babysitter.

There were dozens of reasons why he'd canceled. Yet, she focused on just one.

But as she got ready for her day, she forced herself not to dwell on it.

Henry practically vibrated, he was so excited about spending the day with Ethan. Frankly, she was jealous. Though she was looking forward to the tea, she'd trade it in a New York minute for time with Ethan. Alone.

Her phone rang and she rushed to get it, hoping like a high school girl that it was him. But it turned out to be Griffin.

"Mornin'. I'm just checking in." It was a subtle way of asking whether Brynn had finished his campaign.

She liked his style. It was much better than the usual client, whose vocabulary didn't include subtlety. "I'm just playing around with the finishing touches and waiting for a call from my office with their demographics research, which will help us establish where to place ads."

"Wow. I'd love to see what you've got so far."

"I'm due at Darla's at two. I might be able to squeeze you in before." If she could get Ethan to move up his plans with Henry. "Let me make some arrangements and I'll call you back."

"Great. And Brynn, thank you. I'm pumped about this."

She was too. It was a solid campaign that didn't oversell, but in her opinion was tantalizing enough to whip up interest in Sierra Heights with the right kind of buyers.

She debated over whether to send Ethan a down and dirty text—can you babysit an extra hour? —or call him, which would probably result in a conversation about why he hadn't shown up last night.

Stop being a drama queen.

She called. It took a while for him to answer and when he did she could tell she'd interrupted something. "Bad time?"

"Uh, no. But cell is sketchy out here, so I might lose you."

"Where are you?"

"Fixing a fence on the south border of the ranch. A steer got out this morning and wandered onto Barlow property."

She glanced at the clock. It was ten and she had no idea how long it took to mend a fence. "I hate to ask but is there any way you could take Henry an hour early? Griffin wants to meet over his new campaign. If it won't work, though, don't worry. I can meet with Griffin another time."

"Sure. I promised Roni we'd take the boat out on the lake, do a little fishing. This will give us more time on the water. Henry will love it."

She wondered why Veronica wasn't with Joey but was afraid to ask, convinced that something between Ethan and his ex happened at the party. Something Brynn wasn't ready to hear. "You're a life saver."

She hung up, dissecting the conversation. Had he been distant? Was it weird he hadn't mentioned the night before? She continued to analyze every intonation until he showed up shortly before one to pick up Henry.

She'd dressed up a bit in the kind of clothes she wore to lunches with her friends in the city: a tailored skirt, fitted jacket, high heels and makeup. It was probably over the top by Nugget standards but it was high tea after all. And if she was being honest with herself, she wanted Ethan to see her in something other than jeans and a sweater.

"Wow." He backed up, his eyes gleaming with male appreciation, alleviating some of her earlier anxiety. "You look smokin'."

She laughed unable to remember the last time, if ever, she'd been called "smokin'." "Thank you. And thanks for taking Henry. He's beyond excited. Fishing has become his latest obsession. But, Ethan, I'm worried about the boat. Getting in and out. It won't be easy. And he won't be able to swim."

He stepped closer. "Brynn, you trust me?"

"Yes," which was the absolute truth. But she'd trusted Mason, too.

"I've got a life jacket for Henry but he won't need it. Nothing risky here. I'll get him in and out of the boat, which by the way at full throttle only goes five miles per hour. You don't have anything to worry about."

She hesitated, then acquiesced. Ethan wouldn't do anything to put Henry in harm's way. Unlike Mason, he didn't thrive on adrenaline pumping adventure. He'd seen too much of the damage it could cause. Beyond that, there'd never been a person who'd made her feel safer than he did.

She pulled a light-weight jacket from the hall closet. "Make sure he wears this. It may be spring but it's still chilly."

His lips kicked up. "You got it, Mama Bear." He pulled her in for a hug, even though the children were right there in the living room, and the rest of her uneasiness melted away. She'd worked herself up over nothing.

"How was the party?"

He leaned his shoulder against the wall and in a soft voice said, "Not great to be honest. A lot of tension between Joey's brother and me."

And there it was, the thing that had likely been bothering him last night and had kept him from her door. "Why? Over the divorce?"

"The divorce." He nodded. "Custody of Veronica."

She wanted to say, what did the brother expect? His sister was forging prescriptions under Ethan's name. But she held her tongue, careful when it came to anything regarding Joey. She wasn't altogether clear on the nuances where Ethan's ex-wife was concerned. What she had witnessed was that he refrained from badmouthing her, unlike most exes. To Brynn it was admirable but also confusing where he stood on Joey.

"Did he say anything?"

Ethan let out a mirthless laugh. "The guy never shuts up. But some of what he said hit home."

She could see a mountain of sadness hiding in his hazel eyes. "Is that why you didn't come over last night?"

He sidestepped the question by kissing her. Luckily, the children were oblivious to anything outside of the Sunday cartoon they were riveted to.

"We have company," she reminded him when he took the kiss to the next level, pulling her tightly against his body and plying her mouth with his tongue.

He reluctantly broke away. "I guess we should hit the road and let you get off to your meeting."

But neither of them moved, caught up in each other's spell. From the second she'd fallen for him, she'd known going back to New York would be unbelievably difficult. She now recognized that that had been an understatement. Try gut wrenching.

But would it be the same for him?

"When are we going, Daddy?" Veronica stood on the couch, leaning over the backrest. The cartoon was over and a cereal commercial Brynn had made was playing. An oldy but a goody, she smiled to herself.

Ethan swooped Roni up. "Since when do we stand on furniture? You want to go? Then let's hit the road, daylight's burning."

Ethan herded both kids into his truck and tossed Henry's wheelchair into the back where he'd tied down an aluminum boat.

"Be careful," she called as they drove up the hill. Ethan stuck his arm out the window and waved.

She let out a deep breath. It was the first time she'd been alone since they'd gotten here. A year ago, she would've embraced an afternoon to herself. But now it left her with a sense of foreboding. Counselors told her it was a residual of the accident, a kind of PTSD for the survivors of a catastrophic incident. In the months that followed the crash, when Henry returned to school, Brynn would go into her bedroom, hold Mason's pillow to her nose, and curl up into a ball.

Not today. She gazed out over the majestic pines, took a big whiff of fresh air, and hugged herself. Here, in this magical place, she'd found purpose. She was still working on forgiving Mason and was making strides. Every day, her resentment for him slowly ebbed away.

She found a shawl and although she didn't need it, took it anyway. Griffin wanted to meet at his office above the Gas and Go. The space, an old apartment that had been converted, was as grubby as his mechanic shop. But she suspected Griff liked it that way. Posters of souped-up motorcycles hung on the wall and a big metal desk took up half the floor. There was a small kitchen and a bathroom off the hallway.

Griffin went into the kitchen and stuck his head in the fridge. "You want a soda or a cup of coffee?"

"I'm fine." She opened her laptop at Griffin's desk and pulled up her profile of Sierra Heights' target market.

Griffin hovered over the screen with a cola in his hand. "Show me what you've got."

He pulled over another chair and for the next forty-five minutes she made her pitch. It had been years since she'd met with a client, staying mostly in the background. But going through her proposal in person was exhilarating. She hadn't realized how much she'd missed it.

At the end of her presentation, Griffin rose to his feet and applauded. "Damn, I'm gonna sell some houses."

"That's the plan. We still need to flesh some things out, including the cost of ad buy-ins. But I have staff at the Barnes Group working on that. I'd say in another week, we'll be ready to start."

"Right on!" Griffin pumped his fist in the air.

She noted the time and gathered up her laptop. "I've got to dash. What do you say we meet after I get those numbers? Then we can choose which platforms will give us the most bang for your buck."

"Sounds good."

She made it to the barbershop and found Darla at the front desk, eating Bun Boy fries.

"So good, right?" She slid the basket across the counter to Brynn. "Help yourself."

"None for me, thanks."

She cleaned her hands with a wet wipe and set Brynn up in a chair.

She finger combed the ends of Brynn's hair, turning her face from side to side in the mirror. "You've got too much weight on the bottom. See how it's bringing your face down? Your color looks good, though. Just a root touch up and maybe a few highlights. I'm thinking something in the chestnut family."

"Nothing drastic, though." Brynn hoped she wasn't making a mistake. She went to a great salon in the city and had never noticed that her cut brought her *face down*.

"Nope, I'll just clean you up. You'll see." Darla went to the rear of the barbershop to mix Brynn's color. "How's your son doing?"

Brynn had gotten used to the gossip mill in Nugget. Everyone seemed to know everyone else's business. She didn't mind. Henry's fractures weren't a secret and people genuinely seemed to care about his wellbeing.

"He's holding up." Normally, she would've left it at that, but hairstylists were a lot like priests and bartenders. And soon she was spilling her troubles to Darla like a water spigot.

"Well, you're in good hands," Darla said. "Ethan is world famous. If he can't heal Henry's breaks no one can."

The comment was meant to be reassuring but it made Brynn a little sick to her stomach. The fact was Ethan was her final hope. There was no backup plan. This was it. All the specialists she'd talked to had basically said the stem cell procedure was her best and only option. If it didn't work she had to face the reality that her son wouldn't walk again.

Sensing that the conversation had veered into depressing territory, Darla quickly changed the subject to the Lumber Baron's high tea. "It's the last one for the season, so all the locals are going. Soon, the inn will be crawling with tourists. No room for us yokels."

Apparently, Brynn fell under the yokel category, even though she and Henry were only here temporarily. Oddly, she quite liked being a yokel.

While Darla let Brynn's color set, she gave Ethel, the owner of the Nugget Market, a trim. Unlike the boisterous weekdays when the Nugget Mafia gathered in the barbershop to keep Owen company while he cut hair, the place was quiet. Just Darla's chatter and the swish and snip of her scissors.

"Are you usually open on Sundays?" Brynn asked.

Darla waggled her hand from side to side. "It's on an as-needed basis only. I've got a couple of clients who live in Quincy who can only get here on weekends and like to come after church the second Sunday of every month for their blowouts. It helps to have the flexibility when I'm sharing the shop with my dad, who swears he's going to retire." She snorted and Ethel laughed.

"He's been saying that as long as I can remember," Ethel said.

After Ethel left, Darla washed out Brynn's color and started on her cut. Though Brynn had said nothing drastic, she watched in panic as lock after lock of her dark hair hit the floor. Before Brynn could protest, Darla got out a big round brush and began blowing out her hair.

Afraid to look, she closed her eyes, letting the heat of the dryer lull her into complacency.

Darla flicked off the blow-dryer and straightened the chair so Brynn had a front view in the mirror. "What do you think?"

She slowly opened her eyes and stared at her reflection. Brynn saw exactly what Darla had been talking about. The cut, a series of subtle layers, had given her an instant facelift. It was fabulous. "Wow, you know your stuff."

"So good, right?" Darla rubbed the ends of Brynn's hair with styling gel.

Brynn turned her head from side to side and looked at the back of her head with the help of a handheld mirror. "You're an artist. Seriously, you'd make a fortune in Manhattan."

"Yeah, I get that a lot."

They walked over to the Lumber Baron together to a full house of women, many Brynn knew and some she'd never met.

The furniture in the front parlor had been replaced with at least six round tables. Each one was draped in white linens and set with antique china and silver serving pieces laden with finger sandwiches, pastries, and scones. It was picture perfect. Brynn snapped a few photos with her phone and sent them to her mother, a lover of all things old and traditional.

Maddy waved her over to her table and Darla joined a group of younger women closer to the fireplace, which was roaring even in April.

"Love the do." Donna ran her hands through Brynn's new haircut.

"Darla is beyond talented." Brynn never could've imagined that a small town in the middle of nowhere would be chock full of flair. This hotel, the tea and Sierra Heights were perfect examples.

"We're lucky to have her," Emily said. "Before Darla joined her dad at the barbershop, we all used to trek to Reno."

The conversation flowed like the bottles of wine that were delivered to the table more frequently than the tea. When the discussion came around to Henry, Brynn repeated the same thing she'd told Darla.

Maddy leaned in and gave Brynn a hug. Although they were barely acquaintances, the embrace broke something inside Brynn and much to her mortification she began to cry. Maybe it was because Maddy was a mother with a child close to Henry's age as well. Or perhaps it was simply weeks of pent up worry that needed an escape. Whatever it was, Brynn lost it.

She tried to rush to the bathroom but the eight women at the table, most of them strangers, circled around her like a protective shell. It wasn't so much what they said—because, really, other than empty platitudes what can anyone say to a mother trying to do the best for her child?—it was the outpouring of support that shored her up.

She took that support with her all the way home.

Chapter 23

Over the next several days all Henry talked about was his boat ride with Ethan and Roni and how they caught a fish "this big," which he demonstrated with his arms held wide. Each time he told the story the fish got bigger, reminding Brynn of the old joke.

"Eat up, baby."

She bustled around the kitchen, cleaning up the mess from her weak attempt at making pancakes. They might not look pretty but at least they were edible.

She was still riding the buzz that Henry's test results had come back negative. No osteoporosis and no rickets.

The bad news was they couldn't pin his bone non-unions to anything in particular. Either the stem cell procedure had failed or Henry was a scientific anomaly in that his bone tissue was taking its sweet ass time regenerating.

Even Ethan, who in his persevering, doctorly way had always been cautiously optimistic, admitted to being concerned.

And her time here was running out.

She had committed to returning to the helm of the Barnes Group by May, which was only a week away. Layla and Rich had everything under control. But as the CEO, she couldn't neglect the company much longer. And although there had been no pressure from the Bentley Foundation, the cottage came with an eviction date. Eight weeks, the estimated time it would take for Henry to recover and for Ethan and his team to document the progress.

Ethan.

They'd spent every night together this week but neither had spoken about her leaving. What was there to talk about really? It was an impossible situation. Yet, the idea of living nearly three-thousand miles away from him made her chest squeeze.

"Mom, can we go fishing?"

"You have to do your schoolwork and exercises first. I also have work to do. After that, we'll talk about it."

He started to whine and she gave him the look she'd perfected since he was old enough to talk. When the kitchen was cleaned up, she set him up at the table with his worksheets and grabbed a spot on the couch with her laptop.

There was an email from Rich, detailing plans for the Ohm Super Bowl campaign. She grimaced and picked up her phone.

"I don't like it," she said by way of greeting. "It feels very toxic masculinity."

Rich instantly knew she was talking about the car ad. "Eighty-four percent of the owners of the Model Nine are male, according to Hedges and Company."

"Still, this feels wrong. It feels like a muscle car ad, not an ad for an electric car. This is their car for the masses, right? I think we should be playing up the affordability of it. A Cadillac for the price of a Hyundai, something along those lines."

"I disagree. Fifty-five percent of Model Nine owners live in the nation's top wealthiest zip codes, meaning consumers don't care about price, even though MSRP is around thirty-five thousand. They care about the brand."

He made good points. Still, the tone of the ad turned her off. It was too alpha and too aggressive. "Can we take it down a notch? Maybe not have a guy who looks like Hulk Hogan doing donuts in the snow."

Rich laughed. "You didn't like that idea? The company wants to push the car in the cold states."

"Fine, keep the snow but ditch the donuts. Perhaps a mountainous, snowy road." An image of Nugget instantly popped in her head. "And a cowboy, instead of a gym rat." Ethan came to mind. But cowboys drove trucks not electric cars.

"I'll tweak it. When are you coming home?"

"Soon." She tried to convince herself that it was time, that life had to go back to normal. Henry needed to be in school and she needed to run the company she and Mason had built.

"Good. We miss you."

Did they? She'd been working in the shadows ever since Henry was born. Now she would take the reins. Be the boss.

It had always been her trajectory. As soon as Henry was old enough, she'd planned to go back full-time and run the agency alongside Mason, leading the creative side of the Barnes Group. It had always been that simple.

So, why now had the plan suddenly lost its appeal?

* * * *

Ethan stood at the window with his coffee. He didn't have surgery today and was planning to work from home, something he occasionally did. The plan was to get a few hours in, then sneak off to get in a little alone time with Brynn.

Alma had volunteered to take both kids to town for ice cream at the Bun Boy after Roni got out of school.

The sound of a car coming up the driveway pulled Ethan away from the kitchen to the front porch. It was Lou Ellen's Ford Fusion. He hadn't seen her since the party and it wasn't like her to show up unannounced.

She got out of the car and shielded her eyes as she squinted up at him. "Your office said you were out today, so I thought I'd find you at home."

She could've just picked up the phone. The fact that she hadn't, gave him a sinking feeling. Joey.

"Everything okay?"

"You tell me." She climbed up the stairs.

Thirty years ago, she was the spitting image of her daughter. If not for the dated clothes and the teased hairstyle, he wouldn't have been able to tell one from the other in pictures.

Her face was harder now, with a trail of deep grooves that she tried to cover up with too much makeup. And her hair had gone from blond to brunette to red in the years he'd known her. Today it was a combination of red and brown.

"You have any more of that?" she pointed at his coffee mug.

"Yeah. Come on in."

Alma had gone for her morning walk. It was probably better that way. She liked Lou Ellen even less than she liked Joey.

He poured her a mug, got out the milk, and passed her the sugar.

She gazed around the kitchen, tilting her head back to stare up at the open-beam ceilings. She'd been to the house a handful of times since he, Alma and Veronica had moved in. But she always acted like she was seeing it for the first time, her lips pursed in condemnation for trading up after leaving her daughter.

"Nice party the other night," he said, hoping it would break the ice and she'd say what she'd come to say.

"You left early."

He motioned for her to take a seat at the center island. "I didn't want to keep Roni out too late."

"Was that it?" she asked in her gravely pack-a-day voice. She no longer smoked but still sounded as if she did. "Or was it the woman you've been seeing?"

He stared at her blankly.

"Joey told me. Said you're in love with her or at least you think you are." She waited for him to respond and when he didn't, she continued, "Ethan, you have a chance to put your family back together. A chance for Roni to have both her parents living under the same roof. I understood why you left. I even think it was good for Joey. You leaving and taking Roni was Joey's rock bottom. It gave her the kick in the ass she needed to get into a program. To get clean. But Ethan she's good now. She's worked hard, she goes to her meetings, and she misses her baby. We all do." She glared at him, a reminder that he'd moved Roni fifty miles away from her grandparents. "Before Joey had her problem, you two were good together. Happy. A team."

She took a sip of her coffee. "Think about Veronica. Think about what this is doing to her. You owe it to her to try again with Joey. Whatever you have with this other woman is nothing compared to your family. Family comes first, Ethan."

Her words stabbed at him. Since the dissolution of his marriage, guilt and shame were his constant companions. And his former mother-in-law had pushed his buttons, evoking all those emotions. But she'd also pissed him off.

"Lou Ellen, I love you and Ace but with all due respect it isn't your place to come here and tell me how to care for my family. Joey and I are divorced now and for good reason. Who I choose to see or care about is none of your business."

"I'm just telling you what your own mama would've, bless her soul."

Lou Ellen had never known his mother, who'd died when Ethan was still in college, before he'd met Joey. She had no idea what kind of advice his mother would've doled out. To be hurtful he could've told her what the rest of his family thought about the divorce and Joey but held his tongue. Lou Ellen was only doing what she thought was right.

But this was between him and Joey.

"And I would've told my mother the same thing" as he had with Alma numerous times. "I didn't solicit your advice or your opinion. This is a private matter, Lou Ellen."

"Well, I beg to differ. Joey's my daughter and Veronica is my granddaughter, which makes it a family matter."

"How about we agree to disagree?" It wasn't worth making a federal case out of, though his ex-mother-in-law had a set of balls on her.

"When is she leaving, Ethan? Because the sooner she does the sooner you can get your head on straight."

He assumed Lou Ellen meant Brynn. "Lou," he clasped both her shoulders, "let me walk you out before we both say things we're sorry for."

"Are you throwing me out?"

"Of course not. You know you're always welcome here." He loved Lou Ellen, even if she was butting in where she didn't belong. "But I think it's wise if we both have a cooling off period."

He walked her to her car, opened the driver's door, and waited for her to get in.

She reached up and kissed him on the cheek. "I know you'll do the right thing. You're a good man. That's why Joey loves you so much."

That was the thing. Joey wasn't in love with him and he was no longer in love with Joey. To pretend differently was a lie. Still, everything Lou Ellen had said cut deep. He carried it around with him like a boulder on his shoulder the rest of the day.

"What's wrong?" Brynn asked as she rested her back against his chest on the sofa in the cottage. "You don't seem yourself tonight."

He started to say there was nothing wrong. But one of the things he'd come to value in Brynn was that he could talk to her about anything. Really talk. They'd begun to tell each other things they didn't share with anyone else. Her resentment for her late husband and her guilt over that resentment. His concerns about the toll his divorce would ultimately take on Veronica.

"Lou Ellen, Joey's mother, came to see me today."

"Is that unusual?" She twisted around to look at him. "I mean, I know you're close with your ex in-laws."

"To a degree we're close. I've always sensed some animosity over the fact that I sued Joey for full custody of Roni. On an intellectual level they knew their daughter wasn't in a place to care for a four-year-old. At the same time, it was like a public flogging. The hearing, the lawyers, everything that came out in court. I wouldn't have done it that way if I thought I had an alternative. But at the time, Joey wasn't willing to accept, or at least admit, that her addiction made her a danger to our daughter. Still, I'm sure her parents thought it was an asshole move. And maybe it was."

"No, absolutely not. You were putting Roni first. That's your job as a parent. Going to court was the only way to formalize it. I would've done the same exact thing. So, was that why Lou Ellen came, to complain about the custody arrangement?"

Ethan blew out a breath, regretting that he'd gone down this road. "Yeah and to discuss a new one." Nothing would be gained by telling Brynn the entire truth other than to put her in the middle of a situation that was not her doing.

"How do you feel about Joey sharing custody?"

"That it's inevitable. Joey's clean now, she's a good mother, and Veronica needs her. There's no reason that she shouldn't have joint custody."

"Except that it would kill you."

He let out a wry laugh. "Unfortunately, that's not a good legal argument. Nor is it fair to Roni, or Joey for that matter."

"I'm sorry, Ethan. I can only imagine how difficult this is for you."

"It'll work out." He readjusted her in his arms, snuggling her closer against his chest. She fit there. And for a while he just held her, trying to memorize what absolute contentment felt like. "I wanted to talk to you about Henry."

Brynn's breathing became shallow and she tensed. "No more bad news."

"I've been talking with other researchers about trying the stem cell procedure again."

She jerked in surprise. "You can do that?" She sat forward on the couch and turned to look at him. "I mean have you ever done it a second time?"

"Not for my phase 4 clinical trial, no. But Cedars Sinai is doing similar work with adults. I talked to the doctor heading up their clinical trial and they've had some success repeating the procedure on patients with acute fractures. There's no guarantee that Henry will improve. But it's something worth talking about."

"What kind of success have they had a Cedars?" She was revved up and it worried him. Ethan didn't want to give her false hope. It was just an idea.

"A sixty-percent success rate the second time around. But Brynn these are adults, not juveniles. And in their cases, they didn't even try a second round if they didn't see some improvement the first try." Henry's situation was different.

"But you think it's a possibility, right?"

"I do but with the caveat that it's a long shot."

She steamrolled over his warning. "Do I need to get on your calendar?"

"It wouldn't be me, Brynn. I'd refer you to someone else who is working in the area of stem cells."

Her face fell. "Why? I thought you invented this procedure. I want you, Ethan."

Despite the impossibility of it, he was tempted to give in just to see hope bloom in her cheeks again. "The use of stem cell regeneration is being studied all over the country, Brynn. UC Davis is in clinical trials for adults and John Hopkins has its own experimental procedure. Mine doesn't appear to be effective for Henry. Another might. I have a colleague at Yale who's working with kids. Let's see if we can get Henry in there."

The light went out of her blue eyes. Ethan felt it too. While there was still a slim chance for Henry to heal, the time in his trial was coming to an end.

"How long until we throw in the towel on your study?" she asked, looking as desolate as the first day she'd met him at the hospital.

"Two more weeks. If we don't see marked improvement by then we can safely assume the treatment isn't working." By now there should've been significant progress in Henry's healing but he kept that to himself.

She bowed her head. "You'll call your colleague?"

"Brynn," he wrapped his arms around her, feeling like he'd failed her. Failed Henry. "I'm sorry."

"No one's blaming you, Ethan. You told me from the get-go that it was far from a sure thing. You told me that Henry was amazing just the way he is and you were right. You were absolutely right."

"Henry's great, Brynn. The best son anyone could ask for."

Chapter 24

It took a week. But as promised, Ethan finagled Henry a spot in the Yale trial. They had seven more days to soak up Nugget before catching a flight home. Seven more days to spend with Ethan.

Then, they were scheduled to meet with their new surgeon in Connecticut. New Haven was close enough to Manhattan that they could commute to appointments most of the time. Soon, the life she knew in New York would resume, only this time she'd be going back to work full-time. To the business she loved. To the business she and Mason had nurtured.

Her mother had offered to stay with Henry until Brynn could find reliable childcare. And before they knew it, autumn would be here and Henry would return to school.

She should've been ready—anxious even—to get home, to immerse herself in her old routine and be surrounded by the sights and smells that she'd known her whole life. To see her friends again and meet at the same Sunday café for bagels and coffee.

Normality at last.

But the idea of leaving made her heart ache like there was something broken inside her. This place had been a salve for all she had lost eight months ago. And Ethan . . . she loved him with everything she had.

God, how she would miss him.

"Mom, someone's at the door."

She hadn't heard a car come down the driveway. For a second, she thought maybe Ethan had walked over but just as quickly remembered he had surgery today. She crossed the kitchen and swung open the door to find Donna, Maddy and Emily standing there with a big wicker hamper.

"We come bearing goodies," Donna said and pushed past Brynn, plopping the basket down on the counter.

Maddy and Emily hung back, waiting for an invitation.

"I hope it's okay that we dropped in without calling first." Maddy peeked past the door, looking for signs that they weren't intruding on something private.

Though Brynn and Ethan had tried to be discreet, she suspected there'd been plenty of speculation in town about their relationship.

"Of course it is. Come in. I'll make coffee."

"We thought you could use some friends." Emily took over in the kitchen, setting three more places at the table.

Henry asked if he could read in his room, eager to escape the oozing attention of four women. Lexi's was about all he could take, though he hadn't turned away Emily's brownies.

"First, do your worksheets. And no video games, Henry," Brynn called to the retreating back of his wheelchair.

She caught Donna's pitying glance and knew her sympathy wasn't about the forbidden video games. Would it always be like that? Sorrow for a boy who couldn't walk when Henry was so much more than a pair of working legs.

"Any changes?" Maddy asked and they all knew exactly what she was talking about.

"No." Brynn tried to smile. "But Ethan got Henry into a new trial. He thinks a second round might work this time."

"Well that's promising." Emily unpacked more of the homemade sweets from the basket and arranged the cookies and bars on a plate she found in the cupboard. "Will Ethan continue to oversee Henry's care?"

Brynn shook her head, afraid that they might see the pooling in her eyes. "There is a surgeon at Yale. She comes highly recommended by Ethan."

"Yale?" Donna broke off a piece of biscotti and dipped it in her coffee. "When?"

"Soon. I'm leaving next week."

Maddy put down her cup mid sip and everyone at the table got quiet. "So soon?"

"I've been here since February. And I have an ad agency to run."

"Ah, honey." Donna gripped Brynn's hand. "We're going to miss you and that sweet boy of yours."

Not as much as she would miss them. This town and all of the people in it had filled the emptiness inside her.

Griffin had reminded her that she wasn't just a stay-at-home mom. The ad campaign she'd created for him was drawing attention already. Dana, Griffin's real estate agent, was getting calls left and right for private showings.

From the first day she and Henry moved into the cottage, Alma had been feeding them. Enchiladas, chile relleno, lasagna, mac and cheese.

The women here taught her how to laugh again. How to celebrate all the good things in her life of which there were plenty. She'd always be thankful to them for bringing her into their warm and giving fold.

Then there was Ethan.

These last two months he'd been her shoulder, her sanity and her salvation. He'd been her best friend, an essential part of her being. Without him, she never would have learned to love again.

The thought of giving up all that . . . well, it was impossible to fathom.

"The good news," she heard herself say, "is that you now have a friend to visit when you come to Manhattan."

They nodded and smiled, trying not to turn their visit into a somber goodbye.

Still, she hadn't even left yet and she missed them already.

* * * *

Roni had mentioned that Henry was going home soon. "To New York City," she'd lisped through her two missing teeth. Joey was counting the days. Actually, the minutes.

Once Brynn Barnes was out of the picture, Ethan would get over his infatuation with her and see what was right in front of him. Joey was sure of it. Her ex-husband was the most responsible man she knew. Faithful as Simba. And above all else, he was a family man. He'd do what was right. Joey never doubted that. This thing with Brynn was just a passing fancy. And the sooner she was gone, the sooner Ethan would return to his former loyal self.

Joey turned into the parking lot at The Farm stand near the Circle D Ranch. She'd only learned about the adorable country store the other day from Roni, who'd walked the aisles, tasting the free samples like a regular. Apparently Ethan and Alma brought her to the store frequently enough that Roni and the owner had greeted each other with a big hug.

The place had everything from wine and floral arrangements to fresh produce and deli meats. There was even a section with gift items: mason jar lights, jadeite batter bowls, wooden cake stands and seasonal wreaths.

Last time, Joey noticed a wide array of jams, jellies and baked goods. Today, she'd decided to appeal to Ethan's sweet tooth. They said the way to a man's heart was through his stomach. At this point, she was willing to try anything.

A portable playpen sat in the corner of the store and a toddler with rosy red cheeks and a head full of hair stood inside, watching the owner stock shelves.

"Hey there."

The woman turned around at the sound of Joey's voice and beamed one of those smiles that lit up a room. "Roni's mom. You're back."

"I'm back." Joey waved at the little girl, who in return lifted her chubby hand in the air. "Your daughter?"

"This is Emerson." The woman lifted the child from the playpen. "Say hi to—"

"Joey. Hi Emerson."

"I'm Annie," the woman introduced herself.

Joey couldn't remember if they'd exchanged names last time.

"Welcome to The Farm again, Joey. Can I help you find something? All the citrus is in season right now. We get it from an orchard in the Central Valley. The honey, kale and flowers are from my farm. The avocados are from down south. Mostly everything else comes from around here."

"I'm in the market for something sweet. Maybe one of the pies or some jam."

"I made most of the jam," Annie said. "And the pies are fresh out of the oven from Emily McCreedy."

Joey assumed Emily was someone local. She followed Annie to a table stacked with white boxes filled with pies.

"The apple crumb is to die for but all of them are amazing."

Joey perused the table, checking out the various flavors. Pecan, berry and a lemon meringue that looked tempting. Ethan loved coconut cream but Joey didn't see any. Without it, she was at a loss for a second choice. Then it occurred to her that the only reason she knew about his coconut cream fixation was because it had been her favorite first. She'd introduced him to the pie when they'd started dating and it had become their special dessert.

She mined the depths of her recollection for what his favorites had been before coconut cream had become their tradition. Nothing. As much as she tried, she couldn't remember—or maybe she'd never known in the first place—whether he liked pecan or disliked lemon merengue. A wife should know something as simple as her husband's taste in pastries, shouldn't she?

Upset by the revelation and not exactly sure why—it was pie for goodness sake, not a peanut allergy—she grabbed the apple crumb, paid at the counter, and said goodbye to Annie and Emerson.

Ethan was home when she got there, staring outside the window as if it held the answers to world peace.

"I brought an apple pie from that farm stand down the road. You like apple, right?"

"Huh?" he grunted and seemed to snap out of whatever he'd been contemplating.

"Apple pie. You like it, right?"

He shrugged. "Yeah, sure, who doesn't like apple pie?"

"But it's not your favorite as far as fruit pies go?"

Ethan leaned back in his chair and looked at her like perhaps he was missing something. Like maybe it was a trick question. "What's your sudden obsession with pie? Cherry is my favorite, then probably peach. Apple's good, though. It's pie, you really can't go wrong."

"Do you know what my favorite fruit pie is?"

"Rhubarb." He got up, took the box from her, and shook his head. "Are you okay, Joey?"

"I'm fine," she said but wondered why he'd known her favorite pie but she hadn't known his. She told herself it was a small thing. Insignificant. "Where's Roni?"

"In her room. I don't think she was expecting you."

Joey wasn't sure if that was his veiled way of saying you should've called first. Lately, she'd been dropping in unannounced on weekdays. She didn't have anywhere else to be other than to attend her meetings. The mail-order operator job was only a few hours a day. And seeing Roni kept her going, kept her from falling backwards.

There was also Ethan. She'd thought being around him more might remind him of what they once had. Though when she searched deep for those good times, she mostly remembered the early days. The chase. Her catching the prize.

For his part, he continued to treat her with polite indifference. Occasionally they'd laugh together over something Roni said or even reminisce about an old restaurant they used to haunt. But most of his interactions with her were as impersonal as business transactions. *Are you taking Roni this weekend? Did you get my alimony check? Nothing from the board yet, huh?*

"Alma is having dinner with friends, which leaves Roni and me to fend for ourselves. I was thinking of throwing a tri-tip on the grill." Ethan gave the pie a gentle shake. "You interested in joining us?"

A month ago, the invitation might've given Joey hope. But it was plain to see he was just being courteous. She'd gotten here at dinnertime and had brought dessert. What was he supposed to do, tell her to wait outside until they finished eating? It was on the tip of her tongue to ask why he wasn't busy with his girlfriend. But even as consumed as she was with their relationship, she wasn't that juvenile. And she liked to think she still had some pride.

"Sure," she said. "Why don't I make a salad?"

"Sounds good." He went back to gazing out the window.

Joey wondered where he was today. "Are you all right?"

"Yeah," he mumbled but continued to stare off in the distance.

"Mommy!" Veronica called from the top of the stairs, then ran down so fast Joey feared she'd fall.

"Slow down, Roni." She caught her daughter up in her arms and swung her around. At least someone was happy to see her.

"Are you sleeping over?"

"Not tonight, baby." Joey snuck a peek at Ethan, who was watching them. He looked so torn, so guilt ridden, that her heart folded in half. "Want to help me make a salad and set the table?" she asked Roni.

"I get to peel the cucumbers." Roni ran to the kitchen, her ponytail bouncing against her back.

Joey followed her daughter into the kitchen, leaving Ethan alone with whatever was eating him.

Roni carried the meal with stories about school and a little boy who brought a pet frog to class. Ethan spent most of the evening nodding and pretending to be present. But he was somewhere else entirely. It could've been one of his medical cases. No one ever became immune to a child's suffering. Not even doctors and nurses, who saw it all. But Joey suspected Ethan's melancholy had nothing to do with work and everything to do with the beautiful brunette living down the hill.

You'll get over her, Ethan.

After dinner, Joey gave Roni a bath while Ethan did the dishes.

"Mommy can you move here? I know Geema and Geepa would be sad but we could visit them and they could stay here, too."

"Close your eyes, Roni." Joey cradled Veronica's head under the faucet to rinse her hair.

"Can you, Mommy?"

Joey let out a sigh. "Do you know how much I love you?"

Roni lifted her head and held her arms wide. "This much."

Joey shook her head. "More. To the moon and back."

"I love you to infinity." Roni hung over the tub and gave Joey a wet hug.

Joey clung to her, savoring the sweet smell of Johnson's Baby shampoo as a single tear streaked down her cheek. This was where she should be every night. Bathing and putting her girl to bed. Sleeping only a hallway away when her baby woke up in the middle of the night from a bad dream.

This was the life she'd thrown away for pills.

After tucking Roni in, Joey headed downstairs. It was so quiet she wondered if Ethan had stepped outside. She found him in his study, gazing blankly at a computer screen.

"Are you sure everything is okay?"

"Everything's fine, Joey," he said with an edge to his voice. It wasn't anger just impatience. It was the same voice he'd use on a know-it-all resident who questioned Ethan's diagnosis. Or an emergency room doc who wanted to clear a bed and tried to rush Ethan's time with a patient.

Still, she held up are arms in surrender. "You don't have to bite my head off. I read Roni her bedtime story. She was asleep when I slipped out. I'm taking off."

Knowing he'd been short, his expression turned apologetic. "You sure you want to drive home this late?"

She'd like to stay but it was obvious he was only inviting her to be chivalrous. "It's not even nine yet. I'll be fine."

"Okay, then let me walk you out."

He stood up and she took the opportunity to study him in his faded jeans and sweatshirt. When she'd still worked at the hospital the nurses would surreptitiously fan themselves as he walked by. It had always given her a thrill that he'd chosen her over all the others. He was still as good looking as the day she'd first met him, even with a little gray at his temples.

Still, her heart didn't race the way it used to. She blamed it on the distance he'd put between them. There was a time when all she had to do was crook her finger and he'd do anything to please her.

They got to the front porch where the sweet smell of jasmine glided through the air like perfume. The night was mild, almost balmy. And a full moon cast a magical glow over the front yard, making it seem earlier than it was.

Ethan brushed past her on his way to the stairs. Maybe it was having him so near or the way the evening filled her senses like the Sierra in springtime, but she latched onto his arm to swing him around, went up on tiptoes, flung her arms around his neck, and kissed him.

He stood rigid, then tried to pull away. But Joey wouldn't let him, pressing her body against his and plying his mouth with her lips until it awakened something inside him. Inside her. Until she proved she was the only woman for him and he was the only man for her.

His lips were hard and ungiving. She ground against him, searching for the sweet spot, the spot that used to make both of them wild. In the old days, it hadn't taken much. A touch, a look, even a whisper.

But now . . . nothing.

Suddenly, a pair of bright lights shined in their eyes and he pulled away, ruffled, putting more than an arm's length of distance between them.

"What the hell was that?" He looked at her, baffled, then quickly turned to see where the lights had come from.

Brynn's car sat in the driveway with the motor running. Ethan started to make his way down the stairs. But Brynn backed up her car and rocketed away as fast as she had appeared.

Joey didn't know how much Brynn had seen but it had been enough to make her leave in a hurry.

Chapter 25

"Brynn, open up. It wasn't what you thought. Give me a chance to explain."

Ethan started to bang on the cottage door but Brynn opened it so fast he nearly fell in.

"Shush, Henry's asleep. We had dinner at Griffin's. I stopped by to see if you could help me carry him in. But apparently you were busy." It was said sarcastically but Brynn was hurt. She wouldn't even look at him.

He glanced at Brynn's car. "You got him inside on your own?"

She nodded and moved away from the entrance so he could come inside. Her bag and Henry's jacket were piled on the countertop and other than the hallway light, the cottage was dark.

"I can't stay long. I need to get back to Roni. But what you saw . . . it wasn't what you think."

"No, what was it then? Because from where I was sitting it looked like a kiss."

He wanted to tell her the truth, that it was Joey throwing herself at him. But he couldn't embarrass his ex that way. "It was two people who used to care for each other, proving to themselves that what they once had is gone."

"Is it, though?" Brynn hung Henry's jacket in the coat closet.

"It was gone a long time ago, Brynn. It would be easier if it wasn't, but it is."

She moved through the cottage, putting things away. Ethan got the sense she was trying to keep busy so she wouldn't have to have a real conversation with him.

"I'm sorry you saw what you saw. But it was nothing, Brynn. What Joey and I had is over. I'm in love with you." It was the first time he'd said it aloud but he'd known it for weeks now. Since that first night in the barn.

She stopped tidying the pillows on the sofa and looked at him, her bottom lip trembled. In that moment something changed, he could see it in her sad eyes. Resignation maybe. Or, she thought he was lying.

"I love you, Brynn. Please believe me that nothing happened between Joey and me. That what you saw wasn't what it seemed. I wouldn't do that."

"I know," she said her voice cracking. "You're a good man and I believe you. But you owe it to yourself, to Roni and even to Joey to explore whether you could put the pieces back together. You've said it yourself that it would be easier if you could. It would be the best thing for your family. If Mason were still alive I would try too. If for nothing else for Henry. But only if reconciling makes you happy. You need to be happy, Ethan."

"You make me happy."

She sighed and wiped away a tear with the back of her hand. "I'm leaving, Ethan. I have a home on the other side of the country and a business to run. What you and I have . . . had . . . is something I'll never forget. You taught me to love again. And wherever you are and whoever you're with, know that I will always love you. But this is for the best. Try again with Joey. You loved her once, maybe you can love her again."

She got to her feet, went to the kitchen sink, and stared out the window into darkness.

He started to join her, yearning to feel her in his arms to salve the sadness.

"Go home, Ethan," she said, her voice gentle. "Don't leave Roni alone."

He hiked up the driveway, lost. Eviscerated. Everything Brynn said about her leaving, about Joey was the truth.

But for once in his damned life he wanted to follow his heart not his damned sense of honor.

* * * *

Brynn believed everything she'd told Ethan, right down to her advice to work things out with his ex-wife. Despite the pain Joey's addiction had caused, she was better now and trying hard to redeem herself. Anyone with eyes could see that.

And Joey's love for her daughter . . . well, that was uncontested.

As a mother, Brynn's sympathy for Joey was visceral. No good parent should ever be separated from their child.

So why then did the idea of Ethan and Joey reuniting hurt so much? Just seeing them on the porch, wrapped in an embrace, had been like a dagger through her soul.

But it would be selfish and coldhearted to stand in the way of a reconciliation, she told herself. Together, Ethan and Joey made a home.

* * * *

Joey desperately craved something to take the edge off. Her night had gone from bad to worse. Ethan had completely rejected her advance and had gone running to Brynn the second he'd realized his girlfriend had had a birds-eye view of their kiss. If you could even call it a kiss. It had been more like her mashing her lips against a concrete wall.

Now Joey felt responsible for whatever happened between him and Brynn at the cottage, which was ironic. The whole point of the kiss was to remind Ethan of how hot they once were for each other, so he'd forget about Brynn.

She started to head for the highway but changed her mind. *One drink.* Just one, she told herself. Her problem was pills, not alcohol. So what would be the harm in one vodka tonic?

Her hands shook as she turned the wheel toward the Ponderosa. Hopefully the place was still open. Lord knew the rest of the town pulled up stakes after sunset.

The neon light sign was on when she got there. A couple of men congregated on the sidewalk, near the door. She sat in her car, waiting for them to disperse before getting out. There was nothing rough looking about them. But after being held at gunpoint, she was more skittish these days.

A big rig pulled up alongside her Ford, belching diesel. The brakes made a screeching sound as it came to a stop. Matthew McConaughey was at the wheel, a straw cowboy hat on his head and a day's worth of scruff on his face. His load looked empty and she wondered if he was staying the night at the Lumber Baron on his way to the next stop.

The men were still gathered around the door. One of them was telling a story, Joey could tell from his exaggerated hand gestures. She hopped out of her car anyway and watched as Matthew McConaughey alighted from his 18-wheeler. His brown suede cowboy boots stepped off the running board and a pair of long, denim encased legs followed.

He tipped his hat and graced her with a grin that showed off those pearly whites. "Fancy meeting you here."

She moved in, took a fistful of his collar, flattened him against his trailer, and caught his mouth with hers. He tasted good, like coffee and man. And he felt even better. Big and strong and something else Joey couldn't quite identify. Perhaps a little dangerous but at the same time safe. It didn't make sense but she didn't dwell on it. Instead, she closed her eyes and let him take her away.

Unlike Ethan, he kissed her back, cradling the back of her head with his hands. He angled her face so he could take the kiss deeper, exploring her mouth with his tongue. The scent of his aftershave, or maybe it was just soap, drove her up.

She moved closer, feeling the evidence of his arousal pressing against her. Long and hard. The hot pull of his mouth made her whimper. She could've sworn she heard him laugh but was too enthralled with his kiss to care.

Even the chatter of the men outside the Ponderosa had faded into the background, their voices nothing more than a dull whisper.

His hands moved down her sides and around to her back where his fingers reached her backside. His mouth, hot and hungry, continued to devour her. It was then that she realized that she didn't even know his name.

She started to ask him but his lips had moved to that sensitive spot behind her earlobe and she forgot her own name. He left a trail of kisses across her jaw and recaptured her mouth, his hands skimming the waistband of her jeans.

If they weren't careful they'd be arrested for indecent exposure.

Somewhere in the distance a car backfired, the sound so jarring that they pulled apart. She immediately missed the warmth of his body and the intoxicating pull of his mouth.

"I thought you were married." He cocked one booted foot against his rig and grinned in that slightly sarcastic way of his, giving her naked ring finger a scan for good measure.

"I was." She pressed her key fob to unlock the door. Five more seconds in his presence and she'd follow him to the Lumber Baron or any other place he wanted to go. How could she feel that kind of longing for a stranger and only a mild sensation of nostalgia with the father of her child?

"Yeah?" He gave her a long appraisal. "What does that mean?"

"It means that I'm not anymore." With that she got in her car and drove away.

She was halfway to Reno when she remembered she still didn't know his name.

Chapter 26

The next morning Brynn called Zena and had her change their flight to Wednesday. Even though it was three days earlier than planned, it gave her forty-eight hours to pack. Prolonging her stay would only make saying goodbye that much more difficult. For her and Ethan. It was time for Brynn to put her life back together and for Ethan to figure out his own.

"Mom, can we go the bookstore in Reno today?"

"Sure. As soon as we're done with your doctor's appointment." It was his last one with Ethan. When they got home, Henry had his first appointment with the new surgeon at Yale.

She finished emptying the dishwasher and sat next to Henry on the sofa where he was playing with his smart watch. "I want to talk before we go."

He lifted his head and looked at her with big blue eyes. "Is it about my surgery? Because I don't want another one."

She leaned over and kissed his forehead. "We've been over this, baby. But that's not what I wanted to talk about."

"What then?" He sounded mildly perturbed. She didn't blame him. An eighth of his life had been spent in doctors' offices and hospitals.

"I've booked our flight for Wednesday."

"To go where?" He bowed his head over his watch again, finding it infinitely more interesting than having a conversation with his mother.

"Home, to Manhattan."

His head jerked up. "Why? You said we weren't leaving until Sunday. Dr. Ethan said I could ride Choo Choo this weekend. I don't want to go, Mom. I like it here."

"I know, baby. But we don't live here." How did she explain to an eight-year-old that staying any longer would destroy her? "Don't you want to see your friends?"

He shook his head. "I have new friends. And there are no horses at home."

"Honey, we can't stay here forever. I have to work and you have to go to school."

"What about Dr. Ethan? He's the best doctor I've ever had."

"I know, Henry. But Dr. Ethan says really great things about your new doctor. Don't you think we should at least give her a try?" She tilted her head to the side, hoping to persuade him that their life was in Manhattan.

Scowling, Henry shrugged and went back to his watch.

"We've got to go, buddy." Brynn scooped her purse and keys off the counter while Henry begrudgingly hoisted himself from the sofa into his chair.

On their way out, he reached up and snagged his cowboy hat off the hook at the front door and rested it on his head. It had become a ritual that always made her grin. In the two months they'd been here her son had become a cowboy.

They made the familiar drive to the hospital. She and Henry had been there only a few days earlier for more X-rays. A nurse in purple dinosaur scrubs waved at them on their way to the orthopedic clinic. Brynn recognized her from previous visits and waved back.

She liked to say she'd miss this place but she wouldn't. Just the doctor who in so many ways had changed her life. She wondered if she would miss him forever or if with time he would simply become a fond memory.

"You're here," Marjorie, the receptionist announced. Brynn immediately checked her watch to see if they were late. "You're fine. Right on time. But Dr. Daniels had a break in his schedule and thought you might get here early. Let me check, but I think we can bring you back."

A few seconds later, Ethan appeared at the door and waved them in. They hadn't talked since she'd found him on the porch with Joey and seeing him again reminded her why leaving Nugget early was the right decision. He made her wish for things that were impossible.

"Hey, Henry, how are you doing today?"

It pleased Brynn that at the hospital Ethan made their appointments all about Henry.

"Okay, I guess," Henry said.

"How about your legs? Are they feeling any stronger?" Ethan stopped in front of the first exam room and ushered them in.

"I don't know. I think they feel the same."

"Yeah? Can you hop on the table for me?"

He turned to Brynn and winked like he had a secret. She stared at him quizzically.

Ethan moved to the table where Henry laid lengthwise. "Let me have a look there, buddy." He began manipulating Henry's thighs. "That hurt?"

"No, not a lot."

"But a little bit?"

Henry nodded. "It's just kind of sore."

"That's normal, especially because both legs are out of practice. But you've been doing your exercises, right?" He motioned for Brynn, who'd taken her normal place on the plastic chair in the corner, to join them. "I got your X-rays back and I'm liking what I'm seeing."

Brynn's eyes grew round. "Is there new bone tissue?"

He nodded. "The X-rays show a marked improvement from last time. It's slow but steady. I think we may be on to something and Henry here is just a slow healer."

Brynn was floored by the news. "Does this mean he doesn't need another surgery?"

"I've discussed it with Dr. Rothman and she and I are both of the theory that we should wait and see how things go before rushing into another procedure."

"Does that mean Henry will stay in your clinical trial?" She held her breath.

Ethan adjusted Henry's hat to give it a slight tilt. "Hey, buddy, how'd you like to hang out in the playroom while I talk to your mom?"

"Am I done, then?"

"Yep, you're done." Ethan helped Henry into his chair and had a nurse escort him to the playroom. He shut the door, sat on the table vacated by Henry and gestured for Brynn to take the chair. They were only a few feet away from each other but it seemed like miles. "Dr. Rothman will take it from here."

She started to argue but he held up his hand. "It was an eight to ten-week trial. You know that, Brynn." He pinched the bridge of his nose, his earlier good cheer evaporating before her very eyes. "You want to know what the bitch of it is? As soon as I saw the images, I immediately started making excuses why it would be okay to extend Henry's time. How it would be in the best interest of the study. In the best interest of science." He exhaled and looked at her, tortured. "Thankfully I still have a modicum of sense left. It would be the wrong move for Henry. If he's under Rothman and her team's care, he's guaranteed a spot in her clinical trial if this is as good as it gets and he needs a second round of treatment. She's a brilliant surgeon, Brynn. A brilliant surgeon with fresh eyes who will keep me in the loop every step of the way."

She knew he was right. While today's positive diagnosis had put her over the moon, it was far from conclusive. She wouldn't do anything to risk Henry's future.

Still, it felt like all the air had been sucked from the room. In one fleeting second, she'd gained and lost a valid reason to spend more time with Ethan. Guilt gnawed at her. She should've been celebrating the good news about Henry not dwelling on her disappointment.

"We'll miss you," she said, letting her eyes drop to her shoes. "You've cared for Henry like he was your own. I'll never be able to thank you for all you've done."

"Stop," he said. "You're talking to me as if I were a stranger. You know how much Henry means to me. How much you mean to me." He got off the table and tried to pull her into his arms.

"Don't . . . please. It's too hard, Ethan. Yesterday, I made my peace with leaving. Today . . ." She swallowed, unable to say it. "We're leaving Wednesday," she said at last.

"Wednesday? I thought your flight wasn't until Sunday. Brynn?"

"Dr. Rothman will see us right away, no?" He answered with an imperceptible nod. "Then it's for the best. Otherwise it'll be more days of goodbyes. I can't do it, Ethan. I just can't do it."

"Brynn . . ." he trailed off and rubbed his hand down his face. "What the hell have we done?"

* * * *

Wednesday came too soon.

Brynn spent Tuesday being feted by half of Nugget. Griffin had thrown her and Henry what was supposed to be a small gathering in the Sierra Heights clubhouse. At least thirty people had attended, including Owen, Darla and her husband, a police officer with Nugget PD. The police chief, Maddy and their little girl came too. As did Emily and Clay. Alma, Donna and Brady prepared enough food for a herd of elephants.

Ethan had cleared his schedule to come to the party. Afterward, they'd spent most of the night in each other's arms until Ethan had to creep back to his own bed.

While she cherished every last second they'd spent together, it was agony. Brynn tried not to think about Ethan and Joey reconciling, even though she knew in her heart of hearts they would. In the end, it was the right thing to do, especially if they could make each other happy. For Brynn there was the Barnes Group to run and advertising campaigns to create.

And by this time next year, Henry could very possibly be walking. That's what she had come here for and where she had to focus her energy. Her son.

"You ready?" she asked Henry, who'd returned from the barn with Ethan and Roni for one last goodbye to the horses.

He solemnly nodded and took off his cowboy hat. "You keep this, Dr. Ethan. No one wears a cowboy hat in New York City."

Ethan took the hat and put it back on Henry's head. "Be a trendsetter, buddy."

Henry's eyes filled and he forced the hat into Ethan's hand. "Maybe it'll help you remember me."

"What are you talking about? I'll never forget you, partner. You were my best patient ever." Ethan crouched down so he was eye to eye with Henry and handed him his business card. "You see the phone number and email address on that card? I want you to keep in touch, let me know what you're up to, you hear?"

Henry swiped at his eyes. "I will. And maybe I can come back sometime and ride the horses, even work for you feeding them and cleaning the stalls, like Cody does."

"Anytime you want to wrangle for me, you have a home."

"You can have my room, Henry." Roni danced around him. "I can sleep in the guest room."

Brynn's eyes filled with tears. Life wouldn't be the same without Veronica knocking on her door every day, asking Henry to come out to play.

"Come here, sweet girl. Henry and I have a present for you." Brynn handed Roni a small, prettily wrapped package.

"Can I open it?"

"Of course you can."

Roni tore through the paper, lifted the lid off the box and squealed. "Daddy, look." She lifted the gold heart necklace from the velvet lining, her eyes round. "Can I wear it?"

Ethan nodded and tried for a smile but Brynn had never seen him look so desolate.

"It's just a little something for you to remember Henry by." Brynn put the thin chain around Roni's neck and closed the clasp.

"I'll never forget him." Roni reached her arms up to be hugged and Brynn swooped her into the air, not wanting to let her go.

"What do you say?" Ethan prodded.

"Thank you. I love it!" Roni got down, ran to Henry and threw herself into his chair.

"Careful, careful." Ethan warned but let them say their goodbyes before helping Henry into the car. Roni scampered into the back seat, reluctant to see them off.

Ethan turned to Brynn and whispered, "I want to kiss you."

Even though she and Ethan had said their own tearful private goodbyes the night before, it was awkward with both children there.

"I know. Me too. But it's better this way." Brynn held back tears. "I've got to go, otherwise we'll miss our flight."

He took in a deep breath and let it out slowly. "This is . . ." He scrubbed his hand through his hair unable to finish the sentence. He didn't have to. This was every bit as excruciating for her, too.

"Let's not do this. Please."

With a subtle nod, he opened her car door. As she was getting inside, he bent over and in a soft voice said, "I love you."

It wasn't the words she remembered a week later in her Manhattan penthouse. It was the way his face had lost all its light.

* * * *

Ethan slogged through the next week mostly in a haze. He'd only had two stem cell procedures and had spent most of his office hours catching up on trial documentation. A good portion of most of those days, though, he simply stared into space, wondering what Brynn was doing. Whether she'd gone back to work or was sipping coffee in a café with her best friend, Lexi.

He'd lost track of how many times he'd picked up the phone and started to call her before stopping himself. He'd contact her after Henry's first appointment with Rothman. Until then, he needed to get his head screwed on straight.

"You look like hell." Joey found him in the living room, ostensibly watching television. But it was white noise, he didn't even know what show was playing in the background.

She dried her hands on a dish towel. "You may want to think about shaving and showering. It's past noon and you promised to go riding with Roni."

Ethan forced himself to adjust his recliner to a sitting position. "You going home?" She usually left around this time on Sundays to get a jump on the week. And frankly he wasn't in the mood for her company.

At least she'd backed off since the kiss. Lately, they seemed more distant than ever. She'd come to the house nearly every day this week but spent all her time with Roni.

"Brynn left, huh?" She sat on the arm of the sofa adjacent to his chair, her eyes filled with what could only be described as pity. "I'm sorry, Ethan."

"Isn't this what you wanted?" he asked flatly, trying to keep the edge out of his voice.

She chewed her bottom lip, a habit he used to find endearing. Now though . . . nothing. "I thought it was," she said. "But . . ."

"But what?"

She let out a deep sigh. "I guess I'm wondering if it's my fault that she left."

He was feeling uncharitable enough to say yes but the fact was it wasn't her fault. "Her life is in New York. That's where her company is. But you already know that. So what's your game here, Joey?"

She flinched and he felt like a heel.

"No game, Ethan. Can't you just believe that I don't want you to be miserable?" She rotated from the sofa arm to the chair next to his. "I'm trying to make amends . . . for the kiss . . . for everything." She waited and when he didn't respond said, "If I could take it back I would."

There was nothing to take back. If anything, the kiss had been a gut check that whatever they'd had together was lost. But he didn't want to talk about the kiss, or anything else, right now. He wanted to be alone with his misery.

"I think I'll take that shower." He swiftly rose to his feet and headed to the staircase. But halfway there, he stopped, whirled around and spat, "Brynn thinks I should work things out with you."

It wasn't until he got to his bedroom that he questioned his motives for his outburst. Had he said it to stun her or to shut her up? Or perhaps he just wanted to get it out in the open and show Joey Brynn's capacity for caring. Everywhere he looked Brynn had left an indelible piece of herself, including his heart.

Joey burst through the doors. "I know you don't love me anymore."

"Do you love me?" He held her gaze. "That's the question you should be asking yourself." He already knew the answer and suspected she'd known it for a long time, even before the divorce.

She sat on the edge of his bed and buried her face in her hands. A long time passed in silence before she said, "I love you, Ethan. I'll always love you, but I'm not in love with you." She glanced up, her eyes teary. "I guess that's what you've been trying to tell me all this time. It's just that I

thought what we had . . . companionship, admiration, a daughter we love
. . . was good enough. But . . ."

"But?"

"I don't want to be with someone who doesn't love me."

He sat next to her on the bed. The room grew quiet and it took a long
time for Joey to break the silence. "I deserve more."

"When did you come to this conclusion?" For him it had been the first
night he and Brynn had made love in the barn.

She blew out a breath. "I don't know. The kiss on the front porch
maybe." She shrugged. "Probably even before that. And then there was
the epiphany about pie."

He looked at her and hitched a brow.

"It's too complicated to explain." She leaned back on her elbows and
stared up at the ceiling fan. "In rehab we used to do this exercise in the
middle of this big gymnasium where we sat on yoga mats, closed our
eyes, and visualized our futures. I used to sit there in the darkness, trying
with all my might to imagine what my life would be like. But no matter
how hard I concentrated, I couldn't see it. It was as elusive as a late-night
dream you can't remember in the morning. Instead, my mind always went
to that first Christmas in our house in Reno when Roni was just starting
to walk. The way she would hang on to the wrought iron stair railing and
heft herself up, then let go with both hands. That victorious look on her
face when she realized she was standing all on her own. Remember?"

Of course he remembered. How could he forget?

"That one perfect memory got me through six of the hardest months
of my life. I told myself that it could be like that again. And I mistakenly
turned one idyllic slice of my past into the vision of my future. I know now
that I can't go back. I can only go forward. And other than having Roni
in my life, I don't know what my future holds. What I do know is that I
want it filled with passion and desire and that heart pounding feeling when
you're crazy in love with someone. The feelings I think you and Brynn
have. It would be wrong to settle for anything less."

Joey's words surprised Ethan. They showed that her journey to sobriety
had been more than simply getting clean.

He looked at her, sadness filling his eyes. In so many ways he had let
her down. "All I ever wanted was to be the best man I could be. The best
father, the best husband, the best surgeon. I shouldn't have walked away,
Joey. I'm a doctor for God's sake and I left you sick and broken."

"Oh Ethan." Her lips curved in a tender smile. "Thank goodness you
left. You did what was right for our daughter. I was too self-centered, too

self-destructive to believe that at the time. You were the only adult in our relationship, the only one looking out for Roni's best interests. I was looking out for me. Maybe it was the drugs, maybe it was my own narcissism. But if it wasn't for you leaving, I wouldn't have gotten the help I needed."

He took a deep breath, so conflicted it made his head hurt. "I'm willing to compromise everything just to be with her. What kind of father . . . what kind of person . . . does that make me?"

"It makes you a flesh and blood man, Ethan." She gently touched his arm. "And in my eyes, you're still the best. The best father, the best surgeon, and the best man I've ever known."

He wrapped his arm around her shoulder and pulled her close, knowing that he'd remember this moment forever. "You're pretty damn amazing, that's what I know. And our daughter is lucky to have you."

Chapter 27

"Are you even listening?" Lexi reached for the Margarita pitcher and filled her glass.

"Uh-huh. He looked twenty years older than his Match picture."

"I told you that twenty minutes ago. I have since moved on to real estate. Am I that boring or are you pining away for Doctor Cowboy?"

Brynn took a visual turn around the bar. Lots of well-heeled forty somethings, looking to hook up. The place in all its dark wood glory had been Lexi's choice, not Brynn's. She'd wanted to go to the new gastro pub on 70th but Lexi had called it a mom bar. Brynn wasn't aware there were bars specifically for mothers. What she'd really wanted was a stiff drink in the comfort of her PJs, sacked out in her living room.

But it was probably good to get out. For the last week she'd done nothing but work on the Ohm account, sulk and avoid the phone for fear she'd call Ethan, knowing that the sound of his voice would send her into a downward spiral. She never knew she could miss someone this much.

"I'm distracted thinking about Henry's recovery." It was partly true. Brynn liked Henry's new doctor but had more faith in Ethan. "It's just a lot of change all at once."

It was clear from Lexi's sympathetic expression she wasn't buying it. "You think he went back to his ex-wife?"

That's what she'd told him he should do. So why then did the thought of Ethan and Joey reconciling make her stomach roil? Because she loved him, that's why.

"Do you?" Brynn dipped her finger into the salt on the rim of her glass.

"You would know better. I only met the guy once. The ex, not at all. Does either of them have a Facebook page? We could look. Chances are if they're together again there will be something on one of their pages. A change in their relationship status, a new profile picture of both of them together, something." Lexi reached for her phone.

Brynn put her hand over Lexi's "Don't." Facebook wasn't Ethan's style. Brynn didn't know about Joey but couldn't bear to look.

"So you're just going to let it remain a mystery?"

"Yeah. I think it's best, don't you?"

"I doubt I could resist knowing. But if you can, yes, I think it's better." Lexi rocked her head from side to side in consideration. "Then again maybe it would help you get over him faster?"

Nothing was going to help her get over him. Nothing.

"Let's not talk about this anymore." The conversation was making her queasy. While she wanted all the happiness in the world for Ethan—and Roni—she wasn't ready to embrace him moving on so quickly. She tried to remind herself that Joey had been first in Ethan's life and was the mother of his child, just as Mason was the father of Brynn's.

Lexi leaned in and patted Brynn's shoulder. "Is work a safe topic?"

Brynn groaned. Returning to the Barnes Group had been anticlimactic. Rich and Layla had carried the company after Mason's death without missing a beat. Now that Brynn was going into the office every day, she felt like an interloper.

"It'll take a while before I get into the swing of things," she said, trying to sound positive. "Rich brought in a couple of new clients and I'm focusing on their campaigns. Even though what I should be doing is taking over the company's operation." But it was the creative side of the business that really appealed to her.

"It's only been a week, Brynn. You'll be every bit the CEO that Mason was. You just need time to acclimate. What about Rich and Layla? Is that weird?"

Of course it was weird. For the last eight years she'd stayed in the background while Mason, Rich and Layla ran the show. Now, she was their boss. "We go back a long way. We'll work things out. I owe them so much for keeping things afloat while I dealt with the aftermath of the accident."

"They've been really loyal but it's your company, Brynn. Make your mark."

That was the thing. Her mark was creating campaigns, making creative choices, not running a business. She'd come to understand that about herself in Nugget with Griffin and the Sierra Heights advertising campaign. Nothing had been done by committee or based on a bottom line. It had just been her and the client, doing what she loved. She wasn't so naïve to believe a company the size of the Barnes Group could survive without committees and bottom lines. But the freedom to shed those confines had been heady.

She sipped her Margarita, letting the Tequila burn the back of her throat. "I hope I have a mark to make."

"You do. I know you've been out of the game for a while but you've always been the greatest asset to the Barnes Group. It was your campaigns that put the company on the map."

"Thank you for saying that." Sometimes Brynn wondered if anyone actually knew how important her role had been in those early days of building the firm. People tended to have short memories and it wasn't as if Mason had been tooting her horn, even in the later years when she'd gotten the firm out of a few pickles with clients who'd been unhappy with their campaigns.

Lexi leaned across the table so Brynn could hear her over the roar of the bar. "I know how talented you are, Brynn. Mason had nothing on you."

Brynn's throat clogged. "I never told you this before, Lexi, but things were worse than I let on between Mason and me." She paused to gather her words. "We put on a good act for our friends and family. But toward the end we barely spoke to each other."

"I kind of figured but didn't want to say anything, which I know is shocking. Because like when have I ever shut my big mouth?"

"You knew it was that bad?"

"The shine between you two definitely showed signs of tarnish. But I wasn't sure whether to attribute it to normal wear and tear on a marriage. Both of you were so busy—you with raising Henry and Mason with the agency—that I hoped you'd simply hit a valley in your relationship."

"Why didn't you say something?"

Lexi shrugged. "I guess because you and Mason made me believe true love was possible and I didn't want to burst my own bubble. Maybe it was selfish. But you didn't seem to want to share. How awful was it?"

"Not awful, just lonely. And sad. Somewhere along the line I realized that the only real connection besides Henry we'd ever shared was for advertising. Nothing else. But we had Henry and the business and the penthouse and our friends. And I settled, using a lot of the rationalizations you mentioned. I told myself that our marriage was merely suffering from a mid-life crisis and that when Henry got older we'd make more time for each other. That all relationships fall into a rut."

"I'm sorry, Brynn. I'm sorry I wasn't a better friend. And I'm sorry things didn't work out with Dr. Cowboy. How unfair is life that you meet the guy who knocks you off your feet and he's already spoken for?"

Heartbreakingly unfair.

Though she wanted to down the entire pitcher of Margaritas and go home to have a good cry, she tried to be circumspect. "You know what they say. It's better to have loved and lost than never to have loved at all." Lexi pretended to gag.

* * * *

It was only eight when Brynn got home. She paid the babysitter, helped Henry get ready for bed, and went in the kitchen to make a cup of tea. The room was large and an ode to modern design. When they'd bought the penthouse the kitchen was a tight galley with nary enough cabinets for pots and pans, let alone dishware.

During a massive remodel, she and Mason had blown out walls and expanded the kitchen with an eat-at center island that held a kid-height microwave and beverage fridge. One wall paid homage to Mason's coffee fetish with a plumbed state-of-the-art built-in machine while another wall housed a six-burner Wolf range.

Though Brynn wasn't much of a cook, the kitchen became the heart of their home. As she gazed around it now, it felt sterile, like something in a model home designed to sell the idea of a luxurious lifestyle.

The one in the cottage, though tiny, brimmed with life during their stay in Nugget. Henry and Roni coloring at the breakfast bar while Brynn made hot cocoa. Her and Ethan sharing a conversation while waiting for the kettle to boil. Donna, Maddy and Emily crowding the room with a basket of baked goods.

Lost in the memories, it took a moment for her to hear the buzzer. She glanced at the clock. By now, Lexi was home, likely tucked in bed with a good book. And it was too late for a visitor. It was probably just a reminder from the doorman that the elevator people were due tomorrow for their annual service. Brynn had already arranged to get Henry downstairs early.

She pressed the intercom. "Hey, Al."

"Evening, Ms. Barnes. You have a Dr. Daniels here to see you."

"Here . . . as in the lobby?" She told herself she must've misunderstood.

"Yes, Ma'am. Shall I send him up?"

"Yes . . . yes, please," she said, confused. What was Ethan doing here? When had he purchased a plane ticket? Her head spun with questions while her heart raced.

There was only one reason he'd come on such short notice. Panic rose in her throat.

By the time he stood in her doorway, clutching his Stetson in his hand, she knew. She knew with every bone in her body what he'd come to say. *Joey.* Her stomach lurched and she tried to steady her hands.

He looked wretched. There were dark circles under his eyes, his face was unshaven and his clothes appeared to be slept in. And yet, he took her breath away. No man, not even Mason, had ever had that heart stopping effect on her. For a moment she just stood there, gaping.

"This is a surprise," she finally managed without throwing herself into his arms and pleading for him not to tell her. She wished him all the best. But she just didn't want to know. Not now. Maybe not ever.

"Can I come in?"

"Of course." She moved aside, trying hard not to touch him because if she did, she'd be lost. Broken.

He stepped into the foyer, stared up at the steel and glass staircase and let out a low whistle. "Some place you've got here."

It wasn't anything compared to the Circle D Ranch.

"Thank you." She held her breath and unable to take it any longer said, "What's going on, Ethan?"

"I was in the neighborhood." As a joke it fell flat.

Clearly, he was feeling as nervous as she was.

"Where's Henry?" He peeked around the corner, searching.

She took his hat and placed it on the console table on its crown, like she'd seen him do so many times before. "He's asleep."

Ethan glanced at his watch and looked sheepish. "I forgot the three-hour time difference. Came straight from the airport." Bleary eyed, he shoved his hands in his jeans pockets. She'd never seen him look so tired. So depressed.

"Come in." She led him through the foyer to the great room where he stared out the window at the Manhattan skyline.

"Great view." He turned to her, then gazed back at the lights and skyscrapers. "I could use a drink."

Her heart sunk lower. Clearly, he needed liquor to get through this.

"What would you like?" She moved to the bar in the living room and he followed her, perusing the options. The ordinariness of it, like she was entertaining a guest, felt surreal

"The Bushmills," he said.

She reached for an old-fashioned glass. "Ice?"

"Neat, please."

She poured him a generous two fingers and passed him the glass, amazed that she could keep her hands still.

Unable to hold it any longer, she blurted, "You didn't have to tell me in person, Ethan."

"No, how should've I told you?" He put the glass down on the bar and pulled her into his arms.

"Don't." She tried to wriggle out of his embrace. "Please, don't."

His expression went slack, then she saw dawning. "What did you think I came to say?"

"That you and Joey—"

"No," he interrupted. "I told you I loved you, Brynn. Did you think that would go away the second you and Henry boarded a plane?"

She sagged against him while she let go of the tension that had tightened around her chest like a tourniquet. "I thought you would try again with her. Are you telling me you're not?"

"This has nothing to do with Joey. I came here to try again with you."

She gazed up at him, struggling to comprehend what he was saying, loving him so much that she wanted to believe him with every drop of her being.

He cupped her cheeks with his hands. "I love you, Brynn. I don't want to let you go. Whatever we have to do . . . I just know I can't be without you or else it'll slowly kill me."

"I don't want to let you go either." She buried her face in his chest to hide her tears. "I love you so much, Ethan."

"Then let's make this work." He pulled her closer. "I need you."

She wanted to say yes so badly that her body ached with it. "What about Veronica . . . Joey? As much as I want this, I don't want to be that woman . . . the woman who comes between you and your family."

He leaned down and touched her lips with his. It wasn't quite a kiss but the tenderness of it undid her. "A wise woman told me not to settle. She said I deserved passion and desire, and something about heart-pounding love. That's what I have with you, Brynn."

"Who was this wise woman?" She dragged him to the couch and snuggled next to him.

His mouth slid up in a smile. "Joey."

Brynn did a double take. "Joey?"

"Joey will always be a part of my life just like the memory of Mason will always be part of yours. But you're the one I want to be with, Brynn. You're the one I want to go to bed with every night and wake up to every morning. You're the one I love."

She closed her eyes, letting the words sink in. *You're the one I love.*

"The question is how do we do this? How do we make this work if you and Henry are here and Roni and I are in California?"

They sat there, just gazing into each other's eyes, contemplating the complexities of their separate lives. Though it didn't seem possible, she fell in love with him even more. And in that instant, she knew. She didn't even have to think about it.

"We'll come to Nugget."

His eyes widened in what could only be described as surprise. "What about the Barnes Group?"

"I don't know yet." This was all happening so fast that her head spun with possibilities. "I'll work something out. I just know that I want . . . that I need . . . to be with you." New York didn't feel like her home anymore. Her home was wherever Ethan was.

"Are you sure?" He cupped both sides of her face and in a soft voice said, "It's a big ask." He scrubbed his hand through his hair. "Hell, who am I kidding? It's an impossible ask."

"Nothing is impossible." He'd proven that by choosing her. "I'll have to talk to Rich and Layla but I have some ideas." Ideas that would allow her to work remotely, doing what she enjoyed most.

She beamed, more certain about her decision than anything she'd ever felt before. And feeling so much love she could float on it and touch the sky without ever returning to earth.

"You'd leave this?" He glanced around the room, then leveled his gaze at her. "Your company, your friends?"

She took his hands in hers. "It's not even a contest, Ethan. I choose you. It's that simple. You. Every time."

He pulled her into his arms and kissed her. Unlike before, the kiss was not gentle. It was filled with yearning and need and sweet desperation. "You too," he said against her mouth. "I choose you. Every time."

Epilogue

"Mom, Ethan, watch." Henry raced across the field on Choo Choo's back, a lariat in his hand, chasing after a calf, which seemed more interested in eating grass than escaping.

"Keep your circle tight," Ethan shouted as Henry spun the lasso in the air. "Stay at the steer's flank."

Henry tossed the rope, missing the calf's head by a mile.

"Good try, Henry." Roni sat on the top rail of the corral, waving her hat in the air. "My turn now."

Henry rode up to the fence and Ethan helped him dismount. In a few months, there was a good chance he'd be able to do it himself. His bones had healed enough for him to use a walker and his wheelchair had been relegated to a closet. Both Ethan and Dr. Rothman had agreed to put the other stem cell procedure on hold as it appeared that slowly but surely Henry's fractures were fusing together.

One of his legs was slightly shorter than the other and more than likely he would always have a slight limp. But with physical therapy he'd be able to play sports and become a skilled horseman, his current obsession.

He'd started Nugget Elementary School and came home every day with a funny story about one of his classmates or a teacher, or what they served in the cafeteria. Brynn was amazed that the transition had been so seamless.

A smart man—a pediatric orthopedic surgeon no less—had once told her that children were resilient. Well, Henry had proven that theory beyond her wildest dreams. His appetite was back with a vengeance, his tummy aches were gone, and once a week he saw a grief counselor. She'd made sure to put pictures of Mason on his nightstand in his new bedroom.

While Ethan could never replace Henry's father, her son looked up to him like he'd hung the moon. Both Henry and Roni wanted to be wherever Ethan was. Whether it was down at the barn or curled up on the couch to read a book. Ethan's endless patience never failed to astound her.

Roni switched places with Henry on Choo Choo's back. Ethan showed her how to keep her loop open and warned her not to go too fast. "Easy does it, bonny Roni."

She trotted up to the calf, who by this time was onto their game and not interested in playing along. Ethan jogged out to the calf and slapped its rump to give it a good head start on Roni. The calf trotted across the field and Roni caught up with it only to drop her lasso in the dirt and let out a loud curse.

Brynn choked on a laugh, then called out, "How 'bout burgers and fries at the Bun Boy?"

By the time Ethan got Choo Choo unsaddled and groomed, everyone was starved. They piled into Ethan's old truck and drove to town.

"Guess we'll have to get a minivan," he said as he slipped into a parking space, a big grin lighting his face.

"Maybe when I finish the Toyota campaign, I can get us a deal."

She'd agreed to make Rich and Layla equal partners in the Barnes Group. In exchange, she could focus on the creative end and work from California. Once a month, she planned to make the trek to New York for meetings. So far, it was working out well and Henry would still inherit a third of the company.

Brynn thought it was a good trade off, given that Henry got to grow up in idyllic Nugget with a little sister who adored him and a community that would always look out for him.

And then there was Ethan. They'd both hit the jackpot with Ethan.

Ethan turned to the back seat. "We'll meet you kids inside. Get started on ordering."

The kids hopped out and Roni climbed into the bed of the truck to hand Henry his walker. Brynn watched them make their way to the entrance, happiness spreading through her chest like warm liquid.

"He's doing really great, isn't he?"

"Yep. He's one hell of kid." Ethan pulled Brynn over the console into his lap.

"He is that," she said. "He's also got one hell of a surgeon."

"That's what I hear." He kissed her neck, then worked his way up to the whorl of her ear and whispered, "Thank you for making me the happiest man on the planet."

"The pleasure was all mine."

"Seriously, Brynn, I'll never take for granted the sacrifice you made to be here with Roni and me."

"I'll let you in on a little secret." She snuggled closer. "It wasn't much of a sacrifice. I love you, I love Roni, I love Alma and I love this town." She held her arms wide. "It's where I want to be. And I'm doing exactly what makes me happy."

"You think it's too soon to get hitched? I don't want to make Henry uncomfortable but I'd sure like to make you and me official."

In deference to Mason's death, they'd steered away from announcing an engagement. And Brynn thought Roni still needed time to get used to the idea of having a stepmother. Joey had been kind enough to make things as normal as possible between all of them. Ethan had relaxed the custody order and Joey was spending more and more time with her daughter. She'd even begun to look for a job in Nugget, which Brynn fervently hoped didn't make things messy. Only time would tell.

Still, Brynn couldn't wait to be Ethan's wife.

"Next summer will give us just enough time to plan something big," she told him. "I've never been one for a lot of pomp but I want to invite everyone. Griffin and Lina, the Shepards, the McCreedys, Darla and her husband, the Nugget Mafia, and Donna of course. Heck, the whole town. And by then, Henry will be ready. He already loves you and Roni as much as I do."

Ethan gazed into her eyes. "Next summer it is then. And we'll invite all of Manhattan, too, if that's what you want."

"Ethan," she wrapped her arms around his neck, "all I want is you."

Printed in the United States
by Baker & Taylor Publisher Services